NOCTURNE

Fourth Talisman #1

KAT ROSS

Nocturne

First Edition

Copyright © 2017 by Kat Ross

Map design by Robert Altbauer

ISBN: 978-0-9990481-0-8

To Christa & Jessica

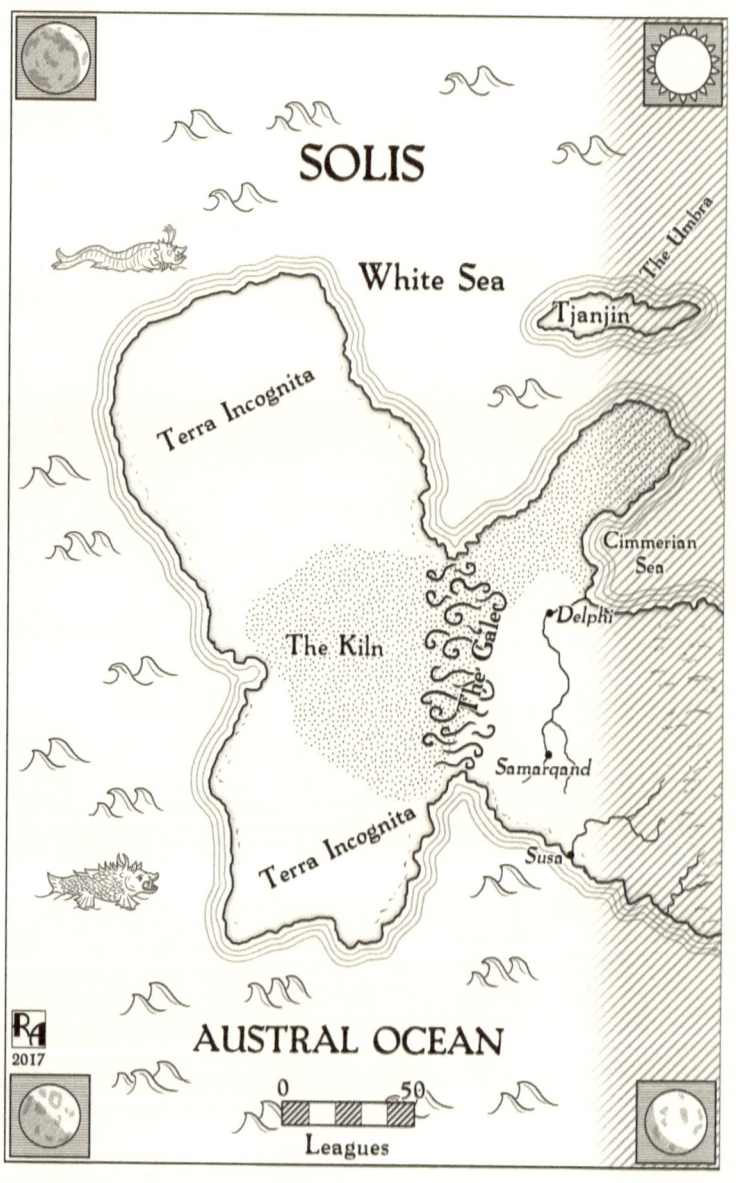

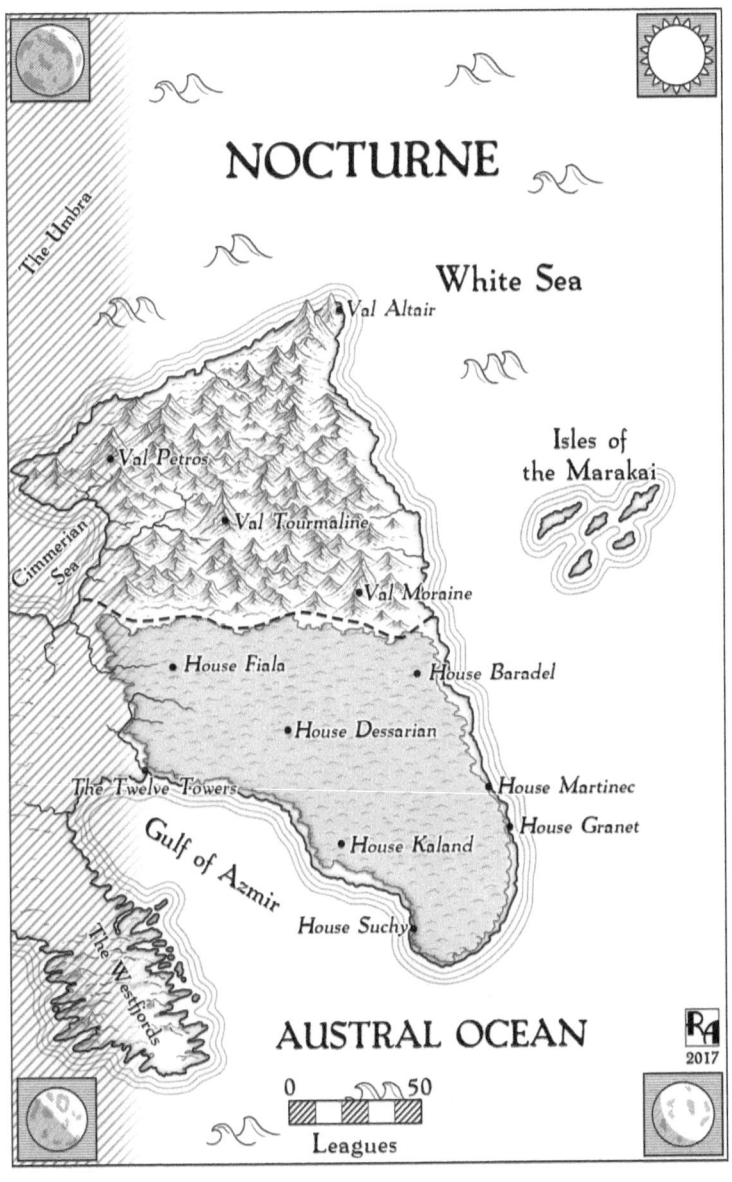

NOCTURNE

White Sea

• Val Altair

The Umbra

Isles of
the Marakai

• Val Petros

Cimmerian Sea

• Val Tourmaline

• Val Moraine

• House Fiala   • House Baradel

• House Dessarian

The Twelve Towers   • House Martinec
                           • House Granet

Gulf of Azmir   • House Kaland

The Westfjords   House Suchy •

AUSTRAL OCEAN   RA
                       2017

0   50

Leagues

CONTENTS

LACUNA

Nazafareen raised the hood of her cloak, tucking errant strands of light brown hair behind her ears. Cool air crept through the crack in the door, redolent of pine and spruce. She waited for six long heartbeats. Nothing stirred in the night. She knew Darius would be occupied in his workshop. Sentries patrolled the Valkirin border farther out, but with care she could avoid them. They weren't looking for anyone leaving.

She slipped into the shadows of the trees. Artemis the Huntress Moon rode at the farthest point of her long elliptical orbit, so distant she looked like another star in the inky heavens. Selene hid behind the mountains to the north. Only cool white Hecate peeked through the leafy canopy above, but she was the smallest of Nocturne's three moons and cast the faintest glimmer of light.

Nazafareen couldn't see in the dark like the daēvas, who had been born to eternal night. She was a child of the sun—even if it was lost to her now. So she made her way with caution, soft rabbit-skin boots silent on the carpet of pine needles. The light of the lumen crystal in her window faded to a pinprick, then vanished altogether. She felt small and alone in the dark wood—

but also blessedly free. Nazafareen had only left the Dessarian compound twice in her time among the daēvas, both occasions unsanctioned. They would never let her roam on her own. Her very presence there was a closely guarded secret.

Once clear of the last line of houses, she relaxed a little. The forest was sparse and open, with little undergrowth to snag her feet. She passed stands of pale bonewood—the daēvas made armor from that—and spreading oaks, skirted shallow pools full of whistling frogs that fell silent at an alien presence. She took the same path she had last time, following a resonance almost too faint to detect, like a snatch of music on the wind.

She climbed a rise. The forest thinned to open meadow and she got her first sight of Hecate, three-quarters full, floating above the distant mountains like a silver coin. Despite chafing at her confinement, Nazafareen had come to love the way the deep twilight softened the edges of things like a velvet cloak. The brightness of the stars and subtle coloring of the moons.

The great forest of the Danai had never known the touch of summer or winter, spring or autumn, but the passage of the seasons could be tracked by the travels of Artemis the Huntress. Her orbit took a full year to complete but when she returned, her light supposedly made it almost as bright as true day—solar day. The tides would surge, covering the land for leagues. Nazafareen hoped to see that. Darius had told her what an *ocean* was, but she still found it hard to imagine so much water.

She crossed the meadow and descended into a thickly wooded valley. Finally, she saw a greenish flicker through the trees ahead. Her steps slowed, the hair on her arms lifting.

She had reached another sort of border.

The gate to the Dominion waited ten paces ahead. It looked like a rectangular doorway with no frame—just a glowing hole in the night. The surface had the shimmery quality of running water.

Nazafareen stepped closer. And closer still.

Two months before, Darius had carried her through the gate

in his arms, nearly dead from her own fey power. Breaker, they called her. A mortal with daēva blood and the ability to shatter magic. She had drawn too much of it.

A lake. A green-eyed man with a scar and an evil sickness inside him. The crowns of trees burning like torches.

She dimly remembered a battle. Her bond with Darius flaring to life and being snuffed out again when they passed through the gate to Nocturne. It was why the daēvas were hiding her. Because that green-eyed man was a Valkirin, the clan that lived in the mountains, and if he ever discovered she still lived....

Nazafareen stared at the gate in queasy fascination. Her own world—her past—lay on the other side, but she had no memory of it. Darius said she'd broken a ward that contained a spell of forgetfulness. The backwash had wiped her own mind clean.

I want to know who I was. Who I am. I have the right.

She sighed, absently rubbing the stump of her missing right hand. It had been a stupid impulse to come here. Fleeing through the gate wouldn't restore what was lost. Magic had erased her past and only magic could restore it.

Darius seemed to think her condition was irreversible, but Nazafareen refused to accept that. Someone, somewhere, knew something and she intended to find them. Except that the daēvas wouldn't let her leave. And part of her didn't want to go. Not without Darius.

She stood before the gate as Hecate set. The lunar night was nearly over. Soon Selene would appear, her bright yellow face heralding the dawn of the lunar day. It was time to return before they found her gone. She started back through the trees, the scant light growing dimmer by the moment. True night was coming, the brief period where none of the three moons was visible. The length of it varied from day to day. The daēvas called it the lacuna and it might last anywhere from a few seconds to an hour or more.

Nazafareen scanned the sky. A thin veil of clouds had swept in.

So much for starlight, she thought. *Let's hope it's a short one tonight.* She pulled her cloak tighter and retraced her steps through the valley, moving as quickly as she dared.

Nazafareen paused at a soft sound behind her, like a breeze rustling the leaves—except that there was no wind. She wished she'd brought the lumen crystal. There were animals in these woods. Mostly small game, but Darius's father Victor had seen wolves near the mountains. Her hand dropped to her belt knife.

One of the frog pools shimmered just ahead. Hecate sank beneath the rim of the sky. The forest seemed to take a last, lingering breath of anticipation. She glimpsed an owl gliding from branch to branch in the canopy. And then the lacuna descended, as dark as the bottom of the sea.

She'd always been safe at home with her lumen crystal when true night fell. Sometimes Darius came by and they played a board game with little wooden animals. The pieces had curving horns and barbed tails and different magical powers. All were cunningly carved to the smallest detail. Nazafareen usually won, though she often cheated when he wasn't looking. A petty victory, but sweet nonetheless.

She glanced up, hoping the clouds would pass. *Just a little starlight to guide me...*

The dry rustling came again, behind her and low to the ground. Moving fast.

Before she could blink, thick coils of scaled muscle wrapped her in an iron grip. Nazafareen grunted, scrabbling for the knife. Her fingers brushed the hilt too late. It slithered higher, pinning her arms. She fought to draw breath against a crushing weight on her chest. The knife slipped from her grasp as she tumbled down a muddy bank. Cold water closed over her head.

Darius had warned her about the forest. She got the feeling he knew about her occasional wanderings. He hadn't said so directly, or even asked her to stop. Perhaps he knew she needed to get away from time to time. That she'd go mad if she didn't.

There are snakes, he said. *By the way.*

Of course, he'd neglected to mention how bloody big they were.

Down they sank to the silty bottom. Nazafareen swallowed her panic and sought the Nexus, that place of nothing and everything where elemental magic could be touched. It wasn't easy with the life being squeezed out of her, but she knew it was her last hope.

She reached for earth and focused on the snake's slender articulated spine. Darius would be able to snap it in an instant. She tried to do the same, bubbles of air slipping through her lips—the last air she might ever taste—but earth was the heaviest element to wield and she'd always been terrible with it. Once, as a lesson, he'd set her to moving grains of sand from one anthill to another. The ants had accomplished the same task much faster.

A glint in the corner of her eye.

Frail moonlight lancing through the water, touching...something.

Her belt knife?

Blood pounding in her temples, she reached for water—and felt it stir feebly in response.

Come, she urged. *Come!*

A weak current lifted the knife, drifting it toward her open hand. As soon as the hilt touched her palm, Nazafareen stabbed at the cold reptilian flesh, driving the blade deep. For an awful moment, the snake clenched tighter. She twisted the knife. And then the coils binding her loosened just enough to pull her arm free. A second later, she plunged the blade into the snake's flat black eye. It sank away into the depths.

Nazafareen dragged herself from the pond and lay on the bank, chest heaving. After long minutes, the frogs resumed their peeping song. She laughed softly, though it hurt. The Valkirins didn't need to come after her. She was doing a fine job getting killed all on her own. If the lacuna had lasted a few seconds longer.... She rolled to her side, wincing. Then she stood and walked back to House Dessarian.

Selene had risen in the west when the first outbuildings came into view. The walls were live white birch, their boles and branches weaving together like clasped fingers to form a leafy roof. Every sixth tree grew crookedly away from its neighbor halfway up the trunk, creating an oval window. The dwellings of House Dessarian were not laid out in orderly rows, the way she heard mortals built their cities. These were haphazard, most barely within shouting distance of each other. Most of the daēvas still slept and no one saw her slinking through the shadows like a wet cat.

Finally, she reached the house they'd given her, smaller than the others but cozy enough.

She opened the door—and found Darius sitting at her kitchen table.

Daēvas looked much like mortals, if a touch...feral. There weren't any obvious differences. It was more the way they moved. Lithe and graceful at rest, blurringly quick when they chose. They were stronger and healed faster. They could wield earth, air and water. But they had a weakness, a fatal one.

Fire.

Which was why the fourth element was banned in Nocturne. Why the daēvas made their home on the dark side of the world.

Nazafareen masked her surprise at finding him there. Darius kept his wavy brown hair short, a holdover from his time as a soldier. As always, she found the intensity of his bright blue gaze disconcerting. He raised an eyebrow at her sodden cloak.

"Where have you been?" he asked in a level tone.

"I felt like a swim," she said, daring him to contradict her.

"Fully dressed?"

"It was a little cool out for my taste."

Darius barked a laugh. "You're an awful liar." His expression grew serious. "It's not safe, Nazafareen. You know that. At least take me with you next time."

She hung her cloak on a peg and sat down across from him.

"I'm sorry, Darius, but I feel a prisoner here. I know that's my own fault. The Danai were kind to take me in. But I...I wanted to see the gate."

He leaned forward, eyes narrowing. "You went all the way to the gate? Are you mad?"

"Just to see it. That's all."

Darius exhaled. "To see it. Why?"

"I don't know." She felt suddenly angry—not at him. At everything. "Curiosity. I don't wish to talk about it."

Darius looked away.

Now you've hurt him.

"What's that?" Nazafareen asked in a softer tone, pointing to a cloth-wrapped bundle on the table.

"A gift. It's why I came."

"May I see it?"

"Of course."

She felt him watching her as she struggled to undo the twine with one hand. Darius knew her too well to offer his help. Finally, she remembered her knife, holding the bundle in place with her stump and slicing it open. The cloth fell away.

"Oh." She looked up at him in delight. "Darius, it's beautiful."

He smiled. "It's called an astrolabe. I made it from yew."

Nazafareen turned the wooden sphere over in her hands. Three moons, each of a different size and distance, spun around it on circles attached to a polar axis.

"I'll show you how to move them to correspond with the heavens," he said with a warm smile. "Then you can track the return of Artemis."

Nazafareen smiled back. There was something stern and unyielding in him that only seemed to soften when they were alone together. She fiddled with the astrolabe for a moment, sliding the moons around and around. It was a clever thing, and cunningly made. His skill with wood amazed her considering the short time they'd been there.

"Thank you," she said solemnly. "It's a wonderful gift. But I have nothing for you."

His gaze held her. "Let me teach you. I enjoy it."

"We've tried—"

"It takes time. And you're stubborn."

"Me?" Nazafareen laughed. "You make a boulder seem pliable." She thought of the snake. "But perhaps it wouldn't hurt."

In truth, she desperately wished she could use elemental power like the daēvas. The Danai—Darius's clan—were especially strong in earth. They nurtured the only forests in the world. The master craftsmen of House Dessarian and the six other houses made furniture and weapons and other items for trade, commanding premium prices for their products.

"Then let us begin with a simple talisman. Extinguish the lumen crystal and then light it again."

They spent the next few hours practicing with air, which Nazafareen found the easiest element to work with. She'd grown more adept at finding the Nexus and could feel the torrents of power swirling around her. The difficulty lay in making them do what she wanted. She could manage the lumen crystal, but trying to move objects—even small ones like their game pieces—left her swearing through gritted teeth. Darius was patient as always, though the man could be *relentless* in his own quiet way. When she finally upended the entire board, not using the power, he laughed and slid his chair back.

"You're tired," he said, rising. "And I have work to do." He paused at the door. "But I want you to promise me you won't return to the gate alone."

Nazafareen stared at him. She wanted to trust him. But the secrets he kept had become a chasm between them that grew wider by the day, even if he refused to see it. All her frustrations boiled over.

"Then tell me everything." She held up her stump. "Tell me how I lost this."

He flinched away from her gaze. "I already have. We were soldiers—"

"Yes, yes. I know the story by heart. Your words hardly vary when you tell it. But it rings false. What was the purpose of the bond? Who forged the cuffs and why? How did you come to be born in my world when your kin are here?"

For a moment, he looked as though he might speak. His eyes searched hers, but then a door seemed to close.

"It doesn't matter," he said with quiet desperation. "Truly it doesn't, Nazafareen."

She folded her arms. "You may think you're protecting me, but the not knowing is worse. Did I do something wrong? Was I some kind of monster?"

"No." He turned away. "Not you."

2

FARAVAHAR

Darius strode into the darkness, hand instinctively dropping to his hip. No sword hung there anymore, yet in moments of anger, he found himself reaching for it just the same.

I am no longer the satrap's dog, sent out with a pat on the head to hunt and kill, he thought savagely. *Those days are over.*

If only she would let it go. Darius would be happy to trade places with her. To not remember the horrors of the empire. If he'd cared to analyze his own reluctance—which he didn't—he might have found a tangled thread of self-loathing at the heart of it. But Darius had learned from an early age to lock his feelings away and try to forget them. It was how he'd survived.

So he went straight to his workroom and picked up a chisel instead, delicately chipping away at a piece of ash he was carving into a figurine. Bonewood swords and bows were the most popular items they traded with the Marakai, but Darius refused to make weapons.

Nazafareen misunderstood. He hadn't lied to her, not precisely. He'd told her they'd served as soldiers to a crumbling empire, what was called a bonded pair. How they had fought the undead Druj together, and even worse things. How Nazafareen had given her hand to save him—though he'd been vague about the details. And how Neblis, the daēva queen who controlled the Druj armies, had summoned her brother Culach through the gate that linked their two worlds. Nazafareen used her power to defeat Culach's invasion but she'd paid a high price, losing her memories and nearly her life.

It was all true.

But her instincts were also correct. Darius had not told her everything.

He paused, the piece of ash in his hand forgotten, and glanced at a small lacquered box in the corner where he kept his cuff. Pure gold and engraved with the image of a snarling griffin, the cuff was a talisman that required fire to work. Once, when Nazafareen wore its match around her wrist, the cuffs had contained their bond. He missed it desperately.

If he told her the truth—all of it—she would see the bond as an evil thing, and he couldn't bear that. So he had...glossed over certain things. And sworn his father Victor and mother Delilah to secrecy about it.

Darius felt himself grow calmer as he shaped the piece of wood, using both tools and trickles of earth power. Working wood was the place where he lost himself, where he escaped from the simmering tension with Nazafareen. He loved her, perhaps too much.

She thinks I love her for who she used to be, but in truth she was the same in all the ways that matter. If only she wasn't so stubborn...

A heavy tread on the stairs announced the arrival of his father.

"I'm heading out to the border," Victor said by way of greet-ing. "I thought you might come."

"I'm busy," Darius replied, briefly glancing up and returning to his work.

He'd said no repeatedly, but Victor wouldn't stop asking. He was a large man, taller than Darius with broad shoulders and black hair. Victor still wore a sword, though the other Danai carried bows. He'd bought one for Darius from the Marakai traders. Darius didn't want it. He'd given it to Nazafareen instead; even one-handed, she was deadly with a blade. Victor hadn't been offended. Instead, he'd taken to sparring with her. The two were much alike in some ways.

"We could use someone with your skill, both as a tracker and fighter," Victor persisted. He glanced out the window. "Galen is coming."

Every day since they'd come to Nocturne, Victor led a patrol to the northern reaches of the forest, where the River Arnor marked the end of the Danai lands and the foothills of the Valkirin mountains began their sharp rise from the earth. Val Moraine, the ancestral seat of their enemies, lay a mere twenty leagues beyond the river. So far, the border had been quiet.

"It's a chance to get to know your brother," Victor said.

"Half-brother," Darius replied. He and Galen had different mothers. Victor didn't see it, but Darius got the impression Galen didn't like him very much. "And I've told you before. I don't wish to be a soldier anymore, not even for you."

His father sighed. "We're doing this to protect Nazafareen."

"Are you?" Darius lay down the chisel and picked up a rasp. "I wonder sometimes."

Victor scowled, his dark brows drawing together. "What does that mean?"

"Never mind."

"Say it."

Darius looked up. "All right. You have a grudge against Culach and his entire holdfast."

His father's dark eyes flashed. "Am I the only one who understands they're still a threat? We should finish them now, while they're weakened. But Tethys won't listen. She's afraid of starting a war."

"And you aren't?" Darius shook his head. "Haven't you had enough of fighting?"

"And what about Nazafareen? Will she hide here forever? That's no life."

The words came too close to what Darius had been thinking himself. He could tell she was nearing a breaking point. Neither of them truly fit in here. The Danai tolerated her for Victor's sake, but she was a mortal—and she had enemies.

"You're right. Which is why I think we should leave."

"And go where?"

Darius had considered the matter carefully. Even if they went to a distant Danai settlement, she could still be found.

"The Isles of the Marakai."

Victor frowned. "Have you discussed this with her?"

"Not yet. I'll ask Tethys first. See if she can make arrangements the next time they come to trade."

"Running away," Victor said with flat disapproval.

"Call it what you will. At least she'll be safe." He gave Victor a long look. "Don't tell her until I talk to Tethys."

Victor shook his head. "You keep too many secrets. It will poison you both."

Darius glanced out the window to where Galen waited with a group of young daēvas. They worshipped Victor. He was a charismatic man, handsome in a brutal way, the hardships he'd suffered writ across his face. Victor was a near legend at House Dessarian. He'd vanished through the gate to the shadowlands more than two hundred years before and his sudden return—with a new wife and son, and mortal girl with strange powers—had caused quite a stir.

Not everyone was glad to see him. Victor had recruited friends for his misadventure, most of whom hadn't come back. But the younger daēvas—the ones who didn't know better—were quite taken with him. Some had even started to wear swords in imitation of their returned hero. Darius knew Victor hadn't told them the whole truth either.

"I'll tell her about the Marakai tomorrow," he said.

"You should tell her all of it." Victor studied him. "If she loves you, it won't change anything."

When Darius didn't respond, he turned and headed back down the stairs, to Galen and the other Danai sentries. Darius watched out the window as they vanished like mist into the woods.

He returned to the figurine he was carving. A bearded man with spreading eagle wings. It was one of the queer aspects of this world that it mirrored the one he had come from in many ways. The faravahar was the symbol of the Prophet, whom the mortals revered in Samarkand—just as they had in the empire. This piece would be shipped off through the Marakai to the Persian cities of Solis, where such religious trinkets were sold on the streets.

Darius used to wear one around his own neck. He'd given it to Nazafareen when they'd ridden into the Dominion to find Victor. He still believed in the Way of the Flame—good thoughts, good words, good deeds—even if he hated the magi. Dark thoughts crowded in again.

Darius picked up the chisel again.

BREAKER

Nazafareen changed out of her wet clothes, pulling on a fresh tunic and trousers. She was still angry but more than that, she felt restless, unmoored. She despised sitting around doing nothing. Victor refused to let her join his patrols lest she be seen. She couldn't learn to shape wood with only one hand. And her only real power was both useless and dangerous. Like the cuffs, the breaking magic drew on fire. Using too much had set a blaze in her own body, an inferno that was only extinguished when she passed through the gate to Nocturne.

But she might have other talents she didn't know about. It all came back to that. If nothing else, restoring her memory would make her feel whole again. Then she could decide where she belonged—Nocturne, or back in her own world.

Nazafareen stared at the scattered playing pieces on the table. She was tired of being told what to do. Tired of waiting for others to move her about as they saw fit. If Darius wouldn't tell her the truth, she'd find someone who would. Not Victor—he made excuses every time she sought him out. And Delilah, Darius's mother, had never liked her.

But Tethys...she might know things.

Nazafareen had met the matriarch of House Dessarian only once, when Tethys came to inspect this mortal woman Victor's son had dragged back with him. She'd uttered a few terse words of welcome, clearly insincere, and then taken her leave in a swirl of green silks. Nazafareen recalled her as tall and whip-thin, with an ability to loom that rivaled Victor's.

Tethys had never come again, but Nazafareen knew where she lived. So she gathered her courage and made her way through the woods to a glen where a ring of junipers poked like spears from the earth. The path led to a narrow gap in the trees. Nazafareen followed it through and paused, inhaling the mingled perfume of a hundred different plants. This must be Tethys's night garden, though it seemed too simple a word for what she'd created. Nazafareen's fingers brushed a tangle of vines with velvety, half-open buds—then yanked back as a hidden thorn pricked her thumb. She sucked on it and tasted blood. *Better to look than touch, perhaps.* All the flowers were dark, bruised colors: eggplant purple, wine red, violet blue. Fireflies flashed on and off in the undergrowth like tiny yellow lanterns.

Nazafareen drew a steadying breath, awed by the fairytale quality of the place. At first glance, the garden seemed to have been left to run riot, but closer inspection revealed a master's hand at work. A subtle order to the chaos. Nazafareen knew all the plants and trees in the Danai lands fed on moonlight. Exactly how was a jealously guarded secret.

She found Tethys kneeling on a patch of newly-turned earth, planting seedlings with glossy heart-shaped leaves. Tethys had the same dark hair and bird-of-prey nose as Victor and looked only a decade older, although her true age was hundreds of years beyond a mortal lifespan.

"I'm sorry to disturb you," Nazafareen said, feeling like an interloper. "I hoped we could speak."

Tethys looked up at her, then patted the dirt with strong, calloused hands. "You think I don't know where you go?" Her voice was dusty and hard as a dry riverbed. "The gate you shattered is warded again. Someone approached it earlier and I'd reckon that someone was you, child."

Nazafareen was twenty years old, but she supposed Tethys would see her as a child still. The daēvas measured such things differently. *So Tethys knows. Well, of course she does.*

"I'm sorry. I meant no harm."

Tethys moved on to the next seedling, handling it as gently as a newborn infant. "Had you stepped through, you could never return."

"I wasn't planning on leaving. I only wanted to see it. And I never meant to shatter your wards in the first place." Nazafareen considered, then added ruefully, "Or maybe I did. That's the problem. I can't remember."

Tethys sighed. "Come, help me. I cannot speak with you like this. I'll get a crick in my neck."

Nazafareen knelt on the ground next to her. Tethys held up a seedling.

"This is feverbane. The seeds are useful for spicing wine or curing evil humors in the blood. Take it."

Nazafareen accepted the seedling with a reverent hand. She poked a hole in the dirt with her finger, then covered the roots and pressed the mound firmly around the fragile plant. Tethys nodded in approval.

"I would ask you some questions, if you're willing."

Tethys gave her a sidelong glance. "And if I'm not?"

"I'll ask them anyway."

The Danai woman smiled, a faint twitch of her thin lips. "Go on, then."

"I know you helped make the ward I broke. Were my memories erased? Or simply sealed away?" She hesitated, fearing the answer. "Could they be restored?"

Tethys picked up another plant and eased it from the pot. "Such a thing has never happened before. But I examined you quite thoroughly before you woke, when Darius first brought you here."

"Yes, he did tell me that. He said I couldn't be cured."

"And that is the truth."

Nazafareen's heart fell.

"Not by me, at least," Tethys added.

"By who then?"

Tethys gave her a hard look. "Are you sure you wish to know? Some people might see it as a gift. A chance to start life anew without the burden of regret."

Nazafareen shook her head. "If I have regrets, they are mine. And how can I learn from them if I don't know what they are? No. I wish to learn the truth." She hesitated. "Has Darius spoken of me?"

"If you're asking whether I'm privy to the secrets he keeps, the answer is no. Darius doesn't confide in me. He may be my grandson, but we hardly know each other."

"Then who can help me?"

Tethys considered her question for a long moment. "The Marakai are the strongest healers among us. Water is the essence of healing and that is their gift. They can accomplish wonders, but we are speaking of physical wounds. Your injury is to the mind."

"The Marakai. You mean the sea daēvas?"

Tethys nodded.

"But they might know a way?"

"They might. Who can say?"

"I think I must go ask them then."

"We send a delegation to the shore of the White Sea twice a year, to trade. I suppose you could go along next time."

Nazafareen tamped down her impatience. "And when will that be?"

"Three more waxings of Selene," Tethys said placidly.

"So long?"

Tethys looked at her strangely. "Long to you perhaps." Her tone sharpened. "Do you have complaints about your treatment here? Are we such poor company?"

"Not at all," Nazafareen said hastily. "And I thank you for the offer. I suppose I'll have to wait then."

They planted the last of the seedlings. Tethys rose to her feet, brushing earth from her hands. She turned to Nazafareen.

"There is something else?" she asked with a touch of asperity.

"What do you know about breaking magic?"

"In Tjanjin, they call it huo mofa. It is a rare ability, and dangerous to the user. But I suppose you know that already."

"But where does it come from? Is there a way to use it safely?"

Tethys eyed her with pity. "I don't know the first. As to the second...better not to touch it at all, don't you think?" She looked pointedly at the path into the woods. "You'd best run along now, child. You oughtn't be wandering alone anyway."

Nazafareen suppressed a sigh and made her farewells.

That's what they all said.

SHE HURRIED ALONG THE DARK PATH, LOST IN THOUGHT. Would Darius go with her to the Marakai? Would he support her in this? If not, she would go anyway.

She threw open her front door and groped for the peg. Moonlight spilled in a broad shaft through the window. She smelled something, queer and cold, like the air just before it snows. That rarely happened in the Danai forest, their magic kept it from freezing despite the lack of sun, but sometimes a storm blew in from the Valkirin range that was too strong even for the daēvas to divert. Then she heard a soft creak from one of her chairs. So Darius had returned. Well, she would ask him now. No point in putting it off. And if he said yes, perhaps they could leave right away.

Nazafareen reached for air and lit the lumen crystal—and froze.

A man sat at her table, but it wasn't Darius. He had long silver hair and a foxlike face. White leathers trimmed with fur covered him from head to foot. A long sword inlaid with jewels rode at his hip. He held her astrolabe in slender, pale fingers.

"Hello, mortal," he said.

Nazafareen opened her mouth to reply and found she couldn't draw breath. Something squeezed her lungs in a cold vise. He stood and walked over to her, frowning. He moved with the prowling grace of a daēva, but not a Danai. Not with those icy looks.

They've found me.

"So young," he murmured, studying her face with luminous green eyes. A shadow of unease flickered across his features. Then his gaze fell to her stump and hardened. "You're the Breaker who burned my clan."

Nazafareen heard the rasp of a sword leaving the scabbard. Black motes danced before her eyes. He had her pinned as neatly as the snake.

How strong he was! She dimly sensed he was using air to hold her, to gag her, simple air, and yet it felt hard as marble. Frantic, she eyed her own sword. It leaned against the wall near the door. She strained and it toppled over, then began to slide ever so slowly across the floor.

The Valkirin watched it with an amused expression.

"You cannot harm me now, can you?" He raised his own blade. Again, she saw a shadow of regret cross his face, quickly stifled. "I vow to make it swift. Swifter than the death you gave my cousins."

The door to the room burst open with an explosive crash, nearly tearing free of its hinges from the violence of the blow. Darius rushed inside. His wintry gaze fell on the Valkirin. Earth magic surged in a roaring, bone-jarring tide. The ground convulsed beneath Nazafareen's feet, clods of dirt scattering outward. The web of air snaring her fell away. She coughed, left hand clutching her throat. The Valkirin vaulted through the window. Darius followed.

Nazafareen grabbed her sword and staggered out the door. The two daēvas streaked through the woods, the assassin's white leathers bright in the darkness. She heard rumbles up ahead and dashed past a jagged crevice where the earth crumbled away into a deep sinkhole, the white tips of tree roots erupting like huge worms.

At last she caught up with them. The Valkirin was trapped on an island of solid ground no more than ten paces wide. Darius stood on the other side of the crevasse. A trickle of blood ran from his nose, the price of throwing all that earth around. His face could have been carved from granite.

"You won't leave these lands," he said with tightly controlled fury. "Sheathe the blade."

The Valkirin lowered his sword slightly but didn't put it away.

"Let me kill her," he pleaded. "It's for the best. For your people and mine. She's a danger to us all!"

"Who sent you?" Darius growled. "Was it Culach?"

The assassin gritted his teeth as fingers snapped like kindling. He switched the sword to his right hand.

Nazafareen ran toward Darius. She heard shouts as the other daēvas caught wind of the attack. Dark shapes pelted through the trees.

"I carry a message from Val Moraine," the Valkirin announced in a ringing tone. "The Avas Danai are harboring a mass murderer. If you don't hand her over—"

Darius crossed the gap between them in one graceful bound.

"And I have an answer," he said.

Nazafareen tossed him her sword and he seized the spinning hilt just in time to parry a blow from the assassin's own blade. There was no cautious circling. No testing of defenses. Instead, they hammered at each other, one blade of bonewood, the other of iron. The assassin was good, but Darius was better. Inch by inch, he pushed the Valkirin toward the yawning pit at his back.

Then the assassin turned to Nazafareen. The ground gave way beneath his heels as he drew a huge breath and blasted it at her. She cried out in surprise as the wave of air lifted her off her feet and threw her backwards.

"Nazafareen!" Darius cried.

She hit the ground just in time to see the assassin aim a vicious kick at Darius's knee. He raised his sword, smashing the hilt into Darius's skull. Nazafareen heard it fracture with a sharp crack. The Valkirin brought his sword back again, this time for a killing stroke—when a black-fletched arrow punched through his chest.

Nazafareen spun and saw Galen three paces behind her, bow in hand, his eyes wide.

The assassin fell back, the glaze of death falling across his foxlike features. Blood bubbled around the arrow in his chest. Somehow he summoned the strength to speak—to her.

"You die," he gasped, staring at her with loathing. "Or they all die."

The words sent ripples through the crowd of daēvas. Victor leapt across the ragged crevice, face a thunderhead, and thrust his sword into the Valkirin's heart.

Nazafareen ran to the edge, but it was too wide and deep for her to cross. Darius lay sprawled in the dirt. Blood matted his hair, a black stain in the moonlight. She felt a stab of sheer terror until she saw his chest rise and fall.

"Don't touch him!" Tethys hurried over. "He cannot be moved, not until I give what healing I can."

Tethys sprang lightly across the gap and knelt beside Darius. Her eyes grew distant. Nazafareen felt complex threads of power weaving around both of them.

"What's happened here?"

Nazafareen turned and saw Delilah, Darius's mother, striding up. She looked nothing like her son except for the intense blue eyes. She'd always been thin to the point of emaciated, but Nazafareen suspected she was stronger than she looked. Delilah never came to see her. It was obvious she had no love of mortals.

"I found the Valkirin in my house," Nazafareen said. "He was about to kill me when Darius came. Darius chased him and they... they fought."

Delilah gave her a long look. "Are you hurt?"

"No, I'm fine."

Victor drew his wife aside. They spoke in low voices. Delilah's inscrutable gaze rested on Nazafareen.

Well, if his mother didn't hate me before, she certainly does now.

When Tethys signaled it was safe to move him, two Danai brought a litter and gently maneuvered Darius back to solid ground. All Nazafareen's earlier anger dissolved into stinging tears that she angrily scrubbed away with a sleeve. She trailed along behind as they carried him to Galen's house, which was the closest. Tethys sat at Darius's bedside and cupped his face, murmuring to herself. Darius stirred feebly, his eyelids fluttering. His face relaxed into sleep.

"He will need a great deal of rest," Tethys said, looking drawn and exhausted herself. "I cannot say when he will wake."

Nazafareen felt her heart unclench a little. Darius would live.

Victor ran a hand through his dark hair. "This provocation cannot go unanswered, Tethys. They violated our borders and nearly killed my son. I warned you this was coming. We should have acted long ago."

Tethys drew herself up. "You were gone for more than two hundred years, Victor," she said evenly. "Things have changed."

"Have they?" he sneered. "They seem exactly the same to me. The Valkirins at our throats and House Dessarian doing nothing to put them down."

"How dare you?" Tethys hissed. "You left me your...*mess* to deal with, which I did. But you have no right to second-guess how I run this house."

"Peace, mother, I'm sorry if I gave offense," Victor said, although he still managed to sound arrogant. "But you heard what he said. If we don't surrender Nazafareen, they'll come in force. The survival of our house is at stake." His temper sounded close to catastrophically snapping. "We know who's behind this. Let me handle it."

Tethys gave a humorless laugh. "I know how you handle things, Victor. Like a rampaging bull."

"And what would you do?"

Tethys's predatory gaze fell on Nazafareen. "Go back to your house, girl," she said sharply. "This is Danai business."

Nazafareen steeled herself for battle.

I won't be treated like a child, not even by this ancient, powerful woman. Let her see this rabbit has teeth.

"It concerns me," Nazafareen said levelly. "I have the right to know what you intend to do."

Tethys opened her mouth to reply when Victor stepped up and laid a hand on her arm.

"She's right," he said softly. "There's little use in keeping secrets now." He raised an eyebrow. "Unless you intend to throw her to the wolves?"

Tethys pursed her thin lips. "Give me more credit than that," she snapped. "Very well. She can stay. But she'll keep quiet."

Nazafareen knew better than to argue the point. She sat down on the floor at the foot of the bed and tried to make herself small, which wasn't difficult.

"As I was saying," Tethys continued, "you seem to have forgotten the fact that they have Mina. We have Ellard. The whole purpose of the hostage arrangement is to keep the peace. It's worked so far."

"Worked?" He laughed mirthlessly. "They just sent an assassin to kill Nazafareen in her own home. Would you call that a breach of the peace?"

Nazafareen covered a smile. Tethys was right—Victor snorted and bellowed and didn't care who he trampled beneath his hooves —but she liked that he was standing up for her.

"It's more complicated than you know, Victor," Tethys said quietly.

"What haven't you told me?"

"Over the last two years, some of us have gone missing. Vanished into thin air."

A frown came over Victor's darkly handsome face.

"How many?"

"Four. Two from House Dessarian, a brother and sister, and one each from House Martinec and House Kaland. They'd gone to assess the far southern groves. It should have been no more than a week's journey. When they didn't return after two, scouts went looking. Not a trace was found." She glanced down at Darius, tucking the blanket around his shoulders with a gentle hand. "And before you start hurling accusations, five Valkirins have vanished too—each one traveling alone. We blamed each other until it became clear we've both suffered losses."

Victor let out a slow breath. The floor creaked under his bulk as he paced the room.

"How could you keep this from me?"

"Because I didn't trust you not to go rushing off again," Tethys said calmly. "If something is indeed hunting daēvas, the clans need to stick together. Or at least not start a war."

"I agree," Delilah said.

It was the first time she'd spoken.

"You don't know the Valkirins—" Victor growled.

Delilah cut him off. "I'm not suggesting we do nothing. But your mother is right. Action taken in anger and haste would be a mistake."

Tethys gave Delilah a nod of approval. "You'd do well to listen to your wife, Victor. She seems to have a modicum of sense. Do I trust the Valkirins? Of course not. They're underhanded and ruthless. Violence is in their blood. But Val Moraine may have acted alone in this. Halldóra of Val Tourmaline is the most reasonable of the bunch. I'll send a bird to her tonight. And then we must convene the Matrium. The other Houses should know of this. It concerns us all."

"Then do it quickly," Victor advised. "Once Culach learns the attempt failed, he'll send more to finish the job." He glanced at Nazafareen. "The Valkirin was waiting for you?"

She nodded.

Victor scrubbed a hand across his jaw. "How did he know which house to go to? And how did he discover you were here in the first place?"

Everyone fell silent. Nazafareen avoided their eyes. Tethys already knew—well, she supposed the others deserved to hear it too.

"I was in the forest yesterday," Nazafareen admitted, shame making her cheeks burn. "I know I shouldn't have gone out alone."

"You shouldn't have gone at all," Delilah muttered, casting her a baleful look.

"I don't disagree," Tethys said dryly. "But the girl isn't to blame. If the Valkirin scout had seen her, he would have killed her on the spot. He'd be halfway back to the mountains before we found the body. He took a great risk coming into the heart of the settlement, and paid the price for it." Her gaze narrowed. "No, it makes no sense. They found out some other way."

"You mean someone told them?" Victor demanded.

"I don't know." Tethys sighed. "We've kept her presence a secret from the other Danai Houses and few here know the full story of what she did. But secrets have a way of slipping out."

"What about Ellard? He's the obvious suspect."

Nazafareen had seen him once, walking with Galen in the

forest. Both moons were full and his silver hair had stood out like a beacon in the darkness. Heart racing, she'd run to Darius's house. Then she learned that Ellard lived here. He'd been swapped as a hostage for Galen's mother long ago and raised at House Dessarian.

"Ellard is bound by wards," Tethys said. "Strong ones. I did it when he first came. If he took any action against us—in word or deed—I would know about it."

"And he wouldn't anyway," Galen put in quickly. "I'm with him all the time. I know him. It's not Ellard, I promise you."

"It's possible a spy slipped past your sentries, Victor," Tethys said. "This assassin seemed to have no trouble."

Victor grunted. "I intend to find out who was on duty tonight. We'll get to the bottom of this."

"What about the body?" Delilah asked.

"There are herbs to preserve the flesh against decay, for a time at least," Tethys said. "I'll see he's attended to."

"We'll keep the corpse as a bargaining chip," Victor said decisively. "They're fussy about their fallen. I heard they have catacombs deep in the mountains dating back a thousand years. A city of the dead. They'll want him back."

Nazafareen wondered if the Danai returned their own dead to the earth. No one had died since she'd been there so she couldn't say what their rites were. But it didn't surprise her that the Valkirins preferred the cold embrace of stone. They had an icy look about them, with their silver hair and white skin. She imagined rows of pale warriors laid out in the darkness of the earth's bones.

"Ellard says his name was Petur," Galen put in. "That he's from Val Moraine."

"Of course he is." Victor sounded irritated. "Who else could be behind this but Culach?"

The way he spoke the name—like a curse—revealed a bitter

hatred that had been carefully tended for years, centuries even. She wondered at its original source.

Culach.

She remembered him from the Dominion. He'd been large and frightening, but he'd carried her when she fell sick. She hadn't been afraid of him then. The fear had come later, after he passed through the gate. He had...changed. Flames burned in his eyes.

The thing inside him had wanted to take Nazafareen too, but she'd driven it back to whatever lightless depths it had come from. The memory raised gooseflesh on her arms.

She'd thought Culach might be dead, but it seemed dead things had a way of coming back—no matter how deeply you dug the hole.

🦑 4 🦐

THE SCARRED MAN

S now beat against the invisible barrier of air sheltering the high holdfast of Val Moraine. The storms rarely paused, a result of the extreme geography on the eastern edge of the dark continent of Nocturne. The currents lifted moist air from the White Sea and carried it over the mountains, where it froze and turned to snow. Val Moraine had been carved out of limestone and glacial ice atop the highest precipice, a testament to the Avas Valkirin's disdain for lowlander luxuries like breathable air.

Even with the poor visibility, the view from the keep was spectacular. Just enough moonlight leaked through the cloud cover to reveal majestic peaks marching to the horizon, and beyond that, the dark, heaving mass of the sea.

Culach could picture it in his mind's eye with perfect clarity. He pulled the furs closer around his naked body. He couldn't stand to wear leathers anymore. The worst of his burns had healed, but they'd left him with an exquisite sensitivity. The lightest touch lit his nerve endings on fire.

His jade eyes faced the stone ceiling, but what he saw was the vast dome of the sky, the spray of stars, hard and cold as jewels in the velvet blackness. He spent his time in this way now. His greatest fear was that he would forget and then there would be nothing left but darkness. So he made sure to remember. To painstakingly summon up the smallest details of things. The luminous blue of the glaciers when Artemis returned from her travels. The pommel of his sword. His sister's eyes.

It angered him that he was already starting to forget her face, and yet he could call up the mortal girl's with no effort at all. She was seared into his memory just as her unholy power had seared his flesh and bone.

He heard light footsteps enter the chamber but didn't turn his head.

"Go away," Culach said.

The footsteps paused, then continued to his bedside. Her scent tickled his nostrils, spicy and feminine.

"I have food."

Culach didn't respond. He heard the rattle of a tray being set on the table near the door.

"Eat it or go hungry," she said. "Your choice."

He willed her to leave. She didn't. Instead, he felt her watching him. Her hair would be in its usual tight braid, draped over one shoulder and brushing her hip. Mina only had two expressions in her repertoire. Haughty disdain, and a studiously blank one that said you were boring her to tears. He wondered which she wore now. Probably the first.

"You've done your duty. Now get out."

"You're a pitiful creature, Culach," she said. "I never liked you, but I wouldn't have thought you'd be so easily broken."

These last few days, she'd made a concerted effort to provoke him. Another of their strategies to get him out of bed. He rolled over and aimed his useless eyes at the spot he guessed her face to be.

"I never liked you either, Mina, though I suppose I should be grateful for small favors. At least I don't have to look at you anymore."

She snorted. "Yes, you've said many times how ugly you find me. It would break my heart if only I found big blonde apes attractive."

He laughed despite himself. It sounded harsh, a raven's carrion cackle. "Ah, Mina. I would never call you ugly. Well, only on the inside."

In fact, she wasn't ugly, just different from every other woman at Val Moraine. Mina was small and dark. He could have picked her up by the scruff of her neck like a kitten.

Culach himself was tall even for a Valkirin. Like all his cousins, he had silver-white hair and green eyes. A winding scar bisected his jaw. That one was old. He'd acquired others of more recent vintage, but they were covered by the furs.

He sat up, fingers fumbling along the floor. Far from icy, the summerstone gave off a pleasant warmth. That and the shields of air surrounding the holdfast were what allowed the clan to live at such high altitude.

"Where's my water?" he demanded. "You moved it."

Mina laughed. "If I wished to torment you, I'd do more than hide your water." She pressed a goblet into his hand, careful not to touch his skin.

Culach took a long drink, then lay back. He knew why she was really here and he wanted to make her leave before she pressed him about it. He wanted to hurt her.

"Did they tell you Victor has returned?" he said. "With his new bride?"

Mina didn't answer, but her brittle silence confirmed he'd landed a blow. Even after all this time, she still pined for her old lover. He wasn't surprised she hadn't heard. Mina had no friends at Val Moraine.

"You lie," she said at last. "Victor is dead."

"Sadly not. He brought a son home with him as well. Your bastard has a half-brother. His name is Darius."

He heard Mina approach the bed. He wondered if she would

slap him. Instead she simply sat on the edge. He held still, willing his expression to stone.

"Thank you for telling me," she said quietly, and Culach suddenly felt ashamed.

"There's nothing you can do about my injuries," he snapped. "If it's all the same to you, lady, I'd prefer to skip this charade every day."

This was the fifth afternoon Mina had come to his chamber with a tray. The eighty-third since he had been carried back through the gate by his brethren, broken and burned.

And blind, though that wasn't even the worst of it.

"It's not my choice," she said. "Your father charged me with trying to heal you and he'll know if I don't try. He seems to believe I have a gift for it."

Culach wouldn't give her the satisfaction of shifting away, of letting her know how much her presence bothered him, but it wasn't easy. He could feel her body heat through the furs. Something brushed his arm like a spider web. He nearly jerked back before he realized it must be her braid.

"I'm beyond healing," he growled.

"Most likely, yes. But I've nothing else to do. Nor do you."

This was true. Mina was a hostage. Traded for Ellard, Culach's third cousin, to keep the peace with the Avas Danai. He'd felt a little sorry for her when she first came to Val Moraine, but that wore off quickly. Mina made no attempt to charm her captors. Quite the opposite. She was prickly and aloof. If she was lonely, she deserved it.

"Don't presume," he snapped. "And if you touch me, I'll break your arm."

She stood up and he nearly wept with relief.

"Fine. I'll tell them you refused me again."

Culach grunted.

"If you wish to starve yourself to death, you're free to. Otherwise, the food is on the table. Don't expect me to feed you."

Her footsteps receded toward the door and he hoped she would leave, but then he heard the chair by the window creak as she sat down.

"I don't want company," Culach said, in case she'd somehow failed to grasp that point. "Especially not yours."

"And I don't want to be here. But they say you are alone too much and I must spend two hours in your rooms each day. I am not accountable to you. Only to them. So I will sit here for two hours."

She didn't ask him anything more about Victor. She didn't ask for news of her son, Galen, or anyone else at House Dessarian. To rely on Culach for information was too humiliating, and Mina was stiff-necked and proud. He didn't think he'd seen her smile once in all the years they'd known each other. She didn't pretend to be a guest at Val Moraine, although that's how she was treated. They didn't need to confine her. Even if she'd wanted to escape, no one walked out of these mountains.

When Culach was younger, he'd disliked Mina for having been Victor's lover. Victor himself had been out of reach, vanished on a sudden journey into the shadowlands, so Culach had been cruel to Mina instead. She always gave back as good as she got. Trading insults had become second nature for them both.

He wondered if Petur had managed to kill the girl. He should have returned by now. Culach curled up on his side and listened to the wind howling against the barrier. He loved Petur like a brother. They'd grown up together, scaling the sheer faces of the massifs and exploring the ancient honeycomb of mine shafts that riddled the mountains. They'd fought together and gotten drunk together.

Petur had volunteered to go when the message arrived saying the girl was alive and living with the Avas Danai. He'd understood the risks, but Culach still felt a stab of guilt. By all rights, it should have been him. Once, he'd been the finest swordsman of all the Valkirin strongholds. Their most cunning strategist. A hero for the ages. Women beat down his door, and a few men too.

He'd been invincible.

Now he was useless. Worse than useless. All because of a slip of a mortal girl not even half his size.

"You need a bath. Desperately."

There was a gentle clink as Mina replaced something on the table. Culach suspected she'd started eating his lunch.

"Are you still here, Mina?"

"You know I am."

"If you don't like the smell, you can always leave."

He could practically see her shaking her head. "You used to be such a heartbreaker. Now you won't even wash your own arse."

It's like she was reading his thoughts.

"Be quiet, Mina."

"It's pathetic. I'm saying that as a friend."

He barked another laugh. This one came out a little less rusty. "A friend, eh?"

"All right, not a friend," she conceded. "The person who has to sit here for two hours a day and smell you."

He casually leaned toward an armpit and decided she might be right.

"Are you offering to fetch water?"

She sighed. "Can't you just wash in snow like the others?"

He pictured her sour expression. "My manhood is shriveled enough already, Mina."

Wonder of wonders, he heard a breathy sound that might have been laughter. The chair scraped back. Footsteps marched to the door. She returned a short time later. Culach heard a bucket rattle down next to his bed. Mina pressed a cloth into his hand.

"I'm not washing you, so don't get your hopes up."

Culach suppressed a groan as he sat up. He felt sore all over. He had to admit it might have something to do with lying in bed for months.

"Turn around," he said gruffly.

Once he would have enjoyed flaunting his body, but he had no idea what it looked like now. Gaunt and wasted at the very least. He tossed the furs aside. Cold air lifted the fine hairs on his belly. He dipped the cloth in the bucket and began to work it over his skin. It felt smooth until he reached his upper chest. He could feel the ridges of scar tissue there.

He rinsed the cloth in the bucket and squeezed it out. Then he ran it over his head. His hair had been badly singed so he'd shorn it at the scalp. The stubble felt strange beneath his hands, like it belonged to somebody else.

"I hope you're enjoying yourself," he said, raising an arm and scrubbing the hollow beneath. "I know you've fantasized about this moment since we first met."

"Eating soup while you wash your balls? You're right, I've thought of nothing else."

"My balls," he exclaimed. "Thanks for reminding me."

Culach lowered the cloth between his legs and waited for a sigh of disgust. When none was forthcoming, he continued about his business. Maybe she really was paying him no attention. The thought was oddly depressing. He might not care for Mina, but despite his sorry state, Culach still didn't relish being ignored.

He finished up. The water had been freezing, the towel rough, but to his surprise, neither caused him agony. His skin tingled and he felt hungry for the first time in days.

"I'll eat something now," he said. "If you haven't devoured it all."

"On the table," Mina replied absently.

He waited for signs of movement. "Bring it over then."

Her voice was maddeningly calm. "You can get it yourself."

Culach suppressed a scowl. A fine nursemaid his father had chosen. There were plenty of women who'd be thrilled to give him a sponge bath and chew his food for him if that's what he asked of them. But he'd been given Mina, who'd despised him from the moment they met. No doubt his father had done it on purpose.

Culach threw the fur over his shoulders and shuffled across the room. He banged into the table, nearly toppling it over, but refused to let her see his frustration. After some cautious groping, his hands closed on the tray.

"What is it?" he asked.

"Beet soup, so try not to trip."

Culach managed to get the tray back to the bed without embarrassing himself further. He didn't dare use a spoon, but drinking straight from the bowl didn't work either as he could feel the soup dribbling into his scraggly beard and probably dying it purple. Culach resolved to shave it off the next day.

Further exploration of the tray revealed a loaf of bread brought in at considerable expense from the bakeries of Solis. He tore it into chunks and washed it down with gulps of water. When he finished, Culach left the tray on the floor and curled into his furs. The food and bath made him drowsy. He was just drifting off when Mina spoke.

"I was thinking," she said in a hesitant voice he'd never heard before. "You've lost your sight. But why can't you use air to probe your surroundings? With practice—"

He cut her off. "I already tried. It doesn't work."

"But—"

Despair gave his voice a brusque edge. "Let it go, Mina."

He'd never admit the truth.

It wasn't the blindness or the scars that kept him hiding in his chambers. He could live with those. But ever since that disastrous day at the lake, Culach had been unable to touch the elements. He was no longer a daēva. Just a maimed creature who dreamt of fire.

The remainder of the two hours elapsed without either of them speaking again. He heard Mina leave and then he was alone again, with only the wind and the faint smell of her for company.

5

A SHIP FROM THE SKY

Nazafareen gripped the trunk of the spruce with her knees, her left hand resting lightly on a branch sticky with sap. From her gently swaying perch at the very top, she could see for twenty leagues or more, the forest spreading out below like a dark green sea. Somewhere beyond the curve of the horizon lay the sun, but it would never rise or set in these skies. Here, the triple moons reigned unchallenged.

Darius said she came from mountain people, nomadic herders who had migrated long distances every year over unforgiving terrain. Nazafareen believed him, not because Darius would never lie to her—in fact, she felt certain he had—but because something inside her loved the high places.

She'd stayed at his bedside for the last six days. Tethys said he would recover, but he hadn't woken up. Not yet. The Valkirin's last words still rang in her ears.

You die, or they all die.

Everyone knew another attack was coming. It was only a matter of time. Tethys had sent word to the other Danai. The ones that shared the Valkirin border—House Baradel and House Fiala—had sent reinforcements and tripled their patrols. Sentries lurked in the trees, watching the skies day and night. The Matrium would be meeting but not for another week—and the outcome was far from certain. Despite the heightened defenses, no one wanted all-out war with the Valkirins, not over a mortal girl. Victor seethed with impatience, but Tethys kept him on a short leash. The other Danai had mostly ignored her. She felt more of an outsider than ever.

I cannot stay here, even if they would shelter me. Every day I remain puts the whole clan in danger.

She could hide deep in the forest, but the Valkirins knew about her now. They'd find her eventually. And once Darius woke up, he certainly would. He could track anything on two legs or four. She wouldn't let him die trying to protect her.

Or she could return through the gate to the Dominion. Nazafareen doubted her enemies would follow—not into the shadowlands. Her own world lay somewhere on the other side, through yet another gate. But the same reason the Valkirins would be loath to follow was why she didn't want to enter the gate herself.

The Dominion was the land of the dead. And other things walked there too, worse than the newly reaped souls—which is why the daēvas had warded it. One of them had been inside the man with the scar—Culach—she felt certain of it. She didn't wish to meet that thing again.

Which left one alternative: go to the Marakai daēvas as she had originally intended. That was certainly the best of the bunch. The problem was that House Dessarian lay far from the coast, at least a hundred leagues. She'd never make it before the Valkirins caught her. Victor said the assassin they sent had come on the back of a winged creature called an abbadax; it was how he'd evaded the sentries.

She remembered his eyes, the pure hatred.

You die, or they all die.

Nazafareen frowned as a shadow flitted in front of Selene's buttery yellow face. She gripped the trunk, leaning forward as far as she could without falling. The moon was almost full and cast a bright light on the treetops. Something floated silently above them, moving fast. The silhouette looked strange. It was far too large for a bird.

Her chest tightened as she scrambled down from the tree. Long practice had made her adept at one-handed climbing. The spruces were the easiest, since they had a multitude of thin branches that grew like a ladder. She dropped the last six feet and set off at a run for the compound of House Dessarian. Would the Valkirins be so brazen as to attack during the lunar day, when everyone was awake? It seemed unlikely, and unlikelier still that they would send only one.

"Nazafareen!"

She turned at Galen's voice. He strode through the trees, ash bow strapped across his broad back. Galen was Darius's half-brother. Both had Victor's bullish build, but Darius had inherited his mother's bright blue eyes while Galen's were dark. He was also a head taller, an advantage he clearly relished.

When Galen spoke to her—or to Darius, for that matter—his voice usually held a subtle hint of mockery. He clearly wasn't thrilled to have a rival for Victor's attention, but it had been Galen who saved Darius's life.

He does have honor, she thought, *even if he hides it well sometimes.*

Nazafareen waited for him to catch up. His face was grave as he jogged out of the shadows.

"What are you doing out here?" he demanded. "You shouldn't be in the woods alone."

Nazafareen ignored the question. "Did you see it?"

Galen nodded. "I saw it."

Her hand rested on the hilt of her sword. "More Valkirins?"

"Perhaps." Galen's eyes held hers. His raven hair shone like a dark mirror in the moonlight. "Once they declare a blood feud, they won't stop until it's done."

She felt a flicker of unease. "We'd better get back then."

Nazafareen knew the terrain well and she ran without hesitation. It warmed her up. The air wasn't terribly cold—not like it would be in the mountains—but it still held a chill and sitting in the tree had stiffened her limbs. Galen quickly pulled ahead. In a minute, he'd vanished down the path ahead.

She scanned the sky, but the foliage was too dense to see anything. Judging by its trajectory, the thing had been heading for a large field on the outskirts of the settlement. It was the only open place for leagues around. Nazafareen adjusted her path and made for the clearing. She sensed it up ahead, a gap in the trees like a missing tooth. Then she heard shouts and knew with relief that others had seen it too and the Danai wouldn't be caught unawares—whatever it was.

She burst out of the forest and skidded to an abrupt stop. To her astonishment, a ship with a sharp upward-curving bow was falling from the sky. It had neither sails nor oars. Nazafareen knew elemental magic could be used to move objects, but not on this scale. As it drew closer, catching Selene's gilded light, she realized the ship hung from a webbing of ropes connected to a large ball of fabric dyed black to artfully blend with the darkness.

The wind whipped the ship this way and that, but its captain seemed experienced enough to keep it out of the treetops. Seconds later, the ship alit in the center of the field and a figure leapt over the side. Other daēvas from House Dessarian were already there, surrounding it, as the great sack of air began to deflate. The captain seized a mooring rope and quickly pounded a stake into the earth. There was much gesticulating but Nazafareen couldn't hear what they were saying. She spotted Galen at the edge of the clearing and ran over.

"A wind ship," he said, staring in fascination. "From the mortal lands."

The mortal lands! Nazafareen caught a quick glimpse of the captain being led away, though she couldn't tell if they were a man or woman. It was the first time she'd seen another human being since coming to Nocturne.

"I thought they stayed on the sunlit side," she said, her curiosity piqued.

"They do," Galen replied thoughtfully.

"Do you think it has anything to do with me?"

He glanced at her with annoyance. "How should I know?"

Nazafareen scowled back. "I just thought—"

Galen spotted Ellard at the fringes of the crowd and shouted his name.

The Valkirin trotted over. With his fair hair and pale complexion, he looked like a snow cat among panthers. Nazafareen watched him approach with extreme wariness. He might be Galen's friend, but his kinsmen had put a blood price on her head. His light eyes lingered on her for a moment. To her surprise, he gave her a polite nod before turning to Galen.

"It's an emissary from Samarqand," Ellard said.

"What does he want?" Galen asked.

"I don't know. I suppose we'll find out."

They turned their backs to Nazafareen, talking quietly together. She stood for a long moment, staring at the wind ship. She needed to find out why this mortal was here, and quickly. From what she'd heard, humans stayed out of daēva business, and vice versa. He was probably here on some other business. But he had a ship.

Nazafareen felt the glimmerings of an idea.

❧ 6 ❧

PARTINGS

Watchful eyes followed Nazafareen as she hurried through the moonlit woods. Every daēva she saw wore a bow and there was an alert tension in their postures, a sense of wariness that made her sad. It had seemed a peaceful place when she first came here.

She assumed the emissary from Samarqand would be brought straight to Tethys. Most likely, Victor would be there too. So she snuck through the fragrant wilderness of Tethys's garden, hood up and keeping to the thickest shadows. The house lay at the end of a narrow path, white birch walls gleaming in the moonlight. Nazafareen was halfway there when she froze. The Valkirin's body had been laid out on a woven mat near the outer wall of junipers. His skin and hair were the same ashen shade. He had sharp cheekbones and a high brow with deeply socketed eyes, but the angular planes of his face were softened in death. Someone had removed Galen's arrow. The white leather coat was ripped and bloody.

Nazafareen walked over to the body and regarded it for a long moment. She thought of Darius, the terrible crack of the sword striking his head. Sudden fury set her heart pounding. She kicked the corpse twice, savagely, then continued around the side of the house, placing each foot with care. Crystals burned in the oval windows, their crisp light casting geometric forms on the ground outside. Nazafareen heard voices and crept closer.

Whatever her other faults might be, Nazafareen wasn't a complete fool. She didn't risk a peek inside. From what she'd seen in her weeks there, daēvas picked up on the slightest sound or movement. So she sat cross-legged on the ground and quietly listened.

"...don't like it."

That was Victor.

"You never like anything," Tethys replied tartly. "But Samarqand has always treated the daēvas fairly. They're our largest market. Where do you think that blade you wear came from? And all the metal tools we use?"

"We trade with the Marakai. They trade with the mortals. That's how it's always been. So why is he here?"

"I don't know, but I intend to find out. And I've kept the boy waiting long enough. You stay put—and try not to start a war with the mortals too. It wouldn't kill you to practice a little diplomacy, Victor."

Nazafareen heard rustling and the gentle closing of a door. A minute later, it opened again and light footsteps entered.

"The Lady Tethys of House Dessarian," a new voice said. It was soft and respectful, with a musical accent.

"If you know my name, young man, I'm afraid you have me at a disadvantage."

"They call me Javid, *Shahbanu*."

"I'm not a queen, let alone an empress." Tethys sounded amused. "And stand up, boy. You needn't prostrate yourself."

"As you say."

His voice sounded half-muffled and Nazafareen's mouth twitched.

"The glowering giant in the corner is my son, Victor."

"It is a most exquisite pleasure to make your acquaintance, Lord Victor of House Dessarian of the Avas Danai."

Victor grunted.

Tethys and the emissary exchanged more empty pleasantries and Nazafareen silently willed them to get to the interesting part —why he was here at all. She knew almost nothing about the mortal lands that lay beyond the the twilit boundary between the light and dark sides. Only that the lands collectively called Solis were very hot and dry.

"I bring gifts for the adornment of your illustrious House."

She heard what must be wooden crates cracking open, followed by other soft sounds she couldn't identify. Nazafareen scanned the shadows. Shrubs concealed her to either side, but if anyone chanced to walk past, they couldn't miss her.

"This is a fine figurine," Tethys said politely. "Bronze?"

The emissary seemed scandalized. "Gold, *Shahbanu*!"

Tethys murmured something noncommittal.

More sounds involving the crates. Nazafareen tensed as she heard air whistle against the edge of a blade, but it was followed by a purr of approval from Victor.

"Nice sword," he said.

"Forged by the masters in Tjanjin."

Grudgingly: "It must be priceless."

"As I mentioned, Lord Victor, my masters are aware of your reputation. They would never insult you with an unworthy blade."

"Wise of them."

More whistling, and the sound of wood chips flying.

"Victor, would you please stop that?" Tethys interrupted dryly. "This is all very nice, but I somehow doubt you came all this way to watch my son reduce the table to kindling."

"The *Shahbanu* is astute. My masters have a proposal for House Dessarian."

"Indeed? Let's hear it then."

Her voice grew louder as she approached the window. Nazafareen held herself perfectly still, hardly daring to breathe.

"I shall be direct. The King's taxes have grown more burdensome every year. The Guild barely ekes out a profit anymore, when we bear all the trouble. It is intolerable."

"So?"

"My masters would offer House Dessarian a secret alliance. There are other routes into Samarqand besides the port of Susa."

"Smuggling, you mean."

"We could offer higher prices for the goods of the Avas Danai if the authorities weren't taking such a large bite. Beneficial for all involved."

"And if the King discovers we've gone behind his back?" Victor demanded.

"The Guild will bear all the risk. There would be no interruption of the normal trade routes. Consider it supplementary income. We could begin with a few small shipments to test the waters, so to speak. But the Guild is particularly interested in bonewood armor and swords."

"Planning a war?"

"Merely preparing for every eventuality," the emissary replied smoothly. "There are concerns about the new Oracle of Delphi."

"Be specific," Tethys said tartly.

"Her prophecies of late have been distinctly...belligerent. She has no love of daēvas either. Some in the Guild feel the Oracle has grown too powerful. By all accounts she holds the Archons in the palm of her hand. I'll be frank, *Shahbanu*. My masters worry that our king is weak. He cares mainly for wine and boys and seems oblivious of the threat to the north."

Nazafareen listened closely. So he wanted to cheat his own king. But who were the Archons? And how was the Oracle a threat to Samarqand? She waited for more details, but Victor gave an ostentatious yawn as though bored by mortal politics.

"Let's cut to the heart of the matter. What incentive are you offering?" he asked.

"Twice the profits you'd normally receive."

"How generous," Tethys replied coldly. "But I'm afraid you've wasted your time. We don't deal with mortals directly. We never have, as I'm sure you're aware. All trade is conducted through the Marakai. Are you suggesting cutting them out? That would surely cause discord between our clans."

"Not at all. We've already approached the Avas Marakai and they're amenable to a bargain. The Oracle is taking a hard line on magic—and anyone who wields it. If she convinces the Archons to seal the port of Delphi, cargo from Samarqand will have go around the entire continent to reach Tjanjin."

Tethys sounded surprised. "Is that truly a possibility?"

"The Guild fears so. It is time we begin to establish alternate routes. If nothing else, my masters wish to convey the clear message that Samarqand does not ally with Delphi. If anything, the Greeks are a common enemy. We will continue to trade with you as always, whatever you decide today."

"Well, that's good to know, I suppose. We need to discuss this further before I give my reply."

"Of course. But by your leave, *Shahbanu*, I hope to depart when Hecate rises. The Guild is anxious for your response and the weather tonight is perfect for flying, clear skies with a light breeze. As much as I am humbled by your gracious hospitality and enchanted by the beauty of your lands, I fear the conditions could change quickly. The Umbra is a fickle place."

"That gives us time to have a quick supper," Tethys said. "I'll admit, I'm intrigued by the offer, especially if the Marakai have already consented. We owe no loyalty to your king. And I want to know more about this Oracle. We pay little attention to mortal affairs, but perhaps that is a mistake."

"You are most wise, *Shahbanu*."

Nazafareen's thoughts raced as she heard them leave the

room. It was a chance that might never come again. A way to cross the Umbra and find the Marakai. This emissary said they were part of the deal. He'd know how to find them.

She briefly considered asking permission but decided against it. The emissary could too easily refuse her—especially if he discovered who her enemies were. But he was only one man and it was a large ship, thirty hands from bow to stern.

If she was sneaky, no one would know she was gone until it was too late.

7

NIGHT FLIGHT

Nazafareen ran back to her little house, cloak flying. Since the Valkirin assassin, she'd become more cautious. Now she paused outside the door and drew a deep, calming breath. It took her three tries before the lumen crystal caught, the light flickering weakly as she struggled to hold the flow. Sometimes it came effortlessly. More often than not, though, reaching for the elements was like cupping water with open fingers. They simply slid away. Darius said it was because she tried too hard; she was supposed to let the power enter her rather than grab for it like a child stealing candy.

Nazafareen peered through the window and made sure the house was empty before entering. Once inside, she found the bag that had held the astrolabe and started packing—not that she had many belongings. Two spare tunics and one pair of pants. A full water skin. A knife and whetstone. Some strips of dried fruit from the larder. She wasted precious minutes searching for the hair-brush Darius had made, but she must have misplaced it.

She took a final look around and buckled on her sword. It wasn't bonewood but iron, forged by the smiths in Solis from ore mined in the mountains of the Valkirins. The pommel and grip were made of gold and engraved with strange animals, half-fish, half-snake. The blade itself was short but perfectly balanced, fitting her hand as though it had been made for her.

Nazafareen wished she could leave Darius a letter of explanation, but didn't know how to read or write. It wasn't a result of her amnesia. He said she'd always been illiterate. In the world they came from, only the magi and the very wealthy received an education.

Nazafareen was about to rush out the door when she turned back.

Should I leave it behind?

Part of her wanted to. But it was the only remnant of her former life as a soldier. The only thing the *other* Nazafareen had owned.

So she went back inside and found the snarling griffin bracelet. Darius had a matching one. Once, the cuffs had bonded them in some strange way she didn't understand—and that Darius refused to explain. The bond had dissolved when they passed through the gate to Nocturne, but she remembered a faint echo of it.

She extinguished the lumen crystal and ran through the forest to his simple two-story house. Certain flowers only bloomed after Selene had risen and she smelled them now, a heady, cloying blend that made her think of the single time Darius had kissed her....

They'd moved him to his own bed once the worst danger had passed. As she'd hoped, he was alone. She sat on the edge of the bed and watched him. Her chest ached, but it was a different sort of pain than when she'd been in the grip of terror. Fear squeezed. Love hurt from the inside out.

A damp curl stuck to his forehead. Nazafareen smoothed it back.

His reticence was infuriating, but she knew he thought he was doing the right thing. *Fool man.* He wouldn't tell her anything of importance, only little snippets, as if that might appease her. Like the fact that Nazafareen meant North Star in the language of the nomads. And that she was fond of figs—whatever *those* were.

He'd made the furniture in her house, beautiful pieces of ebony and white cherry cunningly combined. He said it was a reflection of the world they lived in now—half light, half dark.

She felt bold with him sleeping and no one around, bold enough to kiss his palm. Darius murmured something but didn't wake. She studied the lines of his face, touched his wavy brown hair, his cheek. The heat of his skin almost burned her fingertips.

She thought about what Galen said about blood feuds. The Avas Valkirin wouldn't stop, nor did they issue empty threats.

You die, or they all die.

"I'll find you again someday," she told his sleeping form. "But don't try to follow. It won't do either of us any good."

Now that the moment had come, it was harder to leave than she'd anticipated.

If only he would wake up right now. I would tell him everything.

But he didn't, and she could put it off no longer. Staying would only bring disaster to House Dessarian. The cold air stung her cheeks as she stepped outside into the moonlit evening. Nazafareen pulled her cloak tighter and made her way toward the clearing, the oilskin sack slung over her left shoulder. There was little chance of creeping away unseen, not with everyone on high alert. So she walked with her back straight, not too fast. She glimpsed shadowy shapes in the trees, but she was permitted to move freely within the settlement and none of the sentries challenged her.

A breeze swept through, rattling the leaves. Nazafareen tried to imagine what it would be like to sail through the sky, suspended by ropes from the sack of air keeping the ship aloft. She wasn't afraid of heights, but the thought still sent a slight tingle through the soles of her feet.

Selene was already drifting toward the horizon and Hecate beginning her ascent across the heavens. Nazafareen quickened her pace. She'd spent too long in Darius's room. What if the emissary left early? She'd never make it across the Umbra on foot.

The clearing wasn't far, just a few minutes past the last line of houses and the deep craters Darius had torn in the earth. She darted around a bend just as a gaunt figure stepped directly into her path. Nazafareen dropped the bag and drew her sword, heart racing. Then the figure moved into the moonlight and she recognized Darius's mother.

"I've been looking for you," Delilah said, her cool gaze resting on the bag. "Going somewhere?"

Nazafareen sheathed the sword. "It's not your concern."

"You think not? I'd say it's very much my concern."

Nazafareen concocted and discarded a series of lies. "Oh, very well. Yes, I'm leaving. I don't want to bring war to the clans. Surely you can understand that."

"Tethys would give you sanctuary here."

"I know. But Galen said the Valkirins won't stop once they declare a blood feud. I don't want to put Darius at risk. Or any of you." She picked up the bag and slung it over her shoulder. "It's my choice and I have the right."

Delilah raised an eyebrow. "Let me guess. You think you can go to Samarqand."

Nazafareen glanced at the path, impatient to go. "If I travel by wind ship, I'll leave no trail to follow."

"You think this emissary will take you?"

"That's my business."

"You don't plan to ask, do you?"

Nazafareen lifted her chin. "If I conceal myself, he'll never know the difference."

"And what will happen when you reach Solis and your magic returns?"

"I'll worry about that when it happens," she said stubbornly.

"You should worry about it now." Delilah sighed. "Are you sure you want to do this? You don't have to."

Nazafareen had expected Delilah to be thrilled she was leaving. "I'm sure."

Delilah studied her for a long moment, her face unreadable. "I don't pretend to understand your power or where it comes from. But for the sake of my son, you should let go of your hatred. In the end, it will only poison you."

"I have no hatred."

Delilah laughed. "Liar. I can see it in your face. You hate the Valkirins."

Nazafareen's brows drew together in a frown. She opened her mouth to reply but Delilah cut her off.

"They tried to murder you. They've driven you away from Darius. Of course you hate them." She leaned closer. "Just as I hated King Artaxeros for keeping me as his slave. Just as Victor hates the men who imprisoned him at Gorgon-e Gaz for two hundred years." A shadow crossed her face. "Victor's not the man he used to be. There's a bitterness inside him. I fear war will come no matter what you do."

Nazafareen wasn't sure how to respond. Delilah had never spoken to her so frankly.

"If our enemies are willing to kill, then we must too," she said at last. "I'm not afraid."

Delilah gave her a level look. "That's what worries me." She shook her head. "I'm not a soft woman. I'm merely warning you since no one else will. Victor told me about your temper. You're reckless and impulsive. He thinks it's wonderful, but I don't. And from what I understand, your magic feeds on those traits."

Nazafareen only remembered using it once—that day at the lake with Culach. Her time in the Dominion, just before, was a fragmented dream. A beautiful woman in white who'd called her daughter. Winged creatures with sharp talons. The sound of a monstrous bell tolling....

Nazafareen shook her head. "I'll be fine," she said tersely. "Just because the power exists doesn't mean I have to use it. If I never touch it again, it can't harm me."

As she spoke the words, she knew they were true. No matter what happened, she wouldn't resort to the breaking magic. She could still wield the other elements, to a point, and she had her sword. It would have to be enough.

"All right," Delilah said, sounding unconvinced. "But we have another problem. It will be next to impossible to keep Darius from going after you once he wakes."

Nazafareen felt a stab of guilt, but it was better she did this alone.

I draw danger like flies to a midden heap. And next time, Tethys won't be there to heal him.

"You can tell him I plan to seek out the Marakai. There's a chance they can restore my memories. Tell him...I'll come back when I can."

Delilah's head jerked toward the settlement, though Nazafareen heard nothing except the monotonous chirrup of insects.

"They're coming," she hissed. "I won't stop you, though Darius won't thank me for it. Go, then! Quickly!"

Delilah ran back along the path, black hair trailing down her back in a wild, tangled mane. Nazafareen slipped across the field to the tethered wind ship. The air sack had been partially deflated so the ship wouldn't sail away without its owner. It was made of smooth, lacquered wood that gleamed like polished glass in the moonlight. Nazafareen circled it, searching for a way aboard. She could hear the voices herself now, coming closer. Her heart beat with anxious excitement as she ran her hand along the hull, but it seemed unbroken by any door or toehold.

Nazafareen peeked around the curved prow. Three figures appeared at the edge of the clearing. She recognized the tall, slim figure of Tethys with Victor at her side. He was a physically commanding man, with a lithe, confident stride. Next to him, the human emissary looked practically like a child.

Nazafareen's mouth ran dry as they crossed the open field. She had only moments before they saw her. And she very much doubted the emissary would take her willingly, not with the Valkirins hunting her. She would be sent back to her house and they'd put a guard on her so she couldn't run again.

"...a message from the guild once we reach Samarqand. It's been an exquisite pleasure to conduct business with you, *Shahbanu*."

Hecate rose behind the trio, causing their shadows to lengthen and stretch for the wind ship. Nazafareen's pulse hammered wildly, a rabbit caught in a trap as she hears the hunter's footsteps approach. Her fingers brushed a rope ladder, but it was too late....

"Victor!"

They all turned as Delilah appeared at the edge of the clearing. Nazafareen hauled herself one-handed up the rope ladder and threw herself into a dark corner of the ship.

"What is it, my love?" Victor asked, concern in his voice.

"I just wanted to see the wind ship for myself before it departed," Delilah replied, a trifle breathless. "A fascinating conveyance."

"I would be most pleased to offer you a ride in one should I return to Nocturne," the emissary said. "Would you care to climb aboard and inspect—"

"That won't be necessary," Delilah said quickly. "I don't want to delay you further."

Nazafareen wiggled deeper between what felt like sacks of sand, arranging her cloak so she was covered completely. The emissary made a long-winded, flowery goodbye. Feet thumped down on the deck of the ship. She heard him muttering words to himself, too low to make out. He called directions to Victor, who untied the mooring lines and tossed them aboard. And then she felt the ship lift off from the ground, swaying a bit as the breeze caught it. She wrapped her arms tight around herself. With any luck, she wouldn't be found until they reached Samarqand.

It might have been exciting if she'd been able to see anything, but curled in her dark corner, exhaustion stole over her. She tried not to think about Darius, lying so pale in his bed.

Nazafareen dug through the oilskin bag and found the griffin cuff, slipping it over her stump and around her right forearm. The emblem of a dead king from another world she'd likely never see again. Still, she found the gesture oddly comforting.

8

SHADOW AND FLAME

Culach's eyes spasmed open, a shudder wracking his sweat-soaked body.

He threw the clammy furs off and groped around next to the bed. His hand closed on the pitcher of water Mina had left for him. He drained it in six convulsive swallows. His throat felt raw and parched, as if he'd crawled a hundred leagues through the wastelands of Solis.

He must have drifted off. The last he remembered, Mina had been sitting in her chair, humming a soft, mournful tune. Culach was acutely sensitive to her presence and he knew she was gone. Just a few paces away, beyond the barrier of air, the ever-present wind raged. It moaned against the keep like a restless spirit, cold fingers prying for any chink in the stone.

Culach pressed his palms to his eyes. The dregs of the nightmare lingered, leaving a bitter, almost coppery taste. His heart still raced from the raw emotion of it. Smothering terror. A darkness even heavier than his own blindness.

He had been fleeing across a vast sea of burning sands. Behind him, he heard the roar of some terrible gale, so deep and loud it made his teeth ache. Hunched figures ran to either side of him, but he couldn't make out their faces through the yellow haze. His breath rasped harshly in his ears. His only thought was to escape that wind, but then the sands simply crumbled beneath his feet like water. He sank to his waist, crying out for help. One of the figures paused and briefly looked at him, then kept running. He flailed in panic and only managed to sink deeper.

They were abandoning him.

He watched as the last dwindled to a speck on the shimmering horizon.

He called weakly to air, with no discernible effect. Inch by inch, the sands took him, filling his mouth and eyes. Scalding his skin.

Buried alive.

Culach shuddered at the memory, then froze as he heard a soft exhalation. He wasn't alone after all and it wasn't Mina. He knew her smell.

Who then?

No one else came to see him anymore.

Perhaps it was paranoia brought on by his nightmare, but for the first time, Culach wished he'd kept his sword close at hand. He might not stand a chance against a sighted opponent, but it would be better than dying naked and unarmed in bed.

"Who's there?" he demanded, trying to keep the fear from his voice. "Speak. I've no patience for games."

The chair creaked, a much deeper groan than when Mina sat in it, as though it bore the weight of a man Culach's own considerable size. He caught the faint scent of oiled leather.

"Petur is dead," a gravelly voice said.

Culach's chest loosened at his father's voice, but an instant later the words sunk in. For days, he'd hoped to hear Petur's stride ringing on the stones of the corridor. Once, he'd been certain he heard his friend's laughter, but it must have been a trick of the wind. Through the long hours of his self-imposed confinement, Culach had sought solace in numbness, hoping never to feel anything again, but the avalanche of pain that swept through him shattered that illusion.

Petur. Dead.

His dearest companion. One of the last seasoned soldiers left at Val Moraine.

So many gone. Cousins, aunts and uncles.

His twin sister, Neblis.

Now Petur.

And yet I live on.

"How?" Culach asked.

"Victor's son killed him."

Culach fought the urge to howl his grief at the heavens. Val Moraine was cursed, and the name of that curse was Dessarian.

It was the first time Eirik had come to his chamber in recent memory. Culach's father had no patience for weakness. He was Valkirin through and through, hard as the frozen tundra and pitiless as the tides. But it wasn't Culach's blindness that disgusted his father, he knew. A man couldn't be blamed for an injury taken in war—even if that war proved to be a disastrous mistake. No, what Eirik despised was Culach's refusal to face what he'd become. More than that, to face the fact that he'd led his own mother to her death, along with three-quarters of their holdfast.

Eirik didn't know Culach could no longer touch the elements. No one did.

Culach hadn't felt love for his father in a long time, but he still craved his respect, whatever measure of it was left. So he sat up straight and kept his emotions in check.

"How did you find out?"

"A bird arrived from our informant at House Dessarian this morning."

"And the girl?"

"Still alive."

Culach swore.

"I want to know more about her, Culach. Tell me what happened that day. I've heard it from others but never from you."

Culach drew a breath. He remembered standing before the gate to the other world, rank upon rank of Valkirin soldiers at his back. He remembered raising his sword and saying something about battle and glory, but he didn't remember stepping through. And the next thing he knew, he'd woken up in this chamber wrapped in damp cloths, agony coursing through every nerve.

"She was my prisoner," Culach said, going back to the hours just before the gate, where the ground felt more solid. "She seemed...sick. She was so weak, I had to carry her."

"Yes, yes, I know all that," his father said testily.

"We had just come from the House-Behind-the-Veil. Neblis was gone. I feared the mortals had taken her. Then we found the gate nearby."

Culach closed his eyes against a sudden shooting pain in his forehead. He saw the tall reeds swaying. The fey green glow. Sinuous movement in the murk.

"There was something else..."

He'd avoided thinking about that day. It gave him a queasy feeling in the pit of his stomach. Now the memories were like shards of ice digging into his tender skull.

"What do you mean, something else?" Eirik demanded.

Culach tried to grasp the image (*shadow and flame*), but it slipped between his fingers.

"Her breaking magic must have flared when we passed through the gate. She turned on us." This much was true. His own body was visible proof.

"Must have?"

"I don't remember," Culach admitted. "Not clearly."

Eirik grunted. "It doesn't matter, I suppose. We know what she did and we know where she is. Who's protecting her." His voice grew hoarser. "We gave them a chance. They chose to protect this abomination over the welfare of their own kind. The die is cast. It's time for harsher measures."

"We don't have the resources for another war so soon. Not against the Danai." Culach disliked admitting it, but it was the truth. "They're too strong."

"I'm not talking about an invasion. There are other ways of settling scores. Ancient ways."

A trickle of unease crept up his spine. He waited.

"We can make chimera. A pack of three ought to be sufficient."

Chimera.

"I thought they were just a tale to frighten children."

"Oh, they're real enough."

He wished he could see his father's expression. Would it reveal any shred of doubt? Or was Eirik fully committed to this insane course?

"Even if you could do it, no one has raised a chimera in centuries," Culach said evenly. "For good reason. Are you sure it's wise?"

"Wise?" His father barked a harsh laugh. "Perhaps not. But they've left us no other choice. She's too dangerous and the Dessarian compound is too well-guarded now. It's the only way to be sure."

Culach remembered the stories he'd heard from Gerda, his great-great-grandmother. Chimera were elementals, forces of Nature. Once called into being, they couldn't be unmade, not by iron or magic.

"If we do this, we can't call them back."

Of course Eirik must know this. He just didn't care.

"The Danai have left us no choice," Eirik said again. "And I intend to send a second pack for Victor's son, Darius."

The pain behind Culach's eye sockets ramped up a notch.

"No one wants to avenge Petur more than I do," he said slowly. "But if anyone gets in the pack's way, it will be a slaughter.

The other Houses could retaliate. I'd urge you to think this through."

"I already have. Our quarrel isn't with the Danai as a whole, only House Dessarian. They've been a thorn in our side for too long. If we don't strike first, they will."

His father rose and crossed the room. Culach pictured him standing before the window, silver hair unbound and hanging down his back, deep-set emerald eyes watching the snow fall outside.

"The survival of Val Moraine is at stake," Eirik continued. "If Petur had gotten out quietly, leaving the girl dead in her bed, it might be over. But they caught him and they know we're behind it. Tethys might have been reasonable, but with Victor back... He'll never let such an insult stand. It's them or us now."

Culach considered his father's words. He'd never balked at killing, but something had shifted inside him since that day at the lake. So many had died, and for what? They'd been sent home with their tails between their legs, Neblis's promise of plunder burned to ashes. The truth was, Culach had lost his taste for blood and glory.

But Eirik was right about Victor. His pride wouldn't be able to stand it. Revenge was inevitable at this point. The Valkirins had to hit first and hit hard.

No choice.

"Do it," Culach said, though the unease in his gut hadn't gone away.

His father left without another word. Culach wondered why he'd come in the first place. He could have simply acted on his own. He was master of Val Moraine and answered to no one, not even the heads of the other Valkirin holdfasts. But he'd wanted Culach's sanction for the chimera—probably to share the blame.

HE LAY IN BED FOR A TIME AND MUST HAVE DOZED OFF, because he woke to warm hands stroking his chest. His skin screamed in protest at the contact. Culach struggled upright, his breath coming fast and hard. He grabbed a slender wrist and held it fast.

"Easy now."

A feminine purr. The smell of clove soap and leather, with a sharp tang of iron.

Did no one knock anymore?

He covered his surprise with a scowl.

"What do you want, Katrin?"

"Just looking in. I heard Mina's been giving you baths."

So that was it. Katrin hadn't shown any interest in him until she found out Mina was coming every day. Katrin in a nutshell—she didn't want to be burdened, but she didn't care for the thought of another woman touching him, especially not Mina.

"She brings freezing cold water, which isn't quite the same thing," Culach said. "And I couldn't be better. If that sets your mind at ease, you can leave now."

Katrin twisted her hand free and pulled the furs aside before he could stop her. Culach heard a sharp intake of breath as she saw his scars.

"Do they hurt?"

"No," he lied, yanking the furs back up.

"Did you miss me?"

Wearily: "What do you want?"

She patted his cheek and laughed. "Do I need a reason to come to your rooms now?"

They'd been lovers for many years before he was maimed, although she wasn't faithful and he didn't expect her to be. Katrin had classic Valkirin looks, tall and icy blonde with high cheekbones and broad shoulders. In bed, she was rough and playful. Once he'd found her irresistible, a perfect match for his prodigious appetite.

"I've heard that when one loses sight, other senses become heightened. Is it true, Culach?"

The air stirred against his face as she leaned down and brushed her lips against his. Culach turned his face away.

"I thought you'd be happy to see me," she snapped.

"My father was just here. Petur is dead, at the hands of Victor's whelp. So forgive me if I'm not in the mood."

"Which one?" Katrin's voice took on a hard edge. "Mina's?"

"The other. Darius."

Her hand tightened on his arm. "Eirik will see that Petur is avenged."

Culach considered telling her about the chimera, but then she traced her fingers down his belly. Despite himself, Culach stirred. It was purely involuntary. For some reason, Katrin no longer appealed to him. He told himself it was because she didn't really care for him. She was playing her own game. Katrin had always liked games. She liked to see what she could make men do for her. He tried to push her hand away but she just gave a husky laugh and moved it lower.

"Katrin," he growled.

Naturally, Mina chose that precise moment to arrive with his lunch. He smelled the food and he smelled her hair, like a sprig of fresh juniper.

"I'll come back later," she said quickly.

"No," Katrin said. "Bring me the tray. And he needs a pitcher of water. It's nearly empty."

From the amused edge in her voice, she enjoyed treating Mina like a servant. Culach heard the tray rattle down with more force than necessary.

"Fetch some clean cloths," Katrin said. "I plan to give him a proper bath."

"You can get them yourself."

"So high and mighty, aren't we?" Katrin laughed. "You've always acted like a queen among peasants. But your days on this earth are numbered, Mina. The Danai have a blood debt to pay and you're the nearest currency."

Culach's scowl deepened.

"That's enough, Katrin," he snapped.

"What are you talking about?" Mina demanded.

"She doesn't even know," Katrin crowed. "Tell her, Culach."

"Dammit, Katrin—"

"Victor's son killed Petur."

Mina's voice was barely a whisper.

"Which son?"

"Not your bastard if that's what you're worried about."

The tray clattered to the floor with a tinkle of silverware and breaking crockery. Culach thought Mina had done it until Katrin said, "How clumsy I am. I think you'd better clean it up."

"You can't order me around," Mina replied coldly. "This is Culach's room."

"So it is. And he doesn't want you here either, do you, Culach?"

Culach crossed his arms and stayed silent.

Katrin leaned over him. Her breath whispered against his cheek.

"Tell her to get out. Right now. Or I'm never coming back."

He kept his eyes straight ahead. "Sorry, Katrin."

"So that's how it is?"

"I'm afraid so."

"You truly are a broken creature," Katrin said scornfully. "You deserve each other."

Culach heard her light steps cross the room. The door slammed. An awkward silence descended.

"I'll get another tray," Mina said.

"Don't bother. I'm not hungry."

He listened to the sounds of her cleaning up the mess.

"You have charming taste in bedmates," Mina muttered.

"I didn't ask her to come."

"A roll between the sheets would probably do you good. If not Katrin, how about one of the others? You always had a little harem hanging about as I recall. I can round them up for you."

"No."

"Why not?"

"Enough, Mina."

He rolled to his side. The chair creaked as she sat down.

"Do you really have to stay here?" he demanded. "I'm perfectly fine."

"Eirik says so. You can argue with him if you like. I don't care either way."

"Maybe I will."

He fell asleep to the sound of the wind. The dream was vivid. He stood in a large square at the center of a magnificent city. The buildings were made of some polished material that looked like colored glass, each a different subtle hue that caught the sunlight. Graceful spires stood against the sky and he could hear the rush of water through a multitude of fountains and canals. Tall statues ringed the square itself. He saw the stern features of the Valkirins, the curly hair of the Marakai, the stocky build of the Danai and others he didn't recognize. Each had distinct faces, as though copied from life by a skilled artisan who managed to capture the subjects' personalities in the smallest details of their expressions—the curve of a mouth accustomed to laughter, the stubborn set of a jaw or intensity of a gaze.

Culach turned to the man standing next to him. He had bright red hair and large pale eyes fringed with reddish lashes. A gold circlet nestled amid his curls, plain except for a jeweled serpent above his brow. Ranks of similarly red-haired men and women stood at a respectful distance behind him, and although they carried no weapons, Culach knew from their bearing that they were soldiers, some kind of honor guard.

"The clans have come to parley," Culach said, although it was not his own voice. This sounded raspier, with an eager, obsequious quality he despised instantly.

"So they have," the other man replied lazily.

He gazed across the plaza at a group of perhaps twenty daēvas standing on the opposite side. Their faces were set in grim lines.

"Come forth!" shouted Culach—or whoever it was he seemed to be inhabiting.

Two women and a man stepped out of the crowd, the first silver-haired and pale, the second with olive skin and a long dark braid, and the last with broad shoulders and skin of the richest ebony.

"We demand a truce," the woman with the braid called out. "We offer you a final chance."

The man with the circlet laughed. "How generous of you. And what are the terms?"

"You keep to your lands. We keep to ours. But you must stop this madness."

"And if I refuse?" He sounded amused.

"You will be trapped here forever," said the broad-shouldered man.

Culach's companion turned to him.

"How shall we answer their terms, old friend?"

"Burn them," Culach heard himself say.

The shorter man raised his hand. A single flame danced there, hovering above the palm. He stared at it in fascination for a long moment, then closed his fist. A wall of fire swept across the square. Culach felt a fierce satisfaction. *Burn them all. Every single one.*

He'd expected the daēvas to break, but they stood their ground. The Valkirin of the three who had come forward threw her head back. Her mouth opened. Culach heard the roar of a terrible wind and the flames leapt even higher, then began racing back *toward* him, an inferno a hundred feet high. He threw himself behind one of the statues as it broke over the plaza in a molten wave and continued into the city. He smelled charred flesh, heard screaming. Culach stumbled for the nearest way out, his robes smoking, and then he was in the desert, running toward that hidden sinkhole, the gale howling at his back....

He jolted awake with a gasp, pulse throbbing in his temples.

"I'm here."

It was Mina. Unlike Katrin, she didn't attempt to touch him. He found himself almost wishing she would.

"Another nightmare?" Mina laid a cold cloth across his forehead. "That's the third time this week. Sometimes you call out in your sleep." She hesitated. "I can't make out the words though."

He couldn't always remember the dreams, but Culach knew they were becoming more frequent. As though a door had opened in his mind and he couldn't close it. At first, they had been fragmentary images of fire and yellow sand and intense blue sky. He'd heard of the sun, but its blinding brightness was still overwhelming. Those always ended in smothering darkness.

But recently, the dreams had changed. He no longer floated bodiless but inhabited a particular person. The man with the rasping voice. Worst of all, Culach was becoming convinced the man was not mortal but a daëva.

Except this daëva could work fire.

It wasn't possible. Just a dream, he told himself. He was weaving together disparate strands into a fantasy conjured by his own tortured mind. Every child knew fire was inimical to daëvas, the one element they couldn't work because it would boil the blood in their veins to touch it for even a single instant.

He also knew if he told Mina all this, she would laugh at him.

"I don't remember my dreams," he muttered. "Now if you don't mind, I'll have some lunch. I've decided I'm hungry after all."

He didn't need her hovering over him, watching him. He just wanted to be left alone.

"I was only trying to help—"

"I don't need your help." Culach made his voice harsh. "Your position here is precarious, Mina. Don't make it worse."

There was a lengthy silence, long enough for him to regret his words. He knew he shouldn't take his frustration out on her. She had it hard enough already. He was steeling himself to apologize, but she left before he could say anything more. He wondered if he'd wounded her, but the thought was ridiculous. Mina couldn't care less what he thought. He'd said far worse to her before. And yet Culach felt a twinge of self-loathing as he lay back on his bed, waiting for her to return with his lunch.

He waited a long time.

9
SOMETHING WICKED

Nine daēvas stood in a circle.

Four men and five women—the strongest of those who remained at the mighty stronghold of Val Moraine. A knife made from the yellowed fang of an isbjörn passed from hand to hand. Each stepped forward and made a shallow slice across the palm, their blood joining a pool that shimmered like oil in the moonlight.

The cavern's mouth lay open to the shoulder of the mountain. Just below it, a winding, icy pass led south toward the great forest of the Danai. To the west was the shore of the White Sea and the harbor where the trading ships anchored. On a clear night, when all three moons had risen, one might even catch a glimpse of the barren, rocky Isles of the Marakai. But thick snow-laden clouds obscured the view this morning, wreathing the mountain in grey mist. There hadn't been a clear day in weeks, Eirik reflected, as his third cousin Agathe handed him the knife, her face grave. Val Moraine was truly alone, an island of sanity in a world that seemed to have gone mad.

Eirik was the last to cut himself. He watched his blood drip steadily into the pool. When he felt satisfied it was large enough, he signaled to the others.

This was the moment. If any of them had second thoughts and refused, the effort would fail. In ancient days, Gerda had told him, thirteen were used for the circle. It might be done with nine, but no less. Eirik looked at each daēva in turn. None avoided his gaze. None left. They still trusted him, though he sensed their fear. What they were about to do had been forbidden for centuries.

"Now," Eirik said, drawing a deep breath and reaching for air.

A breeze swept the cavern and the air crackled with invisible lightning as they wove their talents together. Most Avas Valkirin were strongest in air, while the Danai were strongest in earth and the Marakai in water. Gerda said all three elements were needed to make a chimera, but the balance depended on the skills of the makers.

A thin rivulet of blood rose up from the pool like a scarlet serpent. Chips of stone broke loose from the cavern walls and were pulverized to chalky dust that swirled and eddied around the blood, giving it substance. The daēvas joined hands, the wounds on their palms still oozing. They fed their creation with spite and malice and all the secret darkness in their hearts. Eirik thought of his wife Ygraine, who'd died giving birth, and his daughter Neblis, lost to the shadowlands. Of vicious battles won and lost, and his bitter disappointment in his only living heir. Around him, he heard teeth grinding and moans of despair as the others dredged up their own tragedies.

Out of their pain and fear, something shimmered into being in the middle of the circle.

It was bound together by air and thus translucent except for the blood coursing through a network of delicately branching veins and occasional clots of darker matter. Its teeth had the shape and color of icicles.

Freeze my bones. Look at that thing!

"Cage it!" he barked, struggling to master himself. The emotional wounds he'd gouged open still festered, but this was the most dangerous time. Before a chimera had been wedded to its quarry, Gerda said it could turn on its maker.

Eirik started weaving air and earth—as much as he could manage—and after a long moment, the others joined him, some with tears dampening their cheeks. The thing's tail lashed angrily as it lunged...and slammed into an invisible barrier. Only its makers could cage it. No other magic would touch the monstrous thing.

Let it hold, just for a few more seconds...

Eirk approached the cage and extended a single light brown hair, taking care to keep his hand well out of reach. The chimera snuffled. Its hot breath plumed in the air, imprinting the scent in its memory. Even with his sharp daēva eyes, Eirik had trouble seeing it. The thing was a chameleon. It was like looking at a shard of glass through running water. He could only track it when it moved and those clots of darker matter shifted and bunched in its haunches.

The chimera tossed its head back but made no sound.

They repeated the process five more times, until a half dozen of the creatures filled the cavern with dark, unbridled energy and the daēvas themselves were weak from blood loss. The last three were given strands of dark brown hair with a slight wave to it. Eirik had no idea how his informant had obtained them. If the hairs belonged to the wrong people, they would soon be very dead. But the source had never deceived him. All his information had proved to be accurate thus far.

Eirik's shoulders slumped. He felt utterly drained.

Let it be over.

He saw Ygraine's face, not contorted in agony but radiant as she told him she was carrying a child after so many years of fruitlessly trying. Their shared excitement when they discovered in the third month of her pregnancy that it was not one but two—twins. A girl and a boy, the midwife said. Neblis and Culach.

One now vanished, the other crippled, and Ygraine gone to her eternal slumber in the icy crypts.

Would she approve of what he'd done?

He looked at the chimera, pulsing with his own grief and fury.

Goodbye, my love.

Eirik steadied his voice.

"Hunt," he said.

The Valkirins released the cage and hastily stepped back. Hands fell to sword hilts and rested there, even though they'd been told the creatures would only attack if they stood in the way of the quarry. It was an unreasoning fear. But it was impossible to be in the presence of a chimera and not reach for the nearest weapon.

With no power to bind them, the cages fell away to dust. The six creatures stood there for an instant, perfectly motionless. Then they surged as one into the frigid darkness. They made no sound. Chimera only howled when their quarry was within sight.

They were living beings, Eirik knew, with hearts and lungs and brains, but different from all others on the face of the earth. They would not pause except to feed. They needed no rest. They could not be killed or even unmade with the power. They were literally unstoppable. Only when their purpose was completed, the quarry torn to shreds, would they dissolve into their respective elements.

OUTSIDE THE HOLDFAST, IT WAS BLACK AS PITCH. THE HEAVY cloud cover over the mountains prevented any light from leaking through. But the creatures sensed Selene in the sky above and felt a fierce joy at being newly born and having purpose. They would follow the moon to the forest. One quarry was there. The other had already moved on. That didn't concern them. They had nothing but time.

The pack ran down the steep mountainside, breath streaming out in white banners that the wind snatched away without a trace.

10

TO SAMARQAND

O n the eighth day, Darius returned to the world of the living.

By the light of a single lumen crystal, he saw the familiar tangle of leafy branches above his bed, the crooked gap revealing a patch of stars in the quilt of the night sky. A large moth clung to the bark, its wings like pale, delicate lace. His head throbbed. So did his leg, although it was a duller ache.

His mother's face floated over the bed. It split in a huge grin.

"You're awake," she murmured, kissing his cheek. "I've been so worried."

"Nazafareen," he croaked. "Where is she?"

Delilah didn't answer. She poured a cup of water from a wooden jug and held it to his parched lips. Darius took a sip, fighting down nausea. The room spun in a lazy circle. He remembered Nazafareen flying through the air like a dry leaf in the wind. He remembered his knee shattering and then a blackness that felt like death.

Darius sat up too fast and nearly vomited. Delilah made a *tsking* sound and laid a hand on his chest, pushing him back down.

"Where is she?" he asked again.

"Galen killed the Valkirin with an arrow. She's perfectly safe."

Something in her tone sounded cagey. "What do you mean, *perfectly safe?*"

When Delilah didn't answer again, he gripped the edge of the bed and forced himself to sitting. His stomach gave a slow roll but it wasn't as bad as the first time. He gingerly touched his skull and felt a knot above his left ear.

"Tethys," his mother said. "She knit your bones together, but you mustn't exert yourself. It was a serious injury. You need food and rest."

Darius flexed his leg. The joint was still stiff. He threw the covers back.

"Find Nazafareen," he said. "I need to see her."

In fact, he desperately wanted to touch her, smell her, hold her in his arms. If he hadn't been unable to sleep for thinking about her, if he hadn't sensed so much power being worked in her house —far more than Nazafareen could manage—she'd be dead now. He cursed himself for not keeping a closer watch over her. He wouldn't make that mistake again. Whether she liked it or not, Darius intended to put a cot in her room and stay there until this matter with the Valkirins was settled to his satisfaction.

Nazafareen had given her hand for him, although he hadn't yet told her that story. She was the only thing that truly mattered to him in the world. He cared for Delilah, but in truth, he hardly knew either of his parents. The magi had taken him away as an infant to be raised as a soldier-slave.

"Darius," Delilah said carefully. "I need you to stay calm."

Naturally, her words had the opposite effect. His pulse began to hammer.

"What is it?"

Delilah took a breath, tipped her chin up defiantly. He braced himself for what was coming.

"Nazafareen is gone."

"What do you mean *gone?*"

"She left yesterday. She did it to protect you. The Valkirins vowed to kill us all."

He stared at his mother in disbelief. "And you let this happen?"

"I couldn't stop her."

Darius's rage was a cold thing, burrowing like a blade into his heart.

"Of course you could have. You chose not to. Where did she go?"

Darius gained his feet. He felt a thousand years old, but he knew from experience that the stiffness would pass if he forced himself to move. He'd taken worse injuries than this and he'd have to leave right away if he had a chance of catching her before the Valkirins did. Then they would leave this place and never come back. Bone-deep weariness and sorrow washed through him. Delilah knew what Nazafareen meant to him. It was a betrayal of the vilest sort.

"You're not fit to be out of bed," she said gently, laying a hand on his arm.

Darius shook it off. "Where are my boots?"

Delilah folded her arms. "You're a stubborn fool. She knows how to take care of herself. And she said she'd return after things blew over."

He gave a bitter laugh. "They won't blow over. And I'm not waiting."

"You're needed here. She doesn't want you to go after her!"

Darius was no longer paying Delilah the slightest attention. Nazafareen must have headed deeper into the forest. He knew how to track her. If she'd gone through the gate to the land of the dead.... Well, he'd follow. The cold air prickled his bare skin as he grabbed a tunic and pulled it over his head.

"My boots," he snapped. "I need them right now."

Delilah shook her head. There was something like satisfaction on her face as she said, "You won't find her. She's gone."

"Where then?" His blue eyes bored into hers. "Tell me, or I swear—"

"You swear what?"

Victor strode into the room. His father towered over him by six inches and exuded an air of brute authority, but Darius wasn't intimidated. If it came down to it, he knew he was stronger in the power. He'd beaten Victor once before and he'd do it again, if necessary.

"I swear I'll tear this place apart, branch by branch, until I find out where she's gone," he said, locating a pair of trousers and yanking them on.

"You can't follow her," Delilah cut in. "She's gone to Solis."

Darius froze. "Solis? But...she can't." The room swam before his eyes. He remembered Nazafareen dying in his arms as the breaking magic consumed her from the inside out. Only in Nocturne was she safe from it. He bit into his cheek until he tasted blood.

"Which city?" he asked hoarsely.

"Samarqand. But she won't try to touch her magic," Delilah said hastily. "She swore it to me. And she wanted me to tell you she seeks the Marakai. She seems to have some idea that they can heal her mind."

Darius stood stock still for a moment, considering the implications.

Solis. The mortal lands of scorching sun, of forges and fire temples. Darius didn't fear fire the way the other daēvas did. He'd been raised in the empire among humans who followed the Way of the Flame. Fire would kill him if he got too close, but he was practiced at keeping his distance.

Nazafareen hadn't waited for him. The knowledge stung, but perhaps it was no more than he deserved. How badly he had misjudged everything. If only he'd told her his own plans to leave. But he'd kept them secret, and now she was gone.

"She'll never make it. It's too far." His frigid gaze swept over

Delilah. "Your lack of concern for her welfare doesn't surprise me. You never liked Nazafareen." He turned to his father. "But you, Victor? How could you let her do this? The journey through the Umbra is a death sentence." He felt sick. "The Valkirins will catch her long before she reaches the sun lands."

"If she'd been on foot, we would have refused her," Victor said, black eyes flashing like chips of obsidian. "Delilah told me Nazafareen travelled by wind ship."

Darius glared back, keeping his rage on a tight leash.

"And where did she find a bloody wind ship?" he demanded.

"A mortal came, seeking trade concessions. She left with him."

Darius swore and stalked over to a wooden chest. Bolts of pain shot through his leg but he wouldn't let Victor see it. He began tossing extra clothing into a leather rucksack. At the bottom of the chest, he found the griffin cuff. With his back to Victor and Delilah, Darius quickly slipped it into the sack. It might be useless, but he wouldn't leave it behind.

"We're going to war," Victor said through gritted teeth. "Does that mean nothing to you?"

"I thought that was up to the Matrium. Did they meet already?"

"Not yet, but—"

Darius buckled the bag. "Well, I'm sure you can manage it."

"Nazafareen will be among her own kind," Victor said. "I doubt even the Valkirins would chase her halfway across the world. But they won't forgive the fact one of their own is dead. His corpse is lying in Tethys's garden. Galen saved your life and now you'd abandon us in our hour of need? Have you no honor?"

Darius paused. "Do you truly dare to speak of honor, Victor?" he asked softly.

"Stop it, both of you," Delilah snapped. "You're behaving like children."

But Darius couldn't let it go, not this time.

"You're a hypocrite," he spat. "You helped the humans enslave your own people to save Delilah's life. And now you expect me to let Nazafareen walk alone into the lion's den?"

Color suffused Victor's thick neck. "The only one going into the lion's den will be you. The mortals hate and fear us, even if they pretend otherwise. If anyone suspects what you are—"

"They won't," Darius said shortly. "Now get out of my way."

Victor glowered down at him and Darius braced himself for a fight when Galen walked in, shaking glittering flakes of snow from his dark hair.

"I see you've decided to rejoin us." His smile faltered as he looked between them. "What's happening?"

"Ah," Victor said grimly. "My *son* is here."

Galen's eyebrow lifted. "Where are you going?" he asked Darius.

"Samarqand. I need maps."

"Samarqand?" Galen laughed. "No really, where are you going? You look like death warmed over."

"Maps," Darius snarled.

Galen shrugged. "Ellard might have one. I can ask him."

"Do it. Now, please."

"But why—"

"Did you know Nazafareen is gone?"

His half-brother frowned. "Gone? I just saw her yesterday." He paused as understanding dawned. "The wind ship?"

"Yes."

Galen looked as though he might say something more, but the expression on Darius's face discouraged further questions.

"I'll go find Ellard," he said, with a final quick glance at Victor.

Delilah had retreated to the bed, where she watched in silence, hands folded in her lap. Victor sighed heavily and stood aside. He'd never been adept at concealing his emotions and he clearly believed Darius's loyalties were sorely misaligned. But then he'd always believed that.

"Go then," Victor said.

Darius picked up his rucksack and left without another word. He didn't trust himself to speak.

Within a matter of minutes, he'd secured a week's worth of food and water from the kitchens. As promised, Galen found him and handed over a tattered map. Darius quickly surveyed it, committing the details to memory in case he should lose it.

"Thank you." Darius clasped his shoulder. "And thank Ellard."

"I will." He paused. "I hope you find her."

A light snow fell as Darius walked out of the Danai settlement, heading west. Selene had set and Hecate shone weakly through the veil of tattered clouds, her silver light gilding the frost-limned branches. The ground had frozen hard. His breath made little wisps of mist and the silence of the deep woods stretched out before him like a bittersweet secret in the night.

So Nazafareen thought the Marakai daēvas could repair the damage from the spell. Was it possible? And what would happen if they did?

He remembered how she had looked at him in the Dominion, after Neblis filled her with lies. She'd despised him. It had been worse than anything else Neblis had done. Darius didn't think she would blame him for the sins of their past, but she might blame herself. That's how she was.

I will find her. I'll tell her the truth—my side of it, at least—and let her decide.

A bat swooped past his head, hunting insects. Darius watched its erratic, darting flight and briefly touched the Nexus so he could feel its tiny heart beating within its breast. Its wings were fragile as parchment but they kept it aloft. His chest ached for a moment at the marvels of Nature.

Nazafareen was strong and smart. He'd fought at her side for enough years to know that. Even one-handed, she was deadly with a sword. And the wind ships must be swift. She should reach Samarqand by the next day. It would take him much longer on foot, but surely even Nazafareen could manage to stay out of trouble for a week or two.

Surely.

Let Victor have his revenge until he chokes on it. Let the others call me traitor. Let my mother mourn me. Darius didn't care what they thought of him. He'd always held to his own code, one forged in the brutal cauldron of the empire. He was no longer a Water Dog, loyal to King, satrap and Holy Father, but he was still a soldier, with a soldier's discipline and a soldier's honor, and that honor belonged to Nazafareen now. She was still his bonded, whether or not they wore the cuffs, and Darius would find her if it took him the rest of his life.

AN ILL-FATED KNIFE

N azafareen woke to the creaking of ropes. The ship swayed from side to side like a cradle rocked by an overly enthusiastic giant. She didn't know how long they'd been aloft. There was no wind, but the air burned her cheeks, a damp, penetrating cold unlike anything she had ever experienced before, its needle claws finding every gap in her cloak.

She hadn't planned to reveal herself until they reached Samarqand, and not even then if she could find a way to quietly sneak off the ship, but the pendulum-like motion and occasional sudden, brief drops made her stomach roil. Nazafareen swallowed.

I will not vomit, she told herself firmly. I will *not*.

She peered between the bags of sand. The captain of the wind ship had his back to her, standing with his legs braced wide on the deck. He wore a quilted brown coat that came down to his knees and thick fur-lined gloves. As she watched, he peeled one off and took a handful of something gritty from his pocket, tossed it into the air and muttered words under his breath. Reddish sparks danced in the air like a swarm of fireflies. The ship gave a small lurch. He nodded and put the glove back on, steadying himself on one of the ropes.

He's using magic, she thought in astonishment. *Some kind I've never seen before.*

Forks of blue-white lightning illuminated the surrounding clouds, followed almost immediately by a shattering cymbal crash of thunder. The ship moved in tandem with the wind so she couldn't judge its speed, but Nazafareen had the impression they were going very fast. She wondered how far away the ground was. Then the deck gave a sudden, violent lurch. Her head snapped back into one of the sandbags and a small cry of pain escaped her lips.

She shook her head to clear it, pinpoints of light dancing in her vision, when the canvas cloth she hid beneath was yanked back. The captain's eyes widened in shock as he registered the stowaway aboard his vessel.

Now that she saw his face, Nazafareen realized he was closer to her own age, or even younger. He had fine-boned, delicate features, with a mop of chin-length black hair and smooth cheeks that looked like they'd never seen the edge of a razor.

"How in the name of the Holy Father did *you* get here?" he demanded.

She almost drew her short sword right then. What if he threw her overboard? She quickly sized him up. He wasn't much bigger than she was. Nazafareen didn't think he could manage it even if he tried. And he looked more surprised than anything else.

Delilah called me reckless and impulsive. If I put a blade to his throat, we'll be off on the wrong foot, and he might agree to take me without blood being shed.

With this wise thought, Nazafareen crawled out from her hiding place, joints complaining from so many hours in a cramped space. She tried on a penitent smile and found her face to be as stiff from cold as the rest of her.

"I'm sorry, really, but I needed to leave and your ship was the only way out. I've no money to pay for passage, but perhaps I can work it off—"

The boy cut her off. "Are you human or daēva?"

"Human," she answered quickly.

His relief was clear. "What were you doing in the darklands?"

Nazafareen had already concocted the tale she planned to tell in Samarqand, which was loosely based on a story Darius once told her about a poor shepherd girl—although his version also had talking animals and a fortune-teller and a cave full of treasure. Something told her she might want to leave out those bits for credibility's sake.

So Nazafareen said she was from a flyspeck village in Solis, nowhere he'd ever heard of, and ran away when her father pledged her to a much older distant cousin who smelled of onions. She'd hoped to find work in a city, but got lost and went the wrong way, wandering across the Umbra until the daēvas of House Dessarian found her.

"I'd only been there a few weeks, while they decided what to do with me." She grasped a rope and held on for dear life as the ship lurched again. "When you came, I thought I'd save them the trouble."

He gave her a hard stare. "You could have asked first."

"I was afraid you'd say no," she replied, and that was the truth.

"What's your name?"

"Ashraf." Darius said it had been her sister's name.

"All right, listen, Ashraf. My name is Javid and I'm sorry for your troubles, but by all rights, I ought to bring you back. What if the daēvas think I kidnapped you?"

Nazafareen paled. "They won't think that, I swear! I did tell one of them where I went, and she agreed it was for the best. Please don't turn around. You don't understand—"

"I said I ought to." He studied the clouds, heavy with moisture and churning like a vast grey whirlpool. "If I'd found you earlier, perhaps. But it's too much of a risk now. I got lucky with fair weather on the journey over, but the hot currents from the deserts of Solis meet the cold winds of Nocturne in the Umbra. It's notorious for storms." He grinned, revealing crooked white teeth. "I hope you have a head for heights."

Nazafareen pulled her cloak tighter.

"I'll be fine. I climbed trees all the time, the biggest ones I could find."

He chortled. "Trees, eh? And what would you say if I told you we were more than ten thousand paces up right now?"

"Ten...thousand?"

"Give or take."

Nazafareen braced her legs the way Javid did and forced herself to let go of the rope she'd been clutching. She smiled, a portrait of confidence. "That's not as high as I expected."

Amusement glinted in his eyes, but he simply nodded.

"Thank you, Javid. You won't regret it. I'll find a way to pay you."

He shrugged. "I'm afraid you'll be on your own when we get there. I doubt the Guild would look kindly on an unauthorized passenger, especially since my visit was supposed to be secret." He paused. "Did they tell you what was discussed?"

"Oh, no." Which was also the truth, strictly speaking, since she'd been spying. "I've no interest in your business. I just want to get to Samarqand."

He gave her a long look, as if trying to decide whether she was lying. Nazafareen gazed back with wide-eyed innocence.

"Good. Just don't mention it to anyone."

"I don't know anyone there, and I wouldn't even if I did." Nazafareen took in the saucily curving prow and bright brass mooring cleats. She still felt certain she'd seen him use magic. "How do you steer the wind ship?" she asked casually. "Why doesn't it get blown wherever the wind takes it?"

His eyes narrowed in suspicion again. "You have a strange accent. Are you sure you're not Greek?" He studied her face.

"You don't have the look, but I'd wager you're not Persian either."

"I don't know what I am." Now Nazafareen wished she'd asked more questions about the mortal cities. Her ignorance was already causing trouble. "I'm just...just a village girl, like I said. What does it matter?"

"It matters," he replied flatly.

Javid motioned for her to return to the relative shelter of the canvas covering, and Nazafareen complied. He was quiet so long she didn't think he'd speak again. She watched him take readings from various instruments. Dark clouds roiled around them, lit every so often by flashes of lightning.

"The winds at high altitude blow from east to west," he said finally. "That's the direction we're moving in now. A skilled pilot has to find the right current. They're different depending on how high she flies." Javid leaned over the edge, perfectly fearless, as Nazafareen's stomach clenched. "All the wind ships have names. This one is called the *Kyrenia*."

The *Kyrenia*. Nazafareen liked that. It sounded regal.

"You seem very young to have your own ship," she said, hoping flattery would loosen his tongue.

"I am and it's not mine. It belongs to the Merchants' Guild. But no one else was willing to fly across the Umbra into the dark-lands. And if I deliver this contract, they've promised me my own wind ship. I'll be a full captain. There's a fortune to be made in smug—I mean, inter-city trade."

Rain began to pelt down and conversation ceased. Nazafareen huddled under the canvas, where she tried to shelter from the frigid deluge. How small and fragile their little craft seemed in the turbulent sea of clouds, with untold leagues of empty space above and below. Javid scampered around the deck like a monkey, untangling lines and checking instruments. Every now and then, he reached surreptitiously into a pouch at his belt and tossed something into the air, muttering words. Each time, their course altered slightly. His evident skill reassured her, but it was also obvious that the storm was worsening. In the forks of lightning, she saw funnel-shaped clouds in the distance, not grey but a dense, ominous black.

Faster and faster they went. Rotating currents batted the ship like a cat with a mouse. The ropes kept tangling. Suddenly, the ship swooped hard to the right, tilting at a precipitous angle. Nazafareen's heart leapt to her throat. She clung to the nearest line as the sandbags shifted behind her and started sliding across the deck.

"Do you have a knife?" Javid yelled over the roar of the storm.

"Yes!"

He grappled with the webbing of ropes leading up to the sack. Several had twisted together and they'd pulled the ship off balance.

"Good. I want you to cut that line on the starboard side! The one that leads to the—"

A boom of thunder drowned out his words. Nazafareen doubted she would have understood anyway since she had only the most rudimentary grasp of how the ship worked. Letting go of the rail was the hardest thing she'd ever done. She was terrified the ship would lurch again and she'd tumble over the edge.

Nazafareen fumbled for her knife and held it up, sheets of water stinging bare skin where the hood of her cloak had blown back. Two knotted ropes quivered tautly in front of her. She tried to ascertain which one he meant but in the rainy darkness, she couldn't tell what either were attached to.

"This one?" she cried over her shoulder.

He squinted across the deck, then grunted in pain as his own hand caught in the snarl of ropes.

"Are you all right? What's happening?"

Javid's face was white with strain. He dangled helplessly from the rigging.

"Just cut it!"

Taking a deep, terrified breath, Nazafareen seized one at random between her teeth and began sawing with her knife hand. She was almost through when Javid managed to free himself and stumble over. His eyes grew almost comically huge.

"Not that one!" he yelled. "Holy Father, the other!"

Nazafareen stopped cutting, staring dumbly at the rope. Time seemed to slow as it unraveled to a single thread. She blinked and it snapped. There was a terrible groaning sound. Lines slithered and whipped like a nest of angry vipers. Half the ship dropped away from the sack of air above it. She clung to the rope in her good hand, heart beating wildly, the deck tipping beneath her feet. Clouds sped past in a dizzying unchecked descent.

In desperation, Nazafareen opened herself to air magic. She wasn't strong, but she managed to guide a random gust so that it filled the deflating sack, somewhat slowing the ship's headlong plunge. Around and around they spun. Nazafareen held her lifeline with a white-knuckled grip. She screamed for Javid and got no answer. The wind howled in her ears, the earth rushed up to meet her, and she felt sure it was the end of them both.

The ship fell for an eternity. Something slammed hard into the side and then she was rolling on the ground, breathless and battered, her mouth full of sandy dirt. Nazafareen lay dazed. Finally, she rolled over and spat blood. She hurt in many places, but nothing seemed broken. She crawled to her feet.

The ship had continued to drag along the ground after she was ejected and lay some distance away. The prow had broken clean off. It lay in two splintered pieces, with the silken air sack spread out like a shimmering pool of dark water against the flat, barren landscape.

There was no sign of Javid. Sick with fear, Nazafareen seized the edge of the sack and began frantically reeling it in. It was very difficult with only one hand and the wind and rain, but to her intense relief, she finally found him sprawled on his back underneath. A trickle of blood ran down his face from a nasty cut above his eyebrow. She quickly felt his limbs. The worst injury she could see was the cut, which she stanched with a scrap of torn silk.

The ship was beyond repair, but its broken hull could still serve as a shelter. There was nothing else in sight. Just rocks and coarse, mineralized soil that seemed too poor to support even the hardiest lichen. It was the loneliest place she had ever seen, worse even than the Dominion, which at least had trees and streams.

Nazafareen pulled the great mass of the air sack over them both and curled up against the deck, waiting for the storm to pass.

THEY TRIED TO BREAK THE WORLD

C ulach was afraid to fall asleep.

Blindness was no refuge. The dreams came relent-lessly now, even when he was awake—or was he? It was difficult to tell sometimes. He felt the furs against his skin, smelled the ancient wind-blasted stone of the keep, and yet his awareness drifted elsewhere.

Unlike his earlier nightmares, the latest had begun innocu-ously enough. He stood in a lush garden with brightly colored flowers and strange limbless trees. A grand building of rose-hued glass enclosed three sides. The fourth ended at a tawny desert, the edge between grass and sand as sharp and straight as if drawn by a stylus. He strolled over to a fountain near an open archway and glimpsed his reflection. A narrow face with close-set eyes and spiky hair. His mouth had a cruel set to it. He wore loose robes of soft white linen.

Floating along inside this stranger's body, Culach flinched at the rows of flaring torches set in brackets along the palace walls, but they didn't seem to disturb the man. He walked with fluid grace down a pathway where a second man sat on a bench, head in his hands. It was the same who had worn the gold circlet.

"She's refused me again," he said.

"The girl is willful."

The man raised his head and Culach saw madness in his eyes. The volatile rage of a child used to getting his way in all things, who has just been refused his heart's greatest desire.

"She led me on. She made me believe she loved me."

"I know, my lord. It is the Danai nature to be treacherous."

The king crumpled a message in his fist. "She accuses me of murder. Some Danai from House Granet who vanished at the gathering."

"An outrageous insult. Doubtless the man ran off in a fit of jealousy. I hear he sought her favor as well." The advisor sneered. "She clearly encouraged the attentions of many suitors for her own amusement."

"What shall I do?"

"I think punishment might be in order, my lord."

The man considered this, his pale eyes growing distant. Yes, he was mad, but he was also cunning and ruthless and very, very powerful. It radiated from him like heat from the distant dunes.

"What sort of punishment?" he asked at last.

"That depends. What does she love best?"

The man thought on this. "Her precious forests."

"Then that is what she shall lose. To start with."

He nodded, as if it were a small matter.

"See that it's done."

Culach felt the man's satisfaction as he walked back to the white building. He stood in thought for a while. Then he held out a hand. Culach's heart nearly stopped as the flames from one of the torches leapt high, reaching for the man's outstretched fingers. Harsh laughter rang in his ears as his eyes jerked open. But it wasn't true wakefulness.

He found himself in some strange in-between place, surrounded by thick, roiling fog. A pinpoint of light drew him forward. He gripped a flat disc in his hand and knew from the power coursing through the metal that it was some kind of talisman. Other red-haired daēvas in flowing white robes followed behind. The glow intensified and he emerged from a pond in the midst of a thick wood. A Talisman of Folding. It linked two places, so one could travel a thousand leagues in a heartbeat. Culach had heard stories about them from Gerda, though she said they'd been lost for hundreds of years.

It was Culach's last moment of separate awareness. Then his mind blended fully with the body he inhabited, and he saw through the man's eyes, heard his thoughts as if they were his own.

"We are near House Kaland," he said, holding up a fist to signal the others to wait. "Let them come to us."

Sure enough, within a few minutes, six sentries clad in close-fitting green tunics and trousers appeared, bows on their backs. Their faces were wary but they hadn't nocked any arrows. *The fools.*

"Councilor," their leader said in a respectful, if cool, tone. "We weren't expecting you."

Culach smiled, a tightening of the lips across the teeth. "Are you not glad to see your cousins?"

"I know what errand you come on," one of the younger Danai called out angrily. "It is fruitless. She will not return with you."

The leader rounded on him. "Be silent. Let me handle this." He turned back and surveyed the Vatras. "You bring a large party to our lands. May I ask why?"

Sunlight trickled through the ancient trees, dappling the forest floor. Culach found the Nexus and let it fill him. So much life. Every square inch teeming with things that crept and crawled, flew and wriggled. All feeding off each other in a repulsive cycle of death and birth. And the trees! He shuddered as he felt their roots plunging like monstrous tentacles into the earth. Only the Danai could love such a place.

Give me the blazing, lifeless desert. Clean and pure.

"Councilor?" the Danai scout asked. "Your king's petition has been made and answered. More than once. Caecilia is not even here. She's gone and I will not tell you where she went."

Culach nodded, as if considering his words. His smile widened to a rictus. The scout gripped his bow and shared a hard look with the others.

"You mistake my intentions," Culach replied. "We are not here for her. We are here for you."

He held out a hand. Yellow flames flowed along the skin like water.

"Draw!" the leader screamed.

The earth trembled. Bows came up. But it was too late.

The Danai scouts went up like a row of torches. Culach watched their hair wither, their flesh melt from their bones. A bird flew shrieking from a branch. He set it alight in midair, watched the small body plummet to the ground. All around, trees a hundred paces tall erupted into flames. A wind rose, whipping the blaze into an inferno. Sap hit the boiling point and exploded, sending showers of red sparks over his head.

He turned to his companions with savage joy.

"Burn it all."

The Vatras formed a line and started walking toward House Kaland. And so began the harrowing of the Avas Danai forests. Wildfire on a scale never imagined. Daēvas screaming and running from their homes, only to be caught by walls of flame that moved faster than a river in spring flood. People and animals alike turned to torches. He could feel the heat of it on his skin though he remained untouched. Smoke and ashes choked the air.

It was all perfectly realistic except for the fact that he glimpsed a sun in the sky. It was dark red, with a flaring corona from the polluted atmosphere, but he knew it wasn't Selene. It was Solis.

Culach sat up, gasping for breath. His stomach gave a queasy roll and he threw the furs aside, wishing he could leap on Ragnhildur's back and go for a long ride over the mountains. He longed for the icy wind on his face, the stars rushing by overhead.

He must be losing his mind. He'd heard of it happening, even if such disorders were rare among his people. Daēvas who had undergone a deeply traumatic experience unable to get past it. Flinching at shadows for the rest of their long lives. Fleeing from terrors in their own minds.

Culach pressed the heels of his hands against his eyes. He had never been prone to imaginative fancy. Quite the opposite. He was pragmatic and physical, not the sort to have visions.

Visions.

Why had he used that word? Visions implied something real, and this was all utterly bizarre. The Avas Danai forests were intact. Nocturne had no sun. No fire. And red-haired daēvas didn't exist.

He stood and padded over to the air shield. It felt hard and chill beneath his palm. He remembered the view beyond. Once, the whole world spread out before him. He listened to the wind, took comfort in its familiar wild music. *Child of air. Am I still that, even if I can no longer touch it? Will I age and die now, like the mortals?*

Do I even wish to live for hundreds more years, imprisoned in darkness and nightmares?

He no longer stayed in bed all day. That was one thing Mina had done for him. He couldn't stand lying there like a slug while she sat in her chair, so he'd begun fetching things he wanted for himself, as long as they were inside his chamber. He knew every inch of it now and no longer bumped into furniture. Mina was careful to keep everything in precisely the same place.

He hadn't yet ventured into other parts of the keep, but he could begin to imagine doing so, when before it seemed unthinkable.

If only the dreams would leave him alone.

Culach suppressed a yawn. It was bad enough remembering them when he was awake. But when he slept, they seemed real.

He'd be swept away by the raw emotions of terror and horror, heart pounding in his chest, mouth dry as a tomb.

Despite her vow, Katrin had come to see him thrice more, making sure to arrive when Mina was here so she could torment the Danai woman. The last time, he had thrown her out and told her not to return. Rather than getting angry, she'd been condescending.

"You can't forbid me, Culach. And I don't care if you're scarred, you're still pretty enough."

He'd cursed her and she laughed. Mina refrained from commenting after Katrin left, but Culach sensed her private amusement, whether at his predicament or the fact that he had stood up for her, he didn't know.

CULACH HAD COME TO ANTICIPATE THE EXACT TIME MINA arrived every day. When the door opened the next day, he'd dressed himself and was sitting on the edge of the bed.

"What's for lunch?" he asked.

"Soup."

He made a grumbling noise. "Again? Tell them I'm a man, not an invalid. I need real food."

"The cook hates me."

"Has that ever stopped you from complaining?"

He heard a smile in her voice. "No."

Culach felt her eyes on him. He couldn't say how he knew, but he did. He could tell when she was looking out the window or reading, or studying him.

"You aren't sleeping," she said.

"The pain—"

"I don't believe you."

"I don't care."

Her voice drew closer. "Why do you hold it inside?"

"Are you actually asking?"

She sounded a little surprised. "I suppose I am."

"Bad dreams," he replied shortly.

"About what?"

"I don't wish to talk about it."

"I thought we were already doing that."

Culach sighed and went over to the table. He sniffed the bowl. "Honestly, I can't take any more beet soup."

"Don't change the subject." Her skirts whispered as she sat down.

"Fine." He suddenly wanted to tell her. He didn't have to worry about her gossiping because Mina didn't talk to anyone. She already thought he was a fool, or worse. What could it hurt?

"It started with a man," he said.

Culach began to relate his dreams, remembering details as he spoke that he'd forgotten. Mina listened quietly, occasionally prompting him with a question. He found himself opening up, pacing about the room in agitation as he described the total destruction of the great forest.

"Do you think something's...*wrong* with me?" he asked at last.

"You mean, are you going crazy?"

"To be blunt, yes."

"I don't know," she said slowly. "But I've heard this story before, or a version of it anyway."

Culach froze. "What do you mean?"

"My mother used to tell us fairytales. One of them, my favorite, was about a fourth clan of daēvas."

Culach groped for the wall to steady himself. His knees felt weak.

"Did these daēvas...did they...?"

"Work fire? Yes. It was their gift."

He let out a slow breath.

"We never thought it was true, of course. They were an archetype. A myth. The wicked fire workers and their insane king.

They tried to break the world and were beaten back by the other clans."

"Could there be a kernel of truth to it?"

"I've no idea. No one else ever spoke of it. My mother gave the impression it was all very, very long ago."

Culach felt a surge of excitement. He'd been convinced it was all incipient madness. If there was some explanation, he'd grab it like a lifeline.

"I need to learn more." He scrubbed a hand across the silver-gold stubble roughening his jaw. "Who would remember?" Culach snapped his fingers. "Gerda. My great-great-grandmother. You must fetch her."

"Me? Oh no. That woman is nasty."

Culach laughed. It sounded wild and desperate. "Yes, she is. But she's the oldest of us."

"She hasn't left her rooms in decades."

"Then you'll have to convince her."

"And why should I do that?"

"Because if you do, I'll promise to force my father to leave you alone. You won't have to come here anymore."

There was a long silence.

"All right, I'll do it."

Part of him had hoped she'd protest that it wasn't so bad keeping him company. Their enmity had settled into mutual tolerance in recent days. He'd even made her laugh a few times. He thought perhaps she didn't hate him quite so much as she used to. And he had to admit she eased his loneliness. The times Mina came were the best of his day.

But she obviously didn't feel the same way. That was fine. If she could coax his cantankerous grandmother to come for a visit, he would free her from her obligation to him.

"I do have one condition," Mina said.

"Yes?"

"You must let me try to heal you. Only once. Then I can say

truthfully that I made the attempt." Her voice lowered. "I am not completely without honor, whatever you may think."

Culach was taken aback. Did she care for him after all? Or was it simply her stubborn Danai pride?

"Can you stand to be touched?" Mina asked.

Somehow she had always known, although he'd never told her. His heart beat hard.

"If you can't, we'll wait. There's no rush—"

"Yes," he heard himself say. "Please try."

Her footsteps came closer.

"Lie down on the bed," Mina ordered. Her voice was brisk, but he thought he heard a faint tremor in it.

Culach sank back onto the furs. He both craved her touch and was terrified of it. She drew up his tunic, exposing his skin to the chill air. His breath caught as her fingertips settled on his chest, barely touching but enough to send little flares of pain through the tender nerves. She waited, doing nothing more, and his tense muscles relaxed a little.

"I'm going to use all three elements, but mostly water. It's the most important in healing and I've always been uncommonly strong in water for a Danai." She laughed softly. "One of my ancestors probably had an illicit affair with a Marakai."

Culach nodded. He didn't trust himself to speak. She pressed her palm flat against his chest. A warm, tingling sensation spread across his scars. He bit his lip, holding perfectly still.

"Is that all right?"

"Yes." His voice came out hoarse.

"I'm just taking the lay of the land. I won't do anything yet."

The tingling ran down his spine. It was like sinking into a warm bath. He closed his eyes. The heat slowly built and he suddenly wanted to feel more of her against him. To reach out and touch her, taste her mouth. The smell of her was maddening. Katrin's caresses had repulsed him and now he understood why. Culach balled his hands into fists. He tried to think of anything else, but all he could see was Mina's dark eyes, the soft fall of her hair as he unbound her braid....

She gave a soft cry of alarm and jerked back and Culach flushed, thinking she'd noticed his apparently all too obvious desire. But then her hand cupped his face.

"You're severed from elements!" she exclaimed.

Shame and humiliation made him jerk away. That, and the shock in her voice.

"Leave me," he growled.

"I won't tell anyone, I swear."

As usual, Mina had understood immediately what he feared the most.

"Katrin was right," Culach said bitterly. "I am a broken creature. You're free from your *obligation*. I'll speak to Eirik today."

She was silent for a long moment. "Well, this presents something more of a challenge than I anticipated. But I'm not giving up on you yet, Culach."

"What do you mean?" He couldn't bring himself to hope she could fix him.

"I...I'm not sure. But I wish to study this further."

"So I'm to be your pet project? The bird with the broken wing?"

"Call it what you like." She drew the furs over him again. Amusement colored her voice as she added, "I see why the women like you despite your abrasive personality. You have other...attributes."

"Bloody hell, Mina," he grumbled, rolling to his side.

"And I'll try to persuade Gerda to come visit you. Do we have a deal?"

He muttered something.

"I'll take that as a yes."

She started for the door. Culach sat up.

"And tell the cook no more beet soup or I'll come down to the kitchen myself and strangle him with my bare hands."

He heard laughter as her footsteps faded away.

And then Culach was alone again. He knew if he tried to sleep, he would dream of fire and choking sand. So he forced himself out of bed and started pacing, counting his footsteps. Twenty-nine to cross the room to the window, thirty to the other end of the chamber, eighteen back to his bed.

Mina. Damn the woman.

His treacherous body still faintly ached for her. Culach didn't worship any gods, none of the Valkirins did, but if he had, he thought they'd be laughing at him right now.

✣ 13 ✣

SOME NEW DEVILRY

Galen spent the morning hunting deep in the forest with Ellard. By the time Selene had passed her zenith and was sinking toward the trees, they had a brace of rabbits. The Danai generally shunned meat because it couldn't be cooked and raw flesh was tough and distasteful. Most of the daēvas subsisted on the fruits of the forest: nuts, berries, mushrooms, birds' eggs and the like.

But Galen had discovered a method of marinating the rabbits —skinned and finely diced—in bitterlime juice and pepperleaf. It softened the meat and gave it a pleasant citrus flavor. He whistled between his teeth, anticipating supper together. The air grew crisp as they returned to House Dessarian and the pair walked together in companionable silence.

Galen felt at ease with Ellard. They were both outsiders, if in different ways. He glanced over at the slender, silver-haired youth. He'd caught Ellard watching him several times that day. Each time, Ellard had looked away when Galen's eyes met his. But he wondered if perhaps Ellard felt more for him than strictly friends. The idea sent tingles through his belly. He hadn't dared to hope for it, but he'd harbored a secret crush on Ellard for years now.

At first, his attraction had an undeniable whiff of forbidden fruit. The Valkirins were their enemies. And not merely the Valkirins—Val Moraine in particular. A liaison would be deliciously wrong. Besides which, he was curious. What were the Valkirins like? Were they truly as cold and fierce as everyone claimed?

So Galen had volunteered to be the one to shadow Ellard around the Dessarian compound. Like Mina, Ellard would be given a reasonable amount of freedom. It was part of the deal. And he was warded. What harm could he do?

After a week of this, Ellard had approached him and asked in a direct manner if he ever went hunting. And so their friendship began. Galen had gotten to know him. To see past the exotic looks to a man as guarded and lonely as he was—but also kind and decent. Not what he had expected at all.

"You look a thousand leagues away," Ellard said teasingly. Despite the chill, he wore a light cotton shirt with no cloak. His Valkirin blood was thicker than the Danai. Even at rest, Ellard radiated heat. "Drooling at the prospect of a real supper?"

Galen smiled. This time, their gaze held. "Something like that."

Ellard grinned back, but a flush crept into his cheeks. Galen's smile broadened.

Perhaps things were finally going his way. With Darius gone, Galen felt as though he'd shed a burden. Whatever the others believed, he didn't hate Darius on principle. Under other circumstances, he would be grateful for a half-brother. The problem was Darius had everything he didn't.

Galen knew he looked more like Victor—the spitting image, some said. But where it counted—in the power—he had nothing in common with his father. Galen had always been weak in earth magic. Just lifting a pebble left him trembling and exhausted. Air and water came to him easily, but never earth. This was unheard of among the Avas Danai. Earth magic was their affinity. When

Darius tore open deep chasms in the ground to corner the Valkirin assassin, Galen had felt physically ill with envy.

He'd become adept at concealing this handicap. He'd made it clear that he had no interest in tending the great forest, which required deep and subtle earth magic. He took up the bow instead and become a border sentry, a solitary pursuit that kept him away from the other Danai. It had worked—none knew his secret. But it had also been a depressing existence until Ellard came along. Galen hoped someone at Val Moraine was being similarly kind to his mother Mina.

They stopped as Victor strode up. Since Darius had left, their father walked around with a deep scowl on his face. He hadn't mentioned Darius's name once. Their relationship had never seemed warm to Galen, but rather wary, formally polite. Galen was intensely curious about what had happened in the mortal lands beyond the gate, but neither ever spoke of it. That left Delilah, but she was even less friendly than her son.

"We need to speak," Victor said to Galen. His gaze swept over Ellard. "Alone."

If Ellard felt offended, he didn't show it. He gave a brief bow, catching Galen's eye.

"See you later," he said. "I'll start cleaning the rabbits."

Galen turned to his father as Ellard walked into the trees.

"You can trust him," Galen said. "We've been friends for years. Ellard is a good man."

Victor gave him a black look. "He's a Valkirin. Never trust any of them. Come."

They strolled through the compound. Selene was setting, giving way to Hecate. Galen loved this time of the evening. The delicate shift in the quality of the light from a warm, buttery yellow to cool white.

"I've come to a decision," Victor said, pausing beneath a hickory tree. Green nuts crunched beneath his boots. "I'm not waiting for the Matrium. We need to act now."

Galen's chest tightened.

"For one thing, they take too long. I remember how it used to be. Weeks to gather the Houses together and then days of point-less debate. By the time they reach a decision, the Valkirins could have hatched and executed another murderous plot."

"Do you think they'll retaliate?" Galen asked.

"Without doubt. But if we act first, land the first blow...." Victor trailed off as they passed a pair of sentries, who gave curt nods. He continued once they moved out of earshot. "And then there's always the chance they'll refuse me. I have the utmost respect for those women, of course, but they can be overly cautious. And then there's this business about the disappearances. We're supposed to take the Valkirins' word for it that they've lost people, but where's the proof? I wouldn't be surprised if they're behind that too."

"What do you have in mind?" Galen asked.

Victor's jaw clenched. "I'm going to kill Culach and his father Eirik myself. We'll bring a small party, no more than twenty. I want you to come."

Galen swallowed. "It's a great honor—"

"Don't be a fool," Victor snapped. "Killing isn't an honor. It's a burden. But one we must bear." The hard planes of his face soft-ened a touch. "You're one of the only ones I trust. Son."

The word brought a warm flush to Galen's neck.

"But how?" he asked. "Those mountains are impassable. The stronghold of Val Moraine has never been breached, not once."

He knew his history. In the Iron Wars, when three other hold-fasts—Val Altair, Val Tourmaline and Val Petros—had allied to squabble over mining rights, they'd broken their teeth on the walls of Val Moraine. And they were all Valkirins, bred to the alti-tude and harsh conditions. That was how Val Moraine came to be known as the Maiden Keep—because she'd never been taken.

Victor gave a thin smile. "I know a back way in. Now, you must tell no one of this. We leave tomorrow. The whole thing will be done quickly." He fingered the hilt of his sword. "Nazafareen is like a daughter to me. I want her back as much as Darius does. And she won't be safe until her enemies are dead."

Galen's mind raced. "But what about my mother? What if they kill her?"

Victor laid a heavy hand on his shoulder. "Don't worry, we'll catch them by surprise. I won't let that happen. We'll bring Mina home." His eyes grew distant. "I've been an arrogant man, Galen. I've made terrible mistakes. But this is the only way to avert all-out war, do you see that? Val Moraine is already weakened. Kill Culach and his father and we'll behead the snake. They won't have the will to strike back."

Galen was barely listening. He was still fixated on what Victor had said about his mother.

We'll bring her home too.

That was Galen's dearest wish.

He clasped Victor's forearm. "Tomorrow," he said. "We can be there in two days—"

He broke off at Victor's wary expression. They'd reached Darius's house. It was empty and quiet. So very quiet. That's when he realized the birds and insects had fallen silent. Victor flicked his eyes at the front door. It stood slightly ajar. Just an inch or two. Galen couldn't remember if it had been like that when he passed it with Ellard that morning on their way into the forest.

They shared a look. Victor drew his sword. Galen hastily nocked an arrow.

"Has Darius returned?" Galen asked in a low voice.

Victor wordlessly shook his head. He used his blade to ease the door open. The kitchen was neat as a pin. Moonlight spilled through the window, illuminating a bag of onions dangling from a hook over a counter with a wooden chopping block.

Victor stood stock still for a moment. Then he shook his head. "I'll look in the bedroom. You check the second floor."

Galen ascended a circular staircase that wound into the leafy canopy above. The room ran the length of the house, with wide plank floors and a gap at the end where the roof lay open to the stars. A shelf held a collection of orreries and astrolabes. Sawdust danced in the moonbeams, tickling his nose and making him want to sneeze. It was Darius's woodshop. Galen paused before a bench covered with tools. The small table next to it held a half-carved figurine of a girl leaning on her sword, a tiny enigmatic smile on her lips. She had a wide mouth and a determined chin. Her nose was slightly crooked, as if it had been broken and never healed right. *Nazafareen.* Even unfinished, the face was unmistakable.

Sickness twisted in his gut. A black wave of misery and self-loathing.

My mother is probably already dead. And I—

Galen's heart lurched as something stirred in the shadows at the far end of the room. A trick of the light? He instinctively found the Nexus and raised his bow. The calm of the void cleared his mind.

There.

The moonlight caught something. The lash of a tail?

Galen backed toward the stairs, the hair on his arms rising. Something rushed through the shadows and landed on his chest. Hot breath struck his face. And then Victor was there, his blade slashing.

"We're under attack!" he bellowed.

Galen stumbled to his feet. He thought there was more than one, but it was impossible to tell. The moonlight slid and bent around them. The jumble of limbs seemed impossibly wrong, a pattern of light and dark that made no sense. Victor sliced through one of the creatures as if through air. From the corner of his eye, Galen saw curved teeth flash. They meshed together like the bristles of a brush. Jaws snapped, closing on Victor's arm. He lifted it up, shaking, but it clung like a dog with a bone. Galen scrambled for his bow and managed to nock an arrow, loosing it where he thought the thing's eye might be. The missile struck home and it finally let go.

"Get out, boy!" Victor growled.

When Galen didn't respond, he gave him a hard shove. Galen was standing before the window and he tumbled backwards, striking the ground far below on his back. Daēvas ran toward the house from every direction, weapons drawn.

"Galen?" Ellard crouched over him, his face tight with worry. "Are you hurt?"

He shook his head, unable to speak. The fall had knocked his wind out. Ellard gently touched his cheek. Understanding passed between them.

"I'll be back for you," Ellard whispered. "Just sit tight."

Galen reached for his hand to pull him back, but Ellard was already gone, running into the house. Shouts and the sounds of breaking furniture drifted from the upstairs windows. Galen couldn't wield much earth himself, but he sensed it. The daēvas inside were drawing vast quantities of power. Surely, nothing could withstand them. He rolled to his side, tasting blood in his mouth. A moment later, three shadows streaked past, tearing a swath through the crowd and vanishing into the woods. He drew a ragged breath and pushed to his feet, steadying himself on the doorframe.

Two dead daēvas sprawled on the kitchen floor. Galen climbed the stairs. More bodies, all with terrible wounds.

"Ellard?" he called.

Then he saw the glint of silver hair at the end of the room. Galen's heart drummed in his chest as he approached. The sounds around him faded until he stood in a pocket of perfect silence.

Ellard lay on his back, eyes wide and facing the stars. One hand still clutched his bow. His throat had been torn out. Galen thought of the dead rabbits. They'd had the same glassy-eyed stare. His stomach convulsed and he covered his mouth before he retched. A heavy hand fell on his shoulder.

"He saved my life," Victor said gruffly. "You were right. Ellard was a good man."

Galen felt a deep chill in his bones.

"We have to return the body," he said, and his voice sounded strange in his ears. "He needs to be with his clan."

"Of course." Victor squeezed his shoulder. "Of course. But there are other questions we must answer first."

He left the room and Galen followed. He couldn't bear to look at his friend. The angry buzz of the crowd died down a little when they emerged. Victor approached Delilah, whose mouth set in a hard line as she took in his wounds.

"This is some new devilry," he muttered. "Those things were impervious to the power. It only made them stronger." A shadow crossed his face. "And they radiated...sickness. Sickness of the soul."

"Chimera."

They all turned at Tethys' voice. Her stern features lit with a fury that matched Victor's own as she surveyed the carnage.

"What in the Pit is that?" Victor demanded.

"The darkest of elemental magic. It's been forbidden for centuries now. But someone saw fit to violate the laws of nature and bring it back."

"Someone?" Victor seethed. "We know who."

"It could only have been done with a lock of Darius's hair," Tethys muttered. "There's a traitor among us. Probably the same one who told the Valkirins about Nazafareen." She turned to Victor. "And the pack has Darius's scent now. It won't stop until he's dead."

"Gods." Victor's face seemed to crumple in on itself. Then it hardened and his onyx eyes went dead. "When I find whoever did this.... How can the chimera be stopped?"

"Fording a river might throw them off if he goes far enough downstream. But they can't be killed, only eluded."

"Someone has to go after him," Galen said. "To warn him. I'll do it."

Tethys stared at him for a long moment. "Both my grandsons," she murmured, touching his cheek with cool fingers. "Go now, then. Chimera run quickly."

Galen nodded. A wave of nausea rolled through him.

Tethys moved away, gathering the other daēvas in a circle. Galen heard her organizing a search of every house. The Danai looked grim, but none complained.

Victor laid a hand on his shoulder. "I would go with you but...." He lowered his voice. "You recall what I said earlier. It's time to behead the snake. Come, I'll see you off. There's no time to waste."

They hurried to Galen's house, where he hurriedly packed two days of rations and an extra quiver of arrows. He eyed his heaviest wool cloak, but left it hanging on the peg.

"I'm grateful for your help," Victor said awkwardly as they stood outside the door, the dark woods deep and silent around them. "I.... Know that I'm proud of you, Galen." They clasped hands.

Galen's heart thudded in his chest as he ran west toward the Umbra. It didn't slow until he passed deep enough into the woods to change course and veer north.

Toward Val Moraine.

He was woefully unprepared for a journey into the mountains, but Victor would have been suspicious if he'd packed cold weather gear. There was no need for it in the west. But Galen had no intention of going after Darius. He was running for his own life now.

The Valkirins were supposed to give Mina back. That's all he ever wanted. He'd grown up without father or mother, and while Tethys had seen to his needs, she wasn't a particularly warm woman. He never felt he belonged at House Dessarian. When Victor first returned, Galen had been both nervous and overjoyed. But the reunion wasn't what he'd always dreamed of. Victor brought a new wife and son with him. And while he didn't deny that Galen was his, Victor treated him much the same as the other young men. He didn't seem interested in being a father to someone he barely knew.

It had been a bitter disappointment. When Galen learned why Nazafareen had come to House Dessarian and why her presence needed to be kept secret—that she was responsible for Culach's bruising defeat in his quest to plunder the mortal lands beyond the Dominion—an idea had begun to form. Just a little worm of a thought. He'd tried to dismiss it. But it had burrowed deeper, keeping him up nights. Why should Darius have everything and Galen nothing? Who was this mortal woman to put them all at risk? And if the Valkirins found out, would they kill Mina? Was it not his duty to tell them himself? To offer a trade?

The more he chewed over the possibilities, the more he came to see it as a golden opportunity to strike a bargain with the Valkirins. No one need ever know.

One thing led to another. He'd sent a bird to Val Moraine. No response had come and he was starting to think his message hadn't arrived when the assassin appeared. Galen had panicked. Fearful his treachery would be revealed, he'd shot the man with an arrow before he could be taken alive.

But of course that wasn't the end of it.

A few days later, Galen had been ranging near the border when he suddenly found himself bound in flows of air. A Valkirin had stepped out of the trees, pale as death, demanding to know what had happened to Petur. Terrified, Galen placed the blame on Darius. The Valkirin told Galen what he must do if he ever wanted to see his mother again.

Darius was unconscious in Galen's own bed. It had been a simple matter to cut a small lock of his hair. Galen took Nazafareen's from a stolen hairbrush. He was just returning from making the delivery when the wind ship came.

He'd buried the hairbrush in the woods behind his house, but he knew Tethys would find it somehow. She had a way of ferreting out secrets.

And when Victor discovered the truth.... Galen shuddered. His father had been gone in the shadowlands for most of Galen's life and the long absence had only added to Victor's mystique. But Galen had seen his volatile temper erupt on more than one occasion, mostly over minor matters. He couldn't begin to imagine the retribution for such a betrayal.

I should have asked what the Valkirins wanted the hair for.

Now Ellard was dead and he was an exile.

A little voice whispered that the creatures might not have caught Darius yet. That there was still time to turn back. To find Darius and warn him.

My brother.

But he'd seen the look in Victor's eyes. There would be no forgiveness. At least he could see his mother Mina one last time.

So Galen ran.

It was a day to the mountains, less if he pushed hard. Galen fingered his thin cloak. Could he find Val Moraine? And would the Valkirins welcome him?

Know that I'm proud of you.

Too late, father. Too late.

He swallowed a lump in his throat and kept running.

❧ 14 ❧

THE UMBRA

"The Guild will be furious," Javid grumbled as they sifted through the wreckage of the *Kyrenia*. "They'll never trust me with my own ship now."

The wind still moaned across the rocky landscape, bringing occasional gusts of rain, but the main body of the storm had passed by while Javid slept. Now that he'd woken, he was in an ill humor and seemed to blame Nazafareen for their predicament.

"I'm sorry," she said, kicking a splintered chunk of wood from her path. "But you told me to cut the rope."

"The *other* rope."

"I asked you twice," she snapped, her temper fraying. "I said I didn't know which one you meant!"

Javid tucked his hair behind his ears and squatted down to examine a battered navigational instrument, tossing it aside with an expression of disgust. "Fine. I won't waste time arguing about it. We have more immediate problems, such as being stranded in the middle of nowhere."

Clouds scudded across Hecate's pallid face, but a scattering of stars shone overhead. Javid studied them intently for a minute or two. It wasn't quite as dark as in Nocturne, Nazafareen noticed, more like the twilight she remembered from the Dominion—one of the only places besides the forest she *did* remember, even if it was in bits and pieces.

"We were blown considerably off course," he said at last. "I'd say we're only halfway across the Umbra, and much farther north than we should be."

"What does that mean?"

"Well, for one thing, we're nearer to Delphi than Samarqand."

"So let's just go there instead."

Javid laughed. "Oh no, country bumpkin. I don't think so."

Nazafareen rummaged through one of the broken crates. It must be the Oracle, though Ashraf wouldn't know that. "Why not?" she asked.

"Trust me, you don't want to go to Delphi."

Nazafareen eyed the leather pouch at his belt. "What about your magic? Can't you use it to fix the ship?"

He stared at her hard. "What magic?"

"Oh, please. I have eyes."

Javid sighed. "If you're a Greek spy, I don't suppose it matters now. It's called spell dust. Most wind ships have a burner that heats air for the sack. But I couldn't very well bring fire to the darklands, could I? The daēvas would have killed me. So I designed my own version that uses spell magic. It makes the air inside the sack lighter than the air outside, and it can conjure a wind that bears the ship where I wish her to go."

"Can this dust do other things?" She thought of her broken memories.

"Yes, but you'd have to ask an alchemist."

"Where would I find one?"

"Samarqand. And they don't come cheap." Javid checked the pouch. "There isn't much left. Even if there was, I'm not a miracle worker." He looked disconsolately at the shattered hull. "See if you can find any food. It's going to be a long walk."

They spent the next hour picking through every inch of the

wreckage. To her delight, Nazafareen found her sword, but the oilskin bag must have flown out because she saw no sign of it. Javid located a single full water jug; the others had broken.

"Is this all you brought?" she asked, holding up two loaves of bread, a single jar of olives, and a rind of hard white cheese.

Javid raised an eyebrow, then winced as it stretched the clotted cut. "I didn't pack for a long journey by foot. Nor did I anticipate having two mouths to feed. That would have been plenty if you hadn't reduced my ship to kindling."

Nazafareen grunted and buckled on her sword.

"Where'd you get that, village girl?" Javid demanded. "Holy Father, did you steal it from the daēvas?"

"No!" She kicked herself. There was so much she didn't know. *So swords are valuable items in the mortal lands.* "It was given to me. One of the daēvas taught me how to use it. He said a girl alone should be able to defend herself."

Javid gave her a stony stare. "Let's see then."

"What do you mean?"

"Show me how to fight with a sword. Personally, I think you took it to sell in Samarqand." His mouth set in a grim line. "If that's the case, we're turning around right now and walking back to the darklands so you can tell them how sorry you are."

Nazafareen stared back for a long moment. She shrugged. "Okay."

She whipped the sword from its sheath and cut a whistling figure eight around Javid's head. His eyes widened, probably because he thought she was improvising. She did spar with Victor sometimes. And although her memories of people and places were lost, her body remembered how to fight with different blades, and with hand and feet.

Nazafareen held back, deliberately affecting a degree of clumsiness but showing enough skill that he'd believe her story. She must have done a fair job because Javid finally began to clap sardonically, though he was smiling.

"Enough, enough. I see you're familiar with it. Now put it away before one of us gets stabbed." He studied the sword. "It's a finely balanced blade. If you do decide to sell it, I'll tell you where to go to get a fair price."

"I'll never sell it," Nazafareen said fiercely, slipping the sword into its scabbard. "It was a gift."

They started walking across the featureless terrain. At first glance the Umbra appeared perfectly flat, but in fact it was riven by deep gullies and other wind-carved formations. They were forced to go around these, but travel was otherwise easy because there was no vegetation of any kind.

The earth magic that allowed the Avas Danai forest to thrive lay far behind them and without true sunlight, no plant could survive. At first Nazafareen felt exposed on the vast open plain after so many weeks living amid trees. They must be visible for leagues and leagues if anyone was looking. But she soon realized that just as the Umbra was bereft of plant life, there were no animals either. There was nothing at all.

They walked in the monotonous half-light until neither could go any further. Nazafareen slept curled up in her cloak, Javid in his coat. Even if they'd had the means to make a fire, there was no wood to burn. They had to strictly ration the food, so both went to bed hungry and not in the mood for conversation.

Toward the end of the second day, Nazafareen saw a faint glow on the western horizon like it was on the verge of dawn. She waited anxiously for any stirring of magic within her but felt nothing different.

"Tell me about Samarqand," she said.

They'd stopped at a clear, cold stream to refill their water skins. Nazafareen splashed her face, scrubbing the dust off. She still felt sore and knew bruises lurked beneath her tunic.

"The most wondrous city in the world. Rich and fat, just like our King, the Holy Father bless his name." Javid piously brushed forehead, lips and heart with one hand.

She rolled her eyes, but only when he wasn't looking. Nazafareen had told him she didn't care about his business with the Danai, but she knew it had something to do with evading the King's taxes.

"You follow the way of the flame," she said. Darius sometimes made a similar gesture.

"As do all civilized men," he replied airily.

"Is that why you don't like Delphi?"

"The Greeks have their own gods, it's true, but that's not why I dislike them. Delphi and Samarqand are bitter rivals."

"For what?"

Javid took a long drink of water and wiped his mouth. "Money, power, the usual."

"What about the Marakai daēvas? Have you ever met them?"

"Of course. They're the intermediaries between Solis and the darklands."

"So their ships come to Samarqand?"

"The port is in Susa on the White Sea, but it's not far. About fifty leagues by the King's Road." He glanced at her. "Why?"

She shrugged. "Just curious. What are they like?"

Javid considered the question. "My boss says they're honest, though they don't mingle much with outsiders. They take a tenth of what they transport. It's called the Hin. No one knows what the Marakai do with their fortune, though they must be rich as sin." He paused. "They tend to stay on their ships. People can be...funny around them."

"What do you mean?"

"Some still hold a grudge. They don't trust any daēvas at all."

"But why?"

Javid gave her a pitying look. "Listen bumpkin, I guess your parents didn't teach you any history, but the daēvas tried to exterminate us. It was a long time ago, but you don't forget a thing like that."

Nazafareen had no idea what he was talking about.

"They burned our cities to the ground. Thousands died."

"But that doesn't even make any sense! Daēvas abhor fire."

Javid shrugged. "Maybe now they do. I'm just telling you what happened. Like I said, it was a long time ago. Some kind of civil war among the clans and we got caught up in it. Took generations to rebuild."

Nazafareen stood, knuckling the small of her back with her left hand. She didn't believe the story for a moment. The very idea was ridiculous. But she didn't think Ashraf would argue the point.

"You have your spell dust if they try anything," she said lightly.

"Yes, but it's nothing compared to elemental magic. Baby stuff."

He glanced at her, his gaze sliding across her stump and away. He hadn't asked once about the missing hand. And since her foolishness with the sword, she'd made sure to remove the gold cuff and keep it tucked in a pocket of her cloak. No poor village girl would own a piece of jewelry like that.

"Are you truly coming all the way to Samarqand? I thought you'd want to go home to your family after so many...misadventures."

Nazafareen ignored the patronizing tone. "I'm never going back." She thought of Darius and felt a stab of loneliness.

Javid looked at her appraisingly. "Do you have any skills?"

"Like what?"

"Cooking. Sewing. Womanly pursuits."

Nazafareen scowled. "I know how to fight."

"No one hires girl mercenaries. I thought you said you wanted to be a lady's maid."

"Well, I...."

"How about singing? You could get a job at a tavern."

She tried out a snatch of a ballad she'd heard Darius humming. Javid groaned and put his hands over his ears.

"Won't anyone come looking for you when you don't return?"

"Unfortunately not. I told you, no one else is willing to fly across the Umbra. And the nature of my mission was...delicate. If word ever got out, the Guild would deny they even knew me." His teeth gleamed white in the half-light. "Which leaves us fending for ourselves."

She nodded. "I *am* sorry, you know. I was only trying to do what you said."

"I know." He sighed. "So tell me, what was it like living in the darklands?"

"The Danai treated me kindly."

"Then why did you leave?"

"I missed the sun."

This seemed to be the expected answer, for Javid nodded. "I can't imagine living where it's night all the time. I'd go mad."

"Yeah."

"Are there wild animals in the forest?"

"Some. The ones that like the night. Owls and foxes. Possums. They have snakes too." She spread her arms wide. "Really big ones."

"Sounds lovely. I'm sorry I had to leave so soon."

They began walking again. The horizon steadily lightened. After a few hours, they came to the banks of a great river, half a league across. It was slow and meandering on the flat plain, and the air was warm enough that Nazafareen shed her cloak and waded in. Javid explained that there were several rivers leading from the dark side to the light side. Together with the White Sea to the north and the Austral Ocean to the south, they exchanged cold air for hot and moderated the extreme temperatures.

"Of course, the Valkirins live in the mountains, but they have ice water running in their veins," Javid laughed. He'd rolled up his trousers and waded next to her, but kept his quilted coat on. She'd never seen him remove it.

"Aren't you hot?" Nazafareen asked.

Javid shrugged. "I'm used to it."

Nazafareen gazed at the horizon, whose color had lightened to a yellowish pink. For the first time, she felt something stir inside her. It seemed very aware of Javid's leather pouch—and of the cuff she carried. For the metal was no longer cold and dead. It held some kind of flickering, latent force that both attracted and repelled her. The bond with Darius? She'd thought it was broken forever....

Nazafareen stopped walking. The hair on her arms rose as she peered into the twilight behind them, where the sky gently faded from grey to black. Nothing moved on the plain.

"Ashraf?" He stared at her impatiently. "I'm thinking we should make camp—"

"No!"

Javid frowned at the vehemence in her voice.

"Why not? I can hardly walk another step and there's water here."

"We have to keep going. I....I have a funny feeling, Javid. I get them sometimes and they're usually right. We need to leave."

He looked at her strangely but didn't argue. They picked up their packs in silence and started for the lightening horizon again. Nazafareen's shoulder blades itched. She kept looking behind and saw nothing. But she knew what she'd sensed.

Something was back there.

15

CHILDREN OF FIRE

Gerda refused to come to him so Culach was forced to dress and find his way to her chambers. He hadn't been there in years, but he found he remembered the route. She lived in one of the highest, most remote towers of the hold-fast, where the air was so cold and thin Culach had to stamp his feet to keep his toes from freezing. It took ten minutes of knocking before the door opened.

"Who are you?" a harsh voice demanded.

Of course, Gerda knew very well who he was. She just wanted to make him squirm.

"It's me, grandmother," he said patiently. "Culach."

Silence. Then: "What happened to you? You look terrible."

"It's kind of you to inquire after my health. I—"

"Kind? I'm just being honest. And why do you stare at me so blankly, like a simpleton?"

"I lost my sight, grandmother."

He heard her suck her teeth. "That's too bad. My eyesight is still perfect. I can see like a young osprey. Of course, there's nothing much to look at."

Culach had the feeling she was staring at him as she said those last words. An awkward silence descended. Finally, he swallowed what was left of his pride and asked.

"Will you invite me in?"

If he'd thought his condition would evoke pity from the old bat, he was sadly mistaken.

"What for?"

"I need to talk to you."

"You haven't needed to talk to me for three hundred years. I guess I have something you want. You're just like the rest of them."

Culach's bulk shifted in the doorway. Suddenly it seemed a fool's errand. Gerda would laugh in his face and send him on his way. He almost left then, but he'd trudged through what seemed like leagues of corridors to reach her chambers and the thought of returning empty-handed—worse, without even having tried—was too much to bear.

"If you have something to say, spit it out," she said briskly.

"Were there ever daēvas who could work fire?" he asked in a rush.

He heard a sharp intake of breath. Not the question she was anticipating, but she knew something.

"Who told you that?"

"No one. I...I've dreamed of it."

The silence seemed to stretch for an eternity. Then he heard the scrape as she stepped back from the door, the soft creak of hinges rarely used.

"You'd better come in."

Something loosened in his chest as he moved inside. It was even colder than the corridor. Culach liked to think of himself as tough, but Gerda took it to a whole other level.

"When I was a girl, we didn't use shields of air outside the windows," she said in a disapproving tone. "The wind blew straight into the room. Much healthier."

Culach made a noncommittal noise and tried not to shiver. A

disturbingly strong hand closed around his arm and guided him to a chair.

"Tell me everything," she commanded.

"First tell me if it's true. Was there ever a fourth clan?"

He didn't mention the tale Mina had shared—he wanted to see what Gerda knew first. When he was a small boy, she'd been a treasure trove of colorful stories. Eirik never paid him much attention until he was old enough to hold a sword. So he'd visit Gerda. She'd give him a spoonful of too-sweet syrup and a rough pinch on the cheek, neither of which he'd liked very much. But her stories...They were grisly and terrifying, like the tale of the chimera or the eyeless specter that haunted the armory. In other words, *good* stories.

"It's true," she conceded. "They called themselves the Avas Vatras. Children of Fire."

"How could it be?" Culach felt stunned, although he'd known in his heart there was some truth to the visions. They were too vivid, too real. "Do you remember these daēvas?"

"I'm not *that* old." Gerda's voice was dry. "The events we're talking about happened at least a thousand years ago."

Although he'd never dare say it, Culach wouldn't have been surprised to learn Gerda was ten thousand years old. Even in his earliest memories, her hair looked soft and fine as spider silk. It took a very long time for daēvas to show signs of aging, but Gerda's mouth and eyes had a network of deep creases from centuries of wind, cold and ill humor.

"I saw a battle," he said. "Not even a battle, a slaughter. The Avas Danai forests burned down and the seven great houses were driven into exile."

Gerda made a clucking noise with her tongue. "More than the forests burned, boy. Half the world was reduced to ashes. It only ended when the very heavens were sundered in two. Nocturne and Solis."

The knowledge rocked him. "You mean it wasn't always this

way?"

"I heard the tale from my own grandmother, who died before you were born," Gerda said. "She said that long ago, the sun moved across the sky, rising and setting on all lands the way the moons do. That half the day was sunlit and half was dark."

"That's...bizarre."

"To you, perhaps, because you don't know any better. The sundering was the price of defeating the Avas Vatra."

Culach thought of the mad king and his scheming advisor.

"So where are they now? Dead?"

"They must be. No one has heard a peep from them since. Good riddance, I say."

"The Avas Vatra," he repeated, tasting the name on his tongue. "Where did they live?"

"Somewhere out in the desert. West of the mortal cities, I believe, in the part they now call the Kiln."

"I saw a palace surrounded by yellow sand. There were gardens, but none of the flowers or trees were familiar. I saw a city too." He trailed off. "Why am I having these dreams, grandmother?"

"Perhaps because you were exposed to fire."

So Gerda knew about what had happened to him. Culach wasn't surprised.

"You mean...the girl who did this to me might not be human?"

Gerda snickered. "You think the Vatras have come back from the grave for you, boy?"

"She summoned fire, grandmother."

"But she's not of this world, is she? She came through the Dominion."

"That's what Neblis told me."

"Don't jump to conclusions. You know nothing of her world. Perhaps it's perfectly normal for mortals to work fire there."

"Perhaps."

Culach wasn't convinced. He didn't think his sister would have neglected to mention such a thing. And none of it explained why he had dreams of the distant past looping through his head on a nightly basis.

Memories.

That's what they felt like to him. Events witnessed firsthand by the raspy-voiced daēva.

"Do you think it means anything?"

Culach heard the splash of liquid in a goblet, followed by the eye-watering fumes of cheap red wine. Naturally, she didn't offer him any. Gerda took a greedy gulp before answering.

"I don't know, but there is one other part to the story. An important part, mind you. The sundering came later, but their defeat was brought about by three talismans."

"Talismans? What sort?"

"My grandmother didn't know. Only that without them, I wouldn't be sitting here to tell you the story, and you wouldn't even exist."

Culach rubbed his thick brush of inch-long hair. He knew a little about talismans. They were objects that channeled elemental power for a specific purpose, but they were exceedingly rare and Culach had never heard of one powerful enough to freeze the moon and stars in the sky, or to defeat fire-wielding daēvas.

His mind still rebelled at that last part. It was beyond unnatural.

"What happened to these talismans?" he asked, remembering the way the Valkirin woman had somehow turned back the flames.

"Who knows?"

"Someone must."

"Look, kid, there aren't many older than me and I don't know. They must have disappeared after the war."

Culach got the feeling she wasn't telling the whole truth, but he let it go for now. Push Gerda too hard and she might stop talking out of spite.

"What else do you know?" he asked casually, as if he didn't really care either way.

"Not so much. It began with the Avas Danai and the burning of the forests. The houses fled north until they came to our mountains. The Valkirins lived in the foothills then, in timbered holdfasts. The refugees begged for sanctuary and we gave it to them, not realizing the depth of their enemies' rage. When the Avas Vatra came, we had no defense. Imagine seeing a wall of flame a thousand feet high bearing down on you. That's what the Danai brought to our doorstep."

Culach *had* seen it, if only in dreams. He'd always taken the enmity between the clans for granted, a simmering feud that went back generations. The Danai were proud, stubborn, haughty, stiff-necked. Now he understood the roots of the discord.

"The Vatras burned us out too," Gerda continued. "My grandmother said that's why we build above the timberline now, and with stone instead of wood."

Culach flexed frozen fingers against the carved armrests. The chill had sunk deep into his bones. Gerda's rooms felt like a crypt.

"But if the other clans had such powerful talismans, why didn't they use them earlier?"

"Who knows?" She sounded irritated. "That part might not even be true."

"What was the King's name? The Avas Vatra King?"

"There are no records from that time. My grandmother called him the Viper for his cunning and cold-blooded nature, but I don't think she knew his name. It was our darkest chapter, Culach, and once it ended, the clans wanted to forget it had ever happened."

"I've seen him. He had red hair. And he loved with a Danai girl who refused him—"

Gerda clapped her hands, not in delight but like a teacher silencing a rowdy schoolroom.

"Enough talk of the Vatras," she said. "Since you speak of

Danai girls, there is a matter I would address with you, grandson. I hear Victor's old flame has been hanging around."

Culach didn't like hearing Mina described in those terms.

"Eirik's orders," he said shortly.

"For what purpose?"

"He thought she might be able to heal me."

"And has she?"

"No."

"Eirik is a fool sometimes," Gerda sniffed. "Take it from me, you should keep your distance. The Danai never appreciated the help we gave them or the price we paid for it. They only care about their stupid trees." Her tone sharpened to a semi-screech. "Look what they've done now. Darling Petur is dead. And I hear they won't even return the body, those bastards—"

Culach listened to a rambling diatribe about the Avas Danai until he managed to make his excuses and leave, promising to return in a few days. Despite Gerda's deep-seated prejudices, he was burning to share what he'd learned with Mina. There was a mystery here and he intended to solve it. Perhaps once he did, the visions would go away.

His fingers trailed along the wall, guiding him back to his chambers. To an outsider, the keep would be a labyrinth of endless corridors and twisted staircases, most without railings that could prevent a misstep from becoming a shattered skull. But Culach had grown up running through these graceful stone galleries. With a little concentration, he found he could summon a mental map that proved surprisingly accurate.

The return trip to his rooms passed swiftly, but he was struck by how quiet Val Moraine had become. Once the mightiest of all the Valkirin holdfasts, now reduced to two dozen people. And their sacrifice meant nothing since he'd failed to bring Neblis home. Instead, *Victor* returned with a wife and son—along with the mortal girl who had brought ruin upon Val Moraine.

Still, Culach felt the stirrings of a new purpose. Now he knew his dreams were a window into the past. There had to be some reason it had opened for him.

Culach thought back to that moment at the gate. Something had happened, but he couldn't remember what it was. He couldn't even remember being burned. Why? The girl hadn't been near him at that point. He saw her hovering nearby. Her eyes had widened. What had she seen?

Something else was there. The tender skin on his scars prickled.

If there's a connection, I will find it. And Mina will help me.

He hoped she'd be waiting, but his chamber was quiet. He sat on the bed, thinking about what Gerda had said, bursting with questions. What exactly were the talismans she spoke of? How and why was their world sundered into Solis and Nocturne? What had happened to the Avas Vatra? The minutes ticked past and Culach's stomach rumbled. Lunchtime came and went. He began to worry that something had happened to her.

Although Mina had lived at Val Moraine for years, Culach hadn't a clue how she spent her free time. He knew she avoided the places where people tended to gather, because he'd seen her only rarely before his injury. That ruled out any of the great halls, the kitchens, the armory or baths.

Culach wandered through the keep until he found someone who knew where Mina's chambers were, but she wasn't there either.

He leaned against the radiant summerstone wall and gathered his thoughts. Mina had free run of the holdfast since escape was impossible. She could have gone anywhere. But there was one place she might be drawn to.

Culach left her chambers and counted the corridors past the armory until he reached the fourth one. He ran his hands over the stones in the wall, testing them with his fingers until one gave way and a doorway opened. Then he descended a long staircase, winding his way down into the deep heart of the mountain.

The Valkirins' wealth derived from the gemstones and metals they traded with the seafaring Marakai clan. No one wanted ice or snow or rock, but gold? Silver? Iron and nickel? They were worth a fortune to the mortals, whose sunlit lands along the river delta were fertile for farming but barren of ore. So once a month, emissaries from Val Moraine met the Marakai ships on the shore of the White Sea and traded the bounty of the mountains for luxuries like fresh-baked bread, and iron blades and shields.

It required mortal smiths to forge and cast the raw ore, and daēvas to mine the veins. The Valkirins ended up buying back their own metal for twice the price, but no one resented it because that was simply the way of things.

Of course, they didn't rely on the humans for *all* their food, only the dishes that needed cooking. The other clans joked that the Avas Valkirin subsisted on air and their own arrogance. Only the Valkirins themselves knew where their larder came from, but Culach instinctively understood Mina would be drawn there. It was the closest thing she could get to the forests of her own home.

The stone walls grew rougher, the ceiling lowering until it brushed the top of Culach's head. Cold drafts tingled against his skin as he passed secondary tunnels snaking into the mines and he took care at these junctures to stay in the main passage. If he got lost, he might never find the way out. But he remembered the way from his days poaching fruit with Petur and soon he sensed the space opening out around him, his footfalls echoing against distant walls.

"Mina?"

Warm, humid air filled the cavern. Culach thrust his hands out, fingertips brushing leaves and stems as he navigated between the orderly rows of plantings. Despite his newfound confidence, he still couldn't quite believe he'd strayed so far from the safety of his chambers. Was it only a week ago he refused to get out of bed?

Culach knew it was Mina's influence, her prodding and chiding and refusal to treat him like an invalid. He couldn't have borne excessive kindness—or worse, pity. Culach smiled. He'd gotten neither of those things from Mina. Just cool indifference. And it had made him stop wallowing.

Again he called her name and received no response. Perhaps he'd been wrong. Culach drew a deep breath, the air heavy with earth and ripening fruit. The caverns were lit by special lumen crystals that mimicked sunlight. Just as the Danai held the secrets of their forest, the Valkirins hid their groves deep within the mountain, an oasis of soft, fragrant breezes and lush greenery nestled amid leagues of lifeless stone.

And then he caught an unmistakable trace of Mina's scent. A welcoming smile spread across his face as he heard footsteps approach.

"Gerda's charming as ever," he said with a crooked grin. "But she knew some interesting—"

Culach reeled back as a hand cracked across his face. He lost his footing, stumbling backward through dense foliage and slamming into a wall. Mina panted with rage. He knew the rhythms of her breath as well as his own now.

"What the hell was that for?" he demanded, holding a defensive palm out in case she intended to attack him again.

Her voice sounded colder than the frozen waterfall of ice coating the outer walls of the holdfast. "You didn't tell me Eirik sent elementals to House Dessarian. Chimera, Culach. *Chimera*."

Culach tested his jaw. He'd been hit by women on more than one occasion; Mina didn't pull her punches.

"Do you always go around assaulting the blind and infirm?"

He heard her move closer and took an involuntary step back.

"How could you let him do it?" she hissed. "Those things can't be controlled, can't be called back. They'll kill every man, woman and child in the settlement if there's resistance." She swore. "You've both lost your minds. Haven't you shed enough blood?"

Culach winced. He'd been so preoccupied with his own problems he'd hardly spared a thought for the packs of chimera. Of course, they would have reached House Dessarian by now, possibly that very day.

"Who told you?" he asked.

"Your father. He taunted me with it."

Damn you, Eirik.

"They weren't sent after anyone you know," he said quietly. "Victor's other son Darius, and the mortal girl who can work fire. She's a danger to us all, Mina. And the boy killed Petur."

"After Petur tried to kill the girl," Mina pointed out. "And it doesn't matter if I know them or not. They're still my people. My house."

Culach felt a flush of shame. Not that they'd sent the packs, but that he'd hadn't told her himself. Knowing Eirik, Mina had been given the news in the worst way possible and he couldn't blame her for being angry.

"I'm sorry—" he began.

"Do you know why I'm here at Val Moraine, Culach?" Mina asked, and now she simply sounded weary. Lost and alone.

He wanted to take her in his arms, tell her it would be all right, but he knew she despised him more than ever and whatever fragile truce they'd forged had just been irrevocably shattered.

"I volunteered," she said. "When Victor left, I thought you might try to kill Galen, since he was Victor's son."

Culach made a small noise of protest, although the thought had crossed his mind. He'd been livid at the way Victor had treated Culach's twin, and then to have Victor disappear and deprive him of vengeance was a hard rock to swallow.

"Your parents agreed that a hostage swap would help keep the peace between our clans, so I was traded for Ellard. But it was my choice."

"I always thought they forced you."

"Tethys wouldn't have done that. We're not like *you*," she spat.

"I did it for my son. And by the way, I couldn't care less about Victor. He's a self-serving bastard who left me when I was pregnant with his child. But I'm not such a fool that I hold Darius responsible for his father's shortcomings."

"Nor do I," Culach said, though he saw in an instant of clarity that it wasn't entirely true. How deep their hatreds ran—for generations, Danai against Valkirin. And if Gerda could be believed, they'd once been allies against a far more dangerous enemy.

"What if you're wrong?" Mina asked. "What if Darius didn't kill Petur? How can you be certain? But you never think before drawing blood, do you?"

Her doubts came too close to his own. Culach shook them off.

"What's done is done," he said roughly. "Darius and the girl will die and there's no stopping it now."

"And what will happen when you've killed Victor's son? Do you think he won't retaliate?"

"Let him come," Culach snarled.

They stood there for a moment, surrounded by the sweet, sharp smell of apples, and what used to be comfortable silence between them was brittle and charged.

"I hate this place," Mina said finally. "I hate the stone and the cold and the howling wind. All the years I've been here, I consoled myself by thinking I'd see the forest again someday, even if I was old and grey. But I know now that I'll die here. We all will."

Culach felt sick. Like something terrible bore down on them with the inexorable force of an avalanche. He could tell from her voice she was near enough to touch, if he just reached for her.

"I'll help you leave Val Moraine, even if I have to sneak you out. Mina—"

But she was already brushing past him, her footsteps echoing in the empty corridor.

16

A FEY DOORWAY

A cloudless sky arched above as Nazafareen and Javid trudged across the empty landscape of the Umbra. Nazafareen glanced over her shoulder. She saw nothing, but the feeling they were being pursued only grew stronger. She also couldn't deny something was slowly coming to life in her. It wasn't simple instinct but another sense entirely—one that smelled magic.

This sense told her that whatever followed them, it wasn't flesh and blood, not in any normal sense.

"How much farther to Samarqand?" she asked wearily.

"At least another two days."

"We don't have that much time." As soon as she spoke the words, Nazafareen knew them for truth. She surveyed the terrain. It was featureless except for a smudge in the distance where the land began to rise. "Are there any villages? Anything at all?"

Javid snorted. "No one lives out here. I don't know what lies ahead as I've never had the pleasure of crossing the Umbra on foot." He scanned the horizon behind them. "I think you're jumping at shadows, Ashraf. There's nothing out here."

Nazafareen shaded her eyes. The glow to the west had intensified, casting a strange flat light. "What about those hills?"

"I'd say they're a league or so from here."

"Let's head that way. At least we might find some shelter."

Nazafareen picked up her pace.

"What exactly do you think is behind us?" Javid demanded, half jogging to keep up even though he was the taller of the two. "There are no animals out here. There's nothing." He made a sweeping gesture. "Look around."

"I don't know." She squinted her eyes against a gust of wind-blown grit. "You just have to trust me."

She couldn't admit she had daēva blood in her ancestry and was able to touch elemental power. And she certainly couldn't tell him about her breaking magic, which was unheard of and made her a pariah.

"Right," he snapped. "After you stowed away on my ship and then crashed it."

Nazafareen rounded on him. "The storm made your ship crash," she growled. "And you can camp right here if you like. Personally, I'd prefer to live, so I'm going to those hills—"

A distant howl came from the east, high-pitched and excited.

Javid's head snapped around.

"What was that?"

Nazafareen grabbed his arm. "Come *on!*"

They started running. The land gradually began to rise. Nazafareen slipped on a scree of pebbles and fell to one knee. The impact tore her tunic, scraping the skin and drawing blood. Wordlessly, Javid grabbed her hand and yanked her back to her feet.

They didn't hear another howl but the itch between her shoulder blades grew into cold fear as they entered the final stretch. Nazafareen didn't want to look behind, but she had to.

Three shapes closed the distance on the plain. They were the same color as the rocks and hard to see in the twilight, but she had the impression of great speed. Of lithe limbs and muscles bunching and contracting.

Javid saw them too and made a choking sound. Nazafareen knew that to stop and fight in the open would mean death. She ran faster than she ever had in her life, eyes fixed on the dark mouth of a canyon. The things didn't make another sound. She didn't know how far behind they were but didn't dare slow down again to look.

The first hillside loomed. They scrambled up on hands and knees. Some ancient process had buckled the land here, forcing it up into rocky masses with narrow gullies between. Nazafareen sensed something ahead. Different from the creatures that chased them, but it gave her a queer feeling in the pit of her stomach.

"This way," she panted, leading Javid to the left.

Too exhausted to speak, he simply nodded. Perhaps thirty paces back, she heard loose rocks cascading down the hillside. They pelted into the canyon, the sky narrowing to a grey ribbon overhead. Nazafareen could practically touch the rock walls on either side. They'd been worn smooth by wind and rain, exposing layers of brown and grey and pale purple.

Hot panting behind and the click of claws on stone.

The passage twisted and turned. Nazafareen drew her sword. Javid already had his belt knife in hand. His face was ashen.

"What are those things?" she gasped.

"I don't know."

He made the sign of the flame with a shaking hand, fingers touching forehead, lips and heart. She'd seen Darius make a similar gesture. It meant good thoughts, good words and good deeds. A sign of protection.

"We'll make a stand here," Nazafareen said, mouth dry with fear.

Even when she'd heard that dry rustle in the darkness of the forest, felt the snake's scaly coils imprison her body, she'd faced something known. Something *natural*. But there was nothing natural about these creatures. They radiated sickness and malevolence. Pain and fear. She fought a surge of despair.

Why bother fighting? We're going to die here no matter what. The hand holding her sword wavered.

"Ashraf!"

She spun as the first of the creatures loped around the bend, a blur almost too fast to register—and the weak power in her responded with a jolt of pure hatred.

Let them come, a whispering voice in her mind snarled. *Break them. Break them!*

Nazafareen got her sword up just in time. It plunged to the hilt in the thing's chest. The beast made no sound, its jaws snapping at the air. She put a boot on its chest and yanked out the blade. Why, it was light as air! Nazafareen felt a savage joy as it struck the ground. But then it shook itself and rose unsteadily to its feet. The others crept forward. They were translucent but their bodies seemed to constantly change, colors swirling beneath the skin that could have been dirt or rock or water. Crocodilian mouths held an array of gleaming teeth.

Javid just stood there, his eyes dead. She grabbed his shoulders and shook him hard.

"Fight it," she hissed, forcing him to look at her. "It's magic, Javid! They're making you give up. Don't let them!"

He stared at her blankly. The second beast lunged, its claws raking across her thigh. Nazafareen bit down on a scream and kicked it away.

Desperate, she slapped Javid across the face. "Wake up! Wake up, damn you!"

He blinked and seemed to come back to himself a little.

"Come on!" She backed down the narrow passage, Javid behind her. The creatures inched forward. She slashed her sword across the narrow space.

She heard Javid muttering words. It seemed nonsense, but then a cloud of fine, sparkling dust filled the air. A powerful wind rose in the passage, whipping her short hair around her face and battering at the creatures. They squatted on their haunches, untouched, eyes like orbs of quicksilver fixed on Nazafareen.

Javid swore an oath. Blood soaked steadily through her pant leg as they inched backwards. The beasts padded after them.

And then the ground grew softer underfoot, almost silty, like the bottom of a pond. Whatever Nazafareen had sensed was very close now. From the corner of her eye, she saw waist-high reeds swaying in an invisible current. They were still in the canyon, but it felt like *two* places superimposed over each other.

They reached a dead end. Solis rock walls rose up on three sides. The creatures panted, seeming to grin around their gleaming teeth.

And Nazafareen knew what she had sensed.

Behind them, an oblong doorway rose out of the ground. It gave off a faint greenish glow. Nazafareen knew that if she walked around to the back, it would appear precisely the same. A hole in the fabric of the world.

Apparently, Javid knew what it was too.

"Oh no," he said, stopping in his tracks. "We're not going in there."

"Yes, we are."

"It's taboo!"

"Would you prefer to die?"

His eyes darted around, searching the rock walls. "We could try to climb up—"

"We'd never make it."

He opened his mouth, closed it again.

Ten paces ahead, three sets of muscular haunches bunched to leap.

"Now!" Nazafareen snapped.

"Holy Father protect me," Javid said weakly.

He closed his eyes as they stepped through the gate.

17

THE SHADOWLANDS

"You can look now."

Nazafareen watched Javid reluctantly open one eye, then the other. They widened in surprise. The rock canyon had vanished, giving way to a pine forest that reminded her of Nocturne—except it wasn't dark. She could see perfectly well although the light didn't come from any particular direction. The Dominion had no sun, she recalled. No moon or stars. No weather. No birdsong. It was a place outside of time.

"Are we really in the shadowlands?" He looked ill. "Does that mean we're dead?"

Nazafareen suppressed a smile.

"I don't feel dead," she said.

When they first stepped through the gate, she heard the snap of jaws mere inches from the back of her neck. It had been a bad moment. But whatever constructs of dark magic they were, the beasts apparently could not travel through gates.

"At least they didn't follow," she pointed out.

Javid blew out a breath. "They must be native to the Umbra. I had no idea such monsters existed, but no one travels there." He shuddered. "Holy Father, the things that went through my mind. Every wrong I've ever committed.... How did you manage to resist it? I think I would have let them tear my throat out."

She thought of that whispering voice. "I felt it too. But then I...I just got angry."

"Well, your temper saved us." He looked around. They stood in a small clearing, the gate dusting the leaves in golden-green light. "What now? Do we wait for them to leave?"

Nazafareen chose her words carefully. It wouldn't do to admit she'd been here before; that would bring too many questions she couldn't answer.

"What if they don't leave? The only way to know is to step back through the gate. What if they're right on the other side?"

"But we can't stay here!"

"There must be other gates that lead out."

Javid considered this. "I've heard rumors there's one in the King's gardens," he admitted. "The gates are ancient things, though not even the alchemists dare pass through them."

"You see? I think we should try. Even if those monsters were gone, you said it was two more days to the city if we traveled on foot through the Umbra. What if they caught us again?"

Javid hesitated. "Are you sure we haven't leapt from the frying pan to the fire? Everyone knows there are monsters in the shadowlands too. Giants with eyes of flame and iron teeth."

"Then we shall stay on guard," she replied solemnly.

Nazafareen knew she had the ability to sense gates. She closed her eyes and quieted her mind, letting her awareness roam outward. Elemental magic didn't work in the Dominion but her breaking magic did. It seemed to be an inborn talent—or curse, depending how you looked at it. She felt nothing for a long moment, then a faint flicker of power to the east.

"Let's try that way," she suggested.

Javid stared at the gate they had just come through, clearly debating their chances.

"I suppose we have no choice," he grumbled. His face softened as he examined her leg. "Are you sure you can make it?"

"It hurts, but I can walk."

"Wait a second. Give me your cloak."

Javid tore off a strip of cloth from the hem and dipped it in a nearby stream. Then he bound it around her thigh.

"Thank you." She took a few steps. "It helps."

"Maybe you should have a look at it."

"The scratches aren't too deep. I'll do it later. It might be best to get away from the gate first."

They began walking, their footfalls cushioned by a thick carpet of pine needles. Nazafareen doubted that the giants Javid feared were more than a myth to frighten children, but she vaguely remembered other creatures, and they were no less hostile.

"I should be back in the Guild Hall by now," Javid muttered. "Not wandering lost in purgatory."

"I'm sorry I got us into this mess. Truly I am."

In fact, she felt sure the Valkirins had sent those beasts after her. They were bound by magic. That's what she'd sensed in the Umbra. And now she was back in the Dominion—the very place where she'd lost her memories. *I'm running in circles, and poor Javid is being dragged along for the ride.*

He glanced at her. "If you'd asked for passage, I'd have refused you."

She stared down at the ground.

"But who's to say the *Kyrenia* would have weathered that storm? I might have crashed anyway." He frowned at her. "How *did* you know those things were behind us?"

"I don't know. Just a feeling. Don't you ever get those?"

"I suppose. Just like I knew if I didn't leave the darklands that very night, I'd be caught in rough weather." He smiled ruefully. "Though I seem to have underestimated it."

They forded a shallow stream and clambered down a rocky

slope. Not a breeze stirred the air. Despite the dense trees, the place had a lifeless feel. In the Danai forest, she always heard squirrels digging through the leaves and other sounds—the eerie, high cry of a screech owl, the aggressive squabbling of raccoons. Branches creaked, the churring trill of the nightjars rose and fell. But in the Dominion, their footfalls were the only sound.

"How did you come to work for the Guild?" she asked to break the oppressive silence.

"My father apprenticed me when I was twelve. He's a weaver, makes the ropes for the ships. I was hopeless at his trade, but it turns out I have a good head for heights and an aptitude for reading the weather."

"It sounds exciting."

Javid shrugged. "We mainly use them to ferry dignitaries between Samarqand and Susa, and occasionally Delphi. The ships aren't large enough to carry much freight so trade in goods is handled by river barges. But wind ships are much swifter and prestigious for personal travel."

Nazafareen thought about the Marakai. They might demand payment to help her. And Javid said the services of an alchemist were expensive, too. Either way, she would need to survive somehow. At the Danai compound, they'd given her a house to live in and food to eat. But she somehow doubted the same would happen in Samarqand.

"Do they ever hire women?"

He glanced at her. "No. Only men."

"That's not fair."

"Maybe not, but it's the way things are."

"What other jobs are there?"

"You might get work as a scullery in a manor house. I'll see if the Guild would be willing to give you a reference."

"Scullery?"

"A maid. You know, scrubbing pots? Sweeping ashes from the hearth?"

She made a face. "What else?"

"Without any useful skills? It's that or work the streets."

"What does that mean?"

He sighed. "Never mind. Don't worry, Ashraf, I'll find you something. Assuming we live long enough to get there. What about you? Any brothers or sisters?"

"Nine," she said promptly. "Only six are still alive though. The others died horribly in farming accidents."

"Holy Father, I'm sorry!"

"Yeah, I'd rather not talk about it. But I'll tell you about my cousin...Galen. He only bathed once a month and had this wart on the end of his nose with more hair growing out of it than he had on his head."

Javid winced. "I can see why you left."

Nazafareen proceeded to weave an elaborate tapestry of lies she hoped she could remember later. It passed the time and distracted her from all the awful things that could potentially befall them in the Dominion. She was tired of having no memories, so why not invent some?

"You've led a colorful life for a village girl," Javid said dryly, as she finished a tale about nearly being carried off by a giant eagle while fetching water from the well. "I'm amazed you even survived your childhood."

Nazafareen nodded. "I know. But after I brought that old crone's magic chalice back, she lifted the curse and things settled down." She paused. "For a while, at least. Did I tell you about my thirteenth birthday? We were sitting down to a fancy supper when the door burst open and these bandits rushed in. They were so big and hairy I thought they were bears at first. Turned out my brother Victor owed them money...."

The land gently rose and fell. Nazafareen followed the invisible ley line leading to what she felt certain was another gate. It came into view at last, standing alone in a clearing. She could feel the nauseating tug of its power. Nazafareen studied it for a moment, brows drawn down in thought. Every gate she'd seen before had a murky undersea quality in the area just around it. This one looked different. The ground was parched and dry, the vegetation dead. Sand buried the lower half, and the angle seemed slightly off kilter. The surface reflected the surrounding trees like a cloudy mirror.

"I don't know," she said at last.

"Don't know what? Is it a way out?"

"Well, yes, but—"

"Then let's go." Javid glanced around. "I don't like this place. Anywhere has to be better."

"I don't like it either." She sighed. "I suppose if it doesn't go to Samarqand, we can come back through and keep looking."

By unspoken agreement, they clasped hands, Javid's slightly moist and calloused. Two steps and they stood before the gate. Nazafareen saw her own face in its cloudy depths and had a queer, fleeting sensation that *another* Nazafareen stood on the other side, looking out. She hesitated, unnerved, but then Javid gave her hand an impatient tug. Two more steps and they were inside.

Nazafareen knew immediately that she'd made a mistake.

Ahead lay a sun-blasted plain. Waves of ferocious heat blurred the horizon, but she could see tendrils of darkness reaching down from a line of anvil-shaped thunderheads in the distance. They were clouds, she realized, and they appeared to be rotating. The sound they made was unlike anything she'd heard before, a deep, powerful, grinding roar. Wherever these slender cloud-fingers touched the earth, it erupted in a haze of sand that was quickly sucked into the upper reaches of the whirlwind.

Nazafareen tried to step back, pulling Javid with her, but the gate held them fast. Panic squeezed her chest. She couldn't move her limbs or even draw breath to scream, and Nazafareen suddenly knew they would be there for eternity, alive, hands clasped and feet poised to take a step that would never meet the ground.

The talismanic magic of the gate crackled around her like a swarm of maddened wasps. In desperation, she tried moving forward, but it was like pushing against solid stone. She should have listened to her instincts. This gate had been damaged somehow, perhaps because it led to such a forsaken place. Now they were trapped like beasts in a tar pit.

Inside her, something stirred. A dark, destructive force. Near panic, she instinctively shoved it down.

I mustn't touch it again. Not ever!

It wasn't weak the way it had been in the Umbra. No, this was a hungry void in her heart. Not like the elements at all. This power didn't come from the Nexus. This power wanted to *devour* the Nexus. But she could feel her perception subtly shifting.

Nazafareen could *see* the twisted, half-shattered wards holding the gate together. A decaying, tangled mess.

Bloody stupid to have stepped through! Damn Javid for his impatience!

Sudden anger seethed in her gut. Unable to stop herself, she lashed out with the power, yanking at the frayed thread that held the gate together. The buzzing ceased. In the next instant, she found she could move again. She pulled Javid backwards and they both toppled onto the withered grass of the Dominion. The surface of the gate turned a dull black, and she wondered what would have happened if they had been inside when it did.

The thought made her retch. She felt a hand on her shoulder.

"Do you want some water?"

Nazafareen knocked the water skin from his hand.

"Get away from me!" she snarled.

He stepped back, surprise and hurt on his face. Nazafareen glared at him.

All Javid's fault.

Her hand dropped to the hilt of her sword. *I ought to run him through....*

His eyes widened and Nazafareen blinked as if waking from a dream. The fury ebbed, replaced by quiet horror.

What's wrong with me?

"I...I'm sorry," she said. "I didn't mean...."

Nazafareen picked up the water skin and gulped it down, then promptly threw it up again. The next time, she was careful to take only small sips. She finally managed to sit up, wiping her mouth with the hem of her tunic. Cold sweat beaded her brow, but the nausea was passing. She pushed the sleeves of her tunic up and checked her arms. No blackness crept through her veins. Nazafareen closed her eyes in relief. She'd used the power and survived it. How? Had she used only a small amount? She clenched her fist in frustration. If only she knew more. There must be others like her somewhere. If only she could find one.

When she opened her eyes, she saw Javid leaning against one of the trees, watching her warily.

"Better?" he asked.

"Yes. I don't know what happened." She drew a trembling breath. "What was that place on the other side?"

"It must have been the Kiln."

"Oh."

He picked up on her blank look and sighed. "The Kiln is the region of western Solis where the sun is hottest. Permanent noon. The cities are all on the border between Solis and the Umbra, but beyond that lies a brutal desert."

"And those black storm clouds? I've never seen the like."

"They call that the Gale. A barrier of funnels that never goes away. It's impassable."

"I see." She gave a shaky laugh. "I suppose we picked the wrong gate. It seemed...broken somehow."

"Broken?" He shrugged. "All I know is that I'd taken half a step when you pulled me back. I caught a glimpse of it though. You were right to."

"You didn't feel anything else?"

"Like what?"

She shook her head. "Never mind."

Nazafareen tried twice to rise before gaining her feet. Javid pushed off the tree and steadied her with an arm. "I think you need to rest."

She started to protest but he cut her off. "You'll be no use if I have to carry you, Ashraf. One night, that's all. We'll take turns keeping watch." He gave a jaw-cracking yawn. "I'm exhausted too. And if the giants find us, I'll push you toward them so I can get a head start."

She laughed softly. "A mercenary to the end, eh?"

"Absolutely."

They walked until they found a wall of thick brambles growing alongside a stream. Javid used his knife to cut out a hollow place in the center. They both drank some water, and he gave her privacy while she examined the gouges on her leg. They were nasty, but the bleeding had stopped. Nazafareen washed the wounds carefully in the stream, wincing at the sting, and bound her leg up again. Then they both crawled inside the makeshift shelter and spread their cloaks on the ground.

Javid was quiet for a while. Then he said, "I wish you'd tell me the truth, Ashraf. I know the Kiln isn't pleasant, but we were only in it for an instant. Are you sick?"

Nazafareen's heart raced. He wasn't stupid. Of course he would know something was wrong with her. And she could hardly tell him the truth. Then inspiration struck—a way to explain why she sought the Marakai.

"I suffer from fits. The healer in our village said they would likely kill me eventually. That there's no treatment. But I heard the Marakai daēvas are great healers."

"Oh, I didn't realize. I'm sorry, Ashraf."

He looked stricken and she felt bad for lying, but she had no choice. "Do you think they might help?"

"I don't know. Like I said, they keep to themselves. But

perhaps if you offered payment." He thought for a moment. "I don't suppose you have any money?"

She shook her head.

"Well, we'll find a way." He gave her a comforting smile. "I'll take first watch."

"Really, I don't mind. You look half dead."

"You sure?" Javid murmured sleepily.

"It's fine. I'm awake anyway."

So she sat with her sword across her knees while Javid started snoring softly. When she judged two hours had passed, she woke him and rolled herself up in her own cloak.

If there is a Holy Father, watch over us, she prayed. *Help us get out before the Shepherds find us.*

ALL THE FOOD WAS GONE AND HUNGER GNAWED AT HER BELLY as they struck out through the forest. After a few hours, Nazafareen sensed another gate. It wasn't close and they'd left the forest behind and climbed halfway up the flank of a mountain before it came into view on a ledge high above.

Twice they spotted large winged shapes wheeling in the distance and ducked down to hide behind jagged outcroppings of rock. When the flyers moved on, they resumed their climb, this time with greater urgency. But the mountain was trackless and steep, and both were at the end of their strength by the time they reached the ledge.

"I don't care if it goes straight into the Gale," Javid moaned as they stood in the icy wind.

It had a bitter feel and smelled of salt. Nazafareen dimly remembered standing on a similar ledge with a beautiful woman in white. She had silver hair and bare arms.

The Cold Sea, she'd said. *None who seek it ever return....*

"Ashraf?" Javid touched her arm.

She blinked as if waking from a dream.

"I say we try it." Javid stared at the gate, his face grim but determined. "Anything is better than this place."

She drew a deep breath. "Right."

Nazafareen was starting to realize they could starve to death searching for a way out of the Dominion. Water wasn't a problem, in fact it was everywhere—lakes and streams and ponds and rushing rivers criss-crossed the land—but they had yet to find anything edible. The few animals that lived there were more likely to kill them than the other way around.

"Our luck has to change sometime," she said, aiming for a cheerful tone but producing something closer to a whine.

Javid made the sign of the flame and this time Nazafareen joined him. It couldn't hurt. To her relief, this gate looked like the others she'd traversed, glowing faintly, its surface bright and lively like running water. A ring of stunted, windswept bushes surrounded it, but they were living, with small violet berries she figured were probably poisonous.

"I'll go first," she said firmly.

And with that, Nazafareen stepped through.

She braced herself for another shock, but it felt nothing like the gate to the Kiln. Instead, the greenish-grey murk deepened. They moved forward, following a gentle upward slope. Rays of wan sunlight pierced the gloom. Up and up they went, and suddenly Nazafareen's feet left the ground. Her next exhalation produced a delicate fizz of bubbles.

She tried to draw in air and water flooded her nose. She choked and flailed, kicking wildly. After an eternity, her head broke the surface of a marble fountain. She coughed, spewing out a mouthful of water. The bottom of the fountain felt smooth and slightly slimy beneath her hand. It was solid enough. How they had come through it she'd no idea, but that was often the way of gates.

Nazafareen pushed wet hair from her eyes. Above her, shimmering streams of water shot from the beaks of two gilded eagles whose wings spread as though about to launch into flight. Sunlight gleamed on precious stones inlaid in their feathers, producing a gorgeous kaleidoscopic effect.

A moment later, Javid emerged, pale and spluttering. He looked around in wonder. They were atop a flattened hill with sweeping vistas on all sides. Nazafareen saw olive and orange groves dotted with small farmhouses, and the glint of the sea at the edge of the horizon. She followed Javid's gaze to a palatial building perched on the highest point of the hill a short distance away. It was rectangular and made of white marble, with a portico supported by tall, elegant columns. Carved laurels adorned the lintel, flanking the words *Know Thyself*.

"Oh no," Javid said quietly.

Nazafareen tensed. Where had she brought them now? Clearly, it was a mortal city in Solis.

"What is this place?" she hissed.

Javid didn't reply, scrambling out of the fountain and plastering an obsequious grin across his face. A man strode toward them. He had a thick, curly beard and a sword buckled around his considerable waist. Despite his girth, he moved lightly on his feet and gave the impression of having slabs of muscle beneath the fat.

"Here now! Get out of there!"

A meaty hand clamped down on Nazafareen's arm and dragged her over the shallow rim of the fountain. Javid had already dropped to his knees and she quickly imitated him. Luckily, the cloak concealed her short sword. She'd fight if she had to, but not until she had an inkling of where they were and what was going on.

"Faithless pigs!" the man exclaimed, as three more armed men in leather skirts and stiff horsehair helmets ran over from where they'd been standing in the shade of a tree. "Are you drunk? Only a lush or a lunatic would dare pollute the sacred waters."

"Is this Samarqand?" Nazafareen mouthed to Javid, who lay on his belly next to her, a sandal planted firmly on his back.

He gave a tight shake of his head. She saw fear in his eyes.

"Better we were in the Kiln," he whispered. "This is Delphi."

18

THENA AND THE WITCHES

T hena snuck a surreptitious glance through her lashes at the commotion in the plaza. From where she knelt next to the pinewood fire, she could see a slice of stone and sky through the temple's double doors, which had been thrown wide as today was an audience day. It looked like a pair of beggars had tried to bathe in the fountain.

They must be sun-touched to risk the Pythia's wrath, she thought. Depending on the oracle's mood, such an insult could easily buy one a screaming death locked inside the brazen bull. But the Pythia was in her trance, concealed in the recessed inner sanctum, and the Polemarch's soldiers had already taken care of it, dragging the offenders off. They had no idea how lucky they were.

Thena wafted the brazier of incense, thickening the curls of fragrant bay laurel smoke drifting through the chamber. Four other initiates in white robes tended the fire. It was late in the day and only a few men still waited their turn to venture down the winding stairs to the *omphalos* stone, the navel of the world, where the Pythia sat on her tripod to hear their questions.

They looked nervous, those men, sweating in the heat and smoke. They were the least impressive of the day's visitors and thus had been placed at the back of the line, but they seemed determined to wait as long as it took.

The Pythia, also called the Oracle of Delphi and High Priestess of the Temple of Apollo, held audiences twice a month for supplicants who sought her wisdom from far and wide—generals, diplomats, powerful merchants, even a famous poet or two. Usually, the consultations involved practical matters of military strategy and politics, or questions about how to lift curses and which gods needed to be appeased, and in what way. She rarely predicted the future; rather, she gave them advice, which came from the mouth of the god himself.

But no one of any consequence would make an important decision without asking the Pythia first.

When the last supplicant had come and gone, looking suitably shaken, Thena made her way to the sunken space below the level of the temple floor, past the gleaming gold statue of Apollo, to the Pythia's *adyton*, a chamber whose name meant "not to be entered."

"Come, sun daughter."

The Pythia sat on her tripod, her regal, ageless features serene as always. She wore her hair in a thick black braid that hung down her back and brushed the backs of her thighs when she stood. Kohl lined her almond eyes, making them appear larger and emphasizing their rare blue color.

Thena approached and knelt gracefully at her feet. Heady, sulfurous fumes wafted from cracks in the stone floor.

"How does it progress with the Valkirin?" the Pythia asked.

"I believe he's reached a point in his training where he might enter your presence without shaming me," Thena said cautiously.

It had taken her months to break him, but that was typical with the witches. The first thing had been to make him tell her his real name. It was the best way to begin, the Pythia said. Get them to tell you something they knew to be true and that would be considered a relatively harmless piece of information. It loosened their tongues.

Still, Daníel had resisted—longer than she would have thought possible. But Thena had won in the end. She always won.

After she made him tell her his true name, she gave him his new slave name. *Demetrios*. Oh, the hatred in his eyes when she told him. But he answered to it now. He wanted only to please her.

"Bring him to my chambers," the Pythia said. "I would question him about the intentions of the witches. I already know them, of course, but I wish to see if he tries to dissemble."

"Yes, Oracle."

Thena gathered her robes and scurried barefoot from the room.

She frowned as she ascended the stairs and left the temple through a side door, making for the quarters of the initiates. She'd been fooled before by witches who pretended to comply, only to make a desperate escape attempt later. Thena was more careful now. She knew the look on their faces, the precise moment when they surrendered to her will. And she felt certain that Daníel would behave himself.

She'd had him for over a year now.

A tough nut, Daníel was, which made it all the sweeter when he finally cracked. There had been much sobbing and then finally, the calm of acceptance. When he realized he'd never escape and it was a *pleasure* to serve the light instead of the darkness. He kissed the hem of her gown. The hate in his eyes turned to love.

It had been a very special moment.

Thena entered the four-story tower at the edge of the plaza. Once, it had been full of eager young girls, but the new Pythia winnowed their ranks considerably. Only the toughest and most obedient remained, the ones who didn't shirk at carrying out Apollo's will. As a result, only half the rooms were occupied by initiates like Thena.

The other half served a different purpose.

She climbed to the top floor, where bright sunlight poured in golden shafts through the narrow windows. She paused at the third door on the right. The slender bracelet around her wrist seemed to quiver against her skin. She felt his emotions, fearful and anxious to please. Just as it should be.

Thena opened the door. The room was small but pretty with a colorful mural of the sun god Apollo having his feet washed by lovely maidens. Thena remembered the last initiate who'd occupied it, a timid, mousy girl named Leda. When she failed the test to wear the bracelet and wept at the witches' screams, the Pythia had sent her packing. Then stonemasons came to make a few adaptations.

Shackles bound the witch hand and foot to the opposite wall. He kept his face turned away from the sun. If he conducted himself well with the Pythia, Thena resolved to reward him with shutters for the window.

"Hello, Demetrios," she said with a smile.

He was an extraordinary specimen, with hair like beaten silver and eyes of a deep, clear green. Tall and well-proportioned, with smooth skin and animal grace, even chained. A thick collar circled his throat. It had been filigreed with dancing flames, the match of the bracelet around Thena's wrist.

He swallowed painfully, eyes tracking her every movement. The witch was handsome and beguiling, but Thena had sworn her vows at the age of eleven. She was an acolyte of the Temple of Apollo and would never know the touch of a man. This didn't trouble her at all. She was married to her god, who was far more beautiful than any mortal—or even witch.

"Mistress," he said hoarsely.

She laid a palm on his cheek. "Did they bring you water, Demetrios?"

He shook his head. Thena's mouth drew down in anger. She had explicitly told Maia to make sure her collared ones were cared for. It was one thing to inflict the necessary pain to make them pliable. That couldn't be avoided. But denying water once a witch had broken was pointless sadism.

"I'll fetch you some. But first I'm going to bring you to the Oracle. She has questions and you must answer truthfully or there will be consequences. Do you understand?"

He nodded fervently.

"Very good."

She let her hand fall and unlocked the chains that bound him to the stone wall. He stood, back straight, rubbing his wrists. Demetrios stood three hands taller than Thena, with ropes of muscle on his chest and arms. He could snap her neck in seconds. But he did not try to do this, or anything but wait for her next command.

She gave him a tunic of plain roughspun.

"You must put this on. The Pythia demands modesty."

He pulled it over his head. She'd chosen one that was a bit too small, but it covered his manhood at least. It would do for now.

"Come." Thena turned her back and walked to the door, knowing he would follow.

The plaza outside was empty except for the Polemarch's soldiers. Demetrios winced at the light as he trotted along behind her. The soldiers eyed them warily as they passed, but they were Shields of Apollo and used to the sight of the witches. They knew to keep their mouths shut or suffer the Polemarch's wrath. No one must know, else the other witches would surely come in force to attempt a rescue.

Thena passed the high-walled yard where the witches were permitted to take exercise and led Demetrios into the temple. She did not bring him to the adyton—that would be sacrilege. Instead, she led him straight to the personal chambers of the Pythia. The Oracle stood at the window looking out over the city below, her form a dark silhouette.

"You may leave us now, daughter," she said. "Wait outside in the hall in case I have need of you."

Thena understood. She didn't know what the Pythia asked them or why she wanted the witches, only that it was a command from the god himself, who had provided the means of capturing them. Thena never questioned that they were evil. Fire was the instrument of Apollo and the daēvas feared it, had even forbidden its very existence in the darklands. They could only be witches.

The Shields of Apollo, the Polemarch's most elite unit, had taken nine so far, although two were dead by their own hands. One threw herself into the holy fire; the other choked on his chains. The Pythia had been very angry about that, but she didn't blame Thena. They simply needed to be more careful, not rush the process. If a daēva broke too quickly, if their mind snapped rather than surrendering, they were of no use.

Thena had now personally broken five of the witches—more than the other initiates combined. She excelled at it because she understood the need for both cruelty and compassion. She instinctively knew when she was approaching the edge and backed off. Better to be cautious than make a fatal mistake. The witches were hard to catch and they didn't go down easily.

Sometimes Thena prayed to the god to give her strength to continue. It was exhausting to train them because she felt every emotion, every jolt of agony, as if it were her own. She'd learned to block it out, but the anguish took a toll.

She was only twenty and she'd found three white hairs that morning.

Don't be vain, she chided herself as she stood in the hall listening to the murmur of voices through the door. *There are worse things than growing old.*

That she knew firsthand.

19

FOOTPRINTS

Darius walked for two days. Then he decided his leg had healed enough to run, so he did.

The great forest raced past in a blur. He left the lands of House Dessarian and entered those belonging to House Fiala. Their sentries, clad in cloaks of green and brown, greeted him with cautious cordiality. They'd heard of him, of course, but Darius could tell they weren't sure what to make of him. He was one of them, and yet he wasn't. They offered him food, which he politely declined, eager to be on his way.

"Where are you going, cousin?" asked one with a nighthawk feather earring.

"Samarqand."

They looked at each other.

"Any particular reason?"

"I'm following someone."

"Does it have to do with the Valkirins?"

So they'd heard.

"In a way."

"Filthy dogs," another muttered. "Fiala stands with House Dessarian, whatever Tethys chooses to do."

"Thank you. How much further to the Umbra?"

"About thirty leagues. Good luck to you, cousin."

Darius shouldered his rucksack and clasped each of their arms in turn. Then he started running again. At last, the forest thinned out to a featureless plain. He passed the Twelve Towers, a series of sheer cliffs that overlooked the placid waters of the Gulf of Azmir. When the quality of the light grew brighter, going from full night to dusk, Darius knew he was in the Umbra. His sharp eyes scanned the horizon, hoping he might detect a speck sailing through the sky, but he saw nothing. This didn't surprise him. No matter how fast he had travelled—and it was very fast—he couldn't outrun a wind ship.

But the fear that had gripped him since he discovered Nazafareen gone hadn't eased. What was she thinking? She'd come within inches of death the last time she used her power, which she'd drawn from the sun. He'd never forget the shadowy darkness creeping through her veins, the scorching fever and black blood running from her nose. If he'd been a single hour later carrying her through the gate to Nocturne, the fire would have consumed her.

He could only hope she'd keep her word to Delilah not to use the power at all. But he also knew this was easier said than done because power of any kind was seductive by nature.

Darius stopped at a wide river and slaked his thirst. Then he checked his map. The faint glow in the sky would be coming from the west and he had only to follow it to Solis. He set out again, heading for a rise that would afford a view for some leagues around. The Umbra was the most desolate place he had ever seen, even more so than the Great Salt Plain of his birthplace. Other than rock and sand, there was nothing living.

But he could tell from other signs, both large and small, that there had been a different climate at some point in the distant past. Once he'd seen the skeleton of an enormous creature that looked like a whale, its ribcage gleaming white in the half-light.

Darius wondered if the Umbra was the seabed of a primordial ocean, now boiled away to dust.

There was still water in the ground though, he could sense it coursing through aquifers deep beneath the surface. Twice, rain-storms had lashed through, drumming against the parched earth and carving channels that drained the moment the clouds parted. A stark place, not unlovely in its own way, but not a place where he wished to linger either.

Darius gained the hilltop. He squinted into the middle distance. Something was out there. It had been invisible from lower down, but now he saw it clearly, perhaps five leagues away, a dark splotch against the ground. Darius scrambled down the incline and broke into a run again. It took him thirty minutes to reach it.

A downed wind ship.

His heart froze as he poked through the rubble, but there were no bodies or blood. He saw faint traces of footprints heading west, two sets, one smaller than the other, and knew the last belonged to Nazafareen. But the hardpan was poor for tracks and the last rain had washed them away after a short distance.

He thought for a moment. According to the maps, Samarqand was roughly three hundred leagues south, Delphi about a hundred to the north. It would be much closer. He blew out a long calming breath. Then he dimmed his eyes and embraced the Nexus, the place where all things were one.

The map showed a river between Samarqand and Delphi. He reached out for it, let the Nexus guide him. In his mind's eye, he followed its twists and turns north through the wilderness, saw where it led.

An ancient citadel on a hill...

He would go there, he decided. If Nazafareen was forced to walk, it made sense she would take the shorter route.

Delphi, then. He'd heard they had a fire cult, just like the empire.

Perfect.

At least there didn't seem to be any natural predators in the Umbra. And if he hurried, he might catch them. Darius estimated they were only a day or so ahead. He thought briefly of his father. Victor was driven by his own demons. Two centuries he'd spent in the hellhole called Gorgon-e Gaz. It didn't seem to matter that his captors were all dead. He still craved vengeance, but Darius had no use for Victor's cause.

Although the cuffs they'd worn had maimed his body, he would give anything to bond Nazafareen again. Then he wouldn't need to guess. He would know exactly where she was.

Darius's mouth set in a line, his blue eyes like shards of glacial ice.

The Holy Father help anyone who had harmed her.

20

A BLADE IN THE DARK

"We're terribly sorry, captain," Javid said with a weak smile. "It was an honest mistake, I swear."

The soldier glared at them. "Persian heathen! This is the sacred temple of Apollo." He cast a grim look at the huge structure dominating the hilltop. "If the Oracle weren't in the middle of an audience, she'd punish you directly."

Nazafareen felt her magic stir and tamped it down. There was fire in that building. Fire and something else—something nameless that made her uneasy. But the soldier didn't seem to realize they'd come through a gate. She gave him a meek, frightened look.

"I...I had a dizzy spell," she murmured. "I fell in. My brother was only trying to help me."

Javid nodded fervently. "We came to see the famed Temple of Apollo. She's with child, you see. The heat...I was afraid she would drown or I would never have entered the holy waters."

The man scowled. He glanced again at the temple. Nazafareen could see him silently debating his options. If he disturbed the Pythia, who he obviously feared, she might get angry at him too. And no real harm had been done.

"I never want to see your faces on the Acropolis again," he said sternly.

"Never, captain," Javid agreed. "We're pilgrims and intend to leave tomorrow anyway."

The captain waved at the other guards, who returned to their shade tree. Without another word, he escorted them to a long, wide staircase leading down to the city. The sun hung just above the western horizon, painting the sky orange and pink. Nazafareen felt a strange thrill looking at it.

Solis.

"You'd best hurry," the captain said gruffly.

He watched them the whole way down, his meaty arms crossed.

"Welcome to Delphi," Javid muttered as they descended the hill just short of an all-out run.

"What would have happened if he'd brought us to the Pythia?" Nazafareen asked.

Javid shot her a black look. "Nothing good. Especially if she figured out where we came from." He blew out a long breath. "I can't believe there's a gate in front of the Temple of Apollo. They must not know about it else we'd be in cells right now. Magic is strictly forbidden—punishable by death. Holy Father, if they'd found my spell dust...."

Nazafareen fell silent. She hadn't known that—but then, she hadn't expected to end up in Delphi. She could sense the spell dust in his pouch, like a troublesome itch. Her magic didn't like it. She forced the thought away and tried to focus.

So they were in Delphi. Well, it wasn't the end of the world. At least they'd escaped from the Dominion. She simply had to revise her plans.

"Do the Marakai daēvas trade here?" she asked.

"Yes, but it's strictly controlled. The cargo is unloaded at the port on the Cimmerian Sea, then brought downriver by barges."

"How far is the port?"

"About ten leagues."

"That's not too far," she said, brightening. "I could walk it."

"You could, but it's not the distance that's the problem. The Polemarch's soldiers keep the port under lock and key. The Marakai aren't even permitted to come ashore, only their cargo."

"Then what will I do?"

"We have to get to Samarqand. The Marakai trade openly there. You can find them in the streets." He lowered his voice. "We shouldn't speak of daēvas until we're alone. The Oracle's spies are everywhere."

The neighborhood below the temple bustled with shops and crowds of people hurrying to and fro, the air thick with wood smoke and unfamiliar spices. Nazafareen found the tumult doubly jarring after the desolation of the Umbra and the uncanny silence of the shadowlands, but she was glad to be somewhere with life in it at least. As they wandered down a broad boulevard, she studied the inhabitants with interest. The women wore free-flowing bolts of wool pinned at the shoulders with simple brooches, while the men sported belted tunics that came down to their ankles. Cats and dogs darted like fish among the legs of the ambling throngs.

Thanks to the dire state of their clothing and half-starved appearance, most people gave them a wide berth. When Nazafareen paused to admire a palatial home with an archway giving a tantalizing glimpse of a fragrant courtyard shaded by orange trees, a guard stepped out of the shadows and urged them to move on with a flick of his cudgel.

"Don't you know anyone at all here?" Nazafareen asked, wistfully eyeing chunks of fish sizzling on a grill beneath a striped awning. The vendor stared at her hard until she looked away.

"No. Our cities aren't exactly friendly, I told you that."

"How far to Samarqand?"

"Far."

"Can we walk?"

"It would take weeks, and there are bandits in the hills who rob anyone without an armed escort. Better to travel downriver by barge, but that costs money." He gave her a tight smile. "And we don't have any."

"What about a wind ship?" Nazafareen persisted. She could see a few dotting the sky, though the design looked different from the *Kyrenia*, longer and narrower.

Javid gave a hollow laugh. "Passage on one of those would be six times the cost of a barge."

They crossed another main thoroughfare and wandered into a warren of side streets. Sweat trickled down the back of Nazafareen's tunic. Although the sun never moved from its position about six hands above the horizon, the temperature felt like high noon. She was dying to remove her cloak, but a ragged girl with a sword would invite unwanted attention. How she missed the cool forests of Nocturne! Javid was obviously used to it, but Nazafareen's head pounded.

"I'm starving," he said for the hundredth time. "Literally starving. I think I'll die if I don't eat something soon."

"Me too." Right on cue, her stomach emitted a strange creaking sound, like the ropes on a wind ship. Nazafareen struggled to remember the last time she'd had a decent meal. "I wouldn't normally condone stealing—"

"Bad idea. They don't treat thieves kindly here."

They walked on, the smells of fresh bread and roasting meat from open air markets making them both salivate. Nazafareen was starting to feel invisible, a ghost drifting unseen among the living. If the captain at the temple hadn't kicked them out, she might wonder if they hadn't died in the Dominion.

This is hell, she thought glumly. Or purgatory at least.

Even the other beggars ignored them, assuming they had no coins to spare. One man with a missing leg actually looked them up and down and gave a haughty sniff. But the sight gave Nazafareen an idea.

"Wait over there," she said to Javid, pointing to an area of covered stalls. "Pretend to browse."

"What are you up to?" he asked suspiciously.

"Nothing criminal." She unbuckled her sword and handed it to him.

"If you get in trouble, I don't know you," he said, turning on his heel and stalking off towards the colorful awnings of a nearby market.

Nazafareen made a sour face at his back, though she conceded that Javid had fair reason to be angry. If he'd been alone, the wind ship might never have crashed. He would be back home in Samarqand with enough money to buy a wind ship of his own. And she'd led him straight to another ill-chosen gate. Well, she couldn't help the trouble she'd caused, but if her plan worked, she could make it up to him by buying them both breakfast or supper or whatever meal it was time for.

Nazafareen removed her cloak and laid it on the ground. Then she sat down cross-legged and rolled up her sleeves so her stump was clearly visible. It wasn't hard to look pathetic. She hadn't had a proper night's sleep in days. Dirt caked her fingernails and her pants sported a ragged, bloodstained tear.

She cleared her throat a few times, producing a thin croak.

"Help for a poor maimed war orphan," Nazafareen entreated passersby.

Within ten minutes, a well-dressed woman carrying a basket of apples tossed a silver coin at her feet.

"The goddess bless you!" Nazafareen cried.

She'd seen shrines and temples all over the city, some clearly devoted to female deities. It also seemed a safe bet to invoke some nameless conflict. From what Darius said, people were always fighting each other.

The woman smiled. Nazafareen smiled back.

A few hours later, when the crowds began to thin out, she had a modest pile of coins on her cloak. She signaled to Javid, who had been watching her with some amusement.

"How much did you get?"

"I don't know. What are these called?"

"Drachma."

He took the coins and jingled them in his palm. "Not bad. Let's see what we can buy."

The prices were much higher than they expected. Despite Javid's ruthless haggling, they ended up with a few dried figs and two pieces of fish barely big enough to satisfy a cat. Javid grumbled but handed over the money. They found a quiet alley and sat against the wall, savoring every bite of the meager meal.

"I chatted with some of the hawkers while I was waiting for you. There are plenty of barges that go downriver to Samarqand," Javid said, tossing a fishbone in the gutter. Underground clay pipes carried water and waste in Delphi, so the streets were remarkably clean. "I'll find out how much passage costs."

Nazafareen nodded. "If we only eat one meal a day, we might be able to save enough."

He looked down at the sad pile of tiny bones. "One meal a day? We'll waste away to nothing."

"You could beg too."

He glanced at her. "No offense, but I don't think the public would look on an able-bodied young man with the same sympathy." He fingered the cut on his forehead. "They'd probably assume I got this in a tavern brawl."

"What else can you do for money?"

"I'll find something." He leaned forward and lowered his voice. "Just be careful who you talk to here, Ashraf. You can't tell anyone you came from the darklands. Both elemental and spell magic are forbidden in Delphi. They trade with the daēvas, but call them witches behind their backs."

Nazafareen's face hardened. "That's wrong. They're not witches."

"I know, don't get feisty. Anyway, it's nothing to do with us."

She forced herself to meet his gaze. "Right. None of our business."

"I only mentioned it so you don't go blabbing about the dust I used to power the wind ship. It could get us both in trouble."

"I wasn't planning to," she snapped.

He stared at her for a long moment. "Good. Because the sooner we get out of here, the better. People can already tell from my accent that I'm from Samarqand. It's not unusual, of course, merchants and others travel between the cities. But if anyone suspected where we came from or how we got here...." He trailed off. "I'm sorry. I know you're not well. Let's just get some sleep. We'll figure it out tomorrow."

Nazafareen rolled up in her cloak to block out the constant sunlight. The city wasn't far from the edge of the Umbra so the heat was tolerable, but if you kept walking west, you'd eventually find yourself in the Kiln. She remembered that single glimpse of it through the Gate. Surely nothing could survive in such conditions.

Nazafareen set out her cloak first thing and begged until late when the streets grew empty. She earned enough to feed them both with a small pile of silver left over. Javid spent the day scouring the docks for work, hoping to buy their passage with menial labor. But he had no references or experience—wind ships were very different from the ships that plied the river—and returned empty-handed.

"The passage to Samarqand costs twenty drachmas each," he told her as they shared a meal of thin, oily soup with fish heads floating on top, among other nameless grey lumps. "But we ought to have enough in a week or so." He saw her frown and shrugged. "Look at it this way. The skinnier you get, the more money you'll make."

Nazafareen gnawed at a fish head. "Thanks, I feel so much better."

"It's that or sell your sword," he said, eying the blade she kept hidden beneath her cloak.

"Fine. One more week." She tossed the bones away and curled up in a corner.

She wouldn't sell the sword. It had been a present from Darius —though she knew Victor had bought it. And she didn't like feeling defenseless. The Polemarch's soldiers kept order, but there were pickpockets and thieves in Delphi. She had seen one cut a purse the day before and given a shout of warning, but the fellow had melted away into the crowds before his victim could react.

So while things weren't going perfectly, they could have been worse.

Then the other beggars realized Nazafareen was poaching their business.

They banded together and stormed up to her in an angry mob the very next day, demanding she pack up and move. She had no seniority, no claim, and this was the territory of One-Eyed Sinaclos. Fearing she'd be torn to shreds, Nazafareen retreated to a remote spot where almost no one passed by. Her income plummeted. They barely had enough to eat, let alone any coins left over to pay for passage.

"We need to find a new spot," Javid said.

"It's the same everywhere," she responded wearily. "All the busiest markets and thoroughfares are already taken."

He picked at the stitching on his coat sleeve. "I'm sorry I haven't been pulling my weight. There's just no work for strangers from Samarqand."

"I know." She patted his shoulder. "It's not your fault."

"Maybe we should try walking if nothing comes up in the next few days." He sniffed himself and made a face. "I can't live like this for much longer."

"What about the bandits?"

"I'd rather be stabbed than starve. At least it's a quick death."

"You have a point there."

Javid snored softly next to her later that night, but Nazafareen couldn't fall asleep. She was thinking about Darius again. If the Valkirins had come back, she hoped he hadn't done anything heroic and stupid.

Did I do right in leaving him behind? Or was it a terrible mistake?

Sometimes she wasn't sure. The doubts tended to creep up at the quietest hour of the night, when she tossed and turned in her cloak, stomach aching, tunic sticky with sweat. If Darius was here, he would've commandeered one of those barges and we'd be halfway down the river by now, she thought ruefully.

Nazafareen was finally drifting off when a faint cry erupted from the mouth of the alley. She came fully awake at once. She heard low voices, followed by a muffled thump and a weak groan. The area the other beggars had grudgingly ceded to her wasn't far from the docks. It was a mix of taverns and wooden hovels, with the occasional barbershop or other commercial establishment. Once the taverns closed, it was usually very quiet.

Nazafareen buckled on her sword and peeked around the corner.

Four rough-looking youths surrounded an older man. He was tall with a scholarly slope to his shoulders and a curling beard. One of the boys appeared to be trying to tug a ring from his hand. He resisted and earned a sharp blow across the face that knocked him to the ground.

Not my business.

But her feet were already moving, tiptoeing through the shadows. The narrow street was otherwise deserted in both directions. She crouched in a doorway.

"—look like robbery. Gimme that knife."

The tallest youth, who seemed to be their leader, held out a hand. One of his confederates handed him a blade hilt-first.

"Are you going to kill him first or after?"

"First. Then we can take our time stripping the body."

The man on the ground tried to cover his head.

"Please," he said, in a surprisingly calm voice. "Take whatever you like. I don't have much, but there's no need for violence."

They laughed at this.

"No need, old man?" the leader said. "But I'm afraid there is."

"She don't want you around no more—"

"Shut up, Anaxis! You're talking out of turn."

"But he's about to die anyway—"

"I don't care. We're professionals."

The tall one examined the knife. From the way he held it, Nazafareen could tell he knew how to use it, and also that he took pleasure from the power it gave him.

"I don't know what you're talking about," the man on the ground said in a bewildered tone. "Perhaps you've mistaken me for someone else?"

The thug laughed and brought his foot back to deliver a vicious kick to the head. Before it connected, Nazafareen rushed forward and smacked him with the flat of her sword across the temple. He fell like a stone. But his friends had the instincts of boys who'd survived in Delphi's underworld. The nearest one grabbed a hank of her hair and slammed her head into the wall. Stars exploded before her eyes. She lashed out blindly with the sword and heard a grunt of pain. A hand closed on the hilt, trying to wrest the blade away. Nazafareen seized it and gave a vicious twist, snapping the bone. Her vision began to clear. One of the boys was already dragging away their unconscious leader. She locked eyes with the last two. Both were bloodied and one had a broken arm that he cradled with his other hand. She planted her feet wide, trying not to sway.

"You're dead, girl," the tall one hissed.

Quick as lightning, she slashed him across the chest, not a killing blow but enough to part his roughspun tunic and draw blood. He leapt back.

"Come on!" the third one urged. "We'll get her later. I've marked her face. But Maro is hurt bad."

With a last murderous stare, the thugs darted off. In moments, they'd all vanished around a corner. Nazafareen slid her sword into the scabbard and crouched down next to their victim, who was sitting up with one hand cupped over his swollen eye.

"Are you all right?" she asked.

"I would have been much worse if you hadn't come along."

She helped him to his feet. The man looked to be in his late sixties. He had noble, intelligent features and wore a simple belted tunic.

"That was very brave of you."

She shrugged. "I caught them by surprise."

"Many people—most perhaps—would have left me to my fate. Four to one is poor odds, though you seem to have managed it."

"Yes, well.... I don't like bullies."

He smoothed down his thinning grey hair and brushed off his tunic. "My name is Herodotus."

"And mine is Ashraf." The lie came easily now.

He glanced at the scabbard belted around her waist. "I'm no expert on blades, but that looks to be a finely made one."

"I didn't steal it!" Nazafareen said defensively.

Herodotus appeared confused. "I never thought you did."

"Oh. Okay."

"I'm just glad you have some skill with a sword. The gods were watching over me tonight." He took in her ragged appearance. "Still, it's not safe to be on the streets so late—at least for old men like me. Don't you have anywhere to go?"

She briefly gave him the story Javid had concocted, a mix of truth and fiction. They were brother and sister from Samarqand who'd been testing a new wind ship and were blown off course. They had no way of contacting their family back home and were hoping to find work to pay for a river passage.

"I should be going now. My brother will wonder what happened to me. Will you be all right?"

Herodotus gave an embarrassed smile. "Yes. Perhaps it's foolish, but I sometimes take long walks through the city to think. I suppose you can't be too careful these days."

Nazafareen smiled back. "Take a different route next time." She started for the alley.

"Wait!"

She turned back, head cocked.

"You're sleeping in there, aren't you?"

She stared at him, unsure what to say. He seemed harmless enough, but she didn't need anyone prying into their affairs.

"Do you know where the Great Library is?"

Nazafareen shook her head.

"You can get directions at the agora. Come by tomorrow and ask for me. I can offer you scullery work. Nothing glamorous, but you can stay in the servants' quarters and the wages should be enough to help you get home in short order." He smiled apologetically. "I'd give you the money myself, but those lads just took my purse and I'm afraid I'm not a wealthy man."

Nazafareen didn't need to consider his offer for more than a moment. Scullery work beat starving, and she wouldn't turn her nose up at a paying job. Maybe their luck was finally changing.

"Thank you," she cried. "Tomorrow then!"

❧ 21 ❧

CULACH'S FOLLY

Mina came to Culach's chamber each day. She always brought a tray of food and sat quietly in her chair, but she never offered to try healing him again. And she didn't speak a single word, no matter what he said to draw her out.

He tried apologizing innumerable times. He tried to make her laugh. He raged and begged. He deliberately showed off his scars, hoping it might elicit some sympathy. Nothing worked.

The situation made him increasingly desperate, but he didn't return to his bed. Although he had no appetite, he forced himself to eat. Culach also began to rise early and practice with his sword. It was pointless, but the exercise kept him from descending any deeper into self-pity. When he wasn't chewing over the nightmares, he waited with grim anticipation for news from House Dessarian. After two more days passed, he decided to seek out his father. He asked around until he found Eirik in the stables with the abbadax.

The stables were on a broad east-facing ledge of the holdfast. Culach smelled the pungent droppings of the creatures even before he heard their burbling cries. They kept a dozen abbadax at Val Moraine, all trained as hatchlings. They were indispensable in transporting minerals to the coast for trade with the Marakai, and also for scouting the near-impassable mountains.

Culach had loved nothing more than to ride out with Petur, the icy wind tangling in their hair, mist-wreathed peaks streaking by beneath. The abbadax sported stiff, razor sharp feathers, so you had to be very careful where you placed your hands and legs. Petur used to joke that one careless sneeze would leave him a eunuch, but he'd been the most skilled rider of them all, utterly fearless and graceful as an acrobat in the saddle.

"I wouldn't come too close," Eirik said. "We have some new hatchlings and the mothers are already testy from the molting season."

Culach paused, then took three steps further so his father wouldn't think him a coward.

"I thought you might call for me," he said.

"Why?" Eirik sounded genuinely curious.

"To tell me if the chimera completed their task. Since you sought my approval, I thought you'd at least tell me the outcome."

"Approval?" Eirik gave a dry chuckle. "I wouldn't go that far. Frankly, I thought it might cheer you up to know your crippled state was being avenged."

Culach gritted his teeth. His father only wanted to get a rise and he could at least deny him that.

"And?"

"As expected, the trail led straight to House Dessarian. Unfortunately, neither target was there."

"What happened?"

"Six Danai are dead." Eirik sighed. "I only know because Tethys complained to the other holdfasts. They weren't happy we didn't consult them."

Culach felt sick. He should never have been part of this. "What do you mean, they weren't happy?"

"I received nearly identical messages this morning. They say we're on our own."

There were three other Valkirin clans: Val Altair, Val Tourmaline and Val Petros. Since the Iron Wars, their allegiance to Val Moraine had been cemented by the holdfast's indisputable military superiority. With the sword gone from their throats, the other Valkirins would be scheming to seize the mountain's mineral wealth for themselves. Culach wasn't surprised they'd abandoned Val Moraine in her hour of need, but the news still rankled.

And six Danai dead—none of them the ones he'd intended. It was a disaster.

"What are you going to do?"

"Nothing." Eirik's voice sounded strangely detached. "We wait. Oh, and you won't be seeing Mina anymore. I plan to confine her to her chambers."

"Why? It was your idea in the first place. And I need her help."

That was a lie. Culach could manage perfectly well on his own now. But even with her not speaking to him, he treasured Mina's presence each day. Sometimes he thought she was the only thing that kept him from going mad.

His father spoke slowly, as though to a dim-witted child. "Because if Victor tries to take Val Moraine, I'll have to kill her."

"What?"

"That *is* the ultimate point of a hostage, Culach."

If Culach hadn't been blind, he might have ended Eirik right there. A quick knife to the heart. He seethed inwardly, but kept his expression neutral. He could never reveal his feelings. Eirik was fully capable of throwing Mina out a window if he even suspected Culach cared for her.

"And what about Ellard?" he said.

"Ellard is already dead."

The news stunned him, just when he thought it could no longer get worse. "The Danai killed him?"

"No, the chimera."

"Damn you." Culach rubbed his temples. "We've made a terrible mistake."

Eirik's voice was a whipcrack. "No, you made a terrible mistake. You never should have gone to the shadowlands. Do you know what the other strongholds are calling it behind our backs? Culach's Folly. They're already arraying against us now. They smell blood." His father suddenly stepped close and Culach could smell the bitterness on his breath. An old man whose house lay in ruins. "But that doesn't mean we'll roll over and give them our throats."

Perhaps sensing the mood of its master, one of the abbadax gave a piercing, mournful cry.

"Will you seal the keep?" Culach asked.

I have to get her out. Have to get her out tonight....

"It's the obvious course of action," Eirik replied.

Culach kept his face smooth, but his mind raced. If Eirik deployed Val Moraine's defenses, no one would be leaving. There was only one way to stop him, Culach knew. Appeal to his vanity.

"You think we can't handle a few Danai?" He sneered at the last word.

"I'm not certain it will be a *few*," Eirik replied coldly. "And thanks to you, our army was decimated."

"So you'd have us hide in our shell like a turtle? I doubt they'll even make it through the mountains. And if we don't finish Victor now, he'll always be a threat. We'll make Val Moraine their tomb. All of them."

Eirik was silent. Culach held his breath.

"What would you have me do?" he asked at last.

"No enemy has ever breached these walls. The Danai have no abbadax. When they come, it will be through the tunnels. We wait for them there."

"And if their numbers are overwhelming?"

"They won't be. The Danai are cautious. The Matrium would ask for a parley before doing anything. I know Victor Dessarian. He's a hothead. He won't wait for permission, which means he'll have a rag-tag force." Culach sensed his father's hesitation and gave him a final push. "Victor seduced Neblis and led her to her death. All the misfortunes of our house can be laid at his feet. If you wish to avenge her, this is your chance."

Eirik grunted. "Perhaps you're right. Let him come to us. But we must be ready. There isn't much time."

In truth, Culach wasn't so sure they could hold off the Danai at close quarters. But it didn't matter, as long as Mina got out. He had little to live for anyway. If they cut him down, at least it would be a clean death. He forced himself to stay for another hour, mechanically reviewing every entrance to the keep and where to place the defenders, but every particle hummed with the urge to find Mina. He couldn't go with her. He'd only slow her down. But if she was willing to take one of the abbadax, he could show her the proper way to ride without slicing herself to ribbons. It was the only way. She'd never make it on foot.

Culach played the good son, nodding and debating different scenarios—how many men would Victor bring, what would their strategy be—all the while scheming to deprive his shit of a father the pleasure of tossing Mina's head over the battlements. When he finally broke loose, he was in such a state of agitation, he took several wrong turns on his way back to his rooms. One instant and he knew she wasn't there. He searched the keep, finally breaking down and calling her name. He found her rooms. They were empty.

Nearing despair, Culach returned to his own chamber. And there she was, sitting in her chair. He knew because he smelled her hair.

He fell to his knees before her, shaking all over but barely aware of it.

"You have to leave. Now."

"What's happened?" she demanded.

Culach leaned forward, pressing his forehead against her knees. He felt her body tense, but she didn't push him away.

"Calm down. Tell me everything."

Culach raised his sightless eyes. He wished he could see her face.

"You're right to hate us. You were right about everything. And now Eirik intends to murder you." He seized her skirts in his fists. "But I won't let him hurt you, Mina. I swear it."

"And what do you care?"

"I care," he said hoarsely.

"Why?"

The last of his resistance drained away. At least he could find the courage to tell her the truth, even if she hated him for it.

"Because I love you."

"You're only saying that because you're lonely and I've taken care of you."

"No! You're misunderstanding. I...." Culach fumbled for the right words. He'd never been good at this sort of thing. Cutting sarcasm was more his forte. Petur had always been silver-tongued with women. Part of the problem was Culach had never needed to be charming. They wanted him anyway—or perhaps, perversely, *because* he was such an arrogant prick. Now he wished he'd read more poetry instead of sharpening his sword.

"Listen, I don't expect you to feel the same," he said. "But you have to trust me. We'll go to the stables tonight. I know a way no one ever takes. You can be gone before Eirik suspects anything. He could be looking for you right now—"

"Poor tortured man."

Culach felt her fingers slide through his hair. A shock of desire ran down his spine.

"So you love me, eh?" she said wryly.

"Rather desperately."

His breath caught in his throat as she cupped his face.

"Kiss me, Mina," he whispered, praying she wasn't toying with him. It would be a fine revenge indeed for all the crass comments he'd subjected her to over the years. His heart beat hard in his chest as he felt her move closer until their lips were inches apart. His hand found her calf, the skin like warm silk.

"I thought I told you I don't like big blonde apes," she said softly.

Culach's lips curved in a smile. Perhaps Mina didn't care for poetry either.

"Well, I've never liked dark little kittens. They have sharp teeth."

She nipped at his full bottom lip and his fragile self-control crumbled. Culach pulled Mina into his lap and settled her there, legs straddling his waist. He could feel the heat of her.

"And claws," he growled, as she raked her nails down his back.

Then her mouth found his and he sank into the honeyed sweetness of her tongue. She pulled the tunic over his head and kissed each of his scars, and he found the pain was not only bearable but bled into pleasure at her tenderness. He was trying to navigate the complicated fastenings of her dress when the door banged open and they leapt apart.

"Culach." It was the voice of his cousin, Agnar.

"Knock before you barge in next time," he snapped, rising to his feet. Culach did his best to loom, even though fear gripped his heart. Could they have come for her already?

"Your father wants you."

"Why?"

Agnar hesitated.

"Speak it!"

"We found a Danai a few leagues from the holdfast. He's half frozen. I thought he was dead at first."

Culach frowned. "One? Do you know who it is?"

"Your father says.... He says it's her son."

Whose son? Culach didn't know what he was talking about.

Then he heard Mina's gasp and understood that Agnar had gestured to her, momentarily forgetting Culach's blindness.

"Galen? Take us to him now," Culach said, striding for the door.

"But your father only asked for you—"

"It's her *son*," he snarled. "Have you lost all sense of decency?"

Agnar shut up at that.

As they hurried through the chill corridors, he felt a gentle touch on his back. Both guiding and reassuring.

"Thank you," Mina whispered in his ear.

Culach fumbled for her hand and gave it a quick squeeze. *Please let Galen live*, he thought. And then: *Don't let my father kill him too.*

22

TRAPPED

Darius was only a few leagues outside of Delphi when the chimeras caught him.

He'd been running for days, switching to an easy lope that was more realistic than the dead sprint he'd attempted at the start of his journey. His pumping legs ate away at the ground in a steady blur. The monotonous landscape freed his mind to wander and he thought a great deal about Nazafareen. He remembered the first time they'd met four years ago. She'd been so afraid of him, and he of her. She'd driven him half-mad with her stubbornness, and later with the urge to kiss her.

He should have told her everything. Darius resolved to do so as soon as he found her, which should be within the next day or two—assuming he'd chosen correctly and she hadn't gone to Samarqand.

That was the plan, at least.

He shouldn't have stopped to rest.

If he'd just kept going, he might have outpaced them. But his leg had begun to ache again and he didn't know anything was pursuing him until he heard an ear-splitting howl. Darius squinted into the distance. Three pale shadows moved across the plain.

Dogs? When he reached for the Nexus and sought their essential nature, he felt a jolt of shock.

What he discovered was an...emptiness. A black hole in the Nexus. He didn't know what to make of it, so he didn't turn to fight them as he would have done with any other creature, confident that there was nothing faster or deadlier than an armed daēva.

Which saved his life.

They streaked toward him in a tight triangular formation—so far as he could tell, since they were precisely the same color as the rocks. After that first single cry, they fell silent. Ahead, the plain gradually gave way to farmland. The sun was clearly visible now, a large molten ball shimmering above the horizon. Beyond that he could make out the city walls and a large hill rising up in the center with a shining white building perched on its crown.

Could he make it to the walls?

Darius glanced over his shoulder, calculating his own speed and trajectory in relation to his pursuers.

The answer was a resounding no.

In fact, they would catch him before he even reached the first farmhouse.

They were coming fast now, giving everything they had to the final dash, and he was getting a taste of just how bloody quick they could be when they really tried.

But he could be quick too.

Darius scanned the plain, his gaze pausing on what looked like a tooth of rock jutting from the ground perhaps a league away. He veered toward it. The creatures must have been fairly intelligent because they understood what he was doing and redoubled their efforts to catch him before he reached it.

Blood rushed in his ears. He tucked his head and stiffened his fingers to javelins, slicing the air, running, running, the panting right on his heels now, and then the rock loomed before him, black and cracked, at least twenty paces high, and Darius leapt for it.

His nails caught in a tiny crevice halfway up and he clung there, as growls and wet snapping sounds came inches beneath his dangling boots. With a monumental effort, he hauled himself up, inch by inch. The top was a rugged point about four hands across. He straddled it, legs wide, hands gripping a knife-blade of rock.

The things had fallen quiet again. They squatted on their haunches at the base, staring at him with baleful yellow eyes.

The sun beat down. He had no water. No food. It was all gone.

The weight of despair settled on his shoulders like a funeral shroud.

Darius stared dully at the things—like transparent wolves, but even weirder. So close to the the city. So close. But too far for anyone there to see him out here.

You brought this on yourself. You're a fool and liar. You drove her away....

Druj.

The word stabbed him deep. *Druj.* Evil. Impure. Demonic. That's what the magi called him. Even Nazafareen had believed it.

No!

Darius dug his fingers into the rock, terrified to realize how slack they'd become. He was starting to slide off....

He squeezed his eyes shut and sought the Nexus. A void, but bursting with wild energy. The place where the threads of every living creature came together. Despair vanished like mist in the face of bright sunlight.

Every living creature—but not those who waited twenty places below. The Nexus rejected them.

Darius opened his eyes and summoned a gale. He tried smashing them with earth.

Nothing worked.

They absorbed his magic unharmed.

I might be in some trouble, he thought.

❧ 23 ❧

THE BRAZEN BULL

Nazafareen had never seen anything like the Great Library of Delphi.

Javid had helped her find the right neighborhood, then drifted off to wait in a nearby park. Neither had eaten breakfast and Nazafareen felt light-headed as she paused to gather her wits before going in search of their new benefactor. The library was even grander than the Temple of Apollo. It stood alone at the center of a large plaza in the northwestern quadrant of the city, regal and stately as a king's palace—although Javid said that the Greeks didn't have hereditary rulers anymore.

They'd little to do in the evenings but talk, so he set himself the task of educating Ashraf the Hayseed on the history of Solis and its various forms of government. A king ruled Samarqand, but Delphi had three elected bureaucrats known as the Archon Eponymos, the Polemarch and the Archon Basileus.

The Archon Eponymos was the chief magistrate, the Polemarch headed the armed forces, and the Archon Basileus was responsible for civic religious arrangements, such as festivals and the like. Then there was also a popular assembly called the Ecclesia, where all male citizens over the age of twenty could air grievances and vote on things like whether to go to war, or who to elect as the Archons.

It sounded complicated, but Javid claimed everything had run smoothly until the Pythia came along and convinced the Polemarch to crack down on magic. Delphi had never embraced it like Samarqand, but the authorities generally turned a blind eye to philosophers who dabbled in alchemy and other fey arts. The new reasoning was that magic had caused the destruction of the cities and stood in opposition to scientific advancement, which was humanity's proud heritage, while the witches remained literally mired in the dark.

The Pythia despised daēvas to a fanatical degree, spurring all sorts of rumors: her family had been slaughtered by daēvas, or she'd foretold that they planned to invade Solis and was keeping it secret so as not to panic the populace—and so on. The Archon Basileus was completely under her thumb, they said, leaving only the Archon Eponymos to offer any degree of resistance, and he was notoriously corrupt.

So many intrigues, Javid told her with glee. It was worse even than the time of the Tyrants.

The Guild of the Philosophers lay just a few blocks away from the library. Nazafareen had seen those learned men strolling around the grounds, deep in conversation or debate, and felt her own lack of education keenly. But Herodotus had said it was just scullery work and she could manage that, even with only one hand.

Nazafareen climbed the broad stone steps to the entrance, feeling every bit the street urchin in her stinking rags. Once inside, she asked a young scholar where to find Herodotus. He raised an eyebrow at her appearance, but finally condescended to lead her deeper into the honeycomb of scrolls and stacks of parchment. The scholar stopped before a closed door.

"He's teaching a class." He pressed his lips together. "I have work to do, so you can wait here by yourself if you'll promise not to wander off."

Nazafareen nodded obediently. She waited for him to leave, then slipped inside the room and took a seat unnoticed in the back row. It was very warm and stuffy inside, and she listened with half an ear as Herodotus lectured a group of young students about someone named Jamadin, who seemed to be a famous general. But the time he spoke of was long ago and Nazafareen's eyes grew heavy. She woke with a start to find the classroom empty and Herodotus standing in front of her, a bemused expression on his face.

Nazafareen jumped to her feet.

"It's me," she said. "The girl from the alley."

"Of course it is." He gave her a warm smile. "What do you think of the library?"

Herodotus looked different today, with his beard neatly brushed into two large curls and the confident air of a man in his element. But his kindly manner put her at ease.

"Very impressive."

"It's taken years to rebuild the collections. The library was burned to the ground in the Vatra war. Only the stone foundation survived. Of course, there are very few records from that time, but one of the curators managed to smuggle hundreds of the scrolls out and hide them in caves. Still a tragic loss, but at least a fragment of the collection survived."

"The Vatra war?"

He peered down at her. "The fire daēvas, Ashraf. What *do* they teach children in school these days?"

Fire daēvas? Had Javid been telling the truth? Nazafareen felt a chill. Darius had never mentioned them, which seemed very odd. Maybe he'd never heard of them either. As far as Nazafareen knew, there were only three clans: the Avas Marakai, the Avas Danai and the Avas Valkirins. Avas meant *child of*, and Mar meant *sea*, Dan *forest* and Val *mountain*. Did Vat mean *fire*?

"When did this happen?" she asked.

"Why, nearly a thousand years now. We have several treatises on it, if you're interested."

"That's all right, I can't read anyway." She relaxed. A thousand years was a long time, even by daēva standards. "Where are these Vatras now?"

Something flickered in his eyes, there and gone too quickly to identify. "All dead," he said with a bright smile. "So you needn't worry."

An awkward silence descended. Herodotus tugged at his beard, still grinning, though it seemed a bit frozen.

"Are you in charge of the whole library?" Nazafareen asked.

"Oh no, just the cataloguing." He lowered his voice. "My predecessor was overly fond of wine, if you get my drift, so the organization is rather a mess. There are tens of thousands of scrolls and at least half of them have never been properly examined."

"You don't expect me to help with that, do you?" she asked. "As I said, I never learned to read."

"Oh gods, no. We have trained scribes for that. They record the work's title, author and editor as well as its place of origin, length in lines, and whether the manuscript contains a single text or more than one work."

Nazafareen nodded politely. Herodotus clearly relished the finer points of his position.

"Then it must be assigned to a proper category." He ticked them off on long, elegant fingers. "We have rhetoric, law, epic tragedy, comedy, lyric poetry, history, medicine, mathematics, natural science and miscellaneous."

"It sounds marvelous," she said wistfully.

"Oh, it is!" His face fell. "I'm sorry, my dear, but for you I'm afraid it will be scullery work. Sweeping, dusting, that sort of thing." He glanced at her missing hand. "Is that a problem?"

"I can manage."

He smiled. "Very good. You can start right away."

Nazafareen hesitated. "I was wondering if there might be a place for my brother as well."

Herodotus thought for a moment. "You say he's familiar with wind ships?"

"Oh yes, he knows everything about them."

"I have friends in the Philosophers Guild. I'll make inquiries. In the meantime, I think you both can sleep in the servants' quarters. They'll give you fresh clothing as well."

"Thank you for everything. You won't regret it, I swear."

Herodotus looked embarrassed at her gratitude. "I owe you my life, Ashraf. As I said last night, I wish I could simply give you the money you need." He winked at her. "But of all possessions, a friend is the most precious. Come, I'll escort you to the servants' quarters so you can get settled in."

He chatted easily to her as they walked through the library, ignoring the curious stares of the other scholars. The servants' quarters were in a separate building, reachable through a covered passage that crossed the plaza.

"What did you think of the lecture?" he asked as they strolled beneath the portico.

"I only heard the end."

"I'm writing a multi-volume biography of Jamadin, perhaps you know of him?"

Nazafareen shook her head.

"He was the Persian general who founded Samarqand. Long dead now, naturally. But he came through one of the gates from the shadowlands with the remnants of his army. This was after the war."

She looked up sharply. "So he wasn't from this world?"

"No, he came from the lands that lie on the other side of the Dominion. There used to be more travel between them, but it's forbidden now." He glanced around to see if anyone was listening.

It struck Nazafareen as a habitual, unconscious gesture, and she saw the long shadow of the Pythia in it.

Herodotus cleared his throat. "At least the Archon Basileus is an avid supporter of our acquisitions department," he said heartily. "Why, he's even issued an order that all ships making port at Delphi will be searched and any books or scrolls brought straight here for examination. He's particularly interested in the war, although I haven't found much yet. As I said, it was a tumultuous time and most of the records were lost."

They came to the end of the covered walkway and entered a whitewashed building that smelled pleasantly of spices and stew. A small altar to some god held a scattering of fresh flowers.

"Ah, here we are."

The head chamberlain of the library was a vigorous man named Castor who spoke so fast, Nazafareen could hardly keep up with him. Men and women were usually separated by sex, but since she and Javid were brother and sister and the servants' quarters were full, he would allow them to share a single room.

She bathed and changed into a clean tunic laid out on one of the beds. By some miracle, considering the amount of time she'd spent hanging about in filthy alleyways, the scratches on her leg hadn't been infected with evil humors. In fact, they seemed to be healing well. Feeling better than she had in ages, Nazafareen collected Javid from the park, then set about her duties. Now that she wore the garb of a servant, none of the scholars paid her the least bit of attention. She swept and dusted, mopped and polished. Castor seemed pleased with her and best of all, at the end of the day she and Javid sat down to heaping plates of food served at a long trestle table in the kitchens.

There was the fish stew she'd smelled on entering, but they also had bowls of olives and apricots, creamy goat's milk cheese, fresh spring peas and even a cake sweetened with honey. Instead of napkins they wiped their hands on pieces of bread which were tossed to a fat old dog who sprawled under the table.

Six other servants tended to the library. Nazafareen was too tired to remember their names, but they seemed friendly. She stumbled off to bed content and full-bellied, grateful that her good deed had been so generously repaid.

Over the following days, Nazafareen came to know every part of the Great Library, from the lecture halls to the silent study rooms and main collections, which occupied a series of adjoining halls fitted with shelving and thousands of cubbyholes. She'd been ordered never to touch any of the scrolls because some were so old they might crumble to dust, but she couldn't help eying them curiously. How long would it take to read everything in the library, and if you did, would you be the smartest person in the world? It was a question she would have asked Darius, and he might have laughed, but he wouldn't have laughed *at* her, and then they might have had a serious discussion about it.

Darius could read. He could write too. But he never acted snotty about it.

Javid was smart, but he was only interested in wind ships and how to make money. They rarely saw each other since he left early in the morning and spent the evenings prowling the taverns for gossip he could relay to the Merchants' Guild when they reached Samarqand. Nazafareen liked Javid—he had a good heart despite his mercenary tendencies—but she missed Darius more each day.

She'd known from the start that he was concealing things from her and it made her wary of him. They'd kissed once, shortly after she woke from her illness. She'd been swept away by the moment, but then things grew awkward. Darius would start to say something and stop himself, or he'd mention names she had no recollection of. When she asked, he would give only the briefest reply or change the subject entirely. In these moments a distance grew between them.

Had he done something to her? Or she to him? Both? She'd asked herself these questions a thousand times. Speculated about possible reasons, each worse than the last. But if Darius held a grudge against her, why did he save her life?

Nazafareen knew she'd go mad if she kept treading the same barren ground. There was only one thing to do. Save every coin, go to Samarqand, and beg the Marakai for help—on hands and knees, if necessary. If they could not heal her, she would try an alchemist. And if that failed...well, she would worry about that when it happened.

And so her time in Delphi passed. She learned which scholars to avoid because they would snap at her for making the slightest noise or try to make her fetch them things, and which ones were nice. Being the newest and youngest, she was given the dirtiest jobs, but Nazafareen wasn't afraid of hard work. In fact, she preferred it to sitting around begging all day because the time passed much faster.

There were two scholars who she came to particularly dislike. She didn't know their names, but one was thin and balding, and the other had shifty eyes that always seemed to be undressing her. She'd named them the Stork and the Weasel. They stuck together like glue and she began to get the distinct impression they were spies for the Pythia.

Nazafareen had been dusting in a corner behind a shelf of scrolls when she heard them talking. It was in one of the quiet workrooms, where twenty scribes hunched over tables painstakingly copying works with reed pens, the dusty sunlight pouring in golden shafts through windows set high in the wall.

"He has no grasp of politics," the Stork said. "He thinks only of pure scholarship. I suppose his lack of ambition is no harm to our cause, but mark my words, the old fool won't last long."

"I don't trust him," the Weasel replied. "Always poking around in the histories. He claims it's for that biography he's writing, but I wonder sometimes where his loyalties lie."

"He's been warned. If he finds anything, he must bring it straight to Archon Basileus."

Nazafareen saw the Archon once when he came to inspect the library. He had thick dark hair sweeping back from his forehead and a cold gaze that passed over her without pausing. She'd kept her head down, pretending to stare at the ground, but had watched him from the corner of her eye. The Archon Basileus was a man who was very full of himself, she thought. Also a man who shouldn't be underestimated.

"And if he doesn't," the Weasel added, "we shall report it ourselves straightaway."

They must be talking about Herodotus. She didn't see him often because he was usually off rooting around in the farthest, dustiest stacks, but he always had a kind word when their paths crossed. She wondered if she should tell him about the men who whispered behind his back. Nazafareen bit her lip. He might think she'd been eavesdropping on purpose. And she didn't even know their names. Nazafareen resolved to keep her eyes and ears open, but not to get involved unless it seemed unavoidable. Like Javid said, the sooner they left Delphi, the better.

True to his word, Herodotus had found Javid work at the hangar where the wind ships were kept. Javid performed menial labor too, but he had a knack for ferreting out information and he said not everyone agreed with the Pythia. Her ban on magic was a topic of heated debate both within the Philosophers' Guild and the Ecclesia, which was the popular assembly.

Javid told Nazafareen the Philosophers talked about the Pythia in whispers, how she had ensorceled the Polemarch to do her bidding. There were strange goings-on at the Temple, they said. Rumors that she held captive witches and planned to use them as her own personal army—though that seemed too far-fetched to be credible. How could witches be held captive? They were fearsome magic workers and as strong as ten men.

But others believed it was only a matter of time before the daēvas tried to enslave the mortal cities. And only the Pythia could save them.

~

NAZAFAREEN FINGER-COMBED HER HAIR AND LAY DOWN ON her bed of straw. One of the other girls had come down with a fever so instead of her usual duties, she'd been allowed to carry the shopping baskets for Castor that afternoon. He took her to the bustling marketplace called the agora. Afterwards, he bought her a sweet roll and pointed out the bowl-shaped hillside where they held the Ecclesia and the grand palaces of the Archons.

Her store of silver drachma was growing, and with Javid's added to it, they almost had enough to book passage to Samar- qand. Once she got there, Nazafareen could find the Marakai. The thought filled her with both longing and dread. If Darius had withheld so much, it meant her past wasn't pretty. Nazafareen remembered Tethys's warning and wondered if she'd been right.

Some people might see it as a gift. A chance to start life anew without the burden of regret.

Was she foolish to throw that chance away? What if she'd done terrible things?

Nazafareen sighed. If that was the case, she would have to live with it. But she knew she would always be tormented by wondering if she took the cowardly way out.

Either way, she *would* find Darius again.

A knock came at the door and Javid sauntered in, a broad smile on his face.

"I bargained the price down. We leave the day after tomorrow."

She sat up. "That's wonderful."

"It's a wallowing river barge, but we should get there within a week." He grinned. "I'll find work for you somewhere, don't worry. And when I tell the Guild—" He cut off. "Well, let's just say they should be happy with my news. I paid for half the passage in advance. We'll give the captain the rest the morning we sail." He sat on the edge of his bed. "Come on, get up. I think we should celebrate."

"How?"

"There's a performance at the amphitheater tonight," Javid said. "It's the opening of the festival of Dionysus. Let's go see it."

"I don't know."

His brow creased in worry. "Is it your illness?"

"No," she said hastily. "It's not that."

In truth, she was on edge. And she did miss Darius—bitterly.

"Come on then." Javid tugged at her hand. "It's almost our last night in Delphi. Personally, I hope I never return, but I want to be able to say I took in the sights."

She hesitated.

"I'll buy you a sweet roll from that stall you like so much," he said in a wheedling tone.

Nazafareen relented. "All right. I suppose it's early yet."

They left the library and wandered toward the open-air amphitheater, which lay near the base of the Acropolis. When the theatre was full, three actors came out in masks and began performing some drama, sweeping their arms in exaggerated gestures so even those in the furthest seats could grasp the action. Some clever trick of acoustics carried their voices clearly through the amphitheater. Nazafareen guessed it was a tragedy based on the fact that the main character ended up dying in some nasty way, although it was carried out tastefully off stage.

When the play ended and the last mournful strains of the chorus faded away, the crowd swirled out of the amphitheater. Nazafareen stretched, knuckling the small of her back. The stone benches weren't the most comfortable.

"Something's happening," Javid said.

He pointed at the Acropolis. The multiple stairways leading up were all packed with people, pushing and shoving to get to the top.

"Let's go see," he said.

Nazafareen had an uneasy feeling. "I'm not sure—"

But Javid was already striding toward the nearest staircase. Others joined him from every direction, like streams flowing into a river, and she hurried to catch up before the throng swallowed him. Heavy clouds passed before the sun as she caught the back of his tunic.

"I thought we agreed to stay away from there," she hissed. "What if we're recognized?"

"In this crowd?" he laughed. "I don't think so." Javid registered her grim expression. "Come on, we're leaving in two days anyway."

By this point, they were caught in the surging mass and Nazafareen had no choice but to follow him up the worn stone steps. People packed the plaza of the Acropolis from edge to edge. They had expectant, almost eager expressions, like an audience waiting for a show to begin. Nazafareen rose up on tiptoes, straining to see over heads and shoulders, until Javid grasped her hand and plowed a path toward the front, where a black stone altar sat before the temple portico.

There was something on top of it now—a life-sized bronze bull, with curving horns and a gaping mouth. A brazier had been set beneath its belly. Two dozen of the Polemarch's men were arrayed nearby, while others held back the crowd. A balding, middle-aged man stood amid the semicircle of soldiers. He had a distant expression on his face, as if his mind had already fled elsewhere. A drumbeat of distant thunder came from the plain. The air felt heavy and charged. Nazafareen shivered as a chill, rain-freighted breeze lifted the hair on her bare arms.

Then the Pythia emerged from the temple and the crowd instantly fell silent. She wore a deep crimson cloak with the hood up, leaving her eyes in shadow although Nazafareen could just make out her nose and mouth. A young initiate in white stood behind her, slender and stunningly beautiful with raven hair and creamy olive skin.

"This man was caught trying to practice witchcraft," she said in a sorrowful voice. "It is an affront to the god. Apollo has made his will known to me. We must punish this heretic or in turn be punished ourselves."

A murmuring ran through the assembled crowd, like wind rattling naked branches. Beside her, Javid's breath hissed through his teeth.

"I've seen him before," he whispered. "He's one of the philosophers."

The man stood straight-backed and defiant until the Polemarch's soldiers began to drag him toward the bull. Then he let out an animal sound of despair and tried to pull away. One of the soldiers kicked his legs out and they hauled him by his arms, so that his feet dragged in the dust of the plaza. Nazafareen shared a worried look with Javid. She wanted to stop it but didn't know how. Her control of the elements was too weak to do more than summon a light breeze. She couldn't fight that many soldiers. She and Javid would just end up getting arrested themselves.

As the soldiers approached the bull, another stepped forward and opened a panel in the belly. The unfortunate philosopher was bundled inside and a fire lit in the brazier. Within seconds, a terrible bellowing cry erupted from the bull's mouth. At first she thought the creature had somehow come to life. But then Nazafareen realized there must be an acoustic apparatus inside that carried the man's screams and converted them into the roar of a bull.

It went on and on. Nazafareen could feel the pull of the flames, their crackling hunger as they devoured flesh and bone. Against her will, her own breaking magic responded, bubbling up like a witch's brew. Anger burned her throat.

The Pythia's hooded face turned toward her.

"We have to get out of here," Nazafareen gasped.

She grabbed Javid's hand and began pulling him through the crowd, but it was packed cheek by jowl and she thought they'd never make it to the stairs leading down from the Acropolis. She glanced back once. Although the Pythia's eyes remained hidden in the shadow of her cloak, Nazafareen had the distinct impression she was staring at them.

The shrieking bellows of the bull followed them all the way down the stairs to the street below, where Nazafareen doubled over and retched up her sweet bun.

"I'm so sorry," Javid was saying. "I never should have brought you there. I had no idea."

She stood and wiped her mouth. "It's not your fault."

"Holy Father, I've never seen the like." His face was ashen too. "Come on, let's get you back to the library."

"What is she?" Nazafareen asked as they hurried home. "The Pythia?"

"She is the Oracle of Delphi."

"But what's an oracle?"

"Like a seer. You know what that is? They say she has mystical powers granted by the gods. She can see into the future."

"Is it true?"

He shrugged. "I don't know. But what we just witnessed was evil. Our king may not be perfect, but Holy Father...." He trailed off and made the sign of the flame.

Nazafareen shivered despite the heat. She didn't tell him that the Pythia had looked right at them. At her.

Does she know what I am?

✼ 24 ✼

THE STORM

From his perch on the rock five leagues east of Delphi, Darius watched a smudge of smoke rise from the Acropolis. He licked cracked lips and wondered what it meant. Some of the cults worshipped fire. Maybe they were burning an animal as an offering to their gods. When the breeze shifted, he could smell the faint aroma of roasting meat. It made his mouth water.

Wind ships with brightly colored air sacks drifted in the skies above the city, but none came his way. They seemed to avoid the Umbra, moving mainly from north to south.

At the base of the outcropping, three sets of eyes regarded him with maddening patience.

They would wait until he died of thirst or fell asleep. Maybe they hoped he'd finally choose to end his suffering and go willingly to their waiting jaws.

"Sorry to disappoint," Darius rasped with a grim smile.

The beasts simply stared.

It was Darius's sixth day on the rock. He'd retreated to the Nexus, not filled with the power, simply letting it swirl around him. It was the only way to stay sane, to shield himself from their poisonous magic. But he couldn't hide in the Nexus forever—that itself would be a trap. He'd slowly perish without caring or even realizing it was happening.

The constant sunlight helped him stay awake—that and the knowledge that an abrupt end waited a few paces below. Now, after six days of clear weather, a storm was gathering.

It came from the east, from Nocturne. The sky in that direction grew gradually darker anyway so it had taken him a while to notice the black clouds forming. They crept across the plain, achingly slow at first, then with shocking swiftness. Darius watched curtains of rain sweep closer. Knowing his thirst would soon be quenched made it temporarily worse and he swallowed convulsively. The beasts below rose up from their languid haunches and began to circle the pillar of rock, transparent tails swishing.

Finally, the skies above mercifully opened. Darius tipped his head back, savoring the cool, sweet moisture on his lips. It slicked back his hair, washed the dust from his eyes. He drank and drank, scrubbing hands across a week's worth of beard. Swished it around his mouth and spat.

Wind and rain battered his little perch and he let out a howl of savage delight.

The beasts eyed him uncertainly.

He felt alive again.

Darius let his awareness merge with the storm. He could sense the opposing forces of massive warm and cool air currents, see the droplets of water from their birth at the dew point miles above as they plunged through the downdraft, merging with other droplets and growing fatter, until they dashed themselves on the barren earth of the plain.

If he had more talent with air and water, he could push it, feed it, although he didn't know what that would accomplish. The beasts seemed riled up by the storm but not in any way harmed. But Darius's strength was in earth. He clung to his rock, soaked to the bone. Water rushed everywhere. The plain had been so dry, the ground packed so hard, it couldn't absorb the sudden deluge. Arid gullies rapidly became roaring streams. He eyed the fertile green fields outside the city walls. They must irrigate using the river.

Rivers....

Darius felt a faint resonance far beneath the earth. Like calling to like.

He probed with the power, deeper, deeper.

The beasts circled and whined.

There....

Water rushing through darkness.

Darius took a deep breath.

This is going to hurt. A lot.

He filled with earth power, more than he'd ever held before. Enough to do himself some serious damage.

No way around it. I have to go deep.

His senses sharpened to an exquisite, almost excruciating degree. Each raindrop seemed an ocean, each mote of dust a continent. Still he drew power into himself, until he thought his veins would burst with it. He felt a flock of birds winging south, felt the air rushing under his wings, and the blind delving of worms in the earth, and the groves of olive trees drinking the rain through their ancient roots. He was everything and nothing at all, and it left him naked and nearly weeping.

When he could hold no more, Darius unleashed it all in a single blast. Small, delicate bones cracked in his right foot and hand. His third, fourth and seventh ribs gave way a moment later. A rent in the earth opened at the base of the outcropping. The beasts edged back, snarling.

Too shallow.

Darius ruthlessly walled off the pain and drew more. The chasm widened.

So close.

Oh Holy Father, I have to jump down now.

He never knew what would break when he used earth magic. At least it wasn't both legs this time. Before he could think too hard about it, Darius shoved off his perch. He tried to land catlike on the pad of his left foot, but his limbs were numb and tingling from disuse and the right still took some weight. He hit the ground just to the left of the crevice he'd made. A white-hot lance of pain shot straight to his hip socket.

The beasts had been caught by surprise, but they recovered quickly. Darius leapt aside, teeth snapping inches from his cheek, and dove into the crevice. He landed on his back. Sharp rocks dug into his skin. Three heads peered down from above.

This will be your grave if you don't do something.

He opened himself to earth one last time, throwing it back out in a destructive force so vicious and desperate that it vaporized the last layer of rock between him and the cavern below. The ground gave way in a shower of dirt. More bones snapped.

Falling....

Water closed over his head. He fought to the surface and used his last strength to seal the opening he'd made before the beasts could follow.

Rock ground together like a mouth snapping shut. Perfect blackness descended.

He lost the Nexus and full sensation roared back into limbs that hadn't been used in nearly a week. Darius didn't fear pain. He was familiar with it—if not exactly an old friend, a long acquaintance. But this was no ordinary pain. The muscles of his calves tightened into agonizing cramps. His toes curled into tight knots inside his boots. Water filled his mouth. He spat it out with a gasp. Kicking and flailing, Darius struggled to stay afloat as the river carried him away.

❧ 25 ❧

A PIT OF VIPERS

Nazafareen stayed in bed the next day.

She told Castor she'd eaten some bad oysters at the market, but that wasn't the real reason for her queasiness. She knew the Pythia had sensed her. What if she could see Nazafareen's magic?

They would burn her in the brazen bull.

Castor laid a hand on her forehead. He always had a faintly worried look, like a dog with a fickle master. He was afraid of something too. The Pythia? The Archons? It couldn't be Herodotus. Everyone seemed to like him, except for the Stork and the Weasel.

"A bit of a fever, perhaps." Castor's thin lips pursed. "You may rest today."

Javid had offered to stay with her before he left for work that morning, but Nazafareen preferred to be alone. He clearly felt guilty for having dragged her to the execution. She'd given him a wan smile and insisted she'd be fine with a little sleep. But those terrible bellows still rang in her ears. The more she thought about it, the more she loathed the Pythia and the Polemarch and all of them. They deserved to die—horribly.

Just like that day at the lake with the Valkirins.

Nazafareen raised a shaking hand to her eyes. It was wrong to think this way. Delilah had warned her against stoking her temper. But oh, how she would enjoy stuffing that woman into her own torture device and setting it alight!

To her surprise, Herodotus appeared later that afternoon with a pot of mint tea.

"Castor says you're ill," he said, pouring her a cup.

"A bit." Nazafareen sat up. "You didn't have to come."

He pressed a handful of silver drachmas into her palm. "Here's your pay. I added a little extra from my own purse."

Nazafareen was touched by his kindness. "Thank you. My brother found a boat. We leave tomorrow."

"I'm glad. I know you're anxious to get home."

A somewhat awkward silence descended.

"How's your research coming?" she asked to be polite.

His homely face lit up. "Very well! I made a fascinating discovery yesterday in the stacks. A rather colorful memoir by the alchemist Nabu-bal-idinna, who claims he went into the shadowlands and met someone called the Drowned Lady. He had a theory about the gates, you see, that worlds come in linked pairs. Rather like twins, though not identical in every way. Of course, the man was notoriously unreliable, but he said—" Herodotus broke off, a flush creeping up his cheeks. "Well, I won't bore you with the details. But it contradicted other accounts I've read." He cleared his throat. "Anyway, tell me how your brother fares with the philosophers."

Nazafareen wanted to ask more about the Drowned Lady—what an intriguingly dreadful name!—but she could see Herodotus regretted saying as much as he had. Perhaps he didn't want the others to know about it. Scholars were odd, prickly creatures, she had discovered. They cared about the dead far more than the living, and sometimes got into passionate fights over some dusty old scroll that looked like it had been nibbled by mice. Nazafareen wouldn't mind learning to read, but it did seem awfully hard. Most of the scholars had bent backs and bloodshot, watery eyes from peering at squiggly lines all day. Herodotus didn't have their dry, pinched look—like a piece of fruit left too long in the sun—nor was he stern or boring. But it still seemed a high price to pay for knowledge.

They chatted for a while more and Herodotus left. She carefully counted out her money. It came to more than enough to pay the balance of their passage and have some left over for when she arrived in Samarqand. Feeling better, Nazafareen decided to get up and occupy herself with work until suppertime. The hours would creep if she stayed in bed. And this time tomorrow, she'd be outside the city walls and beyond the Pythia's reach.

She found a broom and was crossing the covered passageway when she saw the crimson cloak of the Archon Basileus sweeping toward the front entrance of the library, a contingent of soldiers in tow. Nazafareen froze, then hurried to one of the side entrances.

He was probably there on a routine inspection, like before. Nothing to worry about. But her pulse beat faster as she slipped inside. Over the familiar reverent hush of the library, she heard the drumming of footsteps on stone. Nazafareen trailed unseen behind. A few scholars poked their heads out of doorways to see what the commotion was about, then hastily withdrew like frightened turtles when they saw the Archon. When he reached Herodotus's study, he gave a silent signal. Two soldiers flanked the doorway. Nazafareen hid behind a rack of shelving and peeked through the honeycomb of square holes.

"Herodotus of Delphi!" the Archon said loudly. "Present yourself."

A moment later the old scholar appeared, blinking owlishly. He held a reed pen in his hand and ink stains speckled his white robes. "Archon Basileus. What an unexpected pleasure—"

The Archon cut him off.

"You stand accused of practicing witchcraft. These men witnessed it."

The two scholars Nazafareen had always disliked stepped forward.

"I saw him using spell dust, Archon," the Stork said in an oily, obsequious tone. "It was in the lecture hall, after the students left. We happened to be passing by. He cast a handful of dust into the air and began muttering an incantation."

"A darkness descended," the Weasel added, waving his arms dramatically. "I think he was trying to conjure some kind of devil!"

"This is ridiculous," Herodotus snapped, frowning at them.

"Search his study," the Archon Basileus ordered.

Two soldiers pushed past Herodotus. A moment later, they returned with a drawstring bag and gave it to the Archon. He examined the contents and his face grew smug.

"What do you say now, *Curator*?" Basileus made the last word a sneer.

Herodotus stood up straighter. "I've never seen that before in my life. These charges are outrageous."

Basileus gave a small, cold smile.

"I hereby charge you with treason and conspiracy in the name of the free citizens of this city." He gestured to the soldiers. "Take him."

The Archon's men seized Herodotus by the arms and began dragging him from the Library. Suddenly, a hand clamped over Nazafareen's mouth. She struggled, heart hammering against her ribs, and heard Javid's voice in her ear.

"What's happening?"

He let go of her.

"They've arrested Herodotus," she whispered. "They accused him of witchcraft."

"Holy Father."

"They framed him," she said bitterly. "Those soldiers barely searched his study at all. They knew exactly where to look."

"Why would they do that?"

Nazafareen felt sick. She pointed through one of the holes to the Stork and the Weasel, who stood whispering to each other.

"You see those two? They've never liked him. I heard them talking about him before and I didn't say anything. I should have." Her hand clenched into a fist. "I should have, Javid, and now it's too late." She drew a deep breath. "I have to tell the Archon."

"Did you actually hear them plotting against him?"

"Well, no. Not exactly. But I know they're behind it!"

"Lower your voice," he hissed. "Think, Ashraf. Who will believe you? You're just a servant. They're respected scholars. And if you come forward, the Archon will start asking questions about you. About both of us."

"But—"

"The ship leaves tomorrow and I intend to be on it." His face softened. "If there was any way to help, you know I'd be for it. But unless you have proof.... My advice is to keep your head down and don't talk to anybody. This place is a pit of vipers." He gave her a warning look. "And don't go around saying you think he's innocent. You'll just get us in trouble."

She scowled. "He *is* innocent."

"Then he can prove it at his trial. They do have laws here."

"But—"

"Please." He closed his eyes. "I'm begging you. Just go back to work. I know you like him. I do too. But it's none of our concern."

None of her concern. Perhaps Javid was right, but it still angered her.

"Fine." She grabbed her broom in a white-knuckled grip. "I hate this place."

"So do I. Listen, I have to get back to work. I just came to tell you the boat sails in the late morning tomorrow, so be ready. The captain won't wait around."

"I'll be ready."

He slipped away as the two scholars walked past. They glanced at her with narrowed eyes but didn't pause.

A pit of vipers.

Nazafareen sighed and started sweeping.

✦ 26 ✦

THE HIGH HOLDFAST

Galen had never known such pain.

He curled into a tight ball, his feet throbbing as they defrosted beneath a heavy layer of furs. The skin had gone from greyish-white to an angry red covered with suppurating black blisters. How he wished for the wooden numbness he'd felt when they carried him in. First had come a prickling sensation, followed by intense burning that left him gasping and gritting his teeth.

Everything had gone fine until he reached the mountains. The border with the Valkirin lands was only fifty leagues or so from House Dessarian and there were no other Danai settlements in between except for House Baradel, which lay to the east near the wind-whipped White Sea. When the trees thinned and he saw the smoky blue foothills rising up in the distance, Galen's heart beat faster.

He'd never been so far from home before. Somewhere amid the jagged peaks ahead sat the high holdfast of Val Moraine where his mother Mina lived as a captive. The thought of her gave him courage and he forded the River Arnor with a lighter heart, imagining their reunion and confident he was beyond the reach of Victor and the other Danai.

But Galen had fled wearing only the clothes on his back and soon realized he was hopelessly ill-prepared. He climbed and trekked and climbed some more, the land rising ever higher, the air growing thinner and colder. The Valkirin range seemed to pierce the heavens, a zone of perpetual snow riven by deep, treacherous crevasses. Had he been mortal, he would have died the first day. Galen used delicate probes of water and air to determine whether his next step would land on solid ground or only a thin veneer of ice. It worked but slowed his progress to a crawl.

In the forest, he survived on forage. But in this arctic wasteland, there was nothing but rock and infinite varieties of frozen water. Sometimes the clouds would part for a brief instant and the icy slopes would be dusted with silver-gold moonlight, and Galen found tears freezing on his cheeks for the splendor and majesty of it, even as he felt the life slowly leaching out of him.

He'd naively expected Val Moraine to be visible, clinging like an aerie to one of the peaks, but the range was much vaster than he'd imagined. And when the storms blew through, which they did more often than not, he could scarcely see his own hand in front of his face, let alone pick out a single holdfast across the endless leagues of knife-blade ridges.

At last Galen had sat down to rest and been unable to rise again. In his delirium, when the Valkirin scout found him, he'd thought it was Ellard come back from the dead, and wept and said he was sorry for murdering him. The scout thought he was mad.

And so Galen came to Val Moraine, where his frozen limbs defrosted, first with a tingle, then with roaring agony. He'd screamed for Mina. And now the door to his small chamber had just been thrown open and his mother was rushing toward him, laughing and crying.

She ran her hands over his face and hugged him fiercely to

her breast. Galen breathed in the familiar smell of her and felt himself tremble. All the vile things he'd done, all he'd endured, were worth it just to see her again. She was the one person in the world he loved besides Ellard, and she was the one person who loved him back. The loss of her had been a wound at the core of his being. It had eaten at him for years, until he feared it might swallow him whole. But now they'd found each other again.

Galen bit back the pain in his feet and composed himself. He didn't want her seeing the state he was in.

"How have you come here?" Mina asked in astonishment.

Galen chose his words carefully for they weren't alone. Two Valkirins stood near the door. They all looked alike to Galen: tall and silver-haired with an air of frosty arrogance. But one of the men—the younger one—had a cruel winding scar along his face. Rather than marring his beauty, the defect enhanced it. With his elegantly planed features and full mouth, he might have been too handsome otherwise. The scar made him interesting. He wore a leather coat and trousers in shades of white designed to blend with snow and ice. His emerald eyes looked strangely distant, moving in random patterns around the room. But Galen thought he was listening closely.

The older Valkirin had long hair and wore an iron sword at his hip. His flinty gaze fixed on Galen, his expression giving nothing away.

"I came for you," Galen said to his mother.

She gave him a tremulous smile. "Your timing couldn't be worse. You'll be lucky if they don't kill you. What were you thinking?"

Galen licked his lips. Glanced at the Valkirins.

"I was afraid they might hurt you."

"Why would they do that?"

"Because of that girl. Nazafareen. And what happened to Petur."

"No one would harm me here," Mina said, but Galen saw the lie in her eyes as she glanced quickly at the older man.

"Who is that?" Galen asked in a low voice.

"Eirik Kafsnjór. He's the lord of Val Moraine. The other is his son, Culach. I...I've been caring for him. He was blinded."

Galen knew who Eirik Kafsnjór was. Everyone did. He was famous—or infamous, depending on who you were talking to.

Besides which, Eirik was the one Galen had intended his message for. Galen had used a kestrel, which were accustomed to riding the strong winds over the mountains. Not every daēva could commune with birds, but Galen had the talent. Of all species, birds alone were creatures of air, earth and water and their minds could be joined in the Nexus—after a fashion. They were intelligent but fickle. They refused to carry parchment so you had to give them visual images, which meant the message had to be simple and concise. And if the bird became distracted or hit rough weather, it might never deliver the message at all. Much depended on the skill and experience of the daēva, and the willingness of the bird.

In Galen's case, he had simply given it an image of Nazafareen, the girl with one hand, standing before her home in the woods. He followed with an image of Tethys, to convey the idea of House Dessarian. Finally, he imagined the bird flying to Val Moraine, which Ellard had described for him in detail—though Galen had not told him why he needed the information.

The kestrel had studied him intently, intrigued by the mission. It was a pretty bird, with grey wings and a speckled brown back. It hopped into his hand and he gave it a beetle he'd found under a rock.

Fly, little sister. When you return, I will have more beetles, and perhaps even a mouse.

She'd cocked her head—tan with a grey brow—and hurtled upward into the wind, where she hung suspended for a long moment. Then with a flash of wings, she was gone.

The kestrel had not returned. Until the Valkirin assassin came, he'd been unsure if his message had ever arrived.

"I must speak with your son alone," Eirik said, striding to the bedside.

"Let me stay," Mina said quietly. "Please."

"No."

"Please—"

The one named Culach pushed off the wall and walked to Mina, sheltering her behind him.

"Why can't she stay?" he demanded.

"I have business with this boy. She'll wait in her quarters until called for."

"He's her son."

Eirik's eyes narrowed. "And he's my informant."

Mina looked at Galen in confusion. "What?"

"Never mind, mother," he said hastily. "I'll explain later. Please, just let us speak alone."

"No, I want to know now. What do you mean, *informant?*"

"Your little bastard betrayed House Dessarian," Eirik said with satisfaction.

"You're a liar." She turned to Galen, her face white. "He's lying. Isn't he?"

Galen wanted to crawl under the bed. He opened his mouth but no words came out.

"Enough," Eirik snapped. "We have business to attend to."

Mina looked like she wanted to slap them both but mastered herself.

"Come with me," Culach whispered in her ear. "You can see him later."

Galen's mother gave him a last heartbroken look mingled with disbelieving fury, then stalked out of the room. Culach followed her. The door closed and Galen was face to face with Eirik.

"You will tell me everything, boy," the lord of Val Moraine said coldly. "Everything."

~

In the corridor, Mina shook off Culach's hand.

"Did you know that too?"

"I didn't, I swear to you. Eirik said he received a message, but I had no idea it came from Galen."

Culach himself was still coming to terms with this turn of events. *Damn the boy!* It complicated all his plans.

"We can't talk here," he said. "Come to my rooms."

"So you can tear my clothes off?"

"Bloody hell, Mina, no," he protested, although the prospect was tempting. "Please, I'm begging."

She gave a small sigh and took his hand. They walked in silence back to Culach's chamber. When the door was closed, he heard her stalk over to the window.

"I'm sorry Galen came here and I'm sorry for what he did," he said. "But you still can't stay."

"There's no way out."

"There is. I'll take you to the stables. The abbadax know me. We'll saddle one and send it to House Dessarian."

"And what about my son?"

"I swear to look after him."

"I'm not leaving him in your father's clutches."

"Don't be a fool, Mina. I'm offering you a chance—"

Her voice sounded dead. "It's over, Culach. Eirik has already won."

He clenched his jaw. "Don't say that. Please let me help you."

"No."

"You don't understand. Eirik will kill you before he lets Victor have you."

"I know."

"Don't you even care?"

He felt her eyes on him. "I wish I could have healed you, Culach. You're a better man than I ever suspected."

He had no idea what to say to that. *If only I had my sight. If only I had my power. I'd kill my bastard of a father and then I'd be master of Val Moraine.* All pointless wishes. He couldn't even rage at her stubbornness. If Culach had a son, he wouldn't abandon him either, even if the boy was a lying, treacherous little snake like Galen.

His hearing was sharper, so he detected the pounding of boots in the corridor a few seconds before Mina did. Culach's pulse raced.

"They're coming," he said. "Damn it, seal the door."

"What?"

"Use your earth magic. Do it now!"

She seized his arm. "Culach—"

"Seal the fucking stone, Mina!"

Her grip tightened. Once, he would have felt the flows. Now all he heard was a splintering groan as she drew on her Danai talent to meld the doorframe into the thick keep walls. Culach held her up as she sagged against him. A small cry of pain escaped her lips.

Fists pounded on the door.

Agnar's voice. "Open up!"

"Go to hell," Culach snarled.

It was quiet for a minute while the Valkirins outside absorbed what Mina had done.

Then Eirik spoke, his voice hollow and muffled through the stone. "Think hard, Culach."

"I hope Victor guts you like a fish," Culach yelled.

Silence.

Then: "I hereby cast you out from this clan forever, Culach No-Name. You are no longer a Kafsnjór, nor a Valkirin. You are nothing."

Culach laughed. "That's the worst you can do?"

"No." His voice was eerily calm. "There will be worse. When I get inside, you'll find out just how much worse. I won't kill you.

But your Dessarian bitch?" He gave a thin, deranged cackle. "I only regret you won't be able to watch."

Culach faintly heard footsteps leaving. He carried Mina to his bed and gently laid her down on the furs. How small she was.

"Where's the damage?" he asked softly.

"No broken bones. It hurts, though. Bad."

"You're strong."

She took his hand and laid it against her cheek. "Don't go anywhere, okay?" she mumbled sleepily.

He barked a laugh that half-sounded like a sob. "I won't, Mina."

❧ 27 ❧

A MESSAGE

After a fitful sleep plagued by dreams of the Archon Basileus in his blood-red cloak, Nazafareen dressed in the tunic and trousers she'd been wearing when she crawled out of the fountain on the Acropolis. The night before, she'd sewn a secret pocket into the hem of her pants and safely tucked the griffin cuff inside. Her clothes were clean now, if a little threadbare. She left the servant's cotton shift neatly folded on her bed just as she'd found it.

Nazafareen had been waiting for this day, but she felt no joy at leaving Delphi. Her stomach churned as she said goodbye to Castor. He gave her a weak smile and wished her luck.

A pall hung over the Great Library of Delphi. She could feel it in the downcast eyes of the servants, the way the scribes clumped together in little groups, whispering and neglecting their work. Herodotus had been well-liked by everyone.

For the hundredth time, Nazafareen wished she could do something to help him. When Javid returned late the previous night, he said most of the philosophers thought the charges were false but they didn't dare challenge the Archon Basileus. The old historian's best hope would be with the popular assembly called the Ecclesia, which still held a degree of independence from the Pythia. For while the Basileus might have made the arrest, everyone knew he was carrying out the orders of the Oracle.

Javid had left early to buy some food for the journey. Only men were permitted in the agora until the afternoon, when women and young boys could do their shopping. Nazafareen crossed the wide avenue adjacent to the library and headed for the docks. They were easy to find because everything ran downhill toward the river. The people of Solis judged time by the moons, just like the daēvas, since they were the only large celestial bodies that moved. She knew she had some hours yet before the boat sailed, but couldn't stand being in the library another moment. If she saw those conniving scholars, Nazafareen didn't trust herself not to confront them.

She walked along, lost in dark thoughts, when she saw a girl beckon to her from the half-open gate of one of the stately homes that lined the avenues in this part of town. Nazafareen looked to either side but saw no one else. The girl pointed at her. Nazafareen made a quizzical face and the girl nodded, then slipped into the shadows.

The girl must have mistaken her for someone else. Still, it would be rude to ignore her. Nazafareen paused, then made for the gate and followed a flagstone path to a walled garden at the rear of the house. The light in Delphi slanted low over the buildings, as if the city were perpetually an hour away from sunset, and it dusted the plantings with rose and gold.

The girl waited on a stone bench. She was small with dark olive skin, and wore a wreath of ivy around her head and a short dress made of tawny animal skin. A wooden staff leaned against the bench.

"You're the new servant at the Library," she said.

Nazafareen didn't mention she'd just quit.

"Yes, so what?" she asked cautiously.

"I need you to carry a message."

"Today is my day off."

"A message to Herodotus."

Nazafareen's eyes narrowed. "Who are you?"

"A friend. The message is from his wife and it's urgent he gets it."

Her skepticism mounted. "He never mentioned a wife."

"Well, he wouldn't, would he?" the girl replied with a touch of impatience. "No one knows about her."

Nazafareen scowled.

I don't know what game this girl is playing, but I'm done being used.

"Take it to him yourself," she said, turning away. "I'm late to meet someone."

"Wait!" The girl leapt up, graceful as a cat. "I can't."

Nazafareen inched the cloak back from the hilt of her sword. "Why not?"

"I just can't." She glanced around. "It's too dangerous. They're watching."

Nazafareen felt like she was being tested by some inscrutable deity. If there was any way to help Herodotus, she'd promised herself to do it without hesitation. Now she was being offered that very chance. But she was afraid of the Pythia and even more afraid of missing the boat. Javid might wait for her, but he might not. Then she'd be stranded in Delphi again, this time alone and with no hope of escape.

"Who's *they?*"

The girl merely raised a sardonic eyebrow.

Nazafareen sighed. "How would I even get in to see him?"

"It's every condemned man's right to have visitors. That is the law of Delphi and even the Pythia cannot defy it or she will bring down the wrath of the Ecclesia."

They eyed each other. The girl glanced at Nazafareen's sword. With a casual movement, she picked up the staff and leaned on it.

She's not afraid of me. Not afraid of a blade. That's interesting.

"Why me?" Nazafareen demanded.

"You're new to the city. We can be sure you don't work for *her*."

There was no need to say who the girl meant.

"I don't have much time," Nazafareen said. "It would have to be right now."

The girl seemed relieved. "Now is perfect. He's permitted visitors, so I'm not asking you to take a risk."

Nazafareen doubted this. The girl didn't want to go herself and she might not be telling the truth about why. But Nazafareen knew she could never live with herself if she refused to do this one thing for Herodotus. She wouldn't even be leaving at all if it weren't for him.

"Where are they keeping him?"

"At the Temple of Apollo."

Nazafareen almost changed her mind at this. She assumed he'd be in the Polemarch's dungeons somewhere. She had no desire to put herself directly under the nose of the Pythia. It felt too much like tempting fate.

"Do you know where it is?"

Nazafareen sighed. "I know where it is."

The girl didn't wait for her answer. She thrust a scrap of paper into Nazafareen's palm, along with a silver coin.

"You don't have to pay me."

Nazafareen handed the coin back. The girl raised an eyebrow but took it, tucking it into a pocket.

"Are you sure it's nothing that could get me in trouble?" She disliked admitting she couldn't read it herself.

"I promise you that, Ashraf," the girl said solemnly. "I swear it by the gods, and may I be bound in blood and ashes to the deepest level of the Underworld and have my eyes torn out by the black talons of the Harpies if I speak false."

I'm a fool. Javid would kill me if he knew.

"All right then. I'll do it."

Nazafareen gave the girl one last nod and walked away, and it was only later she realized she'd never given her name.

❧ 28 ❧

BONDED

The river swept Darius along in pitch darkness.

He fought to stay at the center of the current as it wound through its thundering course, for although the rock walls had been worn smooth from eons of water, they were bruising when he found himself flung against them. Now, the channel had narrowed to arm's width. The ceiling nearly brushed his head. If it shrank any more he would surely drown.

Darius had already shed his cloak, though he still held tight to the rucksack. If he'd been a Marakai daēva, he might have had the strength to direct the flow of water, but he was a child of earth and it did him no good here. Still, he felt satisfaction that he'd deprived the beasts of their meal.

To Darius's relief, the river began to broaden. The current slowed and he floated on his back for a while. Then it narrowed again, picking up speed. Water roared in his ears as he floundered to keep his head above the surface. It grew tighter and tighter and then he was forced underwater. His lungs began to burn. Just when he knew he would drown, he saw a dim light overhead and started swimming for it. Moments later, his head broke the surface of a wide, muddy river. Gasping, he crawled from the shallows and pulled himself onto the bank.

Darius let the sun dry his clothes. Then he set out walking for the city of Delphi.

He'd forgotten how noisy mortals were. The sizzle of roasting fish, the clatter of wheeled conveyances, snatches of music punctuated by the pounding of hammers as the city expanded. Shouting, laughing, praying, haggling, ten thousand voices mingling into a vast beehive hum. He hadn't missed it exactly, but it didn't bother him. It was the sound of his boyhood in Karnopolis.

If Nazafareen was here, it might take him days to find her. Then again, people might remember a girl with only one hand. So Darius began asking. He started at the edge of the market and worked his way inward, stopping at each covered stall. No one had seen such a girl.

Until he reached a vendor of sweet rolls.

Yes, he knew a girl with one hand, she worked as a servant for the scholars at the library. Darius wanted to kiss the man. He got directions and hurried over. Would she be angry to see him? Glad? If he could just get her alone somewhere to talk. That's the thing to do, he thought nervously. And if she wished to find the Marakai, he would help her. In truth, he missed having a normal conversation. It hadn't all been bad—not all of it. There was the time at Karon Komai, when he'd argued with Victor and thrown a plate at him with the power, and then Nazafareen came to Darius's room to yell at him.... Well, he supposed that *had* ended rather badly. But not until the next day. The night before had been glorious.

He grinned. And then there was the time he'd been forced to dress as a woman, and Nazafareen as his betrothed. Tijah thought he was very pretty. And Myrri....

His smile died. *It will hurt Nazafareen to remember, but without pain, perhaps there is no joy either. Just as there is no good without evil.*

Darius hurried on. When he saw the stately marble library, he was impressed that Nazafareen had managed to get a job there. Inquiries in the kitchen revealed the disappointing news that she had quit that very morning.

"She said she was returning with her brother to Samarqand," the cook said.

Darius sighed. "Samarqand?"

"Why are you looking for Ashraf?" the man asked suspiciously.

So she was going by her dead sister's name.

"I'm just a friend."

"Well, you should have come earlier. The poor thing was starving by the time Herodotus brought her to us," he grumbled.

"Do you know how she planned to travel?"

"Dunno."

"Thank you for your time then."

"She's a nice girl. I hope you find her."

Darius went outside, thoroughly demoralized. To have come so close and miss her by hours! He sat down at the base of a statue of some naked god with a laurel wreath adorning his brow and thought. At least he knew she was alive and well. He rummaged in his rucksack for the map so he could estimate the distance to Samarqand, when his hand brushed the gold griffin cuff. Darius felt a tingling sensation in his left arm, followed by bone-deep pain. He cried out and a woman passing by looked at him sharply. Darius hunched over, turning his back to her, and clutched his arm. The hand emerging from the sleeve of his tunic had gone withered and grey.

He felt the bond flare to life inside him, but it was a cold, dead thing. Nazafareen wasn't there.

He breathed hard, mastering himself with a monumental effort.

What did it mean?

Darius's mind raced. The cuffs worked again in the sunlands. He couldn't believe she was dead when the cook had just seen her that morning. Could it be that she had her cuff but wasn't wearing it?

His head snapped toward the Acropolis like iron filings drawn to a magnet. The match of his cuff was up there somewhere. And maybe Nazafareen was too.

Darius started running again.

❧ 29 ❧
DANÍEL/DEMETRIOS

Thena was thinking about the witches.

She wasn't supposed to ask what the Pythia wanted them for, but she couldn't help speculating. They had seven at the temple now—five males and two females. Thena held the leashes of three. Very few initiates could wear the bracelet that controlled the collar. The Pythia said it required a special gift from the god.

She had simply appeared one day hours after the old Pythia died sweating and convulsing from a sudden fever. By centuries-old tradition, any woman—rich or poor, young or old—could be named the Oracle if she showed the ability to speak for Apollo. But the moment Thena had laid eyes on the commanding woman who walked barefoot into the temple, the smoke from the brazier wreathing her proud, exotic features, she'd known this would be the new Pythia.

And sure enough, the Archon Basileus had raised her the very next day.

"Go and fetch Demetrios," the Pythia said.

Thena, who had been kneeling at her feet, leapt up.

"Who is Demetrios?" the Polemarch asked.

He was a very fat man, as soft-seeming as the Archon Basileus was hard, but Thena knew that in fact he was not soft at all. He had wanted to do things to the witches that shocked even Thena. The Pythia had forbidden it. She wanted them whole.

"My latest acquisition," she said lazily. "A Valkirin."

"We already have several Valkirins," he grumbled. "And Danai. What we need is a Marakai."

"Yes, but they're hard to catch. They're never alone and they stick to their ships, as you well know. But I have an agent working on it. He is most diligent and I'm confident he will handle the matter."

The Pythia sat atop her tripod, a reminder of her status and power. She'd made the Polemarch stand. He looked uncomfortable but Thena knew he'd never dare complain about it.

"I've heard reports of troubles between the clans," he said. "Over a mortal girl."

At the door, Thena paused, curious.

"Troubles?" the Pythia prompted.

"They claim she can work fire."

The Pythia didn't react, but Thena, who knew her better than anyone, saw the sudden tension in her spine.

"That's impossible," she said calmly.

"Of course it is. I'm merely conveying the rumors. Supposedly she was living with the Danai, but no one knows where she is now."

"Who are your sources?"

"Traders in Tjanjin who heard it from a Marakai ship captain, who in turn heard it from a witch at Val Moraine." Rings flashed on his chubby fingers as he made a dismissive gesture. "Like I said, it's just a rumor. Some wild exaggeration no doubt."

The Pythia noticed Thena hovering by the door. She said nothing, but one look from those blue eyes and Thena hurried from the chamber.

A mortal who could work fire? Thena had never heard of such

a thing. She knew they used spell dust in Samarqand, but the Persians were heathens. Magic was a filthy thing. Only the gods had the right to manipulate the elements.

Thena strode across the plaza, her belted cotton shift swishing around her strong legs. From the top of the Acropolis, she could see for leagues, past the distant edges of the farms to the rocky plain. A few fluffy white clouds drifted in the blue sky just before it deepened to the bruised color of the Umbra. Thena had been born on one of those farms. She supposed her family lived there still, but she hadn't seen them in years. She'd known from an early age that she was meant to have a life of devotion to the gods.

She still remembered being a wide-eyed girl on her father's knee and hearing the tale of how the three sisters, Artemis, Hecate and Selene, had conspired to ensorcel the sun god Apollo, halting his chariot in its path across the sky because they were greedy and it wasn't enough for them to rule for only half the day. So they lured him to a rendezvous and cast a spell on him. Thus the sisters came to rule the darklands unchallenged.

But someday, when the witches were defeated (for naturally, they were the chief allies of the moon goddesses), Apollo would wake from his trance and the normal passage of days and seasons would be restored.

From the moment she'd learned the truth of how the world came to be riven between Nocturne and Solis, Thena had decided she would serve the poor enchanted sun god and do everything she could to free him. And if that required her to traffic with the witches themselves, she wouldn't shirk at her duty.

When Thena opened the door to Demetrios's room, she found him dressed and waiting. He'd known she was coming, just as she'd known he was awake and still sore in his left shoulder from the shackles. Thena had removed them two days ago and covered the windows with shutters as a reward for good behavior. His grass-green eyes absorbed the faint sunlight trickling through the cracks, reflecting it like a cat. Never had he looked so feral.

Demetrios would obey her, Thena was certain of it, and yet there was still something dangerous about him, something that made her uneasy. She felt his sinful magic pulsing at the edge of her awareness.

He couldn't use it against her, not with the iron collar circling his throat. He could only touch the elements if she gave him permission and the Pythia had forbidden it.

They stared at each other for a moment.

"The Oracle wishes to see you," Thena said.

He bowed his head. "As you command."

Thena gave a curt nod. They walked in silence to the audience chamber. The Polemarch blanched when he saw Demetrios—witches had that effect even on generals—but he knew about the bracelet and collar and understood their purpose. To Thena's surprise, the Pythia signaled that she should stay. So she knelt at the Oracle's feet next to Demetrios.

Thena expected her to ask about the mortal who could work fire, but her next words came as a surprise.

"The god tells me there's a witch in the city," the Pythia said.

The Polemarch gave her a sharp look. Demetrios kept his eyes on the floor. It was not a question, therefore he would not speak. Thena had trained him well.

"Come closer," the Pythia ordered.

Demetrios stood in a lithe movement and walked forward until he was within a foot of the tripod. The Pythia reached out and stroked his cheek. His face registered not a whit of emotion.

"Is he here to rescue you?" she asked gently.

"I don't know."

The Pythia made a small gesture to Thena. A second later, Demetrios writhed on the ground, his jaw locked against a scream. The witch's body would show no mark afterward. But through the collar, Thena could make him feel anything she chose. The Pythia allowed it to go on for a while, then made another small gesture. Demetrios sobbed as Thena halted the pain. His pale skin had turned grey.

"I'll ask again. Are you certain you don't know?"

"Please, I don't, Oracle." He reached for the hem of her gown and the Pythia's mouth pursed in distaste.

"Never has a witch come willingly to Delphi," she mused. "There must be a compelling reason for it."

Thena put her arm around Demetrios's broad shoulders and helped him to his feet. He leaned his head against her. She felt the wetness of his tears and stroked his hair. It was good to have a firm hand, but one must also know when to show kindness. She didn't think he knew anything. She'd had him for more than a year. If his brethren had somehow figured out where the missing witches were being taken, it wasn't because he had communicated with them. So he was blameless.

"This witch, he's alone?" the Polemarch demanded. Sweat glistened in the folds of fat around his eyes.

"Yes. He just arrived." The Pythia gave him an icy look. "I want him found."

"Do you know what he looks like?"

She shook her head.

The Polemarch licked his lips, a darting, serpentine movement Thena found revolting. "That makes the task more difficult."

"He'll give himself away. Tell your soldiers to watch for anything unusual."

"What if he's here to harm you, Oracle? I'll order an extra contingent of men to guard the temple." He paused. "Now what of the scholar?"

"We're keeping him in one of the empty animal stalls. I want you to search the library, and his house as well. Bring me anything related to the witches—anything at all, but especially if it pertains to the early history of the clans just after the war."

"I have some of it, although he seems to have hidden the most recent find."

"What does Basileus say?"

"Herodotus was chattering about a scroll he'd found only yesterday. But it wasn't in his office and he's refusing to speak to us."

The Pythia smiled. "Perhaps he'll talk to me."

THE MAIDEN KEEP

Victor came within inches of missing the secret way into Val Moraine.

The company of Danai was on their fifth day in the mountains. They'd followed a rough map Victor had drawn from memory based on the description he'd been given by Culach's sister, Neblis. He wondered if it would still be there after all this time. The Valkirins might have blocked it off. The mountain might have shifted.

Victor shared a look with Delilah. Her sapphire eyes were the only visible part of her. Everything else was wrapped in multiple layers of cloth with a heavy cloak thrown on top. Frost rimed the aperture around her mouth, glittering in the starlight like diamond dust. She hadn't spoken in hours but he knew what she was thinking. If he was wrong, they'd all freeze to death and it wouldn't be long in coming. The same earth magic that nurtured the Danai forest also kept the brutal cold out. But the Valkirin lands had no such protection. Here in the high passes, the frigid darkness cut like a blade. Victor didn't know how anything managed to survive, although he'd heard the thin howling of wolves when Selene rose above the peaks.

They stood in a saddle between two ridges. Victor blew on his numb fingers. He found the Nexus and gently probed the snow ahead, checking for crevasses and weakness in the shelf that could trigger an avalanche. He'd learned the necessity of this the hard way after Ronan had tumbled to his death.

By his calculations, the old mine entrance was in the valley on the other side of the next ridge. But then he sensed a small cavity in the mountainside. The beginning of it was blocked by a rockfall, but a gentle probe with air revealed that it opened into a tunnel. It was dumb luck he'd sensed it. If he'd stopped twenty paces further on, he might never have noticed.

He raised a fist and the other daēvas hurried over. Victor used his hand to clear away the crust of snow covering the entrance. It was only about a foot thick, although it camouflaged the tunnel perfectly. Behind it, darkness yawned. Victor pulled the scarf from his mouth.

"There's a cave-in. I'll try to clear it."

He drew deeply on earth power, felt it resonate in his bones. Too much and he'd be reduced to a bloody lump of flesh. But Victor was very strong and could tolerate a good deal of pain. Only one daēva was stronger and that was his son, Darius. Even so, he struggled to budge the weight of the rock. The injuries he'd taken from the chimera were only half-healed, including a nasty bite on his arm that festered until Tethys gave him a poultice of herbs from her garden.

Delilah's lithe form stepped up next to him. She drew power and helped him pulverize the tightly packed rock. So did a few others. Working together, they cleared the way in a matter of minutes. Victor stepped inside first. The tunnel was tight, with a low ceiling and narrow walls. Since his long imprisonment at Gorgon-e Gaz, Victor hated enclosed spaces. His cell had been much like this: dark and chill. The guards had never broken him, although they'd tried their best. He'd been starved and chained. He'd seen others die and be driven mad. They'd punished him with the cuff again and again. He'd spat in their faces.

They'd never broken him, but he wasn't the same. He had a deep, abiding claustrophobia now. His heart hammered in his chest as he stood in the entrance, looking at the downward-sloping passage. He'd known this was coming, but the oppressive atmosphere nearly unmanned him. Then he sensed the presence of Mithre beside him.

Of all the daēvas Victor had gathered for this unsanctioned mission, only Mithre truly understood. He too had been held at Gorgon-e Gaz. His wolfish gaze took in the tight, dark tunnel.

"Well, they do call her the Maiden Keep," he said finally. "I suppose we should have expected a close fit."

Victor gave a shaky laugh and forced himself to start walking.

The Danai wound their way into the mountain, moving from long-disused tunnels to others that were wider and had smoothly sculpted walls. They encountered no one. Victor held out a lumen crystal to light the way. After a few hours, they reached the catacombs where the Valkirins kept their dead in stone niches carved from the rock, jade eyes open and covered in frost. Victor passed them without interest. Soon enough, Eirik and his son would join their eternal slumber.

The Valkirins would be expecting retaliation—but they didn't even know about the passage he'd found. Neblis had made it herself to sneak out and meet him in the forest so long ago. And Val Moraine had suffered heavy casualties at the lake. The holdfast was already dying. Victor would simply deliver the final blow.

At each junction, he used a little earth magic to orient himself. The tunnel entrance lay several leagues from the holdfast and the intervening distance contained a maze of passages branching out in all directions. A few times, he heard the scurrying of small animals in the darkness, the rasp of claws on stone. Rusted scraps of mining equipment sat abandoned near chutes a man would have to wriggle to pass through. The thought of it made his skin crawl.

Victor focused on the dark passage on front of him. It couldn't be much farther now. The tunnels were frigid, but cold sweat coated his skin beneath the woolen layers. He would face Culach at last. Victor knew the Valkirin was an expert swordsman and very strong in air. He smiled grimly. It would be an interesting match.

Darius should be at my side, but perhaps I was too hard on him. I did terrible things for love too.

Victor glanced back at Delilah. She'd pushed her hood off and her hair fell in a wild black mane down her back.

The Valkirins would regret ever raising a hand against House Dessarian. They'd be living in caves by the time he finished with them. Victor prayed that both his sons still lived, but if he'd learned one thing from the empire, it was that if you wanted justice, you'd better take it yourself.

❧ 31 ❧

THE PRISONER HERODOTUS

Nazafareen hurried through the streets, the message tucked into her sleeve. It was a festival day and a high-spirited procession of young girls passed by carrying loaves of bread and jars of wine. They were cheered on by crowds of cheerfully drunk bystanders. Nazafareen slipped through the press of bodies and cut across a public park where people had gathered to watch a play—this one a comedy, judging by the gales of laughter—despite the dark clouds mounding in the sky toward the Umbra.

As she darted up the steps to the Acropolis, she passed a group of women dancing and spinning with abandon at the base of the staircase. One turned and caught her eye, and she thought the woman might have winked at her, but then the crowd surged around them and the dancers were lost to view.

Selene peeked above the city wall and Nazafareen knew she had until the moon touched the flat roof of the Philosophers Guild to get to the docks, which gave her about two hours. When she reached the plaza, she paused, then approached two soldiers who stood outside the temple, doing her best to look like a frightened servant girl.

"I carry a message for the prisoner Herodotus," she said, keeping her eyes on the stone paving blocks.

"Wait here."

The soldier strode off and returned a few minutes later with his captain. Nazafareen's heart sank as she recognized the burly man who had dragged them from the fountain. She let her hair fall into her face and prayed he wouldn't recognize her.

"What's your name, girl?" he demanded.

"Ashraf," she whispered. "I'm a servant at the library."

"Show me this message." He thrust a hand out.

Nazafareen gave him the scrap of paper. He scanned it with narrowed eyes. She wished she could have read it herself. What if the note said something treasonous? To her vast relief, he handed it back.

"Escort her to the prisoner," the captain said.

They crossed the plaza to another building. She tried not to look at the brazen bull as they passed, tried not to remember the screams so horribly transformed into bellows. Nazafareen felt her own anger rising at the barbarity of it. She drew a steadying breath. And then she was standing before a small, barred window, with Herodotus on the other side. The faint smell of straw and animals drifted out.

"Make it quick," the soldier said, moving away to stand with hands loosely clasped.

Nazafareen nodded.

"Ashraf," Herodotus exclaimed, peering through the bars. "What are you doing here?"

Her heart broke as she looked at him. He had a black eye and his usually neat beard was caked with dried blood.

"I'm so terribly sorry," she whispered. "I carry a message from your wife."

She gave him the note. Herodotus read it once, and then again. His eyes grew watery and Nazafareen looked away in embarrassment.

"Thank you for coming, my dear," he said. "Now you must get away from this place."

She knew he was right, and yet Nazafareen couldn't make her feet move.

"What are they going to do to you?" she asked.

"It depends. I have friends in the Ecclesia. They will argue on my behalf."

"Will it work?"

He smiled slightly. "Probably not."

She felt her own eyes stinging and roughly swiped a sleeve across her face. "Isn't there anything anyone can do?"

"Go, child."

"Those two scholars framed you up, didn't they?"

He turned back.

"I know they did. I wish I could prove it. Why do they hate you?"

"It's nothing that concerns you, Ashraf," Herodotus said gently. He glanced pointedly toward the soldier. "I thought you had a ship to catch."

Her shoulders sagged. "I suppose I do." She took his hand through the bars and gave it a squeeze. "Thank you for all you've done for me."

Herodotus smiled. "Men's fortunes are on a wheel, which in its turning suffers not the same man to prosper forever. My fate is in the gods' hands now, my dear. Fare well."

Nazafareen trudged across the plaza. She felt ill with worry for the old librarian and furious that she couldn't do anything about it. She wished the daēvas *would* conquer Delphi. Even the Valkirins couldn't be as bad as the Pythia and the Archon Basileus. She was rounding the corner of the temple when a hand grabbed her arm. Nazafareen raised a fist to punch her assailant in the face when she saw it was Javid. He made a shushing motion and pulled her around the back of the temple into the deep shadow of a pillar.

"How did you find me?" she hissed.

"I ran into the cook at the agora. He saw you coming up the steps." Javid paused and glanced around. "He said someone was at the library asking about you," he whispered.

She frowned. "Me? Are you sure?"

"Unless there's another girl with only one hand, new to the city," Javid replied grimly.

"One person or more?"

"Just one, I think."

"Do you know what they looked like?"

"He didn't say. I'm sorry, I should have asked. Is it one of your relatives?"

She bit her lip, wishing she could tell him the truth. "I don't know, Javid."

What if it was another Valkirin assassin? But surely the cook would have remarked on it. Nearly everyone in Delphi had dark hair and eyes, and olive skin.

Her heart beat faster. Darius? He would blend in. But how could he have found her? Delilah thought she was going to Samarqand. It was probably just the girl who'd given her the message. Still, she couldn't leave without knowing.

"I have to ask the cook. It might be my...older brother."

"Won't he try to take you home?"

"No, we were always close. But he could have come looking. He's stubborn that way."

Javid blew out a long breath. He glanced at the approaching storm. "Fine, but we'd better hurry. The ship leaves in less than an hour, and they won't wait for us. I already gave the captain all our money to hold the berths."

Impulsively, she got up on her tiptoes and kissed his cheek. It was soft as a girl's.

"Thank you, Javid."

He rolled his eyes, but his face reddened a little. "Don't worry about it." He peeked around the corner of the temple. "Looks like the coast is clear. Let's go."

❧ 32 ❧

QUARRY

The three chimera slipped unnoticed through the city gates.

Amid the noise and general tumult of the festival, no one saw a thing as they slunk through back streets and alleys, transparent bodies now brown as mudbrick, now white as marble. No one saw them, but they left their mark.

In a tavern called the Villa of Good Fortune, a petty squabble escalated into the drawing of blood. Two streets away, a young man spurned by his lover suddenly decided to drink a cup of poison. A group of children who had been giving scraps to a mangy dog turned ugly and started pelting it with stones.

No one saw the chimera, but they left a trail of death and woe.

When the quarry escaped underground, they'd fanned out, speeding across the rocky plain in different directions. The scent had been lost.

But then the wind shifted, and the one who'd turned west caught the stink of him again—faint but unmistakable. It gave a long, high-pitched howl, summoning its brothers. The other pack had peeled away days before to pursue its own quarry—a female— but she wasn't their concern.

Malice burned in their hearts. He was close now. Three sets of eyes turned toward the Acropolis. Very close.

✾ 33 ✾

AN UNBROKEN PITCHER

D arius stood at the edge of the plaza and watched red and yellow flames dance in the braziers flanking the stairway. He wasn't terrified of fire anymore. It fascinated him. He'd seen daēvas consumed by it, including one he'd loved like a sister, but she had gotten too close. He wouldn't make the same mistake.

The cuff around his wrist told him Nazafareen must be nearby. To his intense frustration though, it wasn't as precise as if she'd been bonded to him. He scanned the Acropolis, heart pounding with anticipation.

Of all the places in Delphi, she had to come to the temple of the fire god. *Holy Father, Nazafareen could be a difficult woman to love sometimes.* But then it seemed his luck was changing at last, for Darius saw a flash of honey-colored hair disappear behind the pillars of the temple portico. He strode across the plaza, passing a marble fountain with a pair of golden eagles spewing water from their beaks. Soldiers watched from the shade of a towering plane tree. None challenged him. During afternoon hours, the temple was open to all.

He hurried around the corner, hoping to see Nazafareen, but instead nearly bumped into another young woman. She had striking looks, with dark hair and olive skin. Her mouth opened in an O of surprise as he stepped into her path. The clay pitcher in her hand went flying. Without thinking, Darius reached out and grabbed the handle.

He knew right away that he should have let it smash on the paving stones and cursed his stupidity. He saw in her eyes that he'd moved too quickly, too gracefully. But then her cheeks flushed and she smiled.

"You have nimble hands," she said. "Thank you."

Darius relaxed. She was just a mortal. She'd probably never seen a daēva in her life.

"Perhaps you can help me," he said.

The young woman inclined her head amiably. "If it's within my power."

"I'm looking for a girl."

She raised an eyebrow.

"My cousin."

"There are many girls here."

"This one lacks a right hand. She had an accident as a child."

Her dark eyes lit up. "Why yes, I have seen her. Just a moment ago." Her smile widened. "I'm in a bit of a hurry, but I'll show you if you like."

Darius smiled back, suddenly nervous. Would Nazafareen be glad he came? Or angry? She had a bad temper when it erupted, which was mainly if she thought some injustice had been committed. He also wished to know who this *brother* was the cook had spoken of.

Darius handed her back the pitcher. "Thank you."

He followed her into the cool dimness of the temple. Rush torches burned along the walls, but he'd had years of practice resisting the lure of fire. They descended a winding stone staircase. He smelled incense and sweet pine resin.

"Where is she?"

"Just up here." Dimples pocked her rosy cheeks as she gave him another reassuring smile. "She came to give an offering to Apollo."

Darius stopped. Something was wrong. He felt it in his bones. The passage was deserted. There were no other pilgrims here, no worshippers. Why would Nazafareen come so deep into the temple? She'd renounced her own faith ages ago and he somehow doubted she'd adopted a new one in such a short time. The cook said she intended to leave the city. He grabbed the girl's sleeve.

"What game are you playing?"

She looked flustered. "No game. I told you—"

He leaned in to tell her he wouldn't be going any further when her hand came up. She blew and a cloud of fine, sparkling dust hit his face. Darius coughed, throat stinging. He heard her murmuring words and then sight and hearing deserted him. It was like sinking to the bottom of the sea. He tried not to panic, but his heart beat wildly.

"Hurry!"

"He'll come to any moment now!"

Someone shoved him hard from behind and Darius fell to hands and knees. Fury bloomed in his chest. They had no idea who they were dealing with. He reached through the Nexus and seized earth, intending to pull the Temple of Apollo down around their ears. The ground began to tremble.

"Hurry!"

His vision slowly returned, though it remained blurry around the edges. A shadow moved to his left and Darius lashed out with air, knocking it to the ground. He drew deeper, filled to bursting with power, when a metal collar snapped shut around his neck. The Nexus winked out like a snuffed candle flame. An instant later, agony coursed through his limbs. An alien presence surged into his mind. He felt her fear, mingled with excitement.

Darius found himself on his back, looking up at the girl in

white. Tendrils of dark hair had torn free of her braid, framing her oval face as she stared down at him with a look of triumph. Soldiers flanked her on either side.

"Tell the Pythia we've caught her witch," she said.

❧ 34 ❧

THEY BEND LIGHT

"W hat are you doing here anyway?" Javid asked as they crossed the plaza.

"Some girl found me after I left the library to meet you. She wanted me to carry a message to Herodotus."

He shook his head and made the sign of the flame, a quick touch of forehead, lips and heart. "You're lucky they didn't arrest you too. Did you see him at least?"

Nazafareen scowled. "Yeah. That evil woman is probably going to burn him like she did the other poor philosopher."

"Keep your voice down." He glanced at the group of soldiers ahead but his expression was sympathetic. "That's horrible."

"I know. I wish I could do something." Her gaze roved across the plaza, pausing on the stairs. She had a funny feeling in the pit of her stomach. Just like in the Umbra.

"Javid—"

They both turned as a soldier came running full tilt out of the temple. He gesticulated wildly at the others.

"Holy Father, what's happening now?" Javid moaned.

"No idea, but we'd better get out of here."

She started walking quickly. The fountain lay just ahead, and beyond it the stairs leading down from the Acropolis. The soldiers under the tree scrambled to their feet and dashed for the temple. Nazafareen ducked her head as they came close but it was too late.

"You!"

It was the captain who'd read her message. The one who'd hauled them out of the fountain. Now that she was with Javid, standing before the very scene of their crime, he had no trouble remembering her face.

"Run," Javid hissed.

They turned and dashed for the stairs. Nazafareen glanced back. Two of the soldiers continued toward the temple, but the rest were in hot pursuit.

"We'll make for the alleys near the docks," Javid panted. "We can lose them there."

Nazafareen nodded. She'd always been fast and figured she could outrun a bunch of men in little skirts. They hit the top of the stairs and flew down three at a time. Suddenly, Javid skidded to a stop, grabbing her arm. The sky overhead had grown dark as pitch, but the clouds hadn't yet reached the western horizon and the sun shone directly in her eyes. Nazafareen raised a hand to shade her forehead. It took her a moment to make out what he was looking at.

Three shimmering shapes loped up the staircase.

"Holy Father, I feel them," Javid muttered, his eyes wild.

They passed in and out of shadow and seemed the same color as the stone, but now she could see the faint distortion of light, like ripples across running water.

"I do too," Nazafareen whispered.

Her heart clenched in fear. Dark thoughts tumbled through her mind. The dead Valkirin, and how she'd kicked his corpse. The broken gate. How close she'd come to killing Javid. The bellows of the bull. Roasting flesh. Death and misery.

Nazafareen looked back. The soldiers stood at the top of the stairs, swords drawn.

She closed her eyes. She could feel the creatures—not just the evil miasma they brought, but the complex wards that gave them a semblance of life. No blade would harm them. No magic could stop them.

Except hers.

Break them, a voice in her head screamed.

Her hand shook.

The soldiers charged down the steps. Below, the beasts (*chimera*, the voice growled) devoured the distance, leaping up a flight at a time. Each was the size of a young lion.

Forgive me, she thought, unsure who she meant the words for, and let go of the leash on her magic. It had been straining to break free. Now a lance of white flame leapt from her palm. It struck the first chimera and she heard a faint popping sound, followed by a gush of pinkish, dirty water. The others didn't slow.

Nazafareen started walking down the steps. Again, she raised her hand, and the second chimera dissolved. Shouts erupted behind, but the cold rage that burned in her belly had only one focus. She waited and watched the last one come. She saw it clearly now. The fine network of veins and arteries that carried whatever dark matter it used for blood. The pulsing organs and teeth like needles of ice. It leapt for her throat, and died in a blaze of white flame. The stench of its offal filled her nostrils, rotten as a week-old fish.

"Holy Father."

Javid stood next to her. He was repeating the phrase over and over like an incantation. She saw fear in his eyes, but he hadn't abandoned her. Nazafareen shook loose from her trance and they started down again, but the stairs were covered in the ichor the chimera had left behind. Nazafareen was a full flight ahead when she realized Javid had slipped and fallen. He rolled on the ground, clutching his leg.

"Javid!"

She started back up the stairs but the soldiers reached him first. Four of them lifted him off the ground and rushed back toward the Acropolis. The last two glared at her for a long moment.

She raised a hand, fighting back nausea, and they turned tail and ran. She screamed Javid's name as they disappeared over the hilltop.

"Cowards!" Nazafareen shouted.

It had been a bluff anyway. The soldiers carried no talismans. Her breaking magic was useless against them.

Nazafareen felt the old familiar sickness coming on. She spat, and it sizzled when it struck the stone.

Enough, the voice whispered. *If you die, you'll never help him.*

A small crowd had gathered at the base of the stairs. They gave way before her, staring in superstitious dread and jabbing forked fingers at her but not daring to come close. Nazafareen kept her eyes straight ahead. Down at the docks, the barge would be readying to sail downriver, but she couldn't leave Javid in the Pythia's clutches.

I'll find a way to save him, she thought, stumbling into the warren of side streets. *I just need to rest for a bit first. A quick rest.*

Nazafareen hunched her shoulders, wandering aimlessly. Her legs trembled. Colors seemed too bright, the shapes of things distorted. She swept a hand across her brow, expecting to feel sweat, but it came away dry. *How strange.* Finally, on the verge of collapse, she looked up and dimly realized her feet had brought her to their old alley.

Nazafareen crawled to the end and fell into a dark corner.

Just rest for a bit.

Her eyes slid shut and blackness descended.

35

THE COLD CELLS

Eirik kept his word and returned with reinforcements. The Valkirins managed to shake some dust loose, but failed miserably to pry the door open. Earth and air were elements in perfect opposition and they lacked the strength, even combining their efforts. Eirik cursed his son a final time. Then he left.

Culach lay down next to Mina, who'd fallen into a deep slumber. *Someone* was going to get in eventually. If it was Eirik, Mina would die. If it was Victor, Culach would die.

Not a very good bargain.

But they still had some time left. Whether it was minutes or hours, he didn't know. Culach was just glad he could spend it with her.

He thought about Petur and he thought about his mother, Ygraine, who he never knew but who'd given him her eyes and love of flying. He even thought about Gerda, sitting alone in her frigid rooms. He'd meant to go see her again, but he hadn't gotten around to it. Now he wished he had. Perhaps she was right to be bitter. He wondered if Gerda had ever been young and in love, but it was nearly impossible to imagine her as a girl.

He knew by the deep pitch of the wind and the way the sound rose and fell that it was blowing from the east, from the White Sea. Culach had ridden an abbadax over it once when Artemis returned. She was full and round, twice as large as the other moons. On a normal day, the swells below would have been rough. But under the influence of the giant moon, they looked like small mountains, the trenches between them deep as valleys and cobwebbed with spindrift. The wind had torn at his hair as his mount soared lower and lower, nearly brushing the wave crests. Culach had laughed, full of wild abandon. They'd gone further north than he ever had before. He knew he had to turn back before his mount tired too much to make the return journey, but he'd wanted to keep going. To see what lay beyond the horizon. She would continue if he wanted her to. Finally, he *had* turned back. But part of him always wondered what might have happened if he hadn't.

If he could live one moment forever, it might be that one. When he and Ragnhildur flew out to sea together under the giant moon. Not the victorious battles or drunken fistfights, although he'd enjoyed those too. Just that one moment, before he played it safe.

Or it might be this one right now.

Mina stirred beside him and mumbled something. He found her braid and wove it through his fingers. She fit perfectly against his chest. Culach nuzzled her neck. Suddenly, she bolted upright.

"Galen!" she cried.

He felt her leave the bed. Culach propped himself on one elbow.

"It's all right, Mina. Calm down."

"It's not all right. Nothing is *all right*."

She paced to the window, then back to the bed.

"He could be dead."

"Eirik won't kill him. Galen's on their side, remember?"

She slapped him and he caught her arm, pulling her tight

against him. The top of her head fit just under his chin. Mina struggled like a wild thing so he let her go. His head rocked back as she slapped him again, and then her hands tangled in his hair, pulling him to her mouth. She kissed him hard and shoved him down on the bed.

"I hate you," she said, her breath hot in his ear.

"As long as you don't pity me."

"I've never pitied you. You're an asshole."

But her mouth was smiling against his despite herself. His hands roamed under her thick woolen dress, exploring her back and hips. Compared to Katrin, she was tiny, but her soft curves were delicious. When her tongue found the hollow of his throat, Culach moaned. An avalanche of sensation overwhelmed him. He tipped his head back, trying to catch his breath. Mina straddled his hips.

"You're not broken everywhere," she observed.

He laughed hoarsely. "I don't want to hurt you."

Her fingers touched his mouth. "Hush."

Culach let Mina undress him, which she took her time about. He couldn't see her, but his other senses were heightened to an almost painful degree. The heat of her skin, the salt taste of her sweat. When she finally took him inside her, he felt fire run through his veins, scalding and exquisite. And this time, Culach didn't care if the whole world burned.

HE WOKE TO SHOUTS IN THE HALL, THE RING OF SWORDS, AND finally, the cracking of stone.

"Looks like Victor wins the prize," Culach muttered.

In his heart, he'd been praying for the Danai to come before his father did. At least Victor would give him a quick death and take Mina home where she belonged. He rolled out of bed and groped for his clothes.

"Do you see my sword anywhere, darling?" he asked. "I'd prefer to die with something sharp in my hand."

"Don't be a complete idiot," Mina snapped. "Get behind me."

Culach tried to protest. Then the door shattered. He heard chunks of it roll across the floor.

"Pants?"

Mina thrust a bundle into his hands and he hastily pulled them on.

"Stay back," Mina growled.

Several people entered the room, all of them breathing hard.

"Pick up your sword, you murdering piece of shit, or I'll kill you where you stand."

Culach buttoned his trousers, the cold air raising goosebumps on his skin.

"Give me a minute, Victor. You certainly know how to make a dramatic entrance."

"Get away from him, Mina."

"Fuck you."

Culach smiled.

An unfamiliar, infinitely cold voice said: "Don't talk to my husband that way." And then, "Something's wrong with him, Victor."

"Nothing a few holes can't fix."

"Look at his eyes."

Culach straightened his spine and turned toward Victor's voice. He might be big for a Danai, but Culach was still an inch or two taller. "Would you like to examine me? Come a little closer."

"Gods, he's blind," Victor said in disgust.

"How'd you get in, anyway?"

"Your sweet sister told me a way."

Culach shook his head. "She was always terrible at keeping secrets."

"Can I still execute him?" Victor mused. "He deserves it."

"I have no objection."

That was Victor's new wife.

"You make a charming pair. Oh, did you happen to kill Eirik yet?" Culach asked. "Please say yes."

Victor ignored him. "I don't know." He sounded deeply unhappy. "It seems wrong somehow."

"That's because it is," Mina snarled. "And if you try, I'll crush you with a block of stone."

For a long moment, the only sound was the low, steady roar of the east wind.

"Get on your knees. Now."

Culach assumed Victor was talking to him. He held his hands up and dropped to the floor.

"Bind him."

Rough hands yanked his arms behind his back. He felt cords bite into his wrists.

"This is going better than I expected."

"Shut up." Victor stood over him. "Gods, you're a mess."

"Don't be cruel. I bathed just this morning, with soap and everything—"

Victor kicked him in the ribs and Culach shut up.

"Put him with the other."

"Where's Galen?" Mina demanded. "I want to see him."

"He went after Darius." Victor's tone softened a touch. "Don't worry, Mina. He's a man now. He can handle himself."

"What are you *talking* about?" she snapped. "Galen is here. I..." He heard a sharp intake of breath as she realized her mistake.

"How could he be here? I saw him off myself. He was heading for the Umbra."

A long, deadly silence followed.

"That lying bastard," Victor said in a low voice. "Search the keep. I want him found."

Two sets of boots ran for the door.

"Victor..."

The naked plea in Mina's voice made Culach wince. He felt

sorry for the kid. Galen was about to find himself in a world of pain. Possibly even worse than Culach.

"He just wanted to see his mother," Culach said. "Go easy on him."

Victor gave him another kick, harder this time. "I'm surprised you're standing up for him after what he did."

"What do you mean?"

"The killer you sent? Galen put an arrow in his chest."

Culach felt cold. "Galen shot Petur?"

Not Mina's son. It couldn't be.

Victor gave a bitter laugh. "It seems the little shit betrayed us both."

Culach closed his eyes. The cords were so tight his hands throbbed, but he barely felt it. Any residual satisfaction he felt at Victor's heartbreak evaporated in a wave of remorse.

I'm damned. Well and truly damned. An innocent man is probably dead, and Petur's murderer is here at Val Moraine. I was standing next to him. Culach felt physically ill.

"Galen said Darius did it. That's why we—" he cut himself off.

"Sent the chimera?" Victor grated.

A large hand seized Culach's hair, tipping his head back.

"You need to talk. How do they work?"

"If they have his scent, they'll follow him to the ends of the earth."

"How can they be stopped?"

"They can't," he mumbled. "And there's a second pack."

"What?"

"Eirik sent them after the girl too."

Victor swore.

"I'll go to Samarqand," his wife said at once.

"No."

"One of us has to warn her and Darius both. If they're even still alive. And you're needed here."

"Take someone with you. Lara?"

"Of course," a woman's voice replied.

"I'll meet you both in the armory," Victor said. "Mina, you can come with us or go with him. Make your choice carefully."

"She'll go with you."

"Be quiet, Culach. I'll answer for myself."

"They're obviously lovers," Victor's wife said. "She can't be trusted."

"She's a Danai and a hostage. He could have raped her for all we know."

Culach put on an expression of shame. "She tried to fight me off—"

Mina sighed. "Didn't I tell you to be quiet?"

He heard her light footsteps approach.

"As far as I'm concerned, you're all to blame for this mess."

Her skirts rustled against his skin as she knelt beside him.

"But in balance, Culach is actually less of a bastard than you are, Victor. So I'll stick with him."

Not exactly a declaration of undying love, but Culach would take what he could get.

"At least let Mina keep her rooms—" he pleaded.

"One more word and your ugly head will decorate the battlements. Get him out of here."

The Danai dragged Culach to Val Moraine's cold cells and thrust him inside. Ice coated the interior walls and each breath burned his lungs. His Valkirin blood would keep him from dying, but it wasn't pleasant. He curled his knees to his chest.

After eight hundred and thirty-two years, the Maiden Keep had finally surrendered her virginity to House Dessarian. Culach smiled grimly. He just hoped Eirik was still alive to see it.

36
GHOSTS

Galen dug deeper into the pile of musty furs. He hadn't been able to hobble far with the bandages on. The Valkirins didn't bother to give him any healing and each step felt like knives slicing into his feet. Even if he'd managed to find a way out of Val Moraine, he'd freeze to death within minutes. So he'd found a large bronze chest in the next chamber and climbed in, pulling the lid shut behind him. A temporary refuge but better than nothing.

He just wanted to sleep. To close his eyes and never wake up.

Eirik Kafsnjór had interrogated him on and off for hours after Mina left. Eirik seemed to be expecting Victor, but Galen hadn't told him there was a secret way into the keep. He couldn't do it. He knew his father would come. That Galen was a dead man. He'd known it from the start. But he was weary to the bone of betrayal. Only Victor could save Mina now. She'd done nothing wrong. Whatever his father's flaws, Galen didn't believe Victor would punish Mina for his own sins.

Then he'd heard the clash of swords in a distant corridor and Eirik had dashed off. He hadn't returned.

Why did I come here? If I'd found Darius, I could have warned him and then just...kept going.

But Galen knew he could never live among the mortals. He'd heard of the sun, a thousand times brighter than Selene. It made his eyes ache just to imagine it. The Marakai moved between both worlds, but they were different. He was Danai. A child of the moonlit forest. To live in a crowded, dirty city bathed in constant daylight....

No, better to have seen Mina one last time. At least someone would weep for him.

The door to the chamber creaked open. Galen held his breath.

Footsteps. The lid to the chest flew open. The furs were torn away. He blinked.

Icy blue eyes met his. Galen's testicles tightened.

It had to be Delilah.

Long black hair webbed her thin shoulders. Her lips pulled back from her teeth in a feral snarl.

"If you hadn't saved Darius once, I'd kill you right now," she said, her breath frosting the air. "I still might. But first you're going to face Victor."

Delilah looked like she'd blow away in a stiff breeze, but the hand that seized him was a vise. Galen clambered out, trying to keep the weight on his heels. He said nothing. What was there to say?

"I found him!" Delilah shouted.

Two daëvas—Aedan and Kelyn—stuck their heads in. He'd ranged with them many times near the border. Aedan was one of those who'd taken up the sword. Olive-skinned and beanpole tall, he usually had a quick wit and ready smile. Not now. His hand dropped to the hilt of the blade as if he wanted to draw it. Kelyn —pretty despite a broken front tooth—gave him a grim glare and spat at his feet.

"Go fetch Victor," Delilah said. "But search the prisoner first."

Galen felt a buzz of earth power building around her. She

didn't need to put a blade to his throat. He knew if he moved a muscle, she'd start snapping bones.

Aedan and Kelyn checked him from head to toe, not gently. When Aeden kicked his legs apart, Galen bit down on a scream. He hadn't dared look beneath the bandages, but he knew they covered two lumps of dead, blackened flesh. Satisfied he had no weapons, they left.

The wait seemed interminable. Delilah's eyes never left him, not for an instant. Galen felt like a bug snatched out from under a rock by a sadistic child. Feebly wondering what would come next.

Then Victor came. He stared at Galen for a long time.

"I don't care why you did it," he said finally, his voice dripping with contempt. "I don't know you at all, so I suppose I've no right to expect anything. But you betrayed your own House. Your own clan. You're a murderer."

Galen opened his mouth but found he couldn't speak. Victor turned away in disgust.

"Put him in irons. Not the cold cells. That would be a mercy. Just stick him somewhere I don't have to look at his face."

He dimly sensed daēvas taking his arms. Heard the clank of chains. But his gaze remained fixed on the pale figure standing just behind Victor. Looking at him with those green eyes. Blood stained his mouth. Matted his silver hair. Galen wanted to reach out and wipe it away. To kiss those frozen lips. To breathe life back into that slender body.

Murderer.

He wrenched his eyes away and kept them on the ground as the Danai led him away.

37

PARTHENOI

By the time Nazafareen found their old alley, she could hardly keep to her feet. The ground swam before her eyes as she slumped against the wall. Thunder rumbled in a distant drumroll and the storm finally broke. Sheets of rain swept down. She tore her cloak away. She felt so *hot*. Within moments, it soaked her to the skin. She turned her face to the rain, shivering violently.

She huddled there for what seemed an eternity, sinking in and out of delirium. Minutes might have passed, or hours. The deluge saturated the hard earth and spilled over into puddles. She found her cloak and pulled it over her head, but it didn't keep out the visions.

Trees burning. Screams. The man with the scar. The darkness inside him. She'd tried to cast it out....

Nazafareen woke with a start. The rain had eased to a gentle patter. She rose unsteadily to her feet and wrung out her sodden cloak. In the ribbon of sky above, she saw a patch of blue. She had to get out of the city before they found her. But then she remembered Javid. This was all her fault. The Valkirins must have sent those things after her. She couldn't leave him to the Pythia. If only using the power didn't make her so ill, she'd go back to the Acropolis right now. She wished Darius were here. He'd know just what to do.

I bring death and misfortune everywhere I go.

She sagged against the wall.

Feeling sorry for yourself won't do any good. At least you're still free, which is better than Javid has it.

Then inspiration struck. The girl with the ivy wreath! She was a friend of Herodotus. Maybe she would help. Nazafareen remembered where the house was. If she kept to side streets, she might be able to get there without running into the Polemarch's soldiers. Nazafareen started down the alley when a boy appeared. He smiled.

"Over here!" he shouted.

She froze. She recognized him. One of the thugs who had attacked Herodotus. His arm hung in a makeshift sling and without thinking, she charged, planning to kick his broken bone and shove past, but then she heard running footsteps and three more boys blocked the way.

"I can't believe you were stupid enough to come back here," the leader growled. "We'd all but given up on you."

Nazafareen backed away. She already knew the alley ended behind her in a blank wall. She *had* been stupid to choose a place with only one exit. The leader leapt nimbly over a puddle and pulled a knife from his belt. The others held vicious nail-studded clubs.

"I'm glad we didn't find you before," he said with a grin. "Because the price has gone up. She only wanted the old man last time, but now the Pythia wants you, girl."

Nazafareen reached for her sword and only then realized it was gone. She must have lost it at the Acropolis. She glowered at him.

"Don't try to deny it." He glanced at her missing hand. "She didn't specify dead or alive though." He gave an ugly laugh. "A head's much lighter to carry around, though you don't look like you weigh much anyway."

Nazafareen studied them, calculating the odds. Not good. Not at all. The alley was narrow, but not so narrow they'd have to come at her one at a time. She took another step back, into something squelching and foul.

I'll make them pay dearly for my head at least.

And then she heard a soft grunt of surprise. The leader spun around just in time to catch a staff to the temple. It blurred in tight arcs, just clearing the width of the walls. One of his confederates had already crumpled bonelessly to the ground. The other two brought back their clubs, Nazafareen heard several sharp cracks from the staff, and they too collapsed. It was the girl from the garden.

"Hurry," she hissed. "There are soldiers two streets away."

Nazafareen didn't hesitate. She stepped over the prone bodies and followed. At the entrance to the alley, the girl looked both ways, then waved her forward. They hurried through the deserted streets.

"This way!"

The girl grabbed her arm and yanked her around a corner just as soldiers poured out of a side street.

"Did they see us?" Nazafareen whispered.

"I don't know, but the Pythia's ordered the whole city searched, down to pigsties and outhouses. So move it!"

They ran and ran, narrowly dodging the contingents of soldiers, but Nazafareen had a sinking feeling they were closing in. Soon the buildings grew smaller and shabbier. Trash clogged the streets and they passed several establishments with heavily made-up women and a distinctly seedy air.

"In here."

The girl led her up the steps of an ancient temple. Withered garlands lay on a lichen-coated altar, their petals brown and curled into wisps. Inside, a few stubby candles burned, but they were the only source of illumination. Nazafareen suspected the temple had been grand once. The ceiling soared high above, supported by thick stone pillars. But those too showed signs of age, with large cracks and chips that someone had sloppily plastered over.

She followed the girl to another, larger altar in the center of the chamber. It reeked of cheap wine. The head of a bull stared back at her, but Nazafareen was relieved to find it made of stone rather than brass.

"What is this place?"

"The Temple of Dionysus," the girl replied.

Nazafareen was about to ask why they had come here when a hissing snake slithered out of the bull's mouth. She leapt back. Nazafareen had never cared for snakes and this one looked poisonous, with brown diamond markings against copper scales. The girl smiled as it slid into the shadows.

"Don't mind him. He only bites if you try to pick him up."

She decided she didn't like this place, even if the girl meant well.

"Listen—" Nazafareen began, eyes scanning the ground for any sign of movement.

Voices drifted into the temple. A woman's laughter, followed by breaking crockery. Shouts came from somewhere across the street and were answered by a deep voice that sounded like it was right outside. The girl quickly pressed one of the stones at the base of the altar and a small cavity opened, hardly big enough for a child.

"Get inside," she ordered.

Nazafareen stared at the dark hole. If the snake came out of the bull's mouth, that meant it probably lived under there somewhere.

"You'll be safe, Ashraf. But you must hurry."

Nazafareen swallowed her fear and dove into the hole. The stone sealed shut. She lay in a cramped, stiflingly hot space. She feared she might suffocate, but then she realized she could hear clearly through the bull, and that air could get in that way too.

"*Parthenoi*," a man said gruffly, although there was an edge of respect in his tone.

"Do you intend to ransack the god's holy shrine?" the girl asked calmly.

"I must," he said, sounding uncomfortable. "It is the Polemarch's orders."

"At least leave an offering so Dionysus doesn't curse you."

He grumbled but Nazafareen heard the clink of coins in a bowl.

"Who are you looking for?"

"None of your business."

"Be about it then. We've nothing to hide here."

The search seemed interminable. Nazafareen kept expecting the cold, slick brush of reptilian scales against her skin. She still felt feverish and their mad dash through the streets had used up the little strength she had left. She'd nearly fallen asleep when the first soldier returned.

"Thank you, parthenoi," he said, more politely this time. "Tell the god we meant no harm."

"I have no need. Dionysus sees into men's hearts. He will know if you are blameless."

After several long minutes of silence, the panel slid open. Nazafareen took a deep breath of wine-soaked air and crawled out.

"They won't come back. Not for a while, at least. But we must get you out of the city."

"Why are you risking yourself for me?"

The girl ignored this question, beckoning her through a door to the yard at the back of the temple where a wagon piled with hay waited, two horses already in their traces. She leapt gracefully into the driver's seat and placed her staff on the bench.

"Dig a hole," she said, gesturing to the hay.

Nazafareen crawled into the wagon bed, too tired to do anything but follow this forceful creature's commands. With a lurch, the wagon started off. She tore the hay apart with her hand and burrowed down to the very bottom, pulling it over her head. They rocked along, moving from dirt to paving stones that bumped at each junction in the slabs. The straw scratched and tickled, but Nazafareen decided it was still better than her last hiding place. When they reached the city walls, the girl bantered easily with the guards at the gate. They seemed to know her.

"Open up for the parthenoi!"

The wagon rumbled through the gate and picked up speed, jouncing along country roads. The gentle rocking lulled her into an uneasy slumber. At last, it drew to a halt. Nazafareen opened her eyes.

"You can come out now, Ashraf," the girl called.

She exited the hay wagon the same way she'd gotten in, by burrowing through the straw. When Nazafareen slid down, she brought a scattering of stalks with her. They clung to her clothes and hair like burrs.

"Come on, I'll take you to Kallisto," the girl said, smiling at her appearance.

Nazafareen sighed and brushed herself off. "Thanks for all you've done. But I have a few questions. Where are we? And how did you know where to find me before?" She thought for a moment. "And how do you even know my *name*?"

"I'll answer the third question first, which also answers the second," the girl replied as they walked toward a large, ramshackle farmhouse. "Herodotus told his wife about a brave girl named Ashraf who saved his life. It's the main reason she trusted you to deliver the message. He also mentioned you'd been sleeping rough in an alley by the docks. It took me a while, but I finally found you. Just in time, it seems."

"But won't the Polemarch's soldiers come straight here?"

Charis smiled. "No one knows of their marriage. The note was unsigned. Kallisto is not a fool."

They followed a path through vineyards, where women in headscarves plucked purple and green grapes and tossed them into wicker baskets. They all looked young and strapping.

"As for the first, Kallisto will explain everything."

She nodded as the front door of the house opened and an older woman emerged. Grey braids coiled on top of her head and she leaned on a pine cone-topped staff just like the girl's. She studied Nazafareen with cool, dark eyes. Nazafareen felt a chill. They weren't unfriendly, but they weren't friendly either. And unlike the girl's, her staff had real power; Nazafareen could feel it. Kallisto stood aside without a word and they entered a large, sunny kitchen. Something good-smelling bubbled over a hearth in the corner. Several loaves of fresh bread cooled on the tiled counter.

"Leave us, Charis," Kallisto said.

The girl ducked her head and strode off, slipping behind a curtain that led to the other rooms.

"Sit."

Kallisto pointed to one of the chairs arrayed before a long trestle table.

Suddenly, Nazafareen was tired of doing what these women told her to do. She crossed her arms. It was a petty act of defiance, but all she could muster at the moment.

"I prefer to stand."

"Suit yourself."

Kallisto sat down and folded her hands on the table.

"I gave your message to Herodotus," Nazafareen said. "He looked happy to get it. Well, sad too."

Kallisto inclined her head. "Thank you. Now, I will ask you a question, and I wish a truthful answer."

"How do you know I won't just lie?"

"Because you will hold my staff as you speak. It is a talisman that compels honesty."

"No."

Kallisto smiled sweetly. "Then I'm afraid we'll have to kill you."

"What?"

Nazafareen followed her gaze out the window. The sturdy farm girls she'd seen were no longer toiling in the fields. They'd gathered in a line outside the house with grim faces and staffs in their hands.

"Those are the Maenads. The parthenoi. They serve the god, and they serve me. Oh, and they're impervious to fire. So child, will you answer?"

Nazafareen sighed. These women clearly meant business. And what did she have to hide anymore? She scowled.

"Very well."

She took the staff. It was made of some smooth, pale wood, with carved vines coiling around the shaft. She felt tempted to simply unravel the magic inside, but she'd managed not to break her griffin cuff and she had a feeling Kallisto might be displeased at losing her talisman, so Nazafareen kept a tight rein on herself.

"Ask away."

Kallisto's face grew tense.

"Are you Avas Vatra?"

This was not the question she'd expected.

"A what?"

"Are you a child of fire? A daēva?"

"Me?" Nazafareen laughed. "No. I'm human like you. Though I won't deny I seem to have a strange ability to nullify other magic."

"Ah." Kallisto sat back, a satisfied expression on her face. "So you are a Breaker. I've heard of those. A very rare talent. Very rare indeed."

"Can I put this down now?"

Kallisto waved a hand in assent and Nazafareen gingerly

returned it to its place propped against the table.

"Now that that's settled, would you like a bowl of stew?"

Nazafareen's stomach rumbled. It still felt delicate, but she knew food would do her good.

"Yes, please."

Kallisto ladled out two bowls of vegetable stew and cut thick slices of bread. She set out a bowl of creamy butter and cups of watered wine. They ate in silence. When Nazafareen casually glanced out the window, she saw the young women had returned to their labors.

"I was truthful with you," she said. "Now it's your turn. I want to know what's going on. Who *are* you? And why are you helping me?"

"Fair enough." Kallisto began clearing their plates. "The Maenads are an old cult. One of the oldest. For a thousand years, we've kept watch."

"For what?"

"For the return of the Vatras."

"The fire daēvas, you mean? Herodotus told me a little about them."

"He knows more than any man living, but there are still many things that remain unclear. I fear he discovered something the Pythia wished to keep secret and that's why he was arrested."

"He told me he'd just found a scroll," Nazafareen exclaimed, sitting up straight in her chair. "He came to say goodbye right before the Archon Basileus arrived at the library."

Kallisto turned sharply. "What else did he tell you?"

"Not much, really." She tried to remember. "Just that it was written by an alchemist, Nabu somebody or other, and it surprised him. He said.... He said it contradicted other accounts, about the gates, or maybe the shadowlands. But he didn't say how." Nazafareen leaned forward. "We have to get him out of there. And my friend, Javid, too."

Kallisto raised an eyebrow. "The Persian? He has been accused of supplying the spell dust to Herodotus."

"That's a lie!"

"Calm yourself, child, I know."

Kallisto dried the dishes and stacked them neatly on the counter. Nazafareen watched her movements, brisk and efficient.

"So what are you going to do?"

"The Archon Eponymous—he is the chief magistrate—has ordered them to be tried together before the Ecclesia two weeks hence."

"The Assembly?" Nazafareen brightened. "That's good, isn't it?"

"Perhaps. The Assembly is divided. Many agree with the Pythia. But they stand a fair chance, at least." Kallisto sat down. "The Polemarch and the Archon Basileus are entirely her creatures. But the Archon Eponymous has maintained his distance from the Temple of Delphi. Still, he tends to blow with the wind. And he's guided first by self-interest."

"Then we must help Herodotus make a strong case. I know who set him up. Two scholars. I call them the Stork and the Weasel."

Kallisto gave a grim smile. "Kadmos and Serpedon. They have plotted against Herodotus for years. I'm certain it was they who helped the Pythia arrange for Herodotus's murder at the hands of street toughs. A murder *you* stopped."

Nazafareen felt swept up in deep currents she barely understood. "Why did the Pythia want him dead?"

"She suspected—correctly—that he was hiding information from her. The Pythia has an interest in the Vatras too, though I'm not yet sure why. And she has an interest in *you*. The gods saw fit to bring you and my husband together. A chance meeting. For what purpose? Was it only to save his life, or something more?" Kallisto shook her head. "There are many things I still cannot see. But I will not have a Breaker running loose. You may be a part of this in some way."

Running loose? Nazafareen's jaw tightened.

"I'm a free woman. I will help you, but I will not be your prisoner. And Javid must be part of any bargain we strike."

They stared at each other.

Kallisto inclined her head with a small smile. "They say Breakers have a temper. I suppose I oughtn't test yours. All right. I *invite* you to stay with us for now. But your friend is being held in the Polemarch's dungeons. They are impregnable. There is no way to reach him before the trial." She paused. "You say my husband discovered a scroll. Did he mention anything about the talismans?"

Nazafareen thought back. "I don't think so. Talismans like your staff, you mean?"

"A thousand times more powerful, child. The three talismans that defeated the Vatras a thousand years ago."

"What were they?" Nazafareen found herself intensely curious. "Let me guess. Magic rings!"

Kallisto chuckled. "Not what. *Who.*"

"You mean they're people?"

"Daēvas. One from each of the clans. Valkirin, Danai, Marakai. Air, earth, water. They squabble with each other, but once they were allies."

"But wouldn't the talismans be dead by now?"

"Perhaps. But Herodotus believes the talent may have passed on through the generations. He took the job at the library to further his research. Then the new Pythia came and demanded he hand everything over to *her*." She sighed. "He was never good at keeping his mouth shut. Too enthusiastic."

Nazafareen thought about all this. It was a lot to absorb and she suddenly felt very tired.

"I still don't understand," she said, yawning openly now. "Why do you think the Avas Vatras will come back?"

Kallisto gave her a tight smile. "Because, child, they already have."

38

NAMES

Thena had her speech all prepared. She'd delivered it many times now and knew each word by heart. She kept her expression kind, her voice soft. The other would come later.

Thena always liked to give them a fair chance.

"You can't escape," she said. "You will never get the collar off. Ever. The harder you fight, the worse it will be and I'll still break you in the end. But your life doesn't have to be unpleasant. There are rewards for good behavior. If you do what you're told, you will be treated like a favored pet." She flashed her dimples. "Now. Tell me your name."

The witch hung against the wall, his arms above his head. "What's yours?"

She pursed her lips in annoyance. "My name is Mistress."

"That's not a name."

Thena took a deep breath.

"If you resist, you will experience agony like you never imagined. I can sustain it for hours. Days."

She waited for the usual fear reaction through the bracelet but none came. That was odd. They all pretended defiance at first, but they couldn't conceal how they really felt from her. But then this witch was strange in other ways. When he'd been collared, she felt a thread of power snap. And while his left arm seemed damaged when she met him, now it was unblemished.

"What is your name?"

The witch smiled. "What's yours?"

Thena tilted her head. Then she found the place where the collar joined them and gave it a hard squeeze. His jaw clenched but he made no sound. Still she felt that eerie calm. Thena probed deeper, giving him a taste of what she could do. She felt almost excited. This one would be a challenge worthy of her talents. But in the end, he would break. They all did.

"I'll let you think on it for a while," she said, touching his cheek. "Andros. That's what I shall call you."

She felt his wintry blue eyes on her back as she left.

Thena had realized what he was the moment he'd snatched her jug out of the air. She'd never captured one of the witches herself and it required all of her self-control not to run away. All the acolytes carried a small pouch of spell dust, though, just in case something went wrong. Magic was wicked, but the Pythia said it could be used for very special purposes. She had taught Thena the words to take away sight and hearing, if only for a few seconds.

The Pythia's personal chambers consisted of two rooms, both sparely decorated. The smaller one held a bed and dressing table. The slightly larger one Thena entered now was the audience chamber, where she brought the daēvas for questioning.

The previous Pythia had filled her suite with figurines of jade and ebony, rich tapestries and heavy, ornate furniture. But the new Pythia disdained these things and had them all carted out and given to the poor the day she assumed her office. She kept her rooms as simple as an acolyte's. The only item she had saved was an ivory-inlaid table, which was covered with scrolls and sheets of parchment.

The Oracle of Delphi reclined on a couch, head propped on the armrest and long black braid brushing the floor. She wore a simple length of undyed wool fastened by a brooch at the shoulder. It was in the shape of a serpent and the gold caught the firelight from a brazier in the corner.

"Did he speak?"

"Yes, but he still resists."

She nodded calmly. "I leave him in your capable hands, daughter. You say he knew the girl who escaped?"

"Yes, he asked about her when I met him."

"That's interesting." She thought for a moment. "Bring me the Danai you call Beryl. But show her the new witch first. See how she reacts."

Thena hurried off and fetched Beryl. She had vapid eyes, like a cow, and looked Andros over without interest. He didn't speak to her and Thena saw no spark of recognition in his eyes. When she returned, she reported that it was her opinion the two did not know each other.

"Perhaps," the Pythia said. "There are seven Danai houses after all. Let us ask the witch directly. Beryl?"

The witch's head snapped around. "Yes, Pythia?"

"Do you know the name of the daēva you just saw?"

"No, Pythia."

The Oracle sighed. "Let us move on then."

Thena started for the door, but to her surprise, the Pythia called her back.

"I'm very pleased with you, sun daughter. You thought quickly today."

Thena flushed with pleasure. "I wish only to serve the god."

"And so you shall. I have a task I need your help with. You know how to read and write, yes?"

"I learned at the temple when I first came."

"Excellent. You will be my scribe." The Pythia rose and walked to the ivory-inlaid table. "These are records I've compiled on the various houses and holdfasts. I wish to map the ancestry of the witches, so we may better understand them."

Thena nodded, unsure what was expected of her and afraid she would fail.

The Pythia laughed. "Don't look so worried. I only wish you to write down what Beryl tells me. You can do that surely?"

"Yes." Thena nodded again, relieved. "I can do that."

The Pythia produced a box with ink and a stylus, and a fresh sheet of parchment. Thena took them and sat down cross-legged on the floor.

"Now, Beryl. I want you to focus very hard on these names. Yesterday, I believe we reached back six generations, but you must go farther than that. Am I clear?"

A sheen of sweat coated Beryl's brow.

"Yes, Pythia. I will try my best. But this was long before I was born—"

"Don't make excuses. You haven't failed yet." The Pythia smiled, but it didn't reach her eyes. "It is very important you remember. Here is the first name...."

The Pythia began to speak, with Beryl stammering answers that Thena faithfully recorded. But her mind soon roamed elsewhere. To the room where Andros was chained, awake and brooding. She could feel him, although his state of mind remained a mystery. Why was he so different from the others? What secrets was he hiding?

Thena wrote until her hand cramped and the parchment accumulated into a neat pile. She felt oddly happy. The Pythia favored her, and now she had Andros.

He would be her special project.

39

AN UNLIKELY SAVIOR

T he dungeons of the Polemarch lay deep beneath the Acropolis in an area near the river. As a result, they were eternally swampy and humid. Black mold covered the mortar between the stones and pools of still water provided a lively habitat for the colonies of mosquitoes that thrived on the blood of the unfortunate souls confined there. Many were murderers and thieves, but others had simply said the wrong thing to the wrong person. With its unstable balance of powers and constantly shifting political alliances, the city of Delphi had become a swamp itself—of intrigues and back-stabbing among the Archons, the aristocracy, the philosophers and the assembly, not to mention the multitude of temples, of which the cult of Apollo was easily the most powerful.

From his years navigating the inner workings of the Merchants' Guild and queries in the taverns, Javid understood some of it, not that the knowledge did him any good. He huddled in the corner of one of the larger cells, trying to figure out where exactly he'd gone wrong to end up at such a pass. Had he angered the Holy Father in some way? After a happy conclusion to the negotiations with the daēvas, the trip had been one disaster after another.

He'd had such grand plans. With his own wind ship, he'd intended to start a business dealing in lucrative black market spell dust. Javid had spent the last several years cultivating contacts with the right connections. He still didn't know the physical source of the dust itself, but after tracing a long and convoluted chain of middlemen, he'd finally discovered who ran the whole operation: a powerful noble named Izad Asabana. Discreet inquiries revealed that Asabana had been a nobody only two decades before. Then the king had abruptly elevated him to the royal advisory council and given him a large estate on prime lands near the river—right around the same time spell dust appeared. It had to be because Asabana controlled the source. By law, only the magi and the king were supposed to use the dust, but that didn't stop it from leaking into the black market. And there was a fortune to be made for someone with his own ship who was willing to take risks.

Javid slapped at a mosquito and examined the drop of blood on his palm with resignation. The river barge to Samarkand was long gone. He would probably be executed, or at least horribly tortured. And he had nothing useful to tell his torturers. He figured Ashraf must be a daēva in disguise. There was no other explanation for what he'd witnessed.

"Persian pig."

He looked up, squinting through the eye the Polemarch's soldiers had blackened.

"Turn out your pockets."

The gentleman who stood over him had arms like ham hocks and a bald head shaped like a lumpy potato. Javid hadn't looked in a mirror lately, but he had a feeling this prisoner looked even worse than he did.

"They already took everything." He turned out his pockets with an apologetic smile.

The man grunted. "Get up."

The other prisoners in the cell suddenly found something fascinating to stare at on the grimy walls. Except for one. He'd clearly been there a long time. Javid thought he might be some minor aristocrat because his clothes were of a decent cut and material, though filthy. He had long, dark hair held back by a leather thong and keen grey eyes that observed the proceedings impassively.

Javid sighed and rose to his feet.

"I don't have—"

The man seized the front of his shirt.

"Take your coat off. It's mine now."

Javid's stomach lurched.

"It won't fit you anyway—"

"Take it off."

He tried to shove the man away, but it was like pushing a boulder. They tussled for a moment and the man yanked at his clothing, pulling the coat half off and tearing his shirt. His eyes opened wide. Javid crossed his arms over his chest and backed away, breathing hard.

"Well, look what we got, fellows!" The giant crowed. "Maybe those bastards aren't so bad after all. They gave us a woman."

The others looked up at that, wolves catching the scent of a wounded deer.

"I'm a man," Javid said through gritted teeth, trying to pull his torn coat together.

"Not from what I just saw."

"Stay the hell away from me."

"She says she's a man. Maybe we better check what she's got between her legs."

Javid wildly scanned the faces of the other prisoners. He'd get no help there. They looked agitated. Excited.

"Guards!" he shouted.

The only answer was the steady drip of water.

The giant lunged for him and suddenly the dark-haired man was on his feet. By the time Javid blinked, he'd crossed the distance. A flurry of kicks and punches ensued, so fast Javid could hardly follow it. When the dust cleared, his would-be rapist lay on the floor, out cold, and the other prisoners were examining the grime again.

Javid's heart pounded, unsure what his savior's intentions were. But then the man simply dusted off his hands, adjusted his stained tunic, and returned to his seat in the shadows. After a moment, Javid went over and sat down next to him.

"Thanks for that," he whispered.

The man nodded. "Sometimes old Aknis needs a reminder."

"And I'm not a woman."

He didn't seem to care either way. "Okay."

"What's your name?"

"Katsu."

"I'm Javid."

Javid slapped another mosquito, studying Katsu out of the corner of his eye. His skin was the dusky shade of strong tea and unlined. He couldn't have been more than thirty.

"Where'd you learn to fight like that?"

"Tjanjin."

"Is that where you're from?"

"No."

"What are you here for?"

Only after he asked the question did Javid worry it might be rude. He knew the titles and forms of address for every tier of nobility, both Persian and Greek, along with countless other fine points of court protocol, but he'd never been in a dungeon before and had no idea of the etiquette.

Katsu turned those grey eyes on him.

"I'm a thief. What are *you* here for?"

Javis scratched his head. "I'm not even sure. Wrong choice of friends."

Katsu nodded as though this made perfect sense.

"I'm from Samarqand," Javid added. "I guess you already knew that. I fly wind ships."

This elicited a spark of interest.

"I've heard those are dangerous."

"Not really. It all depends on the wind." As Javid described what it was like to pilot a wind ship, the dungeon walls seemed to recede a little bit. He glossed over any mention of the spell dust, focusing instead on the direction and speed of the various currents and explaining the basic principle, which was simply that the air inside the sack had to be hotter than the air outside, which in turn caused the vessel to rise.

"But how do you land?" Katsu asked.

"There's a valve that slowly releases the air."

In theory, Javid thought ruefully, thinking of the poor *Kyrenia*.

"I would like to see that sometime," the thief mused.

"Look me up if you ever go to Samarqand." Javid doubted either of them would ever see the sun again, but it seemed polite to offer. "You can find me at the Merchant's Guild."

Katsu nodded. "I will."

They heard voices outside. The lock on the great iron-bound door tumbled open and two soldiers stomped in. They surveyed the prisoners, who looked simultaneously hopeful and terrified.

"That one."

They grabbed Javid under the arms. Fear dried his mouth.

"Where are you taking me?"

The soldiers didn't bother to reply, dragging him roughly to the corridor. He shared a last look with Katsu and then the door slammed shut.

❧ 40 ❧

GERDA'S GLOBE

Halldóra spread her hands on the stone table and glared at the two men seated at the other end. She'd been a great beauty once and still boasted high cheekbones and a firm chin, even if her hair had faded from silver to pure white. Bigger men had withered under that gaze, but these two managed to meet it steadily. Runar of Val Petros and Stefán of Val Altair weren't easily cowed.

"I want him found," she said. "Daníel is my only grandson. The heir to Val Tourmaline."

"And we want ours, as you well know. But first we must decide what to do about Eirik Kafsnjór," Runar said. "He's the immediate problem. The man's lost his wits."

The message from Tethys had come a few days before, conveyed by a nightjar. Halldóra could scarcely believe it. Even Eirik wasn't that reckless, was he? But she didn't think Tethys would lie about such a thing. Her clan had always been reasonably cordial toward Val Tourmaline. Hence the emergency meeting.

"Do you think the Dessarians have any chance of taking the holdfast?"

"Of course not," Stefán replied easily. He was short for a

Valkirin, but made up for it in solid girth. "They're *Danai*." He filled the word with contempt. "They probably won't even survive long enough to lay siege. However, it could be a golden opportunity to put Eirik in his place."

Although the Iron Wars lay in the distant past, their bruising defeat had never lost its sting. Val Altair had suffered the greatest losses and everyone knew Stefán still thirsted for revenge. He also coveted the rich seams that ran beneath the mountain, as did they all. Over the centuries, their own mines had slowly depleted, forcing the holdfasts to delve further and deeper. But for some reason, Val Moraine's wealth only multiplied.

"What do you propose?" Halldóra asked.

"Nothing drastic—not yet. We need to assess the situation. I don't care what Eirik does to the Danai, but if he's raising chimera, he could decide to turn some on us."

They fell silent for a moment. Not even during the bloody civil war had any side resorted to chimera. Halldóra didn't know who had discovered their making, it was all too long ago, but she guessed it was sometime after the burning of the timbered holdfasts when the Valkirins were in desperate disarray. It was very old magic, and very dark.

"What if we send a delegation? One from each holdfast. It might help us learn his intentions, while at the same time making it appear we're still loyal to Val Moraine," Runar suggested, stroking his short gold-flecked beard. "In retrospect, it was hasty to turn him away outright. Knowing Eirik, he's probably taken the last message as a declaration of war."

"I like it," Stefán said. "They can promise him anything he asks for." He gave a thin smile. "We have no obligation to deliver, of course. Eirik crossed a line there's no returning from."

Halldóra gazed at the statues flanking the square doorway. Each fifteen hands high, they depicted Tourmaline ancestors long ago consigned to the icy crypts beneath the keep. Hard, stern faces that probably looked the same in frozen death as they had in life. She wondered what they would do in her place. For Halldóra trusted these two about as much as she trusted mad Eirik.

"I suppose it's the best course at this point," she said at last. "We're the closest to Val Moraine and I don't much like having him at my back. Choose your agents, and I'll choose mine. They can fly out as soon as the weather clears." Halldóra's emerald eyes flashed. "Now. Let's talk about Daníel."

EIGHTY LEAGUES TO THE SOUTHEAST, A BLIZZARD LASHED VAL Moraine. Victor Dessarian, the new master of the Maiden Keep, was already wearing all the extra clothes he'd brought in three layers, plus a leather coat he'd found in one of the empty rooms. He still felt cold. He'd always wondered how the Valkirins lived. It turned out the answer was, not very comfortably. Although certain chambers had a little radiant warmth seeping from the walls, it failed to have a discernible effect on the bitterly chill air. The keep itself was austere and unadorned, built only to endure for the ages. He had no intention of relinquishing it, but Gods, he wished for a hot bath.

"I almost envy you," he said to Delilah with a wry smile. "Solis has a certain appeal right now."

She stepped up and kissed him lightly. Victor pulled her close and deepened their embrace, until finally Delilah pushed him away with a reluctant sigh.

"Stay another hour. I'll warm you up. Though I may have to keep half my clothes on."

She laughed. "It's a tempting offer, my love, but Lara is waiting for me and I fear our time has run out. I'll send word as soon as I can."

"Bring Darius back," Victor said, giving her a last lingering kiss. "Bring them both."

Delilah nodded. And then she was gone with a swirl of her dark cloak. Victor felt afraid for her, though he would never say it. Delilah might take it as a sign he didn't have confidence in her. It wasn't that. She'd lived in the empire and knew how to blend in with mortals. But during his long imprisonment, the memory of her was all that kept him going. He refused to even contemplate losing her again—or their son, Darius.

Victor's love for him was a prickly, uncomfortable thing, a thorn in his heart that had eluded every attempt at extraction, burrowing itself deeper despite Darius's maddening aloofness.

There too much of me in the boy, he thought. *And it's not his fault he was made into the satrap's hound. We all did what we had to.*

And paid the price.

Victor laid a palm on one of the slender columns supporting the high ceiling. Other than those columns, Val Moraine had no exterior walls—only leagues of empty air in all directions. At least the shields still held. They must be maintained by talismans woven into the stone. Victor wondered briefly how the Valkirins had managed it. Tethys said the making of talismans was a lost art.

Thick snow obscured the view, but he could just make out the shadowy lines of the nearest peaks. More rose beyond them, and more beyond those. The trackless range of the Valkirins ran unbroken from the White Sea to the Umbra, and north to the tip of the peninsula where Val Altair perched like a hawk's aerie at the end of the known world. He thought he might not stop at taking Val Moraine. Why not roust the Valkirins once and for all?

"Eirik's asking for you."

One of the Danai, a young man about Darius's age, stood in the doorway. Victor's recruits were mostly young and hungry for glory, willing to take risks their elders would scoff at. He'd marked them out right away. They were just as he had been so long ago, when he thought it would be a fine idea to go adventuring in the shadowlands.

"He's still alive, eh?"

"Just barely."

"Shall I see what he wants?"

The young daëva shrugged.

"I suppose I could use a laugh," Victor said, clapping him on the shoulder. "Let's go."

So they made their way to the tower where Eirik Kafsnjór lay dying. When it became clear the keep had fallen, he'd tried to stab himself in the heart with a dagger. Victor managed to deflect the blow—he wouldn't give Eirik the satisfaction of choosing his own end—but the blade had pierced his gut. It was a lethal injury, even for a daëva.

Victor had wanted to throw him into one of the cold cells, but Mithre argued that Eirik would take longer to die if they left him in a bed. Now he lay there, wearing the same blood-soaked clothes and a belligerent expression. His wounds looked horrible, and Victor had to admit a reluctant admiration that the old bastard was clinging on for so long.

"What?" Victor demanded.

It took Eirik a few moments to produce the word.

"Culach," he hissed through broken teeth.

Victor smiled. "He's alive."

Eirik stirred feebly. "You...should..."

"Kill him? Funny, he said the same thing about you. Now, if we're done here, I'll let you get back to the business of dying painfully." He turned to leave, but Eirik grabbed his sleeve. The effort left him gasping. Victor shook the hand off.

"Don't worry, your coward son will get what he deserves."

"No...a different request."

Speaking seemed to be costing Eirik a great deal. His skin had turned ashen.

"Why not?" Victor spread his arms expansively. "Let's hear it."

"My corpse," Eirik rasped. His cloudy gaze moved to the floor, as if he could see through the stone of the keep to the catacombs beneath. "With the others."

"Ah. And if I were in that bed, would you show me the same courtesy?"

Eirik didn't answer, though Victor knew from the faint twist of his lips that he'd heard.

"I thought so."

The former lord of Val Moraine glared up at him, rage and agony hardening his sharp features.

"The holdfasts will come for you, Dessarian," he said in a surprisingly clear voice. "And when that cold hand closes around your throat, my specter will be watching."

Victor nodded. "Fitting last words. Poetic even. Sadly, they're wasted on me." He strode to the door, where the young daēva waited impassively. "When he's gone, feed him to the abbadax."

IN A REMOTE TOWER FAR FROM EIRIK KAFSNJÓR'S DEATHBED, Gerda sat ensconced in her favorite hard chair, mulling over the latest blow fate had dealt her family—or what was left of it. When the Danai came storming in, she'd thrown her hands up and emitted a piteous wail, pretending to be decrepit and senile. After searching her rooms, Victor had left her there with two guards outside, the idiot. For all his faults, Eirik never would have made such a stupid mistake. He would have put the whole hold-fast to the sword. Babies too, not that they had any here.

She poured herself a glass of wine. Gerda had always nurtured high hopes for Culach, but he'd turned out to be as dim-witted as the rest of them. Although she'd been wondering about those dreams he spoke of. Gerda didn't believe in fairy stories, or omens or portents. But she felt troubled nonetheless.

She hadn't told Culach everything she knew, not by a long shot.

She took another gulp of wine and rose, her joints creaking painfully. The guards outside would know if she used too much power, but the talisman required only a thin flow of air. With luck, they wouldn't notice. She went to a secret niche in the stone and retrieved a glass globe on an obsidian stand. Faint runes marked the base, so ancient even Gerda couldn't read them. Inside it, little forks of lightning flickered and grey clouds swirled like smoke. Sometimes she saw clear blue sky or tiny funnels of black wind. Oddly enough, it never seemed to snow.

The talisman had been passed down through the Kafsnjór women for countless generations. No one even knew it existed anymore except for her.

Now she opened herself to air and blew gently at the runes as she asked her question. The talisman didn't always work, or it showed her things she couldn't decipher. If she'd been able to read the runes she might have understood better. Its unreliable nature was the reason she didn't use it often. But she had nothing else to do and figured it was worth a try.

Do the Vatras still live?

The clouds swirled violently. The runes began to give off an eerie blue glow. Gerda kept the question focused in her mind. She prayed the globe would show her nothing, as it did when the answer was negative. Long minutes passed. She was just about to release the power when she realized something *had* changed. The dark slate color remained the same, but now she saw ocean rather than clouds, its surface choppy and rough. The view sped across leagues and leagues of empty water in a dizzying rush. A ship appeared. And standing at the rail, a man.

He had thick hair of a deep, burnt red. Gerda's breath caught in her throat. He wasn't doing anything special, just staring out to sea with a somewhat wistful expression. The view swooped down through the rigging like a gull, arrowing in on his face. Skin tanned deeply by the sun and eyes of a deep oceanic blue. Suddenly he turned and stared directly at her, his gaze widening with surprise. In the split second before she snapped the connection, Gerda thought she saw tiny flames licking at the irises.

She sat back, stunned. Never before had such a thing happened. He had *seen* her spyglass. And that red hair. It couldn't be a coincidence. Gerda's hand shook as she reached for her goblet. It toppled, spilling a crimson pool across the floor.

The hell with it. She decided to just drink from the bottle.

Read on for a sneak peek of Solis, Book #2 in the Fourth Talisman series!

CHAPTER 1

MISTRESS

Thena woke in a cheerful mood.

It was a lovely morning, with an easterly wind carrying cooler air across the Umbra from the darklands. The storm the day before had washed the dust from the Acropolis and left crystalline blue skies in its wake. From the window of her small room, she could see for many leagues. Farms and orchards dotted the countryside outside the city walls. A wide, lazy river meandered among the fields, its waters gleaming like the scales of a serpent. Far beyond, almost at the edge of sight, the fertile delta gave way to a tawny line marking the start of the Kiln, a trackless wasteland that stretched all the way to the western edge of the continent.

When Thena was a child, her mother told her stories about the creatures that stalked the dunes. Scorpions the size of hunting hounds whose pincers snapped bones, and great blind wyrms with armored hides that could smell a human breath from ten leagues away. Multi-jointed monstrosities armed with venom that burned like fire. Her father's farm was one of the most remote and the stories always ended with dire warnings about little girls who wandered too far from home.

Once, her older sister, whom Thena worshipped, had dared her to bring back a bowl of pure sand. Unable to resist the challenge, Thena squared her shoulders and started walking down the dusty road, which was really just a track worn by oxen and wagon wheels, past the neighbors' farms until she reached the last stand of olive trees. They were sad, withered things, clinging to life in nearly barren soil. She stood, bowl in hand, looking out at that great expanse of nothing. All the stories tumbled through her head. She thought she saw a flicker of movement—probably just the waves of heat distorting the air. But her nerve had crumbled and she turned tail and ran all the way home, to the hilarious laughter of her sisters.

Thena pulled a clean woolen shift over her head and gazed down at the rooftops below. The city of Delphi was a hodgepodge of mansions and hovels, teeming markets and grand edifices such as the Akademia, the Great Library and the Philosophers' Guild, with the Temple of Apollo perched atop the Acropolis like a crowning jewel. She always felt important looking down from this high vantage point, like a queen surveying her domain.

Foolish creature, she chided herself. *You may have come a long way for a farmer's daughter, but you're still a humble initiate. Don't tempt the gods with pride and vanity.*

Thena burned a handful of bay laurel leaves and silently asked for Apollo's blessing in the day's endeavors. She hoped the fugitive girl had been caught. The Pythia was in quite a temper about it. But finding her was the Polemarch's task. Thena had a different one.

The Oracle favors me above the others because I am steadfast in my devotion. May the light of truth shine upon us all.

Thena left her rooms and climbed the worn stone stairs to one of the formerly empty chambers. She drew a deep breath and opened the door.

"Good morning," she said brightly. "I trust you had a good rest."

Its new occupant stared at her. Iron manacles pinned his arms above his head. She sensed stiffness in his shoulders but nothing else. Not a shred of emotion. Thena felt confident this would soon change. Apollo had arranged for this witch to cross her path. He was a gift from the god.

"I know you're Danai." She smiled. "You have the look."

The witch looked no older than twenty, though that meant nothing. The Pythia said they aged much more slowly than mortals and lived for hundreds of years. This one had short, wavy brown hair and blue eyes. They regarded her coldly.

"As I told you yesterday, your new name will be Andros." She bustled over to the shutters, throwing them wide. He winced as the sunlight hit his face. "And we shall get to know each other very well in the coming weeks. Better than you've ever known anyone in your life. But first you shall tell me your old name. I need it for the records, you see."

She studied him. He wasn't as handsome as the exotic Valkirin witches, with their silver hair and golden skin, but he had a stern face some might find attractive. Thena cared little about such things. She was betrothed to the sun god. He even spoke to her directly sometimes, though she kept this secret. The Oracle might think Thena was lying—or worse, challenging her authority as the voice of the god on earth.

"I'm waiting," she prompted, showing her dimples. "Tell me your name and I'll get you a nice cool drink of water."

"What's yours?" he asked hoarsely.

"Mistress."

He laughed.

Thena nodded serenely. She'd played this game before. They were still in the opening moves. The very beginning. If he'd known what was in store for him, he wouldn't be so cavalier. But they never did. The witches all thought they were hard until Thena taught them differently.

"Do you know how many daēvas I've broken?" she asked

calmly. "Five so far. I'm the best at it. Everyone says so." She fingered the thin gold bracelets around her wrist.

"And yet you have doubts," he said.

Her brow furrowed. "What?"

"I sense it in your heart." The sun caught his eyes, turning them a blazing sapphire. "You're scared."

"That's ridiculous," she snapped.

"Is it? The bond cuts both ways, you know."

"It's not a *bond*, it's a leash. And I've had enough of your impudence. First lesson: Mind your manners."

She gave him the sensation of fire on the soles of his feet. His eyes widened, but that's all. Absolutely nothing came through the bracelet. She held it for a count of ten, then released the flow.

"What's your old name, Andros?"

A long moment passed before he replied. When it came, his voice was tinged with mild curiosity.

"Are you afraid of the Oracle? That she'll punish you if you fail? I suppose I don't blame you. Five's not bad, but it sounds like you're still new at this. If I were you—"

Thena stepped forward and wrapped a leather strap around his mouth. She struggled for composure, only speaking when she was certain she matched his calm.

Remember your rules.

"I'm sorry we're getting off on such a bad foot," she said. "Truly, I wish it were otherwise, mainly for your sake. All I needed to know today was your name, but since that's apparently too much to ask, I'm forced to give you a proper demonstration of what your collar can do." She paused. Her pulse thudded in her ears. "I want you to remember, you brought this about. This is *your* doing."

No fear from him. No anger. Not even quiet defiance.

Nothing.

Her mouth set.

"Someday, we'll be very good friends," she said, reaching into the bracelet where his spirit lived. "But for now...Well, I'm sorry, Andros."

And she was. More than he would ever know.

Darius watched her leave some hours later, only slumping in his chains after the door shut behind her. He felt so tired. It was the only thing he allowed himself to feel, but the exhaustion was too great to block out.

Darius wasn't new at this game either.

He could sense his power, an ocean of it, tantalizingly close yet on the other side of a high, thick wall, and that wall was *her*.

She did feel remorse—not much, but a little. If the collar worked anything like the cuffs he'd worn as a Water Dog, she would suffer an echo of his pain. By the time she'd left, her emotions had been a furious, red-hot tangle he hadn't cared to decipher. Darius steeled himself when it began, fleeing to hiding places in his mind he hadn't visited in a very long time. It helped him to dull some of it. Some, but not all.

The pain isn't real, he whispered through cracked lips. *Not real.*

She'd been surprised at his ability to read her and didn't seem to fully grasp what it meant, or be able to shield herself from him. A small advantage, but Darius would use it.

He rested his head against the wall and tried to arrange his thoughts. The cult of Apollo had taken him prisoner. Somehow, the Oracle had discovered the secret of bonding a daēva. She used a collar instead of a cuff, but the mechanism must be the same. And she already had others. The woman said so and he didn't think she was lying. He'd felt a swell of satisfaction through the bond when she said she'd broken five.

Darius shifted in his chains, muscles screaming.

Your own stupidity got you into this mess. You underestimated them because they were mortals.

Delilah warned him, but he hadn't listened.

How long did you last in Delphi before getting caught? Two hours?

Darius remembered the woman's face when he'd caught her pitcher. Shock, quickly masked. He'd been so impatient to find Nazafareen, he let his guard down. Only for an instant, but there you had it.

She'd taken the griffin cuff away. He might never find Nazafareen now.

Darius severed that train of thought, locking it away in a dark corner of his mind. *Too dangerous.* He wouldn't give his captor a single shred of emotion.

And he wouldn't give her his name.

CHAPTER 2

THE MAENADS

Sharp knocking roused Nazafareen from a deathlike slumber. One eye cracked open. Her hair felt glued to the side of her face, probably by drool, and her mouth tasted of wet ashes. She groaned and sat up. A clay jar painted bright turquoise sat on a table next to a window. Outside, a flock of blackbirds erupted squawking from orderly rows of grapevines bound to stakes. It took several long moments to remember where she was.

"Hang on," she mumbled, as the knocking carried on without pause. "I'm coming."

A low sun slanted through the window, pooling on the wood floor and warming it beneath her bare feet. Nazafareen used the stump of her right arm to push open the door. Her left hand worked on unsticking the clump of hair.

"Oh good, you're awake," Kallisto said pleasantly, as if she hadn't just been pounding on the door. The wife of Herodotus and leader of the cult of the Maenads looked like a plump housewife except for a hard and knowing gleam in her dark eyes. Braids streaked with grey formed a pile on top of her head. They'd been combed with oil that gave off a sweet, smoky scent.

"How long have I been sleeping?" Nazafareen asked with a jaw-cracking yawn.

"Three days."

"Three *days?*"

"I tried to wake you." Kallisto shrugged. "You clearly weren't dead so I decided you needed the rest. But time grows short. We must speak of certain matters involving the Oracle and other things as well."

Nazafareen's temples started to pound.

"Have you heard any news from the city? Has the Pythia... burned anyone?"

"No, child." Kallisto gave her a reassuring smile. "I won't claim your friend is safe, nor my husband, but she's keeping them alive to stand trial. I don't think she'll harm either of them until judgment is passed. Why don't you come down and meet me in the kitchen? And try not to fall asleep face-down on the table this time." She strode off, her ankle-length wool gown billowing behind her.

Nazafareen nodded distractedly. Alive was better than dead, but Javid languished in the Polemarch's dungeon while she'd been dozing away in a soft bed. It was all her fault, though she didn't know what she could have done differently. They'd been trapped on the stairs between the Temple soldiers and the chimera. She remembered killing the beasts—or perhaps *unmaking* was a better word. Then Javid had slipped in the resulting mess and the soldiers carried him off.

Nazafareen picked up the jug and was grateful to find it filled with clean water. She downed the entire thing in one long draught and immediately discovered other pressing needs, which another, larger pot in the corner took care of. She wanted to wash but the water was gone, so she made her way down to the kitchen, feeling vaguely grimy but somewhat more alert.

Kallisto had already laid out a breakfast of grilled fish, golden apricots soaked in honey, and a loaf of yeasty brown bread on the scarred wooden table. She added bowls of olives and grapes, and a soft slab of goat's cheese. Nazafareen tore into the food like a starving dog, eating until her pants felt uncomfortably tight. She washed it down with a cup of heavily watered wine.

"Thank you, that was excellent," she said, stifling a small burp. "I'll clean up."

She felt Kallisto's gaze on her back as she rinsed the plates and stacked them on the counter. Through the kitchen windows, she could see several mudbrick outbuildings nestled in groves of trees. Movement near one of them caught her eye. Four young women stood at the edge of a dirt yard watching as two others sparred with staffs. They wore short fawn-colored dresses that exposed muscled thighs and calves. The combatants fought with a controlled ferocity that impressed her. Faint cracks carried across the yard as they parried each other's blows. The staffs whirled in deadly, blurring arcs that must have been eight or nine hands in length. One of the women lunged, sweeping the staff at her opponent's feet. The second leapt over it, nimble as a cat. Another flurry of strikes and counterstrikes ensued and Nazafareen, utterly enthralled, forgot all about the dirty dishes. She feared they'd take each other's heads off, or at least shatter some bones.

"I'd like to learn how to do that," she murmured as the two finally broke apart and clapped each other amiably on the back.

"Why would you need a weapon?" Kallisto sounded puzzled. "You can work magic."

"Not very well." She returned to the plates, rinsing them from a clay pitcher. "And it carries a price."

"You killed the chimera."

Nazafareen gave her a sharp look. "What were they?"

"Old darklands magic. Very nasty." Kallisto tilted her head. "Someone sent them for you?"

"I think so, yes. Javid and I escaped them in the Umbra, but they must have found me again." Nazafareen sank into a chair. "I suppose I ought to tell you everything."

"That would be a great deal indeed," Kallisto laughed. "Let's start with how you came to Delphi."

Nazafareen did so. The story wasn't a very long one, since her memories only began a few months before.

"Ashraf isn't my real name," she admitted. "I think it was my sister's. You can call me Nazafareen."

Kallisto had listened in silence while she dried the plates with a cloth and replaced them in a cupboard.

"So, Nazafareen, you've angered the Valkirins. They're a touchy bunch, from what I know of daēvas. And you traveled through the Underworld?" Kallisto made a sign with her hand, extending the pinky and forefinger like a pitchfork. "Herodotus would pester you for hours if he knew. He has all sorts of theories about the gates."

"We had no choice," Nazafareen said simply. "It wasn't so bad really, except that the first gate we found opened into the Kiln."

"You saw the *Kiln?*"

"I think so. It's rightly named. The place felt like an oven." She shifted in her chair at the memory. "Javid said it was the hottest part of Solis, where the sun sits at high noon all day."

"It is that," Kallisto replied thoughtfully, sipping from her wine cup. "But it's something else too. The prison of the Vatras."

"Prison?"

"The other clans sealed them away. That's what ended the war. Few remember anymore, but we Maenads do. The Gale pens them in from the east. An impassable line of storms."

Nazafareen thought of the black storm clouds she'd seen writhing on the horizon.

"There was something wrong with the gate. It almost trapped us inside. I think it was damaged somehow. I had to use my breaking magic to shatter the wards."

Again, Kallisto made the forked sign with her hand. "You were lucky to escape. But I imagine if the gate had been whole and open, the Vatras would have come through long ago. Better it's sealed."

Nazafareen felt replete and sleepy again after the heavy meal. Sitting in Kallisto's bright, good-smelling kitchen, the dangers of the Kiln seemed very far away. She listened to the distant sounds of sparring with half an ear, but she couldn't deny a strong curiosity about this fire-working clan of daēvas no one had seen for a thousand years.

"Why can't the Vatras get out some other way?" she asked.

Kallisto smiled. "You don't know much geography, do you?" She took an olive and placed it on the table. "This is the Kiln." Another olive, to the right. "This is the Gale." Now a few grapes, to the top and left, forming a semicircle. "The White Sea. Do you know why they call it that, girl?"

Nazafareen shook her head.

"Because the wind whips it to such a froth, only the Marakai dare sail its waters. And here"—the last grape, placed carefully at the bottom—"the Austral Ocean. Full of sea monsters and smashers that turn ships to kindling."

Nazafareen studied the arrangement, like the bars of a cage.

"Looks foolproof to me. But then I seem to remember you saying something about the Vatras coming back?"

"Yes, that was right before you hit the table." Kallisto gave her a sly grin.

"If they're loose, why aren't they taking their revenge?"

"I don't know. I think it must be because they are not loose yet—or not all of them. But I've seen one."

Nazafareen leaned forward, eyes wide. "You have? Where?"

"In visions sent by the god. We drink wine and perform the ecstatic dance. Sometimes Dionysus visits me, or shows me things."

Nazafareen scratched her ear. "Ah, okay."

"You don't believe?" Kallisto asked mildly.

Daēvas didn't drink intoxicating beverages. Darius said they dulled the Nexus. But from what Nazafareen had seen sleeping in the alley with Javid, mortals had no such reservations, and they behaved quite oddly when they stumbled out of the warren of taverns near the docks.

"That you see things after you drink a lot of wine? No, I can believe that."

Kallisto shrugged. She didn't seem offended. "What will be, will be, whether we believe in it or not. But I wish to know, does your offer still stand?"

"My offer?" Nazafareen struggled to remember.

"To help me find proof of Herodotus's innocence?"

"Oh yes, of course," she replied with feeling. "I will do whatever I can. And if he is to be tried with Javid, I suppose helping one will help them both."

"Good. It won't be a simple matter, but I believe you were right. Our best chance is to focus on Kadmos and Serpedon. Someone placed that spell dust in Herodotus's study and I'll wager it was them."

Nazafareen frowned. Three days of sleep had left her head stuffed with wool.

"The Stork and the Weasel?" Kallisto prompted.

"Oh, those two." She scowled. "I never liked them. And I saw them whispering together when Herodotus was arrested."

Kallisto made a noise of disgust. "Kadmos has been appointed the new Curator of the Great Library. Clearly a reward for his treachery. But he must have obtained the spell dust somewhere."

"I can sense it if I'm close enough." Nazafareen thought for a moment. "Maybe he has more hidden away. It's worth looking."

Kallisto nodded and pushed her chair back. "I'll find out where they both live. The parthenoi will help. Would you like to meet them?"

Nazafareen nodded. "What are...*parthenoi?*"

"The word simply means virgin warriors," Kallisto replied. Her lips twitched. "They are certainly the second, though I cannot vouch entirely for the first. But Dionysus is a forgiving father in such matters. Come, they've been waiting for you to wake."

Kallisto led her out the kitchen door and over to the yard. The women stopped sparring and silently watched them approach.

"Charis you already know," Kallisto said, gesturing to the slight, olive-skinned girl who had brought Nazafareen there in the wagon. "The rest of you, introduce yourselves."

They glanced at each other.

"Rhea," said a tall woman with long, blue-black hair. Her voice was velvety and cultured, and she seemed older than the others— mid-twenties, Nazafareen guessed. She had sharp cheekbones and arresting grey eyes.

She holds herself like a warrior queen and she spoke first. The leader of this little group?

The next two looked like twins, with square jaws and pug noses. Unlike the other Maenads, who all had dusky skin, they were fair and freckled. They spoke almost in unison.

"Adeia."

"Alcippe."

The shortest of the bunch eyed Nazafareen up and down. She had piercing eyes and a belligerent air.

"Megaera," she growled.

"And I'm Cyrene." A heavyset, pretty girl with a multitude of braids like Kallisto, she was the only one besides Charis to smile.

Nazafareen gave a tentative smile in return. "Nice to meet all of you."

She sensed nothing unusual about their staffs, which meant only Kallisto's was a talisman. Nazafareen felt relieved. At least she wouldn't accidentally destroy anything valuable—these women didn't seem like the forgiving types. Yet something about them tickled her memory.

"You were dancing at the base of the Acropolis," she

exclaimed. "And you...." She turned to the tall, elegant one named Rhea. "You winked at me!"

Rhea smiled mischievously, but then her face grew solemn. "After you passed, we felt the chimera." There was no fear in her grey eyes, just revulsion. "They were pure darkness. I've never seen the like."

"We saw you destroy them," one of the twins put in, idly twirling her staff. "But we were across the square and by the time we pushed through the crowd, you'd vanished."

"So we all split up and started searching," the other twin said.

"But I'm the one who thought of the alley by the docks," Charis added with a hint of smugness.

Cyrene's almond eyes widened. "And now the Pythia is hunting you. She's declared that any who aid or shelter you will be put to death."

Nazafareen stiffened.

"If you're her enemy...well then, you're *our* friend."

Cyrene said it so earnestly that Nazafareen relaxed. "Thank you. I saw you all fighting before. It was impressive."

"We've trained since we were children," Charis put in. "I could show you a few things if you like."

Nazafareen beamed. "I would. Very much."

"Another time, perhaps," Kallisto said briskly. "We have work to do. Megaera, take Rhea and watch the library. There are two scholars there. I'll describe them for you. You're to follow them and see where they go. Do nothing! Just follow and be discreet." She turned to the twins. "You two, go make an offering at the Temple of Apollo. Take note of how many soldiers are posted and where. If it's possible to free Herodotus, I won't wait." She looked at the girl with almond eyes. "Cyrene, go to the taverns by the river. The Polemarch's guards drink wine there when they're off duty. See if you can find out any news about the Persian prisoner from Samarqand."

"What about me?" Charis demanded.

Kallisto sniffed. "You'll show Nazafareen the bathhouse and find her a change of clothes."

The first five Maenads gathered around Kallisto, peppering her with questions. Charis beckoned and Nazafareen followed her toward a small, thatch-roofed building at the rear of the farmhouse. Something nagged at her and she suddenly remembered what it was.

"I've been meaning to ask," Nazafareen said. "Did you come looking for me at the library the morning I carried the message to Herodotus?"

Charis glanced over her shoulder. "No, I didn't dare go inside. I waited for you to come out and followed. The people who live in that manor house are benefactors of our temple. I knew it would be safe for us to speak in their garden, away from prying eyes."

"So you never asked the cook about me?"

Charis shook her head. They entered the bathhouse and she winched up a bucket from a small stone well. A plain wood bench was pushed up against one wall. Shafts of sunlight poured in through a round window set high above the door.

"Someone was looking for me," Nazafareen admitted. "I'm afraid it might have been a Valkirin daēva. They hold a grudge against me."

"You have a lot of enemies," Charis observed, setting the sloshing bucket on the ground.

"I seem to have a talent for it," Nazafareen agreed.

"Well, they won't find you here." The Maenad grinned and handed her a block of clay mixed with sand. "Scrub with this first. Then rinse with the water." She gestured to a small jug of oil and a flat, hook-shaped instrument. "That's a strigil. You put the oil on your skin and scrape it off like so." She mimed running it up and down her body.

They have a strange way of bathing, Nazafareen thought, but she gamely peeled off her clothes and got to work. *Have I ever done this before? Perhaps I bathed with a...strigil every day in my own world.*

At the library she'd used the basin of water in her room, sneaking quick ablutions when Javid wasn't around.

I will find the Marakai, and then I will find Darius too, she swore to herself, vigorously rubbing the clay over a week's worth of grime.

But first I must fix the terrible mess I've made.

When the soldiers dragged him from the Polemarch's cells, Javid had expected to be handed over to some sort of hulking leather-hooded torturer named Uthos, or possibly Nagog. So he was somewhat relieved to find himself escorted out of the prison and thrown shackled into the back of a smelly cart. It lurched around the ring road that circled Delphi, but his spirits sank once again when he realized it was ascending a narrow incline carved into the eastern side of the Acropolis.

He whispered a prayer to the Holy Father and composed himself. Javid had dealt with all varieties of dignitaries, diplomats, aristocrats and filthy rich egomaniacs, but he had never encountered even a minor prophetess, let alone the Oracle of Delphi herself. He wondered if her reputation was exaggerated or if she really could see into the hearts of men. Hopefully the former, as he intended to call on all his considerable flair for perjury, dissembling and prevarication. In other words, he would not go down without lying through his teeth.

The cart halted before the Temple of Apollo, where custody of the prisoner was transferred to the soldiers there. A brief discussion ensued about whether the Pythia wanted him right away, or if he should be thrown in a cell next to "the old man." One of the soldiers hurried inside and returned to report that she did indeed want the Persian immediately.

And so Javid found himself face-down on the carpet in a full prostration.

"On your feet, heathen," a feminine voice ordered softly.

"I fear to look upon your face, O Most Holy Oracle and Mouthpiece of the Glorious Sun God!" he cried. "I am not worthy!"

"Just get up."

She didn't sound impressed. Javid clambered to his knees, keeping his gaze locked on the floor. Certain monarchs—his own king included—could be very touchy about direct eye contact from inferiors. It was always better to be cautious than cause accidental offense.

"You were here yesterday."

It wasn't a question. Javid could see the tip of a slippered foot just ahead.

"I don't deny it, Most Radiant One."

"Your companion is a witch. She used magic. There were dozens of witnesses."

The Pythia had a strange accent he had never heard before and Javid thought he knew them all.

"She did, Oracle. But I had no idea she was a witch." This much was true. "I've only known her a short time, I swear it on the honor of my mother and sisters, and may the Holy Father curse my offspring for twelve generations if—"

"I know who you are, Javid of the Merchants' Guild of Samarqand."

He bowed his head.

"Why are you in Delphi?"

He kept silent for a moment as though engaged in some internal struggle. Then he allowed his shoulders to sag—just a little bit. "I was on a secret mission to test a new type of wind ship, Holy Oracle."

"What sort?"

He sensed her leaning forward.

"A special fabric for the sack that doesn't tear so easily. It would be worth a fortune to the Guild. But they didn't wish anyone to know of the discovery, at least until it was proven, so they sent me into the Umbra."

"Go on."

"The ship crashed. If you look, you'll find it. I had to walk out." He paused. "That's when I met the witch."

"Her name?"

"She said it was Alanna, O Illustrious Seer."

"And where is she now?"

"If I knew that, I would tell you so you do not punish me further. But as you must have been informed, she fled when I was arrested. I shouldn't have run, but I was frightened."

"The captain of my guard says he hauled you out of the sacred fountain two weeks ago. What were you doing?"

Javid smiled weakly at the carpet. It was worked with a pattern of orange and red sunbursts. "One cannot come to Delphi without visiting the Temple of Apollo. It is the city's most famous shrine."

He felt her eyes on him but didn't dare look up to gauge her expression. *Does she know about the gate? Is she simply toying with me?* He kept his mouth shut and tried not to sweat.

"How long were you together?" she asked finally.

"Only a few days, Oracle."

"What else did she tell you?"

"In truth, I saw little of her. All I wanted was to raise money for my passage home." He hesitated. "She did say something about returning to the darklands—"

"But why was she *here*?" The Pythia's voice hardened. "Why did she deliver a message to the heretic Herodotus?" She held up a scrap of parchment. "It says only, *Take heart, beloved.* The note is unsigned. Who is it from? It cannot be the girl. He is old enough to be her grandfather!"

"I swear, I do not know, O Renowned—"

"Be quiet." The slipper began tapping the floor. "Shall I give you to the Polemarch? He says all Persians lie. It is their nature. But he is quite efficient at extracting the truth."

Javid felt the blood drain from his face. He had heard stories in the taverns about the Polemarch. "That is your choice, Oracle. But I have no reason to deceive you. If you know who I am, you know I am a respected emissary of the Guild. Our only traffic with the witches is the same as Delphi's, for trade purposes. I come from a good family." He knew he was babbling now, but couldn't help it. "This has all been a series of unfortunate misunderstandings!"

"Calm yourself. I didn't say I would." The Pythia abruptly stood. "Not all of us are uncivilized here. Yet I can say with certainty that you are a liar and not a very good one at that."

She moved closer, until she was standing directly above him. Javid felt a fingertip lift his chin. He squeezed his eyes shut.

"Look at me."

He took a breath and opened them. The Pythia stared down at him.

She's so young! And pretty too.

But a coldness lurked behind those pale eyes. A knowing depth beyond her years. Javid could easily imagine her reducing powerful men to stammering fools.

"You carried a pouch of spell dust. No doubt that is where the heretic Herodotus obtained it."

"Spell dust is legal in Samarqand—" he whispered.

"But not in Delphi." She gave a chilly smile. "Not in Delphi. One last question, emissary of the Merchants' Guild. Why were you being pursued by chimera?"

"Chimera?" He felt himself caught by those cold eyes, a fly in a web as the spider creeps near, and Javid struggled to understand what she was saying.

"The magical beasts," the Pythia snapped.

"Alanna had a sword," he blurted. "I think she stole it from the daēvas! I mean, the witches. Perhaps they wanted it back."

"A sword." The Pythia left her hand drop and gestured to the soldiers who guarded the door. "Take him back to the dungeons. He will stand trial before the Ecclesia for conspiracy."

Javid's heart raced. "Wait! Conspiracy to do what? I am innocent, O Sacred Priestess!"

But the Pythia had already left the room. He hastily got to his feet before the soldiers dragged him out on his knees. As they escorted him back to the wagon, Javid expected to feel a mild surge of relief. He hadn't been beaten or tortured. And they would give him a trial at least. Instead, he felt a deep sense of unease.

The Pythia's blue eyes had flickered when she accused him of giving the spell dust to Herodotus. *She knew*. She knew he was innocent.

And she didn't care.

CHAPTER 3

THE GAMBLER

The abbadax regarded Victor Dessarian for a long moment. Unblinking topaz eyes gleamed with malevolent intelligence. Its serpentine neck reared back, the head inches from brushing the ceiling.

Gods, they're big, Victor thought. He cracked frozen knuckles and kept his gaze riveted on the abbadax. *I wonder if they can smell fear?*

Red-gold feathers along its back rose to a stiff razor-sharp crest. The hooked beak opened for a sibilant hiss.

"That's the first warning," Mithre remarked, leaning against the wall just beside the heavy oak door leading back into the keep. "Well, the only warning really."

Victor held his ground as the creature flexed a taloned claw and took a step forward.

"Easy, girl," he said soothingly, holding his palms out.

"It's a male, actually."

"You're not helping," Victor growled under his breath, which curled upward like smoke in the frigid air.

He could barely feel his limbs and he'd been in the stables for less than a minute. Cut into the side of the mountain, the row of five pens lay open to the sky on one side so the abbadax could hunt for food and take off without hindrance. If necessary, the stables could be secured by an iron portcullis, which was raised and lowered by means of a winch. The entrance had filled with drifting snow from the blizzard that engulfed the keep, but the far reaches of the cavern remained dry. The bones of animals, small and large, lay scattered about the floor. Others had been used to build nests, held together by some kind of greenish goop. The arctic temperatures dampened the smell, but he could still guess what *that* was. Each pen had a stout door leading into the holdfast.

The good news was that despite the fact that the portcullis had been left open, the abbadax had stayed. Victor assumed they'd been raised by the Valkirins as hatchlings and considered the stables home. The bad news was that no one could get near them.

"The males seem somewhat less aggressive than the females," Mithre said with a crooked grin. "That's not saying much though."

The abbadax turned its head and regarded him with reptilian inscrutability. The black-haired daēva tightened the grip on his sword hilt.

"Too bad you don't have a treat for it. A nice fat hare might—"

The abbadax shrieked in fury and flared its sharp-edged wings, slashing at the air where Victor had stood a moment before. Mithre slammed the door shut and helped the new lord of Val Moraine to his feet. A moment later, it shook on its hinges as something large struck the wood.

"I told you there was only one warning."

Victor glared at him, shivering violently. "You talk too much."

"Maybe you'd have better luck with one of the hatchlings—if you can get past mommy, that is." Pointy white teeth flashed in a wolfish grin.

"Laugh if you will, but we have serious problems."

It pained Victor to admit it, but his grand dream of taking Val Moraine was rapidly becoming a nightmare. Seizing the Maiden Keep from its handful of defenders had turned out to be the easy part. Holding it was another thing entirely. Victor had originally planned to kill Eirik and Culach and leave, but now he found he didn't want to relinquish Val Moraine. It was too great a prize.

"Then let's go home," Mithre said, as though reading his thoughts.

"No."

"The others are getting restless. Hungry too."

"They'll live."

Mithre shrugged. "Yes, but for how much longer? Your reputation as a dashing adventurer is keeping them in line for now, but you may find yourself facing a mutiny if we don't replenish the supplies. Last I heard, the kitchens were down to a few grotty onions." He paused. "Then there's the matter of the Matrium."

The ruling council of the seven Avas Danai houses, the Matrium had no great fondness for Victor Dessarian—even before he snuck off to invade Val Moraine without waiting for their sanction. He briefly remembered the day so long ago he'd left for the shadowlands, what the Danai called the Ael sa'Vrach. Raisa and Tethys and the others waited at the gate, faces set in stark disapproval, to give him one last warning.

Any who pass through it will be cursed to forget where they came from. The doorway will be sealed. There is no returning.

It was this ward Nazafareen had broken more than two hundred years later.

Well, Victor *had* returned. He had his memories back, though Nazafareen had lost hers. But he would not forget what they had done.

Victor shook snow from his dark hair and peeled off his gloves, tucking them into the belt of his leather coat. "I'll handle those women."

Mithre looked at him skeptically, a glance down his long aquiline nose Victor always found irritating. Mithre had been one of the daëvas who followed Victor through the gate. Against all odds, they were still friends.

"How? You cut them out and they're not going to help you now. Not even Tethys. *Especially* not Tethys."

Victor rubbed his forehead. It ached all the time, probably from the altitude.

"You learned about the message?" he asked wearily.

It had arrived that morning via a bright-eyed snow bunting. Victor didn't know how the bird found its way inside—through the stables perhaps. It swooped into Eirik's study, shat on the table, and disgorged a torrent of wordless rage. If Victor had harbored any doubts about the sender, the bunting shared a memory of his mother strapping him as a young boy for some long-forgotten offense.

"No, but I can imagine. You're screwed, Victor. And I am too."

They looked at each other and barked a laugh. Mithre had been imprisoned with Victor at Gorgon-e Gaz. Val Moraine was still heaven compared to that infamous fortress by the sea. They wandered together down the corridor, boots echoing on the stone. Lumen crystals set at intervals of twenty paces cast pools of alternating light and darkness. It was marginally warmer inside, but Victor had still suffered until he relented and followed Mithre's lead, donning the fur-lined leathers of the Valkirins.

"If you're talking a lengthy occupation, we need a plan," Mithre said.

"I'll tame the abbadax," Victor insisted stubbornly. "We can use them to resupply."

"Or your frozen corpse will resupply the abbadax. My gold's on the latter."

Victor shot him a wounded look. "You're a font of helpful advice."

Mithre's hand jerked him to a sudden stop. "Go see the old woman."

Victor rolled his eyes. That was the final thorn in his side—the troublesome prisoners he'd been saddled with. Much simpler to just kill them, but he hadn't gotten around to actually doing it. Maybe he was growing soft, but he didn't care for summary executions—even of Valkirins. He still hadn't decided what to do with Culach so he'd left him to rot in the cold cells.

Victor wished Delilah were there. Gods, he missed his wife. It had been over two weeks since she and Lara left to find Darius. He managed all right during the day, but at night, alone in his cold chamber, Victor would toss and turn, beset by dark visions.

And then there was the matter of Gerda Kafsnjór.

"She's been kicking up a fuss for days," Mithre said. "Says she has an offer for you."

Victor snorted. "She'd say anything to lure me into that grubby crypt she calls home. I'd rather kiss a wight." He pretended to consider the matter. "Or even a revenant. They couldn't smell any worse."

Mithre didn't smile. "We're out of options. What if she knows something useful?"

"She doesn't."

Victor started walking again and Mithre fell into step beside him. They were of a height, both raven-haired and in the prime of life, but Mithre was built like a rapier while Victor had the brawn and heft of a broadsword. Victor knew his friend's wit was equally nimble, though he could be blunt as a rusty axe when he deemed it necessary.

"You're a coward, plain and simple, Dessarian. Did you know the others are drawing lots for who has to guard her room? One of the losers offered to trade his bow yesterday—"

They passed through one of the dark patches. Victor's eyes gathered the dim light like a cat. "Fine. Will you at least come with me?"

Mithre grimaced with patently insincere remorse. "I'm not sure our friendship extends that far...."

"Bloody hell!"

Victor stormed off, taking the stairs to the tower two at a time and muttering under his breath all the way. When he reached Gerda's frost-rimed aerie in the northeastern corner of the keep, the two young Danai outside looked relieved to see him.

"She's quiet now," one whispered. "But earlier she threatened to throw herself from the edge of the barrier if you didn't come."

Threat? More like a blessing.

"Do you find that such a disagreeable prospect?" Victor asked softly. "Maybe I should come back later—"

But Gerda must have had hearing like a bat, for now he heard her shrill voice through the door.

"Dessarian? Are you out there?"

"Gods." He sighed and rubbed his hands together briskly to warm them up. "Go ahead. Open the door."

The Danai looked at each other, then at Victor with something close to pity. They threw the newly installed bolt and stood aside.

Gerda saw the door swing wide and hurried back to her chair. She squinted so the idiot would think her eyesight was poor.

"Who's there?" she cried. "Is it the butcher who murdered my family?"

Victor Dessarian entered the room, an annoyed expression on his face. He was a piece of work, Gerda could tell right away. Big and cocky.

"Eirik butchered himself," he snapped. "And your blind grandson is still alive. He didn't seem worth the effort of killing."

"Great-great-grandson," Gerda corrected tartly.

Victor crossed his arms and tried to suppress a shiver. "What do you want?"

"I want to see him."

"No."

She beat her breast and wailed, to no discernible effect. Ever the pragmatist, Gerda decided to change tack.

"Getting hungry?" she asked slyly.

"Why?"

"I know where the food is," she replied in a sing-song cadence.

Victor snorted. "Don't waste my time."

"There's plenty. Fields of it! How do you think we live here, nitwit? Oh, I'm sorry, *Lord* Victor of Val Moraine." She lurched from her chair and started bowing and scraping.

"Stop that." Victor stepped back, alarm on his face.

Gerda hobbled back to her chair. She grinned.

"Still got all my teeth," she declared. "But you won't, once the scurvy sets in."

Victor's eyes narrowed. "What are you talking about, old woman?"

"You'll never find it. Not in a million years." She took her time pouring a cup of wine while Victor waited with obvious impatience. "Not unless I tell you."

"Let me guess. I permit you to see Culach first, and then you reveal this secret bounty."

"Maybe you're not such a nitwit after all." She took a sip and smacked her lips.

"Why should I trust you?"

"I'm just a decrepit old widow lady," she croaked. "Husband dead! Children dead! The Dessarian wolves baying at the door. All I have left is my darling Culach." She stretched a trembling hand out. "Already, the room grows dim. The frayed thread of life grows thin—"

"Once more," Victor interrupted coldly. "Why should I trust you?"

Gerda dropped her hand. "Why not? What do you have to lose?"

"My self-respect, for one thing."

She sniffed. "Only a Danai would rather starve than give an inch."

"And only a Valkirin would attempt such a childish ruse," he shot back.

They stared at each with mutual loathing for a long moment.

"Go ahead, *Lord* Victor. Feast on ice and stone. There might be a few spiders lying around too. I hear boot leather isn't too bad if you soak it for a couple of days."

Victor laughed. "I wish I could say it's been a pleasure to make your acquaintance, madam." He gave her an ironic bow. "But I can honestly say I would indeed rather eat my own boots than repeat the experience."

"Oh, you'll be back." She smiled. "And don't forget to shut the door on your way out." She fanned herself. "You're letting the hot air in."

As soon as the idiot left, Gerda leapt spryly from her chair and retrieved her globe from its hiding place. The guards outside seemed none the wiser that she was using small amounts of power. For all his preening and posturing, the idiot didn't run a very tight invasion.

She blew on the runes, feeding them a weave of air. They began to glow. Right away, the image of blue skies shifted, as if the talisman had been waiting for her call. It sped across the sea and swooped into the window of a ramshackle building too quickly for her to make out any details about the place. As usual, the globe sought out the same red-haired man. Gerda couldn't be sure he was a Vatra, but she intended to spy on him until she found out.

The moment he appeared, she eased the flow of the power so she wouldn't get too close and alert him to her presence. She could see the back of his head as he crouched down and threw a set of dice in a corner crowded with scruffy men. Mortals, by the looks of them, with the glossy black hair and tilted eyes of Tjanjin.

Gerda watched him for a while. Judging by the scowls on the other men's faces and the growing pile of coins in front of him, he seemed to be on a winning streak. Finally, after much gesticulating, another player produced a fresh set of dice. It didn't do any good. If he was a cheat, he was a clever cheat. This wasn't the first time she'd seen him fleecing mortals and Gerda had decided to name him the Gambler.

She was starting to grow bored when a Marakai entered and sat down at a table. Gerda recognized him as the sea clan not only by his ebony skin and curly hair, but the graceful way he moved, like a cat slinking through a kennel of slobbery dogs. She could tell from a subtle shift of the Gambler's shoulders that he noticed the newcomer out of the corner of his eye, but he continued to dice for a few minutes more. Finally, he rose and sat down at the Marakai's table.

Interesting.

Gerda didn't know much about the sea clan. She figured they were dim-witted, mentally unstable, or both. Who else would choose to sail the White Sea, with rogue waves a hundred paces high and denizens of the briny deep that could smash a ship to splinters with a single tentacle? Of course, as the only clan to deal with both daëvas and humans, they got rich off everyone else. That made sense. But Gerda couldn't imagine living on the pitching deck of a ship any more than she could imagine living in the sunlit mortal cities, or the dank, mossy forests of the Danai.

Give me stone and snow and sky, and I'm content, she thought. *Preferably with the idiot's corpse on a spike to improve the view.*

The Marakai conferred with the red-haired man over mugs of wine that neither of them touched. The Marakai looked around the tavern in a shifty-eyed manner, but his attitude toward the

Gambler was deferential. How Gerda wished she could hear what they were saying! She gripped the globe with gnarled fingers, conscious that the man might become aware of her presence at any moment. He had only caught her the one time, but the look in his eyes had been enough to take care it didn't happen again.

At last the Gambler rose and left without a backward glance, though a small smile played on his lips. The globe followed him—at a safe distance—to a moonlit harbor where a few small fishing vessels floated at anchor. Gerda frowned. He must be on the twilight side of Tjanjin. The island straddled the Umbra and its eastern half had a reputation for bawdy houses, dust lairs and other dens of iniquity. It was where you went when you didn't want people seeing your face too clearly.

The Gambler stood on a sandy crescent of beach, looking out at the sea. He nodded to himself and muttered something. Hecate sat low on the horizon, casting a glimmering silver net across the bay. Then Gerda saw movement in the shadows. It was four of the men he'd been dicing with. The biggest, a stocky fellow in a sleeveless shirt and baggy breeches, stabbed a meaty finger into the Gambler's chest. She couldn't hear what was said, but it seemed fairly obvious they were accusing him of cheating. The Gambler looked amused.

Gerda drew a sharp breath as one of the others, a rat-faced creature who'd been sidling around behind, suddenly produced a knife and darted in like a striking snake. Without turning his head, the Gambler's hand shot out, seizing his attacker's knife arm. He did nothing else, but the man's mouth gaped in a silent scream. Gerda squinted. Was his flesh...smoking? The others stood there dumbfounded until flames started licking at the crotches of their trousers. The Gambler laughed as they dropped and rolled around flailing on the sand. Then he strolled off down the beach, lazy and lithe as a sun-warmed tiger.

Gerda let the weaving go and sat back, sucking her teeth.

No wonder he won all the time. He was probably using air to tip the dice.

She poured herself a cup of wine and took a thoughtful sip. So they *were* loose. But why was a Vatra wasting his time in dingy taverns on the other side of the world? And where were the rest of them? Could he be the last of his kind?

Perhaps further observations with the globe would clarify matters. Either way, no one else knew the truth and she intended to keep it that way until she saw how to turn it to her own advantage.

Gerda smiled. The Vatras' revenge might be a thousand years in the making, but she'd make sure Victor Dessarian got his fair share of it.

Culach woke to someone banging on the bars of the next cell. It could have been a shoe, or maybe a piece of rock she'd worked loose. He'd been dreaming again, of the burning city and the desert and the last agonizing moments of the king's councilor.

"Shut up!" a woman's voice yelled. "Shut up, shut up, *shut up*!"

"You shut up," he growled, groping for the wall and leaning against it.

For a moment, blessed silence reigned.

"I thought Victor came to kill you. So why is the job unfinished?"

"He talked himself out of it."

"Felt sorry for you, huh?"

"I thought you wanted me to shut up."

He heard a soft exhalation and guessed she was standing at the bars. Each cell had a grill set into the door at eye level so the jailers could inspect the prisoner inside.

"Well, if I have to listen to you muttering and moaning for another night, I'll come over there and do it myself."

"Be my guest," Culach replied wearily.

Of all the cold cells, they had to put him next to Katrin.

She'd never once asked what his nightmares were about. Empathy wasn't Katrin's strong suit. Instead, she just yelled and pounded on things until he woke up. It had become an almost farcical routine.

"Those Danai bastards," she muttered. "How did they get in? *How?*"

Culach assumed she was talking to herself, but he answered anyway.

"Neblis. She told Victor about some secret passage."

Katrin made a noise of disgust.

"I wish you'd found her. So I could kill the bitch."

Culach stretched his arms over his head and winced. His ribs still ached from Victor's vigorous kicking.

"We've established why I'm here," he said. "Blindness has its advantages. But I never figured you for the type to get taken prisoner."

In fact, Katrin was the best they had. She trained for hours on end against anyone willing to spar with her, man or woman. The knowledge of her superiority with a blade—and even unarmed—had never bothered him. Katrin was better than *everyone*.

"The fuckers knocked me out with a chunk of stone," she said. "I still have a lump on my head the size of.... Hey, do you remember that hailstorm we had a couple years ago? With those balls of ice that smashed right through the hull of the Marakai ship?"

They'd gone to the shore to trade with the sea daēvas. The coastline west of the Isles was wild and barren, but there were coves where the Marakai could drop anchor. That particular day, a nasty storm had blown in from the White Sea. They'd been stupid enough to try flying the abbadax through it. Culach gave a slight smile. He'd been black and blue for days, but it still made a good story.

"I remember."

"Like that."

"Ouch."

Culach stood and walked to the cell door, curling his fingers through the grill. The corridor was quiet. No other voices, not even a cough or a whisper.

"Who else is alive?" he asked.

"No idea."

"Do you think the other holdfasts will come to our aid?"

"What do you care?" she asked bitterly. "I heard you protected our only hostage."

"Eirik was going to slaughter her in cold blood," Culach snarled. "And it would have done nothing to stop the Dessarians. You're just..." He trailed off.

"Jealous?" Katrin's anger turned to genuine amusement. "Oh, Culach. I think we have bigger problems, don't you?" She chuckled. "Men have astoundingly high opinions of themselves. I hate to say it, but your cock has nothing on your ego in terms of size."

"Point taken."

"You were a pleasant diversion, but Agnes, for example, was *far* better at—"

"I get it."

Katrin went on for a while, dissecting his manly prowess in excruciating detail and comparing it to various other lovers she'd acquired over the years. Culach mostly stopped listening. She was doing it out of boredom and frustration, and simply because she was Katrin.

He scrubbed a hand across his mouth. His beard itched maddeningly but he doubted the Dessarians would be giving him a razor anytime soon. They came through every quarter hour, pausing before the cells to do a head count before continuing on. No one wanted to linger amid the thick sheets of ice and vicious little drafts that crept through fine cracks in the stone walls. The cold cells faced east, toward the White Sea. When the wind hit the mountains, it picked up speed. By the time it crossed leagues of barren peaks, that wind felt like a knife to the throat. And there were no shields on this side of the holdfast, which also held the stables.

In a strange way, Culach's dreams—bad as they often were—had become an escape from his dire reality. Even the recurrent nightmare of being buried alive had grown familiar, though it still jolted him awake with a pounding heart. But that one came less frequently now. He still dreamt of the king's councilor and had learned the man's name: Farrumohr.

Culach suspected he was reliving Farrumohr's memories in reverse order from the moment of his death. In the dreams he rode along like a passive observer, but he felt Farrumohr's emotions and even absorbed some of his knowledge. He was beginning to understand what had occurred so long ago that led to the sundering of Nocturne and Solis, and the downfall of the once powerful Vatras.

As so often happens, it began with a beautiful woman.

A dry desert wind whipped the brightly colored pennants streaming from hundreds of tents. Daēvas from every clan milled around the plaza, laughing and exchanging news and gifts with old friends. They were celebrating the annual return of Artemis. Twice as large and luminous as the other moons, she sailed high as the sun set, bathing the surrounding city in soft light that shimmered on the rooftops and spires. Some of the buildings looked like colossal, ancient trees, others like breaking waves, and still others resembled jagged mountains. Together, they created a metropolis like none the world had ever seen, a tribute to the wild and the tame, to both Nature and civilization.

Once a year, all the clans came together in the glass capital of the Vatras, power-forged from the desert sands. The Vatras were the only clan to have built a city—clear evidence of their superiority over the other races. As he looked out through Farrumohr's eyes, Culach felt the man's malice. They were all parasites who exploited the Vatras' generosity. But things were about to change.

Farrumohr sat on a raised pavilion on the western side of the plaza, an untouched cup of wine in his hand. Culach sensed his bitterness as he watched the merrymaking, though the man maintained a frozen smile that made Culach's cheeks ache. His gaze wandered to the area where the Danai had erected their camp. Both the ebony-skinned Marakai and the fair Valkirins mingled with their cousins, as well as a number of flame-haired Vatras. But Farrumohr's attention rested on one woman. She stood with a knot of people, smiling at some joke. She was small, like Mina, and darkly beautiful.

Farrumohr leaned closer to the king, who sat at his left watching the proceedings with an indulgent air. Gaius was a striking man, with sharp cheekbones and almost feline eyes. His hair spilled down his back like a river of flame. He wore no jewelry except for the serpent crown. Farrumohr had ordered it specially made when he took the throne. A reminder that even the mighty could be felled by a careless step.

"There she is, my lord."

Gaius turned. "What?"

"The girl I told you about. Caecelia."

Farrumohr's thoughts were a tangle of envy, hatred and bitter longing, but Culach understood in a flash of insight what undercurrents swirled around the king and his advisor. The king needed an heir. Farrumohr had managed to find fault with every potential Vatra courtier, urging an alliance with one of the other clans through marriage. It would be a first step toward bringing the four together under a single ruler.

"Where?" the king asked languidly.

"Near the third tent. She's wearing green."

Farrumohr watched the king search her out. Much work had

gone into this particular selection. It was unusual for the clans to intermarry, though not unheard of. If she was rejected, Farrumohr would have to start his search from scratch again, a prospect he didn't relish.

Then Gaius paused and his features stilled. Farrumohr heard the faintest hitch in his breath.

"She is...intriguing," Gaius murmured, his pale blue eyes locked on Caecelia.

Farrumohr smiled. "I'm sure she would be honored to dine with you, my lord. In fact, I've heard she admires you greatly."

This was a lie. In fact, the woman was in love with another Danai. It was partly for this reason that Farrumohr had chosen her.

"Does she?" Reddish lashes blinked rapidly.

"Oh, yes. You shall have your pick, of course, but I cannot imagine any woman refusing you."

Except for Caecilia.

Farrumohr knew Gaius had a weakness for dark-haired women. Caecilia of House Martinec would be irresistible. She was young and lithe, charming and intelligent. Her home lay on the White Sea, near the Valkirin border. He'd heard she loved to walk the sandy shoreline in the mornings and swim in the tepid water. Even if she hadn't already given her heart to another, she was not the sort of woman who would happy living in the desert. And she was strong-willed. Stubborn to a fault. She wouldn't accept a marriage for political reasons, no matter how much her family pressured her. In other words, Caecilia was ideal for Farrumohr's purposes.

He rose and crossed the plaza, the crowds parting like he was some kind of diseased beggar. The group turned at his approach, smiles dying on their faces—even those of his own clan. His lips tightened. He had never given them cause to dislike him, but they did anyway. Instinctively.

Farrumohr's grin stretched wider and he made a flowery bow.

"The king extends his personal welcome," he said to Caecilia.

She stared at him, then glanced at the others uncertainly. A handsome Danai with fiery black eyes took a step closer to her. That one would be trouble, Farrumohr thought. He *wanted* trouble but not right away. Not until the hook was set.

"Please thank Lord Gaius for me," she said graciously, turning away.

Farrumohr laid a hand on her arm, enjoying her slight flinch. "Oh, I will. But he wishes you to dine with him. He would like to hear news of House Martinec."

Caecilia hesitated.

"You would not insult our king in his own city, would you?" Farrumohr asked softly. "It is simply a meal. He wishes to get to know all of his..." Farrumohr nearly said *subjects* but caught himself. "Cousins. That is the purpose of the gathering of Artemis, is it not?"

Her dark brows drew down. "Oh, very well," she said carelessly.

The black-eyed daëva opened his mouth to say something but she quelled him with a hard look.

"Tell Gaius I would be honored. We leave tomorrow anyway."

Farrumohr bared his teeth. "So soon? But the gathering lasts another three days."

"Yes." She made an apologetic face, the little liar. "There are... matters I must attend to. They cannot wait."

"How unfortunate. Still, he will be pleased to meet you. Come to the pavilion within the hour. I assure you, Lord Gaius is delightful company."

She nodded, clearly eager for him to be gone.

This would not do.

Farrumohr leaned closer, pulling her aside so the others wouldn't hear.

"Between us, the poor king has been ill lately. I fear...well, I shan't say it, but I fear the worst. Your kindness would mean the world to him."

"Oh!" Her pretty eyes widened. "I am sorry," she said in a softer tone. "Please tell him it would be my great pleasure to sit at his table."

Farrumohr sighed. "You are as big-hearted as they say. This could be his last...Never mind. But you have my personal thanks. And please, don't mention it, especially to the king. He doesn't wish anyone to know. He can't stand the thought of being pitied."

"Of course not," she replied sympathetically.

He felt their eyes on his back as he walked away. The other daēvas avoided him, but he heard their whispers. *Viper*. For once, it didn't bother him. Soon enough, they would learn their place.

Later, at dinner, Caecilia played her part perfectly. She listened when Gaius spoke, laughed at his jests and filled his cup when it grew empty. The king basked in her attention as the black-eyed daēva smoldered at a table in the very rear of the pavilion.

Lumen crystals in every color cast the tables in rainbow hues. The porcelain was from Tjanjin, the gold-chased goblets from Samarqand. At Farrumohr's urging, Gaius had spared no expense for the occasion. Each clan was served delicacies that would appeal to their particular palate. The Marakai dined on freshly grilled fish, the Valkirins on cold soups and stews, while the Danai devoured platters of fruit and poached bird's eggs. Wine flowed from talismanic casks that never grew empty. Laughter and snatches of song—battle dirges from the Valkirins, lighter fare from the others—rang through the tent as the feast went on through the night.

Farrumohr observed the proceedings with his frozen smile, though it never touched his eyes. As attendants in livery cleared the last plates, he leaned over to King Gaius.

"Perhaps my lord should tell Caecilia he wishes to take the night air," he hissed.

Too much wine had flushed Gaius's face a rosy pink. His eyes were slightly unfocused.

"A fine idea," he said loudly. He extended his arm. "My lady? Would you allow me to escort you to the gardens? There are flowers that only bloom in darkness."

She bit her lip. "I am growing tired—"

"Just a brief stroll. You would not refuse me that? They are very close."

"I suppose a quick walk would be all right," she muttered.

Gaius grinned. His serpent crown sat slightly askew and a sheen of sweat coated his brow, but his legs were steady enough as he rose and offered Caecilia his arm. She took it with obvious reluctance, though Gaius didn't seem to notice.

"I know you Danai love your forests," he said, "but you'll find the desert has its own stark beauty." His gaze lingered on her for a moment. "I look forward to showing you."

Caecilia tensed but allowed herself to be led from the tent. Farrumohr grinned as they disappeared. It faded when he saw the black-eyed daëva rise from his table, a glower on his face. Farrumohr glanced around. The food and wine had worked their magic. Unused to such rich fare, half the daëvas sat with chins propped on hands, eyes drooping. The others still laughed and jested, toasting each other with the last of the wine. In short, no one was paying the slightest bit of attention. He followed the man, catching up to him when he reached a fountain at the entrance to the gardens.

"Danai," Farrumohr called softly.

The daëva turned and his scowl deepened. "What do you want, Viper?"

"Let the girl make up her own mind." He held his hands up. "That's all."

The Danai laughed. "Caecilia knows her mind already. That is not what troubles me. But I've heard things about your king—"

A faint scream rent the darkness. The Danai turned to run

and Farrumohr held out a hand. Flames burst from the man's back. From his mouth and eyes. He flailed soundlessly, the flesh melting from his bones. Farrumohr sagged to his knees. Fire drained the wielder's own life force. It was all he could do to haul the smoking corpse into the trees. Then he used the last of his energy to char it to greasy ash. The wind would do the rest.

∾

Get your copy of Solis at any major bookseller!

ABOUT THE AUTHOR

Kat Ross worked as a journalist at the United Nations for ten years before happily falling back into what she likes best: making stuff up. She's the author of the Nightmarked series, the Lingua Magika trilogy, the Fourth Element and Fourth Talisman fantasy series, the Gaslamp Gothic mysteries, and the dystopian thriller *Some Fine Day*. She loves myths, monsters and doomsday scenarios.

www.katrossbooks.com
kat@katrossbooks.com

facebook.com/KatRossAuthor
instagram.com/katross2014
pinterest.com/katrosswriter
bookbub.com/authors/kat-ross

ALSO BY KAT ROSS

A Bad Breed

The Necromancer's Bride

Dead Ringer

Balthazar's Bane

The Scarlet Thread

The Beast of Loch Ness